The soldiers in the arena saw what was happening and closed on the Rift . . . too late.

Marsh and Cooper sailed down, the top edge of the net caught, the ropes pulled tight, and their fall turned into a swing that arced over the arena floor, past the guards, and flung them straight through the Rift.

Into the Blood.

Also available from D. J. MacHale

PENDRAGON

JOURNAL OF AN ADVENTURE
THROUGH TIME AND SPACE

Book One: The Merchant of Death

Book Two: The Lost City of Faar

Book Three: The Never War

Book Four: The Reality Bug

Book Five: Black Water

Book Six: The Rivers of Zadaa

Book Seven: The Quillan Games

Book Eight: The Pilgrims of Rayne

Book Nine: Raven Rise

Book Ten: The Soldiers of Halla

MORPHEUS ROAD

Book One: The Light

Book Two: The Black

Book Three: The Blood

MORPHEUS ROAD
THE BLOOD

D. J. MACHALE

Aladdin
New York London Toronto Sydney New Delhi

ALADDIN

An imprint of Simon & Schuster Children's Publishing Division
1230 Avenue of the Americas, New York, NY 10020
First Aladdin paperback edition April 2013
Copyright © 2012 by D.J. MacHale
All rights reserved, including the right of reproduction
in whole or in part in any form.
ALADDIN is a trademark of Simon & Schuster, Inc.,
and related logo is a registered trademark of Simon & Schuster, Inc.
Also available in an Aladdin hardcover edition.
For information about special discounts for bulk purchases,
please contact Simon & Schuster Special Sales at 1-866-506-1949
or business@simonandschuster.com.
The Simon & Schuster Speakers Bureau can bring authors to your live event.
For more information or to book an event contact the Simon & Schuster Speakers Bureau
at 1-866-248-3049 or visit our website at www.simonspeakers.com.
Designed by Sammy Yuen Jr.
The text of this book was set in Apollo MT.
Manufactured in the United States of America 0313 OFF
2 4 6 8 10 9 7 5 3 1
The Library of Congress has cataloged the hardcover edition as follows:
MacHale, D. J.
The blood / D. J. MacHale. — 1st Aladdin hardcover ed.
p. cm. — (Morpheus Road ; [bk. 3])
Summary: A final showdown is in order between best friends Marshall and Cooper and
the terrifying villain Damon, who's more determined than ever to break down the walls
between the worlds of the living and the dead. Marshall is forced to make a brave and
shocking choice when the battle is on the line, and he and Cooper might be
rewarded with help from someone quite unexpected.
ISBN 978-1-4169-6518-3 (hc)
[1. Horror stories. 2. Supernatural—Fiction. 3. Death—Fiction.] I. Title.
PZ7.M177535Bm 2012
[Fic]—dc23
2012000564
ISBN 978-1-4169-6521-3 (pbk)
ISBN 978-1-4424-5235-0 (eBook)

For Alex and Samantha Galvao

Foreword

Well, kids, we've come to the end of another saga.

You know that feeling you get when you finish reading a really good book and you're a little bit sad that it's over? The same thing happens when you write one. Maybe that's one of the reasons I like to write stories that play out over multiple books. You only have to read (or write) "The End" once. But eventually those words have to show up, and you'll find them here in *The Blood*.

One of the great things about a trilogy (as opposed to a monumental ten-book epic *cough* Pendragon *cough*) is that it isn't that difficult to perceive it as one big story. That's certainly how I treated Morpheus Road. It is one story told in three chapters. Many readers who read *The Light* had many questions after finishing it. What they didn't know was that most of those questions would be answered in the very next book, *The Black*. Those books were two different pieces of a very big puzzle. The final piece of that puzzle you now hold in your hands. The true extent of Damon's wicked plan will be revealed (Muhahahahaha) and when you have finished reading *The Blood*, your journey along the Morpheus Road will be complete.

Before we take the next step, I'd like to once again thank the many people who have helped bring my books to you. A big thank-you goes to the folks at Simon & Schuster for allowing me to complete the trilogy. My colleagues Richard Curtis, Peter Nelson, and Mark Wetzstein will always have my gratitude for their support, expertise, and friendship. I'd also like to thank the great folks at Brilliance Audio for the terrific audio versions of Morpheus Road. Nick Podehl's reading of the story has been no less than perfect.

One of the great joys for an author is getting the chance to meet so many of the wonderful librarians and teachers who encourage reading while feeding the imaginations and intellect of young people everywhere. We *all* owe them a great debt of gratitude. Also, the many booksellers from stores both small and massive are wonderful guides who help steer young readers to the books that will best suit them. Thanks to you all.

My wife, Eve, and daughter, Keaton, are always there for me, and for that I am truly grateful. Now if only Keaton would start reading my books! All in good time . . . all in good time.

And of course the biggest thank-you must go to the readers who have not only traveled the Morpheus Road, but have been with me since as far back as *The Merchant of Death*. (Though it's kind of strange to hear "I grew up with your books!" Yikes. It doesn't seem like I've been writing them for that long!) I love reading all your e-mails and posts and hearing your thoughts about my stories. The best is when I actually land in a city where we can meet face-to-face. There's nothing better than talking to a reader who simply says, "I love your books." That truly is one of the great things about being an author. Thank you all.

Now, back to the business at hand. For those who may have forgotten . . .

In the Black (the place *and* the book), Cooper and the Guardians of the Rift had nearly been wiped out in a valiant attempt to keep Damon from controlling the portal between lives. They were saved by the Watchers, who not only swept Damon's forces into the Blood (the place, not the book) but sealed the Rift forever.

In the Light (the place *and* the book), Marshall finally stood up to Damon in his quest to force him to find the poleax. (Remember the legions of the living dead in the cemetery?) Marsh and Sydney became a couple (probably the most surprising twist of the whole story), and the hauntings ended. Weeks went by without a single ghostly-doing and Marsh was beginning to believe that the nightmare was over.

He was wrong.

No sooner did he let his guard down than he was visited by the three apparitions: the ghosts of Zoe, Eugene Foley . . . and his mother, Ree. Then a fourth ghost appeared. Cooper. Only this time Marsh was able to see and hear him. Cooper announced that Damon wasn't done and whether they liked it or not, it was going to be up to them to stop him. Together.

It was turning out to be a tumultuous summer, and the worst had yet to come.

Now it's here.

Have fun.

—D. J. MacHale

1

Sydney Foley was about to die.

Impending doom rarely telegraphs itself, which meant she was blissfully unaware of the fact that a chain of events had been set in motion that would likely end with her being cast, violently, to the next stop along the Morpheus Road.

Sydney had been working all summer as an algebra tutor at Stony Brook Junior High. It was a job that would normally warrant battle pay for most hapless young tutors, but Sydney had no trouble handling the challenge.

"I'm smarter than you," she would announce at the beginning of each class. "So either pay attention and learn something or zone out and I'll see you back here next summer. Your choice. I get paid either way."

Sydney wasn't subtle. She intimidated the girls and mesmerized the normally hyperkinetic boys, who quietly admitted that there were worse ways to spend time than staring at a hot teacher like Sydney . . . even if she was lecturing about exponents and factoring.

When her lesson ended on that particular day, she decided to stay in the classroom and grab a little study time. Her goal was to gain early acceptance to Stanford University, and Sydney never fell short of her goals, even if it meant spending a beautiful summer afternoon in an empty classroom calculating the effect of gravity on linear acceleration. She stared at the open book, glassy-eyed, thinking about how she would rather be lying on the beach with her boyfriend.

"Bored," she texted him. "Come visit me at SBJH. I'll be your best friend."

Two months before, the idea that she would be texting Marshall Seaver and calling him her boyfriend was about as likely as her not getting into Stanford. The events of the early summer had changed that. Drastically. The two were thrown together by the tragic death of her brother, Cooper . . . and by the haunting. Sharing sorrow and terror tends to forge a bond between people, and to the surprise of everyone who knew anything about either of them, Marsh and Sydney had become inseparable.

Sydney stared at her phone. There was no reply from Marsh, which was odd. He was usually quick on the draw when it came to returning her texts. With a shrug she reluctantly turned back to her study guide for the twentieth time, and for the twentieth time her mind wandered. She gazed out at a sea of unoccupied desks, suddenly feeling very alone.

Not lonely alone . . . vulnerable alone.

It was too quiet.

Schools were always full of noise and activity, even during lunch. Especially during lunch. Quiet wasn't normal, even during summer school. She thought maybe everyone had gone out to eat, but the entire school couldn't have emptied out so quickly. Something felt off. It raised the small hairs on the back of her neck. That didn't happen often, so when it did, she paid attention. Quickly she gathered her books, phone, and purse and started for the door.

That's when the smell hit her. It was a stagnant, dead smell. The room had grown warm, as if the air-conditioning had failed. Small beads of sweat formed on her upper lip. Her eyes started to burn and tear up.

What the heck?

She stood in front of her desk, trying to understand what was happening, when her eye caught movement. She glanced up to the air duct near the ceiling to see tendrils of smoke drifting from the grate.

Fire, was her first thought.

Get the hell out, was her second.

She ran for the door, but before pulling it open she flashed on a boring fire safety lecture she'd gotten in third grade. She stopped, cautiously placed her hand on the wooden door . . . and felt heat.

"Oh man," she gasped.

She touched the metal doorknob and quickly recoiled. It was searing hot. There could be only one reason: The building was on fire. She took a quick look through the narrow vertical glass window in the door to see that the corridor was filled with smoke. The fire was close. She didn't panic. Sydney never panicked. Glancing around she saw a red fire alarm on the wall next to the door. She had always wondered what would happen if she pulled one of those. She was about to find out. Sydney lunged for it and yanked the lever down, breaking the thin glass tube that seemed to have no purpose. She held her breath and waited, expecting the harsh blare of an alarm to break the eerie silence. Seconds passed. No alarm sounded.

"Seriously?" she exclaimed as she fumbled for her purse to grab her cell. "A fire *and* a defective alarm?"

Her fear about being alone was suddenly justified. If the alarm didn't work, she could be the only one who knew about the fire because she just so happened to be in the middle of it. The wispy vapors turned to dark, thick smoke that poured from the air-conditioning vent. Digging for her phone, she hurried toward the only other possible escape route . . . the door at the rear of the classroom. She found the phone, wiped tears from her burning eyes, and punched in 911.

Seconds passed. There was no answer. Sydney shook the phone in frustration.

"How is that possible?" she screamed.

She had full bars and the battery was charged. Why hadn't the call gone through? She stopped worrying about alerting people who weren't there and decided to focus on joining them. She got to the back door, praying that the fire hadn't moved that way. She was about to put her hand on the door to check for heat, and realized she needn't bother. Looking out through the window, she saw flames. The fire was burning right outside the classroom.

Sydney stared at the dancing flames, mesmerized, unbelieving. How could a fire spread so quickly? She leaned in to the window, until her nose nearly touched the glass, to stare into a corridor that had become a furnace. It was almost pretty the way the orange flames twisted and danced . . . as they drew closer, coming to burn her alive. It was hypnotic, but not so much that she forgot how much trouble she was in. The flames would soon be in the classroom. She was trapped and knew if she stayed put the fire would only get worse. She knew what she had to do . . . run through the flames. It was crazy, but better than doing nothing.

While keeping her eyes on the flames through the window, she reached for the doorknob, but stopped when she

"Ready or not!" the voice taunted as the skeletal face appeared through the wall of flame, floating closer.

Sydney focused and made a decision. Burning to death would be worse than falling and being smashed like a china doll. She had to jump. She took a breath, leaned out of the window and pushed off . . .

. . . as strong hands gripped her ankles from behind.

"No!" she screamed, fearing that the skeleton was trying to pull her back into the inferno.

She kicked violently, desperate to get away from its grasp and out into space.

"Stop!" came a voice from behind. "What are you doing?"

The voice cut through her panic. She recognized it. It wasn't the flaming skeleton. But then, who? Was it a trick to make her think she would be better off giving up and allowing herself to be incinerated? She looked to the ground far below and imagined herself lying in a broken heap. It was too much to bear. She gave in and let the grabbing hands do their work. She was pulled roughly back through the window frame and over the bookcase until she fell rudely to the floor. With the little presence of mind she had left, she twisted from the grasp of her assailant and spun to see . . . Marsh.

"My god, Sydney. What are you doing?" he cried in panic.

Sydney's sense of reality had been wrenched inside out. Seeing Marsh sitting on the floor across from her made even less sense than being grabbed by a flaming skeleton. She stared at him in shock, not sure if he was real or a hallucination that would soon burst into flames. Glancing around quickly, she saw that the smoke had cleared. All of it. Could it have been sucked out of the windows so quickly? A look past Marsh gave her the answer:

The door was still there. The fire . . . wasn't. Nothing had been burned. The floor was intact. People were gathered saw movement outside in the corridor. It was a dark shadow that floated in hazy contrast to the brilliant fire. Her hopes soared. Was it a firefighter battling through the blaze, coming to her rescue? She leaned forward, trying to make out detail of the shadow as it drew closer.

"Hurry up!" she screamed.

The dark silhouette was nearly there. The smoke was getting thick inside the classroom, making Sydney's eyes sting, but she could still make out the vague form of a person. She leaned in closer to the window, hoping to see the face of a heroic, handsome firefighter looking back at her. The shadow floated right up to the glass and snapped into focus, inches from her face.

Sydney screamed.

The face was that of a burning skeletal head with its mouth open in a ghastly howl. Its flesh was on fire, turning black as it burned away from the bone to expose the charred skull beneath. Its hollow eyes were focused directly on Sydney.

Sydney threw herself backward, tripped over a chair, and landed on the floor. If she had hurt herself, she didn't know it. Her mind was spinning too quickly. Who was that? *What* was that? Some poor guy trapped out in the corridor? She scrambled to her feet and ran back for the door to open it and let the tortured victim into the room, though she knew it would be too late. He was a goner. Still, she had to try. She reached for the door and was about to turn the handle . . . as the narrow window in the door smashed in, spewing shattered glass and dark, choking smoke into the room.

Sydney jumped back again, hacking out a cough as a new wave of acrid smoke filled her lungs.

The burning skull pushed through the frame where the glass had been and glanced around the room until it spotted Sydney, and offered a ghastly grin.

"Unlock the door, Sydney," the skull commanded in a dry, gravelly voice.

Most people would have snapped. Not Sydney. She had been through too much that summer and had seen things far worse. She now realized the truth: The only victim was her.

"Bite me," she snarled, and turned away, looking for another escape route.

She ran into a large storage closet in the back of the class, hoping it would lead to an adjoining classroom. No luck. Dead end. She quickly realized that if she was going to get out of the building, there was only one way to go. The window.

A low bookcase ran the length of the classroom across from the doors. Above the bookcase were five large sealed windows. Beneath each was a small hinged window that opened in. None were large enough to crawl out of. Sydney yanked them all open, hoping the smoke would be sucked out before she choked to death.

"That's right," the flaming skeleton cackled. "Feed the flames . . . feed the flames."

"Shut up!" Sydney barked. She leaned down to a window and screamed to the outside world.

"Help! Somebody! I'm trapped in here! Help!"

"This is a race you're going to lose," the fiery ghoul taunted as it rattled the door, trying to get in.

The classroom was on the fourth floor. It was a long way down to the parking lot. The empty parking lot. There were no fire trucks or ambulances racing to save the building. Or her. Sydney had to make a choice. Fast. She looked back to the door to see the skull peering through the broken window, only now the wooden door was ablaze. It would soon burn through, allowing the fire to leap inside, along with the ghastly creature.

The decision wasn't a hard one. She grabbed a desk chair,

wound up, and heaved it at one of the large windows. The chair hit the glass, bounced off, and clattered back to the floor.

The demon laughed. "Or you could just die gracefully."

Sydney ignored the taunt. She picked up another chair and heaved it at the window. This time the glass splintered as it rejected the chair. Sydney felt the heat at her back. It wouldn't be long before the room was engulfed . . . or she died from smoke inhalation. She coughed, wiped her eyes, and kept fighting. She picked up another chair and whirled it into the glass. A spiderweb of cracks spread across the pane.

Sydney was getting dizzy as the smoke grew so thick, it became hard to see the windows. She grabbed another chair, summoned her strength, and hurled the chair forward. This time the glass shattered and the chair kept going, sailing out into space and falling to the pavement far below. The thick smoke rushed through the jagged opening, creating a swirling storm inside the room. Without stopping to admire her work, she grabbed another chair and used the legs to punch out the remaining glass from the window frame.

She climbed up onto the bookcase and leaned out to see a sheer wall of windows with no ledges or handholds to grab on to. Four stories down was hard pavement.

Sydney couldn't imagine what it would be like to fall so far. How should she land? What possible way could she hit and survive without breaking her legs? Or her back? As the choking smoke rushed past her and out the window, Sydney stood frozen, paralyzed with fear.

There was a wrenching sound, followed by a loud crack of splintering wood as the classroom door blew down. She instantly felt a tremendous rush of heat as the last barrier between her and the flames was removed. Sydney whipped around to see a wave of fire rush into the classroom moving impossibly fast, eating up the desks and the floor, revealing the beams beneath and the classroom below.

outside, staring into the room with curiosity, wondering what all the yelling was about.

Sydney looked up to the window she had thrown the chair through. That was no illusion. She had indeed smashed through the window to escape, but from what? There was no flaming ghoul, no smoke, no fire. The only threat was the shattered window that Sydney had nearly jumped through . . . to escape a fate that wasn't real.

"Go away!" Marsh shouted to the people in the corridor. "Close the door!"

They scattered, not sure what they were seeing. To them it looked as though the unflappable Sydney Foley had inexplicably flapped and tossed a chair through the window for no reason.

Marsh tentatively crawled closer to her, trying not to scare her any further.

"What happened, Syd?" he asked calmly.

Sydney finally accepted that she was no longer in danger. At least not from Marsh. She relaxed and threw her arms around him, holding him close, grateful to be alive and for his being there for her. But she didn't cry. Sydney never cried.

She did her best to steady her voice and said, "You didn't answer my text."

"Yeah, I did. I was already on my way."

"The fire alarm didn't work."

Marsh didn't have to reply to that. Sydney's focus had returned enough so that she was able to register a blaring horn. The fire alarm was working just fine. She hadn't heard it . . . or had been prevented from hearing it. Another harsh sound intruded. It was the urgent shriek of a siren from a rapidly approaching police car.

Sydney said, "I guess that means my 911 call went through too."

"Did you think the building was on fire?" Marsh said as calmly as if asking for the time of day.

"Isn't it?" she asked tentatively.

Marsh shook his head.

"You didn't see anything?" Sydney asked, though she knew the answer.

Marsh surveyed the room and ended by staring at the smashed window.

"No," he said with a frown. "And I can guess why."

He pulled away from her, reached into his pack, and took out a tennis-ball-size golden sphere that was covered with carved symbols.

Sydney nodded. She understood.

"He's back," she said soberly.

"Damn right he's back," came a bold reply from the other side of the room.

Marsh and Sydney turned quickly to see that someone else had arrived.

"It's about time he showed himself," the new arrival added.

"He tried to kill me," Sydney declared. "Why would he do that?"

"Because he couldn't get to *me*," Marsh said, holding up the golden ball. "This wouldn't let him."

"So it's starting again?" Sydney asked, with a slight crack to her usually strong voice.

"It never ended," the new arrival corrected. "But this time is different."

"How?" Marsh asked.

"This time he's not getting away."

"Bold talk . . . for a dead guy," Sydney said to her brother.

"Hey, it's good to be a ghost," Cooper Foley replied. He walked over to the smashed window and added, "Can't wait to see how you're going to explain this."

Marsh took a deep breath and said, "That'll be the least of our problems."

2

"He was trying to kill me," Sydney bellowed as she paced angrily. "Why else would he create the whole fire illusion? And the flaming skull. That was a particularly gruesome touch, by the way."

"It's not about you, Syd," Marsh said calmly. "If I wasn't protected by the crucible, he would have come after me."

"So you're saying I shouldn't take it personally?" she countered, exasperated. "That doesn't make me feel any better."

Marsh walked to her and took both of her hands. "Take it any way you want," he said softly. "But take the crucible."

Sydney was ready to argue, but when she looked into Marsh's eyes, she softened. He had that kind of effect on her.

She touched his cheek with genuine affection and said, "I can't do that."

"Yeah, you can. I don't want you to be in danger when it's me he's after."

"And that's why you have to keep it," Sydney said. "If he went after me like that, I can't imagine what he'd do to you."

Marsh pulled Sydney toward him and the two kissed.

Marsh then reached into the pocket of his hoodie and pulled out the golden orb that contained the blood of Alexander the Great. He held it out to Sydney and whispered, "Please. Take it."

Sydney shook her head and pushed it away. "I can't. I love you."

"I love you too. That's why you have to."

"Stop!" Cooper shouted, exasperated. "Take it. No, *you* take it. I love you. I love you more. Kissy-kissy. Jeez. If I weren't already dead, I'd have to kill myself just so I could roll over in my grave."

Sydney squinted at her brother. "You'd think death would have made you less obnoxious."

"Sorry," Coop shot back. "And speaking of obnoxious, I don't know what freaks me out more, Damon showing up or you two being all lovey. So strange."

"Said the ghost," Sydney said sarcastically.

Cooper and Sydney may have looked alike, with their dark hair and blue eyes, but their polar opposite styles usually put them at each other's throats. Coop's death did nothing to change that. Though Cooper was a spirit, Marsh looked more like the sore thumb with his blond hair and brown eyes.

The three were in the living room of Marsh's house in the suburban town of Stony Brook, Connecticut. It was a home that had always been so comfortable. So normal. It was a safe haven for Marsh until a malevolent spirit had turned it into a house of horrors.

"This is a no-brainer," Coop declared. "There's one crucible and two of you, so just stay together. You're practically joined at the hip anyway."

"You don't . . . watch us, do you?" Sydney asked with disgust.

"Give me a break," Cooper shot back. "Like I don't have enough to deal with."

"That's not practical," Marsh said, and held out the golden ball to Sydney. "When we're together, we'll be fine. When we're apart, Sydney keeps it."

"But I won't," Sydney argued.

"Give it to me," Cooper ordered, and tried to grab it, but his hand traveled through Marsh's like a beam of light passing through a solid object.

"Damn," he said in frustration. "Can this get any older?"

Marsh and Sydney were the only two beings in the Light who could see Cooper. To them he appeared the same as any other person, though he was anything but.

"Forget the crucible," Sydney exclaimed as she pulled Marsh toward the couch. "It can't protect either of us forever. This is about Damon."

"Agreed," Marsh said.

The two sat close to each other. Sydney kept a firm grip on Marsh's hand out of affection . . . and for security. Her nerves were still frayed.

"I'm way ahead of the curve on this," Coop declared. "I'll handle Damon."

"That gives me exactly zero confidence," Sydney said coldly.

"Let's hear what he has to say," Marsh offered.

Sydney bit her tongue and forced a smile.

"Okay, Mr. Afterlife," she said to Cooper. "How exactly are you going to 'handle' Damon?"

Cooper had already shared with them the entire story

of his adventures with Damon in the Black. There were no secrets between them.

"First I have to find him," Cooper began. "I have no idea where he is."

"So much for being ahead of the curve," Sydney said.

Coop ignored her and continued, "I haven't seen him since his army was sucked into the Blood, but I've seen the damage he's caused since. The guy wants revenge. On me. That much is obvious from the way he busted up my vision in the Black."

"How did he do that if his army was sent to the Blood?" Marsh asked.

"I don't know," Coop admitted. "And I don't know what happened to the spirits who were with me . . . my grand-father, Maggie Salinger, Zoe, and—"

"And my mother," Marsh said.

"Yeah. They're just . . . gone. Damon must be respon-sible, but as to where they are . . . your guess is as good as mine."

Sydney suggested, "Maybe he took them to his own vision."

"Okay, I lied. Your guess *isn't* as good as mine," Cooper said curtly. "I told you, his vision doesn't exist anymore. The Watchers took it from him. Damon's flying loose some-where."

"Maybe they all moved on to the next life," Marsh offered hopefully. "You know, the place you go after the Black?"

Coop squinted at him. "Do you *really* think that hap-pened?"

Marsh thought for a moment. "No."

Coop said, "I think Damon knows exactly where they are so he can use them to get what he wants."

"The poleax," Sydney declared.

"Yeah, the poleax," Coop confirmed. "For that he needs *you*, Ralph."

"But I don't know where his sword is!" Marsh declared with frustration.

"Maybe not, but he thinks you can find it."

"That's insane," Marsh grumbled.

Sydney asked, "And what happens if Damon gets it?"

Coop took a tired breath and turned serious. "The guy has something to prove. He feels as though he was never given his due as a general in Alexander's army and wants a second chance."

"To do what?" Sydney asked. "When did he fight for Alexander? Two thousand years ago?"

"Doesn't matter," Coop said quickly. "Time has no meaning in the Black. You can find spirits who lived yesterday or centuries ago. For all I know, Alexander himself is still floating around someplace and Damon wants to show him what a bad little soldier-boy he can really be."

"But why does he need that sword to prove that?" Marsh asked.

"That weapon holds the spiritual power of all those he killed in life. He can use it to tear open another Rift between the Light and the Black. Between the living and the dead. The Black is a very real place, but the spirits are . . . spirits. Not flesh and blood. I think for Damon to prove himself as a warrior, he'll have to do it here in the Light against living soldiers."

"So he wants to tear open a new Rift, come into the Light, and start a war?" Sydney asked. "Won't he be, like, two thousand years out of his league?"

"I don't know, Sydney," Coop said impatiently. "Maybe he'll get his ass kicked, but that's not the point. Can you imagine if a doorway was created between two worlds so that spirits could come back to reclaim their lives? There are millions of spirits in the Black. Billions. What would happen if the dam opened up and the Light was overrun by its own history?"

The three fell silent, imagining the possibility.

Marsh finally said, "Armageddon."

"Something like that," Coop agreed. "That's why the Watchers gave me the ability to be seen by you guys. My being here is totally against the way things work, but it seems like it's fallen on us to stop Damon."

Marsh said, "Because I'm the one he's coming after to find the poleax."

"And he killed me to get to you," Coop added. "Let's not forget that."

Sydney asked, "Why don't the Watchers stop him?"

"I think the only thing they can do is send him to the Blood, but that's the last thing they want because it'll put Damon back together with his army. No, they want Damon destroyed, and I don't think they have that ability."

"And we do?" Sydney asked.

"Not 'we.' Me. I'm a spirit. I can move through the Black and use one of those spirit-killing swords on that bastard. That's how this is going to end. It's the only way it *can* end."

"So what are we supposed to do?" Sydney asked.

"Nothing," Cooper answered quickly. "I mean it. Nothing. Stay together and keep the crucible with you. As long as you two have that thing, Damon is powerless over you."

"No," Marsh said flatly.

Cooper shot him a quick, surprised look. "What do you mean 'no'? I told you—"

Marsh stood up to face his friend. "I heard what you said, Coop. I get it. But I'm not going to sit around doing nothing. None of this would have happened if my mother hadn't gone digging around under that temple and destroyed the first crucible."

"So what?" Coop shot back. "This is serious, Ralph. We're not playing army."

"Do you really think I'm playing?"

"No, I don't," Coop said, backing down. "But I mean, c'mon, you're in way over your head."

"I'll be the judge of that," Marsh said quickly.

Coop walked away from Marsh, his mind racing, trying to come up with the right thing to say.

"Look," he said sharply. "I may be a spirit but I can't be hunting for Damon in the Black and babysitting you at the same time."

"I don't need a babysitter," Marsh said, bristling.

"No? How many times did I bail your butt out when Damon was coming after you?"

"This is as much my battle as it is yours," Marsh said through gritted teeth. "You may think I'm still a little kid that you have to coax into trusting himself, but things have changed."

"I'm sorry, Marsh," Cooper said, softening. "I know you've been through a lot and you aren't the same guy you were before and blah, blah, blah, but this is way more important than you trying to prove something to yourself."

"Do *not* put me in the same category as Damon," Marsh snapped.

"That's not what I meant—"

"I don't care what you meant. I'm telling you that I'm going to do what I can to make this right. You're just running around like you always do, thinking you can handle anything. Well, you can't. Damon got you. He killed you, remember? You're in as far over your head as I am. The only difference is that you won't admit it."

The two stood toe-to-toe, neither backing down.

"Okay, Ralph," Coop said coldly. "I'm going to the Black

to track down and kill a demon. What are *you* going to do?"

"I'm going to find Ennis Mobley," Marsh said with authority.

"Why?" Coop asked with surprise.

"You haven't thought of everything, Coop. You never do. There were six crucibles. One was broken in Damon's tomb when my mother and Ennis found it. The second one I broke. Your grandfather broke the third in the Black. The fourth I've got right here, and the fifth is protecting the poleax, which is why Damon can't find it himself. That leaves one more. If these things have as much power over Damon as you say, I think we should try to find it, and who has a better chance of knowing where it is than the guy who found them all in the first place?"

Coop started to argue, but held back.

Sydney smiled. "He's got you there, spirit boy."

"All right," Coop said. "Go for it. But stay close to my sister. And keep that crucible with you. I don't want to have to come back here to save either of you. Again."

"Just worry about yourself," Marsh said coldly.

A colorful, swirling mist appeared behind Cooper.

"What I'm worried about is ending this, and there's only one way that can happen. Damon has to be destroyed."

"So stop talking and find him," Sydney called out.

Cooper took a step backward and disappeared into the mist.

Marsh and Sydney stared wide-eyed at the colorful cloud as it quickly vanished.

"Well," Sydney said with a sigh. "That went well."

"Here," Marsh said, holding out the crucible.

Sydney pushed his hand aside and wrapped her arms around his neck. Marsh hugged her close.

"You know the strangest part?" she asked.

"There's more?" Marsh asked with mock surprise.

Sydney chuckled. "Something good has actually come out of this."

"Enlighten me. Please."

"If none of this had happened, I'd still think you were a geek."

Marsh smiled.

"Actually," Sydney added. "I *still* think you're a geek, but now you're *my* geek."

"Good . . . I think."

"I love the way you're stepping up," she said, turning serious. "But I also know how scared you are."

Marsh shrugged but didn't disagree.

"We're in this together, Seaver," Sydney said. "I have no idea how this will play out but there's one thing I'm sure of: If my brother is going to finish Damon, then somewhere, somehow, he's going to need your help . . . and you're going to need mine."

She leaned forward and the two kissed.

Marsh held her close, enjoying the last few seconds of sanity before their lives would, once again, be turned inside out.

3

In spite of his bold promises, Cooper had no idea where to begin his quest.

Though he had all of time and history at his disposal, he felt as if he had to work fast. Damon was a brilliant tactician and Coop had no doubt that he had already formed a plan. The fact that he had resurfaced and gone after Sydney proved it. Damon was very much back in business. In desperation Coop began by trying to track down the spirits that had disappeared. He had no doubt that they would somehow factor into Damon's plan, and finding them was crucial.

He first went to the vision of Marsh's mother, Ree Seaver, the spiritual leader of the Guardians of the Rift. From Marsh's house in the Light he stepped through the veil between lives, between the Light and the Black, and entered Grand Central Terminal. Or what was left of it after the battle between Damon's soldiers and the Guardians. Nothing had changed since he was there last. The vision of the 1970s' version of the train terminal was a wreck. A bombed-out war zone. The train engine that had jumped the track and crashed into the passenger concourse still stood amid the rubble of crushed granite and cement. The entrance to the building was destroyed. The vintage army tank that had caused so much damage still stood where it had fired on the Guardians during the battle. There was an eerie quiet that made the tumultuous scene appear that much more impossible.

Coop walked to the center of the promenade, kicking through the remains of the pulverized information booth, to confirm that the Rift into the Light that Damon had cut centuries before was indeed no longer there. Seeing the empty floor where the Rift once existed was the only visible proof of the Guardian's victory.

As he stood in the center of that cavernous building, he was overwhelmed by a sense of emptiness. Ree was gone. The Guardians were gone. It was a dead, abandoned vision. As forlorn a feeling as that was, the fact that it still existed gave him hope. If her vision was there he felt certain that Ree's spirit still existed in the Black. Somewhere.

Cooper descended the stairs to the subway tracks beneath the terminal where Ree's private rail car stood. Empty. There was nothing there to give him any ideas about where else to search for her. He thought of walking to the warehouse where the Guardians had first captured him and Maggie, but knew what he would find there. Nothing. Wherever Ree Seaver was, it wasn't in her own vision.

He thought of Zoe, the daughter of Adeipho, Damon's enemy. With one step he left the train car and stepped onto a rocky beach on the shore of a calm ocean. The air was warm, the sky brilliant blue, and the sun hot and welcoming. He turned to see that he was in an ancient fishing village some-where in Greece. Coop figured it had to be the vision of where Zoe lived in the Light when Adeipho fought alongside Damon a few centuries before the year zero. It wasn't much more than a collection of crudely constructed huts surrounded by palm trees. The tranquil beach was scattered with small wooden boats and jumbles of fishing nets.

What Coop didn't see . . . was people. Like Grand Central, this vision was empty. As much as his curiosity tempted him to explore the village, Coop didn't know enough about Zoe to know what clues to look for that might help him find her. Instead he thought of his grandfather.

With one step he was back in the familiar front yard of Eugene Foley. It was a cool fall day, just like always. The autumn-colored trees swayed in a slight breeze. The scene wasn't as eerie as the others, for Gramps didn't normally have other people populating his vision. His white farm-house and tomato garden looked as inviting and normal as always . . . except that Gramps wasn't there. Coop was about to walk up to the house, when he glanced to the house next door. Maggie's house. He turned and headed for it, vaulting over the split rail fence that separated the two properties.

When he came down on the other side, he had made the transition from his grandfather's vision to Maggie's. The sky had grown darker and the season had made the transforma-tion from fall to early winter. The colorful leaves were gone and a chilly wind rustled Coop's hair as he stood between Maggie's house and the barn where her parents had died.

"Hey!" he yelled, not expecting an answer.

It struck him that since he had communicated with the Watcher in Damon's lost vision, he hadn't seen any other Watcher in the Black. Anywhere. He didn't expect them to be observing empty visions, but he had hoped they were still looking out for him. He glanced around, wishing he would see one of the dark-clad figures standing in the distance in their usual pose, silently observing.

Nobody was there. They had asked for his help and then left him on his own.

Coop strode toward Maggie's house, not at all sure what it was he was looking for. Damon had done something with these spirits, of that he was sure. Was it for revenge? Or part of a devious plan for a counterattack? The sickening truth was, it was probably both.

Coop was about to climb the stairs that led to Maggie's porch, when his foot crunched on something that sounded like broken glass. He lifted his shoe to see the remains of the vessel that had once contained the blood of Alexander the Great. It was one of the six crucibles that were created by ancient priests upon Alexander's death as a curse to keep Damon from coming back through the Rift. The crucibles had done their job for a few thousand years.

Cooper knelt down and picked up one of the larger pieces. It was all that was left of the crucible that had protected the Rift in Ree's vision. He and Maggie had stolen it to try and force the Guardians into a battle with Damon and his soldiers. Instead Coop's plan backfired and Damon demanded that he break it or he would kill Marsh and Sydney. Coop would have smashed it to save his sister and best friend, but never got the chance. His grandfather had taken that difficult decision away and broken it himself . . . right there in front of Maggie's house.

Coop examined a sharp piece of golden glass. It had a streak of blood inside that had already dried to a dark brown. It was a gruesome artifact . . . that reminded him of another grisly relic. Thousands of years before, in their final battle in the Light, Damon had severed Adeipho's ear and kept the flesh as a barbaric memento. Damon had given the ghastly artifact to Cooper, telling him that it had a strong connection with Adeipho (obviously) and by using it Coop would be able to track down Adeipho's spirit.

The crucible had a strong connection with Damon. It had been one of the items that had cursed him for centuries. Was it possible? Would the connection between Damon and the crucible be strong enough to track him down? Coop clutched the glass, feeling the sharp edges digging into his palm. He closed his eyes and thought of Damon, his two sharp teeth and his malevolent laugh. Without opening his eyes he stood up and took a step.

The air grew instantly colder and the sky went dark. Cooper opened his eyes to see that he had arrived in another vision. One he had never been to and wasn't familiar with.

He couldn't help but smile. The hunt was on.

He stuck the glass shard into his jeans pocket and made a slow turn to see that he was in a dense pine forest. A sharp wind blasted through the trees, whipping the branches about and kicking up leaves that danced through the air. The sky was clear and the moon was full, which made it easy to see. The challenge was to know which way to go and what to look for. He wasn't about to shout out: "Hello? Damon? Ready or not, here I come!"

Rather than pick a random direction that might have taken him the wrong way, he folded his arms and listened. Within seconds his patience was rewarded when he heard the faint sound of music. It was a single flute playing a soft, sad solo.

"Gotcha," Coop said, and headed toward the sound.

Moving through the trees was no problem. The moon offered plenty of light. With each step he grew closer to the source of the mysterious, haunting tune while his mind raced ahead to what he might find when he reached it. He didn't know where he was, or *when* he was. Whose vision was this? Most important, why was Damon there? For all

Coop knew, Damon had armies hidden throughout the Black. The vision could have been a staging area for a massive counterattack and he could have been walking into a situation that he had no hope of handling without one of the black spirit-killing swords. If he'd had any other option, he would have taken it.

Within minutes he came to the edge of a clearing and a small village that was surrounded by a low stone wall. The collection of huts within the circle were constructed with stone and earth. They were circular and had thatched roofs that came to a tall point. Wherever he was, it didn't look like a vision from the twenty-first century. Or the twentieth. The structures were ancient-looking. Unlike the previous visions he had searched, this vision was very much alive, that much he could tell from the smoke that curled up and out of holes in the points of the roofs that acted as crude chimneys. Rather than the welcoming smell of burning wood, Coop was hit with an odor that was more like scorched earth.

Man, what are they burning? he thought. *Old shoes?*

The haunting flute song continued, luring him deeper into the ancient village. He scrambled over the stone wall, passed one hut, and entered a loose circle of similar huts that were clustered around a stone well. A wooden two-wheeled cart stood nearby with an empty yoke for a horse or ox. Wooden buckets were scattered about, along with piles of black chunks that looked like dried cow pies. There were no people, though most of the huts had a warm glow coming from within, which meant that the town was populated but had closed up for the night.

The music was coming from a hut on the far side of the circle. Coop followed it like a moth drawn to a candle. He thought of walking up to the wooden door and knocking but wanted to know what he was getting himself into first, so he moved cautiously around to the side of the hut to try and get a peek inside. He circled the round structure, looking for a window that would allow him to peer inside, but there were none.

He had come all the way around to the front and was about to reach the door when—

"Stop there!" came a threatening shout.

Coop froze, and before he could react, strong hands grabbed him from behind, trapping him in a bear hug. Coop struggled to get free but it was no use. The powerful attacker was in charge. He whipped Cooper around and brought him face-to-face with a massive, bearded man in peasant clothing.

"Who be ya?" the man in front of Coop bellowed through green-stained teeth.

Cooper was too stunned to think of a clever answer. "I . . . I'm just passing through" was all he managed to say.

"Passin' through?" the man repeated mockingly. "And ya just so happened to come right to the home of Riagan?"

"Uh . . . yeah. I mean, I followed the music."

Cooper couldn't move, which meant he couldn't step away and leave the vision. He was totally at the mercy of these men. While one held Cooper tight, the other strode to the door and pounded it with his fist. Instantly the flute music stopped.

"Come," a voice commanded from inside.

The huge man pushed open the door, and Coop was wrestled inside by the other. Fighting back would have been futile so he didn't even try.

"We found another," the man in front announced.

Sitting on a tall bench on the far side of the hut was the musician. He was an old man with long gray hair and rough-hewn brown clothes. In his hand was a wooden recorder. He too had a beard but looked cleaner and more put together than the two beasts who had jumped Coop. He gave Cooper an appraising look, then nodded to the others.

"Be still, Maedoc," he said calmly. "I will be honoring his visit."

The taller man, Maedoc, gave Cooper an angry glance, then nodded to the guy who was holding him, and Coop was roughly shoved across the room.

Coop managed to stay on his feet and whip around, ready to fight, but the sight of the two hulking men wearing ratty clothes and looking like they had the kind of strength that came from a lifetime of heavy work made him think twice about doing anything stupid.

"We stand ready," Maedoc said.

"Thank you," the musician replied.

The two men left, reluctantly, throwing angry glares back at Cooper.

Cooper smiled and waved back. He then took a quick scan of the hut.

A fire burned in the center, directly under the ventilation hole in the roof. Crude wooden furniture was scattered about. There was a table and a chair that looked as if a heavy weight had landed and destroyed them. The legs were splayed and the wood was freshly splintered.

Something had happened in that hut. Something violent.

Coop continued to turn slowly until his eyes set on something that appeared out of place. A long wooden table was set up along one wall, and was loaded with the makings of an incredible feast. There were wooden bowls brimming with fruit, loaves of freshly baked bread, bunches of succulent vegetables, crackling roasted meats, and pitchers filled with wine. A candle burned at either end, adding a touch of elegance. Running parallel to this table and pushed right against it was another. It might have been a bench for sitting except for the fact that it was on the same level as the brimming table. This second table was empty except for a single pillow on one end, as if ready for a corpulent king to recline and partake of the incredible feast.

It was an incongruous display of abundance in the peasant-like hut.

"You having a party?" Coop asked.

The old man glanced to the table and snickered. He put the recorder down on the bench and walked to the fire.

"Forgive the rough treatment," he said politely with a thick Irish accent. "They be protecting me. Me name is Riagan, though I suppose you already be knowing that."

"What are they protecting you from?" Coop asked. "Hungry neighbors?"

Riagan glanced at the feast and frowned. "That feast be the last thing me neighbors be wanting. Those coming here seek something far different, but they be wasting their time, as be you."

He tossed a flat brick of black earth onto the fire, making sparks fly. Coop cringed. It was a chunk of that cow-flop-looking stuff he saw in piles outside that was burning and producing the foul smell that permeated the village.

"I'm searching too," Coop said. "Not for food, for a man."

Riagan gave Coop a sad smile. "Course you be," he said, sounding tired. "They all be. But I have to be telling ya the same as I told 'em all: He no longer be here."

Coop's heart sank. The glass shard had led him to the right place, but too late.

"Wait," Coop said. "Other people are looking for him?"

"Surprised are ya?" Riagan said. "People been coming here for generations, from every corner of the Black and every type of vision there be. Same as when we lived in the Light. They all be after the same thing . . . that no longer be here."

The man sat back down on his bench and picked up his

recorder. "So you might as well go back to where you came from and make way for the next poor soul I'll be having to disappoint."

He started to play again, but Coop ran in front of him.

"Whoa, wait. What do you think I'm looking for?"

The old man shrugged. "Redemption? Salvation? Call it what you like. All be the same."

Coop's mind raced.

"No, it isn't," Coop said. "We're talking about two different things."

"I think not," the old man said, irritated. "The only reason anyone be coming here is to seek me brother."

Coop took a surprised step back. "Damon's your brother?"

"Damon?" Riagan said, confused. "Me brother's name is Brennus. He goes by no other."

Cooper backed away from Riagan, scanning the hut, trying to understand what it was he had stumbled onto.

"I . . . I don't get it," Coop mumbled. He felt the sharp shard of glass from the crucible in his pocket. "Damon must have come here."

"Perhaps this Damon be seeking Brennus as well," Riagan replied. "Many pass this way. I never learn all the names. Turning them back be my fate now, and I suppose it be deserved. It be a penance I been paying for longer than I care to remember."

"That must be it," Coop declared. "Damon was here, maybe looking for your brother. He must have, or why else would the crucible have led me here?"

"I know of no crucible."

"Damon was a warrior," Coop explained, his excitement growing. "From ancient Macedonia. He's short and stocky. His face is covered with scars. And, oh yeah, major detail: His two front teeth are sharpened to points."

Riagan's eyes widened with understanding . . . and fear. He backed off the bench, knocking it over as if trying to get as far away from Cooper as possible.

"That devil be the one you seek?" he asked fearfully.

"So he *was* here!" Cooper exclaimed.

"Aye!" Riagan replied. "When he learned Brennus was here no longer, he turned into a wild man. Certain he was that I be holding back the truth, but on whatever small scrap of honor I be keeping, I swore to him I know not where me brother has gone."

"Let me guess. Damon didn't like that."

"Flew into a rage, he did," Riagan said, pointing to the damaged furniture. "Threatened to end me if I did not speak the truth, but I told him I'd be welcoming the end rather than having to spend another second in this cursed vision. I begged him to lead me that way."

"So he left you alone, right?"

Riagan nodded, his lips quivering. "The life I led was not a good one. Ashamed I am for me part in Brennus's crimes. If I could take back what I done, I would. But since that cannot be, I deserve whatever punishment is fair. That I accept. But trapped here in such a nightmare for all eternity is a fate beyond cruel."

Riagan dropped to his knees in front of Cooper, grabbing at Coop's black T-shirt.

"Help me, lad," he cried. "Can you end me? I be too weak for the Blood, but even that would be a far sight better than this limbo. I beg ya. Destroy me if you can."

Cooper pushed Riagan away, and the old man fell to his elbows on the dirt floor, sobbing.

"Who is your brother?" Coop asked. "What's so special about him that he can offer salvation?"

Riagan sobbed, "You truly do not know?"

"No!"

"Then I will not be the one to reveal such dark truths."

"Oh no, you can't do that," Coop yelled with frustration. He grabbed Riagan by the back of his shirt and pulled him to his feet. "Why was Damon looking for him? There's no way he cared about redemption. There has to be another reason."

Riagan looked deep into Cooper's eyes. Cooper saw how tortured the old spirit was.

"Damon is truly who you seek?" he asked. "Not Brennus?"

"Yes," Coop said, and pushed him away.

The tortured spirit shuffled to a table, where he picked up a worn brown leather glove.

"He pulled this from his hand before he started on me," Riagan explained with disdain. "Said he wanted to feel me bones break when he struck me."

"That's about his speed."

Riagan tossed the glove to Cooper as if he didn't want to touch it any longer. Coop caught it awkwardly.

"That should help you find the devil," Riagan said. "But do not be telling him ya got it from me."

"Don't worry."

"Now go," Riagan demanded. "It makes me fearful havin' a spirit here that be party to that beast."

"Not until you tell me what your brother does here," Coop said.

"Maedoc!" Riagan suddenly shouted.

The door flew open, and the two bearded guards tumbled in.

"Help me!" Riagan called out.

The two peasants charged for Cooper, but Coop was too fast. He clutched the leather glove and took a quick step backward out of the vision. He wasn't even thinking of where he might go. It was more about not being there anymore. He backed out of Riagan's dark vision . . .

. . . into bright, warm sunlight. Replacing the quiet of the pine forest was a rush of sound that swept over him like a massive, charging wave. Coop covered his head and fell to the ground to protect himself from whatever was headed his way.

The sound grew to a quick crescendo, then died back down to a steady roar. Without looking, Coop knew exactly what the sound was. He'd heard it many times before.

It was cheering. Big crowd cheering.

He cautiously peeked out from under his arms to see that he was next to a massive structure. A stadium. The roaring sound was the white noise of excited fans, coming from inside. Another cheer went up. Coop figured that somebody must have scored a touchdown or hit a home run. He stood slowly and heard another sound. Something was headed toward him, fast. He turned quickly to see a man on horseback charging his way. Coop had to dive away or he would have been trampled.

"Dude!" he called to the oblivious rider. "What the heck!"

The rider didn't react. Cooper saw that he was wearing armor of some sort, with a golden helmet.

His first thought: *Mascot*. What team had a Roman centurion-looking mascot? Michigan State? USC? Coop had no idea what Damon would be doing in somebody's vision of a college football game. He looked out at the parking lot for answers and saw . . . it wasn't a parking lot. Rather than pavement, the stadium was surrounded by acres of grass and lush, flowering gardens. Far beyond the stadium he saw an immense arch, behind which were more massive structures held up by soaring columns. Next to the arch was a tremendous bronze statue that rivaled the Statue of Liberty in size, only this was a naked guy with a wreath of laurel wrapped around his head.

Not USC, he thought. *Not even close.*

People from many different eras milled about. He saw modern soldiers and ancient warriors. There were men wearing everything from business suits, to togas, to shorts and sneakers. Some women were dressed as if they were going to the opera, while others wore matching brightly colored warm-up suits. As confusing as the sight was, it made sense. This was the Black. If there was a big game going on in somebody's vision, why wouldn't people from different visions and times come to watch? It was all so strangely explainable. The real question was: Whose vision was it and where exactly was he?

And where was Damon?

The answer came in the form of a platoon of soldiers. They marched in formation leading a horse-drawn cart that was carrying people. Prisoners. The men being transported wore dirty white tunics and shackles around their ankles. The soldiers had spears and wore gleaming ceremonial armor. They led the wagon through the archway and into the stadium, disappearing into the dark depths.

Cooper realized where he was.

Not a stadium, he said to himself. *At least not like any stadium I've been to.*

It made perfect sense. It was just the kind of place that Damon would appreciate. Seeing innocent people being fed to lions was right up his alley. Without stopping to imagine the carnage he might encounter inside, Cooper jogged toward the huge structure that up until that moment he had only seen in pictures, in movies, and in ruins.

It was the Colosseum in ancient Rome.

4

"I cannot come to the phone at this time," announced the familiar male voice with the unmistakable lilting Jamaican accent. "Please leave a message after you hear the tone."

The tone sounded, followed immediately by an annoying computer voice that declared, "Message box full."

Marsh had made at least a dozen calls and hit the same dead end each time. He kept hoping that Ennis would eventually pick up. Or clear out his mailbox. He didn't bother texting because Ennis's phone was a relic and didn't have that capability. With no way to make contact, Marsh had no choice but to hunt him down in person.

He and Sydney rode the commuter train into New York City from Stony Brook with the plan of going to Ennis's apartment in the East Village in Lower Manhattan.

"How can you be sure he's even in town?" Sydney asked.

"I can't," was Marsh's curt answer.

"So this could be a total waste of time."

Marsh stared out the window. "It could, but I don't know what else to do, Syd."

He said this with such a strong sense of pain and frustration that it made Sydney's heart ache. She could see how much pressure he was under, so she went against her normal instincts and didn't press him. She knew that for the most part this was his show, and though she was usually one to take command, she decided to take a backseat for once and follow his lead. That's how much she cared about him.

Sydney tried to remember him as the nerdy little guy who used to hang around the house with her little brother playing Nintendo and futilely trying to impress her by showing off his knowledge of all things Batman. She barely gave him a second thought back then. Now that she had feelings for him, she wished she could see through to that young, immature guy once more just to remember the way he used to get so excited over something so silly.

But too much had happened since then. Marsh had become a different guy.

Sydney chuckled to herself.

"What's funny?" he asked.

She held his hand and said, "I was just thinking about when we were kids and how you used to get all twitchy-nervous when I was around."

Marsh smiled. "I didn't think you knew I existed."

"I knew. I just thought you were annoying, so I avoided you."

"Gee, thanks."

"But I don't make you nervous anymore."

Marsh nodded thoughtfully. "Yeah, you do. It's just . . ."

His voice trailed off.

"Just what?" she asked.

Marsh shrugged. "There are other things I'm a lot more nervous about."

Reality had returned, quickly. Sydney nodded sadly and put her head on his shoulder. They rode the rest of the way in silence.

Marsh wasn't used to getting around in the city, so when they arrived at Grand Central Terminal (the real one, not Ree's vision in the Black), Sydney took charge and found them a cab. It wasn't difficult. Sydney was hard to miss in her jean shorts, and a cab nearly caused a huge accident by careening across three lanes of traffic on Lexington Avenue to get to her. Sydney and Marsh hopped in with a cabbie who didn't try to hide his disappointment when he realized that Sydney was with a guy.

"Where to?" he asked dourly.

"You know McSorley's?" Marsh asked.

"Doesn't everybody?" was the cabbie's sharp reply.

"Then let's go," Marsh commanded.

Marsh wasn't sure of Ennis's exact address. He'd been there several times with his mother but she had always led the way. He only knew it was near a place that was considered the oldest saloon in New York City. McSorley's Old Ale House.

Sydney watched Marsh as he stared out the window. Though she felt he wanted to be alone with his thoughts, she also wanted to help.

"What do you think he'll say?" she finally asked, unable to contain herself any longer.

Marsh didn't answer right away. Sydney wasn't sure if he was ignoring her or thinking about his answer.

"Marsh?"

"I don't know," he finally said, keeping his gaze out the window. "Hopefully he's got another piece of the puzzle."

"But you've already talked to him about the crucibles. What makes you think he'll tell you any more now than he did before?"

Marsh snapped a look to Sydney. His steely gaze surprised her.

"I don't know," he said curtly. "If I could think of something better to do, I would do it."

Marsh's harsh answer surprised Sydney. She didn't take attitude from anybody, and her first instinct was to fire back at him. Instead she took a breath and let it go, telling herself that it was the stress talking.

They didn't speak again until the cab stopped in front of the old tavern. Marsh paid the cabbie and got out. He knew exactly where he was going. Sydney followed, walking east. The tension in his body seemed to grow with each step. Sydney saw that he was clenching his fists. She chose not to ask him about it.

They finally came to a ten-story brick apartment building. Marsh stopped in front and looked up to the highest floors.

"This is it," he said to nobody in particular.

He climbed the few steps of the stoop to the front door and entered the vestibule. Sydney followed without question and watched as Marsh scanned the rows of buttons on the ancient security panel. Each had a name penciled in next to the number of the apartment. Marsh scanned the list until he found the name Mobley.

"10H," Sydney said, reading. "Top floor, of course. The elevator better work."

Marsh pressed the button on the call panel. They waited. No answer. Marsh pressed it again, harder.

"He could be off on an assignment," Sydney offered.

Marsh was about to press the button a third time when an elderly woman came out of the door that led to the lobby.

Sydney grabbed the door before it swung closed and gave the old lady a disarming smile.

"Forgot our keys again," she said sweetly.

"Welcome to my life," the old woman growled, and continued on out to the street.

Sydney winked at Marsh and the two went inside. To Sydney's relief the elevator worked.

"You okay?" she asked as they slowly rose in the creaky old lift.

He nodded.

Sydney didn't believe him.

They got out on the tenth floor, where Marsh led them down the narrow corridor to the door marked 10H.

"Smells like boiled cabbage," Sydney said, wrinkling her nose.

Marsh pressed the doorbell and waited.

"Ennis?" he called.

No response.

"He's probably not here," Sydney offered.

Marsh dug out his cell phone. He punched in a number, and a moment later they heard the electronic chime of a ringing phone coming from inside Ennis's apartment.

Marsh looked to Sydney and smiled with satisfaction. "If his cell's here, he's here."

For a brief moment Sydney saw the old Marsh, who was tickled at his ability to be an ingenious sleuth. He knocked on the door again.

"Ennis? It's Marsh. I've been trying to get hold of you for days."

Still no answer.

"Suppose something's happened to him," Sydney said soberly. "I mean, what if he's in there but . . ."

She didn't finish the thought as Marsh pounded on the door in frustration.

"C'mon, Ennis! It's me!"

He was about to try and force the door open, when he stopped suddenly and put his ear to it.

"What?" Sydney asked, confused.

"I heard something. Somebody's in there," he replied, then shouted, "Ennis?"

They heard a whisper that was barely loud enough to reach through the door.

"Marshmallow?"

The voice was faint, but unmistakable.

"Yes! It's me. Open the door."

The door didn't open.

"C'mon, Ennis," Marsh implored. "We gotta talk."

In a voice so small it sounded as if it could be that of a frightened child rather than a forty-year-old man, Ennis said, "How do I know it is really you?"

"Who else would it be?" Marsh argued impatiently.

He gave Sydney a "What is his problem?" look.

"What do you expect?" she said in reply. "He's been dealing with this longer than you."

Marsh thought for a moment, then softened.

"It's me, Ennis," he said. "I promise."

"Who is that with you?" Ennis asked.

"My friend Sydney. You know her. She's Cooper's sister."

"Hi, Ennis," she said.

Marsh added, "If it wasn't us—I mean, if it was Damon—we wouldn't need for you to open the door. We'd just come in. Right?"

"That proves nothing," Ennis replied. "I have seen too many tricks."

Marsh and Sydney exchanged worried looks.

"Something happened to him," she said.

"C'mon, Ennis!" Marsh shouted with frustration.

Sydney put her hand on Marsh's shoulder to calm him, and said, "Ennis? If it was Damon out here, would we have the crucible you gave us in the cemetery?"

There was a long pause, then Ennis asked, "You have the crucible?"

"Yes," Marsh said, giving Sydney a big smile and a thumbs-up.

Sydney beamed.

"Show me," he said while tapping the door near the peephole.

Sydney dug into her shoulder bag, pulled out the golden orb, and held it up to the lens in the door. Seconds later the door was unlocked and yanked open.

"Quickly," Ennis commanded.

They both hurried inside, and as soon as they crossed the threshold, Ennis slammed the door shut and locked it tight.

"What's going on?" Marsh asked.

Ennis threw his arms around Marsh.

"I am so sorry for that. I no longer know what to think and who to trust."

Marsh patted Ennis soothingly on the back. "It's cool," he said. "I get it. I *really* get it."

Ennis was crying. Sydney kept her distance, not wanting to intrude on the emotional moment. She glanced around the apartment to see that it was empty. There was no furniture, lamps, rugs, or anything else that would normally be found in a home. The only sign that a person actually lived there was a dirty blanket lying in the corner surrounded by empty Doritos bags. It looked more like the temporary shelter of a squatter than someone's home.

"You moving out?" Sydney asked.

Ennis pulled away from Marsh and tried to compose himself by wiping away his tears.

Marsh was shocked to see that Ennis was a mess. His

mother's friend and associate was normally an impeccably neat guy who ironed his clothes and kept his hair trimmed short. Ennis hardly looked like the same person. His clothes looked as though he had been sleeping in them for weeks, with grease stains on the front of his normally arctic-white shirt. His hollow cheeks were unshaven. Worse still, his eyes were bloodshot and tired, his dark skin gray. Flecks of gray had appeared in his black hair.

"I am not moving," he replied. "I have gotten rid of everything other than what I need to get by."

"Why?" Sydney asked.

"To give him less ammunition to use against me," was his grim answer.

Sydney and Marsh exchanged dark looks.

"You look bad, Ennis," Marsh said. "What's been going on?"

Ennis collected himself and cleared his throat, trying to regain whatever dignity he had left.

"I gave up the crucible," he said, pointing to the golden ball that Sydney clutched. "That left me, how should I describe it? Exposed."

"Damon's been haunting you?" Marsh asked.

Ennis managed an ironic smile. "'Haunting' is a gentle way of putting it."

He led them into the bedroom, where there was a single mattress on the floor, along with more empty bags of chips. He quickly closed the door behind them, which shut out most of the light since the window blinds were closed tight.

Sydney stayed close to Marsh. She didn't fear Ennis as much as what he was about to tell them.

"This has become my world," Ennis explained. "I do not leave the apartment unless it is absolutely necessary. Mostly it is to buy food."

"Why all the chips?" Sydney asked.

"Soft bags cannot harm me," he explained. "I cannot say the same for glass jars or metal cans or sharp utensils. I was afraid of what I might be tricked into doing with them, so I got rid of it all. I know, that sounds like the ramblings of a madman."

"Why didn't you tell me?" Marsh asked. "You could have come to Stony Brook. The crucible could have protected all of us!"

"I considered it," Ennis admitted. "A few times I even left for the train station. But each time I was turned back by . . . circumstances."

"Damon," Sydney said with a gasp. "He's keeping you isolated."

"Why don't you answer your phone?" Marsh asked.

"Because I never know who might be calling," was his sober answer.

Marsh knew what that meant. He'd gotten plenty of unwanted phone calls courtesy of Damon the Butcher.

"Have you told your father about Damon?" Ennis asked.

"No," Marsh answered quickly. "And I'm not going to. The more who know, the more will be in danger. I've heard that way too many times, and I believe it."

"You cannot battle this alone," Ennis warned.

"I'm not. I've got Sydney . . . and Cooper."

On hearing the name of Marsh's dead best friend, Ennis's eyes opened wide.

"You must tell me all that has happened," he implored.

They sat down, though Sydney and Marsh chose the floor over the soiled mattress. It took only a few minutes for Marsh to relate the story of his battle with Gravedigger and Cooper's adventure in the Black. Ennis listened without interrupting. He soaked up every word. Nodding. Understanding. Every so often he winced, mostly when Marsh told him about what his mother had been through in the Black.

Marsh's tale ended with Sydney's near death at school, and their plan to find Damon and destroy him.

Marsh finished with, "Hearing it all like that makes it sound so incredibly impossible."

"Yet we know it is not," Ennis said, tired. "Words cannot begin to express how miserable I feel over what I so foolishly started."

"Don't be sorry," Marsh declared. "Help us."

He took the golden ball from Sydney, held it up and continued, "You discovered the poleax and the crucibles in the tomb that protected the Rift. There were six. Three are broken. This is the fourth. Do you know where the other two are?"

Ennis looked uncomfortable, as if it were a question he didn't want to answer. He stood and went to the window to peer outside in case someone might be listening in, even though they were ten floors up. Satisfied, he closed the blinds and then went into the bathroom to splash water on his face.

Sydney whispered to Marsh, "He's gone off the deep end."

"We all have," Marsh replied.

Ennis came back into the room and said, "I do not know where they might be. When I left the tomb in Greece, I brought out only three."

"You told me the one I broke belonged to my mother and you promised her you'd give it to me to keep me safe. But that wasn't how it happened, was it?"

"No," Ennis admitted. "I told you that so you would appreciate its importance. I did not divulge the whole story because I was holding out hope that you would not be touched by this horror and never learn the truth. It was foolish of me to think it would be that simple."

Sydney said, "So what about the other crucibles?"

Ennis rubbed his chin nervously.

"One has to be with the poleax," Marsh declared. "That's why Damon can't see it. My mother believes you took the weapon out of Damon's tomb, Ennis. Did you?"

Sydney and Marsh stared at Ennis, waiting for a response.

Ennis kept his eyes on the floor.

"C'mon, man," Sydney blurted out impatiently. "Did you take the poleax and hide it with a crucible or not?"

Ennis frowned and nodded. "I did."

Hearing those words and the reality they revealed made Marsh's head spin. "My god," he said, stunned. "All this time. Damon's been coming after me but you're the one who knows."

"And I will not tell you where it is," Ennis added. "That knowledge would only put you in more danger."

"More danger?" Sydney bellowed, and jumped to her feet. "Are you serious? How can we be in any more danger than this?"

"You have no idea, miss," Ennis said. "Look at me. I cannot sleep because he invades my thoughts with such horribly vivid visions that it is impossible to know if I am awake or dreaming. I have been tortured by visits from my dead parents, who implore me to tell Damon where his weapon is hidden. I know they are only shadows, but they are torturous just the same. He has shown me images of a fantastic feast, knowing how hungry I am. He has sent me home to a glorious, warm beach, enticing me with the promise of paradise, but it is all an illusion to further the torture. I have not given in because I know that if he finds the poleax, it would create horrors that go far beyond what I have had to deal with. I consider this my punishment for disturbing the tomb . . . for forcing your mother to disturb the tomb. For that I deserve whatever horror he sends my way. But I will not let him beat me. The secret of the poleax will go with me to my own grave."

Marsh stood up and looked Ennis square in the eye. "That's noble, Ennis, but taking the secret to your grave won't end it. Your dying would only move you closer to Damon."

Ennis snapped a surprised look to Marsh. He opened his mouth to speak, but no words came out. Marsh saw a spark of clarity in Ennis's otherwise dead gaze, as if a thought had come to him. Something he hadn't considered before.

Sydney said, "Kinda hard to wrap your brain around, isn't it?"

"Perhaps," Ennis replied thoughtfully.

"So then, what about the sixth crucible?" Sydney said, pressing.

"I am afraid that I do not know where it is," Ennis admitted. "That is the truth. My guess is that it went through the Rift during the earthquake and is somewhere in the Black. If not, it could be buried in the rubble near the Necromanteio."

"Swell," Sydney said, deflated. "So to find it we either have to mount an excavation project in Greece . . . or die."

Ennis nodded knowingly. "If it has gone through to the Black, perhaps Cooper will locate it. Find it, and you will have even more leverage over Damon."

"It's not about leverage," Marsh argued. "Damon must be destroyed and I think we'll need the poleax to do it."

Ennis's eyes grew wide with surprise. "Is that why you want to locate the weapon? To use it against Damon? Please do not tell me that is your plan."

"It's a thought," Marsh answered with a shrug.

"Whoa, wait," Sydney cried. "That's news to me."

"I want to know where it is, Syd," Marsh said adamantly. "We can't keep guessing."

"Yes, we can," Sydney argued. "As long as Damon is guessing too. If we don't know where the poleax is, he can't force us to get it."

"Tell that to Damon!" Marsh shot back. "That hasn't stopped him from terrorizing us."

"And what happens if we find it?" Sydney argued. "There'd be no stopping him from coming after us."

"Except that we'd have two crucibles. And maybe we could turn the poleax on him. That's what Coop was thinking."

"No!" Ennis cried. "It is far too dangerous."

"But it might be our only chance," Marsh argued.

"Then there is no chance," Ennis said soberly. "Please. I want you to go now."

He hurried out of the bedroom, headed for the front door. Marsh and Sydney followed.

"Come with us," Sydney said. "This crucible can protect you too."

"No," Ennis said with finality. "I do not wish to be shielded from Damon. I want to confront him. I need to confront him."

"You can't fight him," Marsh argued. "You know that."

"Perhaps not," Ennis said. "Or perhaps I am stronger than you think."

"I think you're incredibly strong," Marsh cried. "We need your help. Please come with us."

"I will help," Ennis said calmly. "In my way."

For the first time since they had arrived, Ennis looked at peace. It actually troubled Marsh to see the sudden change in his attitude.

"What are you going to do, Ennis?" Marsh asked suspiciously.

"What I must," he replied. "As must you. Take care of yourself and do not seek out the poleax."

Marsh searched Ennis's eyes, looking for a clue as to what was going through his mind.

"I want to know what you're thinking," Marsh said.

"Do not worry about me," was Ennis's reply. "Concern yourself with making the best use of the opportunities that present themselves to you. That is what I plan to do."

Marsh nodded.

"Wait. That's it?" Sydney interjected. "We can't leave him here! As soon as the crucible is gone, Damon will go after him again."

Ennis gave Sydney a warm smile and said, "And I will welcome that."

Sydney looked to Marsh and cried, "He's crazy."

"Maybe a little," Ennis said. "But for the first time since I pulled myself from the rubble of that tomb, I believe there will be an end to this nightmare."

"Seriously? What gives you that impression?" Sydney demanded.

"Because I believe that Damon has met his match," he said. "In all of us."

Marsh took Sydney's hand and led her to the door. "Let's go."

"No!" Sydney protested. "We can't just leave him. Marsh! Make him come with us!"

Marsh shook his head. "He's made up his mind."

"I don't believe this," Sydney screamed. "He's your friend!"

"And he wants us to go, so let's go."

"I will see you soon enough," Ennis assured her. "I promise."

"Come with us, Ennis. Please," Sydney begged. "You can stay at Marsh's house. We'll all be together, with the crucible."

"Good-bye, miss," Ennis said. "Good-bye, Marshmallow."

Marsh stood in the doorway, holding eye contact with Ennis.

"Be careful," he cautioned.

Ennis nodded, then closed his apartment door and locked it up tight.

Ennis was no longer afraid.

He'd spent every moment since the first crucible was broken in the cursed tomb fearing the spirit that he had accidentally freed. He had watched Terri Seaver die as she slipped out of his grasp to fall into the Rift. That memory was far more haunting than anything Damon had since conjured. He feared for Ree's soul, and for the lives of her family. He feared for the havoc that Damon might cause in both this world and the next. And he feared for himself. It was the least of his fears, but the most present. He had lived in unceasing terror from the moment the first crucible had been broken on the rocky floor of Damon's tomb.

But he wasn't afraid anymore.

Hearing the story of Damon's haunting of Marsh and of Cooper's trip to the Black gave him the confidence to believe he no longer had to be a victim. He didn't know for certain what the future might hold, but he drew strength from the fact that whatever it was, he could deal with it and quite possibly make a difference.

He was drained. And hungry. He went to the kitchen to see if there were any unopened bags of Doritos. He was about to push open the swinging door, when he heard a sound coming from within. It was the steady drip . . . drip . . . drip of a leaky faucet. He entered the kitchen to see that the faucet was indeed dripping. Strange. That had never happened before. Had he not cranked it all the way off? He tightened the handle and began his search for a fresh bag of chips . . . when he heard another dripping sound.

He left the kitchen and headed down the hallway to the

bathroom. The hollow plunking sound grew louder, echoing through the empty apartment. He entered the bathroom to see another leaky faucet. Stepping up to the sink, he saw his wan reflection in the mirror. The man who stared back at him looked like a stranger. He had lost weight and his hair had grown gray, but that was minor compared to the haunted look he saw in his own eyes. Strangely, that too gave him confidence. He felt hardened. After all he had been through, he felt ready to take the next step.

"I believe I am ready," he said aloud to himself.

There were decisions to be made and he needed to think clearly, so he opened up the cold water valve and splashed his face. There were no towels left in the room, so he crooked his elbow and wiped his face down with the sleeve of his soiled shirt. Standing up, he looked back at the mirror . . .

. . . and came face-to-face with Damon of Epirus. The scarred apparition stared back at him, smiling hideously and baring his pointed front teeth.

"I believe it is time we met," the vision said.

The water spigot exploded, sending a high-powered jet of water into the room. Ennis backed away in surprise. His legs hit the edge of the bathtub and he fell inside. He landed on his back and looked up to see the shower head explode the same way, spewing a pressurized jet of water down on him. The tub faucets were next, shooting off the wall as gallons of water spewed into the room . . . more water than seemed possible. The toilet was next. It was rocked off of its base by a geyser of water that shot high and hit the ceiling, sending water cascading back into the room.

It took Ennis several seconds to gather his wits and pull himself out of the tub. There was so much water spewing into the room from so many sources that the small bathroom began to fill up. In seconds the water level had reached his ankles. Ennis splashed for the door and grabbed the handle but it wouldn't turn. He was locked inside. He yanked desperately on the knob but the door wouldn't budge. There was one large window in the bathroom. Ennis went for it and struggled to lift it but the window would not open.

The water had reached his knees and was rising fast. A strange calm came over Ennis. He had made a decision. A tough decision, but in that insane moment of impossibility he finally felt clarity. It was a good feeling. The children were right. Hiding wasn't an option. The fear wouldn't go away. Action had to be taken or they'd be lost.

He didn't panic. It was as if he understood that what was happening was impossible, but he didn't care. He closed his eyes, took a deep breath to keep his heart from racing, and moved deliberately to the sink. Looking into the mirror, he saw that the spirit was gone, though he knew Damon was still there. Somewhere. As water poured down over him, he pulled open the mirror that covered the medicine cabinet. Inside was a black Sharpie pen. He grabbed it, then glanced down to see that the water had reached his waist. Floating on the surface were several empty potato chip bags. He grabbed one and tore it apart until he had a rough piece of white plastic the size of a playing card. The vanity was already underwater so Ennis had to put the paper against the tiled wall in order to write on it. It took only a few seconds to scribble the message with the black marker. Satisfied that his words were legible, he tossed the pen and squeezed the paper into his hand.

Above the sound of roaring water, Ennis heard another sound that was even more incongruous. It was the sweet sound of steel drum music. Being Jamaican, he was as familiar with the sound as he was with any other instrument. Rather than question why he was hearing it, he let the music calm him. The song reminded him of when he was a boy. Of soft white sand and warm tropical water. He turned to look out the window, but rather than seeing a view of New York, Ennis saw the shore of his home. A bright blue fishing boat sat beneath a small grove of palm trees on a white-sand beach under a warm Jamaican sun.

The water had reached Ennis's chest. It wouldn't be long before it filled the room. He briefly wondered if it was possible to drown in an illusion. He focused on the window. On home. Ennis wanted to be there. He knew in his heart that he could make it. He also knew that he would first have to make another stop. It was a stop he was prepared to make. That he *wanted* to make.

He was tired of being a victim.

Marsh and Sydney hurried away from Ennis's building, headed back toward McSorley's to grab a cab to Grand Central.

"This is wrong," Sydney declared angrily. "How can you just walk away and leave him unprotected like that?"

"It's what he wanted."

"He's out of his mind! Nobody can make rational choices when they're in such bad shape. This was a totally wasted—"

She was cut off by the sound of smashing glass that was quickly followed by a terrified scream.

Marsh stopped short. "Oh my god," he muttered to himself.

He didn't have to look to know what was happening.

Sydney did. She spun back toward Ennis's building in time to see a dark figure plummeting from the tenth floor.

"No!" she screamed, and took off running back to the building.

Marsh steeled himself and followed.

Mercifully, neither saw the impact. The woman on the street who had screamed wasn't as lucky. She was coming out of a bodega and saw the whole thing . . . from the first sight of a man diving headfirst through the shattered glass ten stories above, to the horrifying plummet, and finally to the sickening crash as he landed in a narrow patch of grass, barely missing a spiked fence.

Sydney ran up to the woman, who stared straight ahead in shock, pointing to the building. Sydney ran across the street, barely aware of the traffic that was screeching to a stop all around her. She only slowed when she saw the crumpled mass that was once a human being. She stopped several feet away, not able to bring herself to go any closer.

"Ennis?" she called out.

There was no response.

Marsh ran past her and went right to his friend. Looking down, he tried to convince himself that Ennis was simply unconscious. But his spine was twisted into an impossible angle that said otherwise. Marsh knelt down and forced himself to look at Ennis's face. He expected to see an expression frozen with fear but instead saw a man at peace.

"You knew," Sydney said as she tentatively approached Marsh from behind. "You knew he was going to do this."

"I didn't," Marsh countered.

"Yes, you did," Sydney insisted, holding back tears.

A far-off siren sounded. The authorities were on their way.

"This was inevitable," Marsh said. "From the moment Ennis and my mom cracked the seal on that tomb. One way or another, Ennis was doomed."

"And we did nothing to help him," Sydney said with disgust.

The siren grew louder. Soon the police would come and take Ennis away. There would be questions. Marsh's dad would have to come. Marsh didn't care. His only concern was that the mechanics of putting Ennis to rest would take them away from their mission.

From Ennis's mission.

Marsh saw that Ennis had something clutched in his hand. A white piece of paper. Was it a suicide note? It had to have significance. Why else would he be holding it while jumping out of a window to his death? Marsh reached for it and gently removed it from Ennis's still-warm grasp.

"Don't touch that," Sydney commanded.

Marsh ignored her. Ennis's fingers gave up the paper easily. It looked to have been torn from a bag of chips. On one side was the colorful print from the product. Marsh flipped it to see that there was writing on the other side. Two simple words.

Marsh read them and frowned. The words were familiar but he didn't know why. He looked down at Ennis, relieved that the man's eyes were closed.

"Ennis," Marsh whispered. "Find Mom for me."

He stood up and handed the torn paper to Sydney.

"What's this?" she asked.

"Ennis's last words."

Sydney looked at the torn paper to see the two curious words.

Lignum vitae.

5

Cooper was torn between the thrill of seeing the ancient wonder of the Colosseum in its original glory and figuring out a plan to find Damon.

Whoever's vision he had found himself in, it was on a day when the Colosseum was rocking. Coop could hear the roar of what seemed like multiple thousands of spectators, who were inside cheering whatever mayhem was on display. The area around the stadium was also busy with hundreds of people milling about and chatting. It was like a game day tailgate scene . . . gladiator style.

This vision was by far the most populated that Cooper had been to. Seeing the eclectic mix of spirits from so many eras made him realize that the Colosseum was just as big a tourist attraction in the Black as it was in the Light. He wondered if that applied to other interesting spots too. Could one spend their time in the Black bouncing from the Grand Canyon to the Great Wall of China and then make a quick side trip to Niagara Falls before hitting Disneyland? It made Coop think that he could be having a lot more fun in the Black than he had been.

He stuck Damon's glove into the back pocket of his jeans and wandered toward the Colosseum, gazing up at the structure that was both familiar and alien. Though he had seen many pictures of the ruined structure, it took some imagination to recognize the iconic, crumbling image as it existed in modern day through the complete, pristine facade he now faced. It was four stories high with a ring of tall arches on the first three, many of which held large marble statues. The circular building was intact, unlike the contemporary ruins, where one whole side had collapsed. The exterior was light brown limestone that was constructed with such care to detail that it made Cooper lament the fact that the actual structure in the Light had crumbled into such disrepair.

"It was called the Flavian Amphitheater," a man announced.

A skinny guy wearing shorts, black knee socks, and sandals approached Coop holding a travel guide. The guy had on a loud aloha shirt and a New York Mets cap . . . not exactly a classic Roman look. It was more of a classic geek-tourist look.

He continued, "Opened in 80 AD. They started calling it the Colosseum after that guy." He jerked his thumb toward the giant bronze statue that stood a few yards away. "The Emperor Nero. That statue is called the Colossus of Nero. Hence, the Colosseum."

He looked up from his guide book to Coop, squinting against the bright sun. "Isn't that fascinating?"

"No," Coop said flatly.

The man shrugged and went back to his reading.

"Does that book tell you whose vision this is?" Coop asked.

"No. But it does say that the structure could hold up to fifty-five thousand spectators, which is roughly the capacity of Shea Stadium."

"Or Citi Field," Coop said.

The man gave Coop a curious look. "What's Citi Field?"

"The new Shea."

The man looked stunned. "No! Shea is gone?"

"Hold on to your socks—so is the old Yankee Stadium."

The guy's jaw dropped. "But I've only been dead a couple of years!"

"Yeah, well, life goes on. What year is this?"

The man scanned the surroundings. "My guess is it's pretty close to when they first opened for business. Did you know that to celebrate its opening they slaughtered over five thousand animals?"

"No," Coop said coldly. "And I don't think that's fascinating either."

"And they held a hundred straight days of competition. Right now they've got gladiators going at it inside. I took a peek but it's a tad barbaric for my taste. They outlawed gladiator battles in 438, so this vision is somewhere between 80 and 438. AD."

"That's, like, a 350-year window," Coop said. "What kind of tour guide are you?"

The guy straightened up, offended. "Just trying to help."

He turned with a huff and hurried off in search of some other vision-hopping spirit to impress with his wealth of Roman trivia. Coop figured that if Damon had come to this vision, his reasons must have something to do with the action inside the Colosseum, so that's where he had to go.

Entering the ancient stadium was simple. No ticket was required. He wandered through a tall archway into the cool of the shade beneath the seats and made his way toward the arena.

"Man," he marveled aloud. "It's just like a stadium back at home."

The general design concept was the same, but rather than steel and cement the Colosseum was constructed with wood, marble, and limestone. Coop pushed past bystanders to make his way through a long tunnel until he re-emerged into the hot sun . . . and was instantly dazzled by the spectacle of the arena. The mix of the familiar and the bizarre was overwhelming. He was on the lowest level, the same level as the competition. He looked up and around at the imposing structure to see that it was packed with cheering fans, and not all of them were citizens of ancient Rome. The raucous crowd had come from every other vision and age imaginable. There were soldiers from many different eras and countries, who sat in small groups, possibly having died together. The majority of the spectators were men, but there was also a peppering of women. Ladies with parasols sat next to primitive tribesmen in colorful wraps. They wore every kind of headgear imaginable, from turbans to feathered crowns, baseball caps to helmets, burkas to sun visors.

"Peanuts!" Coop shouted, though he didn't expect to have a vendor toss him a bag. That was one of the few obvious differences between an event in ancient Rome and a baseball game at home. No vending.

Though the spectators were as varied as could be, they all seemed to have one thing in common: They were all caught up in the excitement of the contest that was playing out on the floor of the arena. Coop walked down to the brick wall that surrounded the competition area and peered over the top to see that a fight was under way.

Man, right out of the movies, he thought.

Two gladiators in full armor were hammering away at each other with oversize swords. There wasn't much elegance to the fight. It was a brutal battle of strength and stamina. Whoever ran out of gas first would lose. If it had been an actual battle in ancient Rome, a loss would have meant death. In the Black the worst that would happen is that the loser would experience the pain of being skewered and then have to endure the shame of defeat. Knowing that neither of the contenders was actually in danger of dying took some of the thrill of the fight away for Cooper.

But not for the other spectators, who were leaning over from every level as if trying to get closer to the fight, while screaming commands and encouragement.

No wonder they're all still stuck in the Black, Coop thought. *They're vicious.*

Above him, on the second level, Cooper saw what looked to be an open-air royal luxury box with several men and women sitting in elaborate carved chairs. Unlike the rest of the stadium, which was in a fever pitch, these people looked totally bored, as if the sight of two huge men beating each other's brains out was an everyday occurrence . . . which it probably was.

In the center of the box, seated in an elaborate golden throne, was a rotund man in a toga who casually ate from a tray of fruit.

Coop grabbed a U.S. sailor who was walking by and asked, "Who's that guy?"

The sailor looked up and said, "Emperor Titus. This is his show."

"It's his vision?" Coop asked.

"Yeah. He's been putting on these battles forever."

Coop said, "Staging battles to the death isn't exactly a smart way to get out of the Black."

The sailor shrugged. "Like I should care about him? Gotta go, pal. I got money riding on this fight."

The sailor kept walking. Cooper thought the guy wouldn't be getting out of the Black anytime soon either.

It wasn't that Coop felt as though everybody should be running around the Black picking flowers and spreading sunshine, but the people in that stadium were out for blood . . . not exactly proof that they were working hard toward becoming evolved spirits.

Coop looked up to the emperor's box to see Titus watching the fight with a satisfied smile. Was this the guy Damon came here for? It seemed as though he enjoyed human suffering as much as Damon, which meant the two would have a lot in common. Coop decided that he would have to speak with Emperor Titus.

A cheer erupted from half of the crowd. The other half groaned with disappointment. Cooper glanced into the arena to see that one of the gladiators was on his back with a sword sticking out of his chest. The victorious gladiator stood over his fallen victim, raising his fists in celebration. The people in the stadium were out of control, either cheering or booing.

The winning gladiator grabbed the handle of his sword and yanked it out of his victim. There was no blood. Spirits didn't bleed. The losing gladiator sat up and struggled to his feet while clutching his wound. As soon as he stood, the entire crowd jeered. Losers got no respect.

It was an ugly glimpse into the darker side of the human psyche. Coop couldn't imagine being there in the days when blood was actually spilled.

A trumpet fanfare blasted through the stadium. It was the call for the next battle. Coop took it as his chance. While people milled about, stretching their legs between bouts, he made his way back through the tunnel and found a set of stairs leading up to the next level and the emperor's box. His plan was to try and get to the emperor during the next battle while all eyes were focused on the gladiators. He sprinted up the narrow stairway and came out onto a wide walkway that circled the Colosseum, just like in a modern stadium. The only thing missing was the hot dog concessions. He ran until he came upon a tunnel that would bring him close to the emperor's box and was happy to see that there were no guards stationed at the mouth. He ducked into the narrow tunnel and sprinted until he reached the far end. Peeking out, he saw that he was only a few aisles away from the emperor's box. Perfect. He stayed in the shadow of the tunnel, waiting for his chance.

The trumpets sounded again and two gladiators entered the arena from opposite ends. He couldn't have cared less who they were. If they wanted to fight it out in the afterlife, that was their choice. It was probably how they lived and died in the Light anyway.

The crowd let out a cheer. The previous fight had been forgotten and they were getting themselves fired up for a little more old-fashioned gladiator thumping. The two combatants walked slowly to the center of the sand-covered arena. One guy was big, with full armor and a shaved head. The other gladiator was a foot shorter with long curly black hair. He wasn't a close match to the other guy, either in height or weight. It was obvious which fighter had the advantage. Coop hoped the fight would last long enough so that he could get a few words in with the emperor. He stepped out from the cool shadow of the tunnel into the burning hot sun, headed for the emperor's box. No guards were there, either. There was no need to protect the emperor, seeing as he was already dead. Along with everybody else. Coop was a few steps away from the box when he glanced down to the arena to try and judge when the fight might begin.

The two gladiators stood face-to-face in the center of the ring.

Coop got a better look at them both—and froze. He stared at the two combatants, hoping he was wrong about what he was seeing. As with the previous fight, the gladiators were armed with swords and shields. But unlike in the previous battle, the swords looked different. They were smaller. They didn't catch the light of the sun.

They were black.

"Oh man," Coop gasped. Instead of continuing on to the emperor's box, Coop ran down the steep steps past rows of benches packed with eager spectators and right up to the edge of the second level. He wanted to get a better look at the gladiators and their swords in the hope that he was wrong.

He wasn't. The weapons they carried were not made from ordinary metal. They were black spirit-killing swords that had come through the Rift from the Light into the Black. The barbaric spectacle had suddenly taken on a more ominous tone. The loser of this battle wouldn't be able to pull the sword from their gut, shrug, and live to fight another day. The spirit who got pierced by one of those swords would be destroyed. For good.

Did those gladiators know the power of the weapons they held? Did the spectators know that this time they actually were going to witness a battle to the death? Was this why Damon had come to this vision, to bring his lust for destruction to yet another vision?

The gladiators circled each other. Until that moment the back of the gladiator with the long hair was to Cooper. As they moved, they exchanged places and Cooper caught a glimpse of the face of the smaller combatant.

It made his knees grow weak.

"My god," he muttered.

The small gladiator . . . was Zoe.

He had found one of the missing spirits, and wished he hadn't. Any doubt Coop had about Damon being in that vision was gone. Zoe was about to be destroyed in a very public way, but to what end? Revenge against her father, Adeipho? Retribution for having lost the Rift? Or was it just another example of Damon's sadism? Whatever the reason, Zoe would have no chance against her massive opponent.

Coop turned and sprinted up the stairs to the emperor's box. He only had seconds before the battle would begin. He vaulted over the low wooden rail and landed directly in front of the only guard who was there to protect the boss. Before the oblivious guard could react, Coop jabbed one punch to his throat and followed with a solid hook to his cheek. The stunned guard's head snapped to the side as he tumbled to his knees, clutching his throat.

If the emperor was surprised, he didn't show it. He turned in his ornately carved golden throne and peered down his nose at Cooper as if he were no more of a threat than a fly that someone beneath his station should have swatted for him.

"Your . . . Emperor-ness-Majesty, whatever," Coop huffed, catching his breath. "You can't let them fight. Not with those weapons. This isn't for show. Those black swords could destroy them."

The emperor tilted his head like a curious cat, trying to understand why a strange guy from a modern vision had dared to intrude on his personal spectacle.

"Please," Coop begged. "Stop the fight."

Titus opened his mouth to speak, but was interrupted by another spectator who was sitting in the far corner of the royal box.

"I see you have taken the bait," the man declared.

The hair went up on the back of Coop's neck. He knew the voice. He spun quickly to see that the spectator had risen to face him.

"The glove, please," the man said, holding out his hand.

Coop pulled the glove from his back pocket, held it out . . . and dropped it on the floor.

The spectator didn't react.

"Bait?" Cooper repeated. "You wanted me to find you?"

"Of course," the man said with a sly smile that revealed his pointed front teeth. He reached down, picked up the glove, and slipped his hand into it. "And now that you are here, the next act of our little drama can begin."

Cooper's hunt was officially over.

Damon of Epirus was back in the game.

6

"Stop the fight," Coop demanded.

"You are assuming I have that power," Damon replied coyly.

"Give me a break. This is all about you. How else would they have gotten the black swords?"

Damon glanced to the arena floor, where Zoe and the gladiator stood poised, ready to do battle.

"I suppose it could be stopped," Damon said, sounding less than enthused. "But why disappoint all of these spirits who are so looking forward to the contest? It isn't often that they can actually witness a true fight to the death."

The crowd had grown eerily quiet as if holding a collective breath in anticipation of the impending battle. Many eyes were on Coop and Damon, fascinated by the standoff that was being played out in the emperor's box.

"What's the point?" Coop asked. "Revenge?"

Damon chuckled. "Revenge against the daughter of Adeipho is a bonus, yes, but nothing more. My ultimate goal remains the same."

"The poleax," Coop declared.

"And you can help me get it."

"What if I don't?"

Damon took a threatening step closer to Cooper.

"Do not make the mistake of thinking you have gained an advantage by my having lost the Rift."

"You lost your army too," Coop said, not backing down. "Let's not forget that little detail."

Damon shook his head in wonder.

"As always, so confident. But why?" He gestured down to the arena floor and said, "Because you have found the daughter of the traitor Adeipho? Congratulations. But what of the others? The girl Maggie. And Foley, your grandfather? And of course the Seaver woman. Where could they be?"

Cooper had all he could do to hold himself back from lashing out and drilling his fist into Damon's smug face.

"I hold all of their lives in my hand, including that annoying urchin down there who is about to meet her end. Tell me, Foley, are you willing to risk their eternals souls?"

Cooper's body tensed as his anger grew.

"And then of course there is your sister," Damon continued. "The poor girl nearly leaped to her death from that burning building. How much longer will her luck, and the luck of Marshall Seaver, last?"

"It isn't luck," Cooper said. "The crucible is protecting them."

"For now, but they are young. Most of their natural lives still lie before them. All it would take is one mistake over that lifetime, and they'd be mine. It could be ten minutes from now, or ten years. I am nothing if not patient. And I promise you, they *will* make a mistake, and when they do, I will be there waiting . . . as I was with Ennis Mobley."

"Ennis? What about him?" Coop asked, not able to hide his surprise.

"Didn't you know?" Damon asked with mock surprise. "He has journeyed farther along the Morpheus Road."

"You killed him too?" Coop declared, rocked.

Damon shrugged and said, "The choice was his."

Cooper took an impulse step toward Damon, but stopped himself quickly. He knew he had to stay in control.

"You have the power, Foley," Damon continued. "Especially now that you can communicate with your friends in the Light. Find the poleax, deliver it to me, and those you care about will be safe."

They were back to square one. As they stood facing each other under the hot sun, and the hotter gaze of thousands of spectators, Coop knew that there would be no reasoning with Damon. No negotiation. There was only one way to stop him, and that was by doing what Coop did best.

He looked to the emperor and said, "You have no idea what trouble you're getting into with this guy."

Emperor Titus shrugged and said, "Perhaps trouble is what I seek."

That was all Coop needed to hear. He was on his own. Before another word could be spoken, he swooped down and grabbed the spear from the guard he had knocked senseless.

"Oh must you?" Damon whined with annoyance.

Coop didn't attack. He ran. Leaping out of the box, he sprinted down the stone stairs, two at a time, headed for the edge of the balcony.

"Begin the contest!" Damon bellowed to the emperor.

Obediently Emperor Titus raised his right hand. Trumpets sounded and the stadium erupted with ecstatic cheers. They were going to have their battle.

Several Roman soldiers ran down the stairs to stop Cooper, but too late. He reached the edge of the balcony, looked over, and saw what he needed. A heavy rope net hung straight down from the balcony to protect the spectators below from stray weapons that might fly into the stands. Coop used it as a ladder. He tossed the spear over the edge, flung his legs over, grabbed on to the netting, and quickly climbed down.

None of the spectators moved to stop him. Their attention was focused on the arena and the fight that had finally begun.

As Coop hit the lower level and recovered the spear, a cheer erupted for the big gladiator who was pummeling Zoe. The girl valiantly held up her shield to defend herself against his vicious blows but was hopelessly overmatched.

Clutching the spear, Cooper sprinted for the brick wall that surrounded the arena. While still running, he tossed the spear over the wall and then hit the bricks, digging the toes of his red Pumas into the mortar seams. He quickly climbed to the top and vaulted to the other side, landing in the dry sand of the arena.

Several spectators cheered as they realized the game had taken on a new wrinkle. Coop grabbed the spear and sprinted toward the center of the arena, and the battle. The screams from the crowd grew louder. Some cheered him on while others were trying to warn the gladiators that a new contestant was about to enter the fray.

Coop had no time to plan his strategy. He was a street fighter, not a trained warrior. If he had stopped to think about how to attack the gladiator, he wouldn't have done what he did. Coop was flying on adrenaline, fear . . . and hate. To him the gladiator who was hammering away at Zoe represented Damon. It made what he had to do that much easier.

Zoe fell to the ground, holding up her shield in defense. She was exhausted.

The gladiator raised his sword high, ready to end the battle with one final blow.

Zoe valiantly lifted her shield to protect herself.

The gladiator bellowed with bloodlust . . . and the scream caught in his throat as he froze, holding the sword poised high.

Zoe stared up at him, confused. What had happened? Why hadn't he finished her? She dropped her eyes and saw the reason: A pointed metal blade stuck out from his chest. Behind him, Cooper stood with both hands on the shaft of the spear.

"This won't stop him for long," Coop said quickly. "We gotta go."

The gladiator dropped to his knees in a haze of pain and confusion. He wasn't going to die, he was going to get angry.

"Fool!" Zoe scolded.

"Uh . . . what?" Coop replied, stunned.

The gladiator had gathered his wits and let out an angry holler that echoed through the stadium.

"Follow!" Zoe commanded, and took off running, sprinting for the gladiator's entrance to the arena.

Coop let go of the spear and followed quickly.

The boos rained down on them. The spirit spectators had expected a battle to the death, not a cowardly sprint for freedom.

Several soldiers clambered over the brick wall and into the arena to give chase.

Zoe hit the tunnel that led beneath the stands and didn't stop. Cooper was right behind.

"You should not have interfered!" she screamed angrily.

"Hey, I just saved you!" Coop yelled back.

"And condemned the others to death."

"What others?"

Zoe led Cooper into the bowels of the Colosseum, following a twisted route through narrow stone passageways and down steep wooden stairways. The rank smell of animals and sour sweat grew stronger the farther they descended.

"What do you mean?" Coop gasped as they ran. "Who's condemned?"

"Your friend Maggie."

"Where is she?" Coop yelled back, stunned.

"Here," Zoe answered. "Damon threatened to destroy them if I did not do battle."

"Them?"

"Your grandfather is here as well."

Coop didn't know whether to be relieved or horrified. "But . . . why don't you all just leave? It's not like he can lock you up."

"We stayed to protect Ree," Zoe answered, breathless. "Now you've condemned them all."

They hit the lowest subterranean level, where the only light came through narrow slits in the walls that allowed in a small hint of the sun. The tight corridor opened up into a wide paddock that was lined with cages. The floor was wet and the animal smell so strong that Coop had to fight to keep from gagging.

They were met by the angry growls of surprised lions, who resented the intrusion on their nap time. One male lion lunged at the bars of his cage, biting at the wooden bars. Coop instinctively jumped away, but slammed into the opposite cage that held an annoyed bear that tried to reach its paw out to slash him.

Zoe didn't stop running, so Coop had to collect himself quickly and keep moving. He passed more cages that were homes to tigers, hippos, and even a few ostriches. All were there to provide amusement for the bloodthirsty spectators in the arena above, the same as when the Colosseum was open for business in the Light centuries before.

Beyond the paddock they moved through an equally dank corridor of cells that were used to house slaves bound for the arena. None were occupied. Spirits in the Black had choices, and none chose to be torn apart by lions for the amusement of others. The stretch of dark cells gave way to a wider corridor with better ventilation and light. These were the cells where the gladiators prepared for battle. Each room had a crude bed, table, and chair. They weren't luxurious, but were far more comfortable than the slave quarters. These too were empty.

Zoe ran into the final room that was lined with several large cells. It was the place where the most popular and successful gladiators prepped. Cooper entered the spacious area to see that Zoe had stopped and was standing in the open doorway to one of the cells. Coop skidded to a stop and gulped air that was hot and worse than stale, but he was grateful to be away from the animals and their overwhelming stink.

"We have to make a decision," Zoe said to someone inside. "Now, before Damon returns."

"Who's in there?" Coop called out.

A moment later Maggie Salinger stepped out of the cell. Her face brightened the moment she spotted her exhausted friend.

"Coop!" she exclaimed with joy.

Maggie ran to him and the two hugged. She didn't seem to care that he was drenched with sweat.

Coop held her close. It wasn't until that moment that he realized how much he had missed her . . . and how much he wanted to hold her. And protect her.

"So much has happened," she whispered.

"I know," he said. "We've got to get out of here."

"No can do," came a gruff voice.

Coop looked over Maggie's shoulder to see his grandfather, Eugene Foley, stepping out of the cell next to Zoe.

"You okay?" he asked Zoe.

Zoe nodded.

Foley gave her a grandfatherly pat on the shoulder, then looked to Coop and said, "So? Where've you been?"

Coop reluctantly pulled himself away from Maggie and went to his gramps. The two hugged with genuine warmth.

"Looking for you," was Coop's answer.

"This Damon fella is bad news," Gramps said.

"You think?" Coop replied. He glanced into the cell and added, "Where's Ree?"

The others exchanged dark looks.

"Not here," Zoe answered.

"We don't know where Damon took her," Foley added. "He said if any of us tried to return to our own visions, he'd kill her."

Zoe added, "That is why we cannot leave."

Maggie looked to Coop with tired eyes and said, "The killing has to stop somewhere."

Coop pulled away from the group and surveyed the cell area. "So nobody can leave for fear Damon will destroy someone else. He probably said the same thing to Ree."

"Gotta give him credit," Foley said. "He knows we wouldn't let that happen, so here we stay."

Agitated growls and barks came from the animal pens.

"They're coming," Zoe announced.

"Get out of here," Coop said, thinking fast. "All of you. Go to Zoe's vision. She's got one of the black swords now. She can protect you there."

"No," Zoe said flatly. "We cannot endanger Ree."

"If he wants to kill her, he'll do it no matter what you do," Coop said.

"But—," Zoe argued.

"It's not about you guys," Coop shot back. "It's about getting me to do what he wants. That's the real reason he's been keeping you here."

"What if you're wrong, son?" Foley asked.

Coop didn't have a quick answer. He wanted to show confidence, but the best he could do was act in the moment and make the best possible choice. "Then I'm wrong. But we've got to take control, and as long as he's got you, he's got power over all of us."

The others exchanged nervous looks.

"Zoe, what happened to the other Guardians?" Coop asked quickly. "The ones that survived the battle at the Rift?"

"They have all returned to their own visions," she answered.

"What about the spirit swords that were left in Ree's vision when Damon's soldiers went into the Blood?"

"The Guardians still have them, but what good can the swords do if they are scattered throughout the Black?"

Coop processed that information, then said, "All right. Go to your vision; take Maggie and Gramps and don't allow Damon to enter."

"I'm afraid that ship has sailed," Gramps said. "Damon can pretty much go wherever he wants no matter what anybody allows him to do."

"Then find someplace there that you can defend and wait until you hear from me."

The sounds of shouts and scuffling feet grew louder.

"You gotta go," Coop declared.

Maggie grabbed Cooper's hands and looked him straight in the eye. "What are you going to do?"

Coop started to give a quick answer, but held back and offered an honest one instead. "I don't know."

Maggie looked grim and Coop gave her a quick hug.

"They are coming!" Zoe shouted, pointing to the stretch of gladiator cells they had just run through.

"Go!" Coop demanded. "I'll see you soon."

There wasn't time for more talk. A swirling wall of color appeared behind each of the spirits as they took a step backward . . . and disappeared.

All but Cooper.

The gladiator who Cooper had impaled was the first to enter the room. He boldly strode forward with one thought in mind: execution. He still had the black sword and raised it to strike.

Coop was about to step out of the vision, when . . .

"Stop!" Damon commanded.

The gladiator cringed and shook with rage, but he stopped. Several more Roman soldiers with traditional spears entered and spread throughout the room, followed by Damon, who strode in quickly.

Cooper was prepared to blast out of that vision at the first sign of trouble but needed any clue he could get as to Damon's strategy, so he waited.

Damon went right to the large cell and stuck his head in to inspect it.

"Taking attendance?" Coop asked. "Don't bother. They're gone."

Damon scanned the empty cell, then spun to Cooper.

Coop felt his rage. He glanced to the gladiator with the black sword in case Damon gave him the order to attack.

Instead Damon smiled.

As Coop had seen so many times before, Damon's emotions swung wildly. It was just one of the many signs of his insanity.

"No matter," Damon said with a shrug. "I can easily hunt them down."

Coop said, "You could, but isn't it more fun this way?"

Damon laughed, genuinely. "Perhaps. But rest assured I'll be keeping a much closer watch on Ree Seaver."

"Where is she, anyway?" Coop asked casually.

Damon wagged a finger at Cooper as if chastising him for being a naughty boy. "Still so sure of yourself. It's what I like about you. I'm sorry to have to tell you this, but in spite of the debacle at the Rift, nothing has changed."

"Except that your entire army was sucked into the Blood," Coop shot back.

"Do you seriously believe my strength comes from those few spirits? There are countless spirits in the Black who clamor to join me. I watched as you observed the faces of the spectators in the arena. You saw their rage. Their hunger. These are spirits who cannot accept that their fates are being determined by so-called superior beings."

"The Watchers?" Coop said.

"Yes. Watchers. Why should they have the right to judge us? To judge anyone? Billions have accepted their decisions throughout time without question. I say we should each determine our own future, and I am not alone."

"So that's why you're in this vision? To recruit more soldiers? What did you promise Emperor Titus? The greatest spectacle of all time?"

Damon gave Cooper a sly smile. "That is *exactly* what I promised him."

"Did you also tell him that you really don't care about how the Watchers have run things? Did you tell him that you're just using that as an excuse to get the spirits fired up so that you can get what you really want?"

"And what do you believe that is?" Damon asked, smug.

"One last battle to prove something . . . mostly to yourself. So sad."

Damon stiffened.

Coop had tweaked a nerve, so he continued to push.

"And how does Brennus fit into your plans? I hear you went all snaky when you didn't find him in Riagan's vision."

Damon twisted his head slightly, as if trying to wrap his mind around the question and the fact that Coop knew enough to ask it.

Cooper offered him a smug smile.

"Brennus," Damon said thoughtfully. "A name you overheard that could mean anything . . . or nothing. We will leave it at that."

Damon waddled up to Cooper and patted him on the cheek. He stood a good foot shorter than Coop and quite a bit wider . . . not at all the intimidating warrior he envisioned himself to be.

Coop had to hold himself back from hitting the guy.

"I need you to do something for me," Damon said.

"I'm not going to tell Marsh to find the poleax," Coop spat. "Give it up."

"Then deliver a message to him for me. Since he is in possession of a crucible, I am unable to do so myself."

"You're kidding me, right?"

"Not at all. Tell him that I grow impatient. Make him understand that unless he locates the poleax and delivers it to me, I will destroy his mother."

"I'm not going to tell him that," Coop shot back.

Damon backed away from Cooper with a knowing smile. "But you will, for I am quite serious about making good on my threat. What kind of friend would you be to keep that information to yourself?"

Cooper fought to keep his rage under control.

"You're a miserable bastard," he said, seething.

"Characterize me any way you'd like," Damon said casually. "But you cannot deny that I know how to get what I want, and I want the poleax. Deliver the message, or Ree Seaver dies."

Damon strode from the room, followed by the Roman soldiers. The last to leave was the gladiator, who stayed long enough to give another thought to slicing into Cooper with the black sword.

"This is not over," he warned, then turned and exited.

Cooper was left alone, standing in the bowels of an ancient stadium that was the vision of an emperor who'd lived in the Light somewhere around the year eighty. He closed his eyes, desperately trying to control his feelings of fear and frustration. Finally, he couldn't contain himself any longer and let out an anguished scream.

"Where are you?" he shouted.

The animals in their cages roared back an answer, but it wasn't what Coop wanted. What he desperately needed. He staggered about looking for something he knew wasn't there.

"Why aren't you here? Help me! Why don't you stop him?"

It was futile.

Not a single Watcher appeared. Or answered.

7

It was the second funeral of the summer and no easier than the first.

Ennis Mobley was laid to rest in the same cemetery as Cooper Foley. And Terri Seaver. Ennis had no family living in the States. His only relative was an elderly aunt who lived in Kingston, Jamaica, who Marsh's father, Michael, flew up for the service.

Ennis's closest friends were the Seaver family, so Michael took charge as soon as he learned of the tragedy and handled all the arrangements. There was a simple service at the funeral home in Stony Brook that was well attended by Ennis's friends and colleagues. He was loved and respected by many.

Cooper was there, though only Marsh and Sydney knew of his presence. He stood beside them throughout. While the three grieved for Ennis, thoughts of Damon and the true reason for Ennis's death were never far away.

Ennis's final journey in the Light was to the cemetery. Neither Marsh nor Sydney could bring themselves to go. Michael understood. They had just been there to bury Cooper, so he didn't insist that they pay the place another visit.

What Michael didn't realize was that for Marsh and Sydney, the horrifying memories of the cemetery had little to do with Cooper's funeral. The two had confronted the full fury of Damon's frightening visions that day, and neither wanted to set foot in that graveyard ever again . . . alive or dead or anywhere in between. So when the services ended, Sydney and Marsh drove home while Michael and the rest of the mourners brought Ennis to his grave.

Coop hadn't said much throughout the service, out of respect for Ennis. That ended on the trip back to the Foleys' house, when he quickly related all that he had seen in the Black.

"So Damon's building another army," he announced to complete his tale. "He's making it out like it's some kind of revolution against the authority of the Watchers, and there are plenty of idiots who believe him."

"Who is Brennus?" Marsh asked absently.

"I don't know, but he sounded like a bad dude, and Damon sure wants to find him."

"And Damon can't just step into Brennus's vision in the Black?"

"He can. He did. But Brennus wasn't there."

"Where was he?"

"I don't know, Ralph," Coop said, frustrated. "I'm not the afterlife expert here."

"Maybe Ennis can help you," Marsh offered.

Sydney shot him a quick look, as if surprised that Marsh would have said such a thing.

Marsh ignored her.

"To do what?" Coop asked.

"He thinks the sixth crucible might be in the Black. Maybe he can find it. And maybe he can find my mother."

"Maybe," Coop echoed, with no enthusiasm. "I'll have to look him up. He should be landing in the Black and losing his mind right about now."

"Where do you think my mom is?" Marsh asked.

"I don't know, Ralph," Coop said impatiently. "I don't know anything."

"Was there a clue in anything Damon said about her?" Marsh asked, pressing.

Cooper didn't answer.

"Coop?" Marsh prodded.

"No!" Cooper snapped. "Give me a break. I'm lucky I found the others."

"Easy," Marsh cautioned. "I'm just trying to think it all through."

"Yeah, well, me too," Coop countered. He said nothing about Damon's threat to Ree.

"Are you all right?" Marsh asked. "You don't sound right."

"I'm fine . . . for a dead guy."

"That's not what I meant."

"I'm going to Zoe's vision," Coop said, changing the subject. "I'll be back soon. You two are staying together, right?"

Neither answered.

"Hey!" Coop shouted. "You hear me?"

"Don't worry," Marsh said with assurance. "We'll be fine."

"Wish I could believe that." With that, Cooper disappeared in a swirl of color . . . without having delivered Damon's threat to Marsh.

Marsh and Sydney drove on in silence. It was becoming a habit.

Since the day Sydney had nearly been killed at school,

Marsh had been sleeping at her house on the living room couch so they could both be near the crucible. His dad didn't mind because he knew the Foleys were there to chaperone. He was thrilled that Marsh was finally getting a life, and a girlfriend. The excuse Sydney gave to her parents was that Marsh's room was being repainted. If that had been true, it would have been the longest painting job in history, but the Foleys didn't question Marsh, because they thought of him as their second son and liked having him around. Especially since Cooper's death.

Sydney did too . . . at least until the day Ennis had died.

Sydney pulled the car up to the curb in front of her house and killed the engine. She turned to Marsh and finally said the words she had been holding in for days.

"You knew," she said with disdain.

"Excuse me?" Marsh replied innocently.

"You knew he was going to kill himself."

"That's just stupid," Marsh said, and got out of the car, headed for the house.

Sydney jumped out and followed.

"How could you have let that happen?" she demanded. "He was your friend."

"I—I didn't know," Marsh said, stammering. "How could I?"

Sydney grabbed him by the arm and spun him around, forcing him to look at her.

Marsh hadn't experienced the legendary fury of Sydney Foley since the two of them began their unlikely romance, so the moment was surprising yet strangely familiar.

"That's a lie!" she screamed. "I wanted to stay and protect him with the crucible, but you insisted that we leave."

"He wanted us to go," Marsh said defensively. "I did what he asked."

"I should have known," Sydney lamented. "As soon as

you told him that his dying would get him closer to Damon, something changed. I saw it and so did you, but you understood what it meant. You told him to be careful. And when you looked down on his dead body, you asked him to find your mother. Is that why you let him do it? To help find your mother?"

"Stop," Marsh demanded. "This isn't my fault. I didn't start any of this."

"I know, but it doesn't give you the right to look the other way and let someone die."

Marsh couldn't stand still. He walked toward the house, then quickly spun back and faced Sydney.

"Don't you dare judge me!" he yelled. "You have no idea what it's like to have so much at stake!"

Sydney was ready to erupt but held her temper and responded with measured words.

"I know exactly what it's like. And because I care about you, I *haven't* judged you. I backed off. I gave you space. I barely offered my opinion, and you know full well that isn't me. But I did it because I thought that's what you needed. I did it because I love you and I love my stupid brother and because I'm scared. But I'm not going to do it anymore."

"What does that mean?"

"Damon is a cold-blooded bastard who has no respect for life. I will not sink to his level, even if you can."

Marsh recoiled as if Sydney had physically slapped him.

Sydney dug into her shoulder bag, pulled out the crucible, and jammed it into Marsh's hand. "Go home. I'll take my chances alone."

She turned quickly and started back for the car.

"Sydney?" Marsh called.

Sydney stopped walking but didn't turn back to him. Marsh approached her from behind and leaned over her shoulder.

"You're right," he said. "Okay? I had an idea that something like this might happen. But you know what? It's what he wanted. He was haunted. Not just by Damon, but by knowing that his actions killed my mother and set this nightmare in motion. He was doomed from the start, Sydney. There was nothing we could do to change that. Ennis has moved on, and maybe he's got a better chance of being at peace now than he had in life."

"It wasn't about him," Sydney said without looking at Marsh. "It was about you. You let a man die because it might help you. And that makes you no better than Damon."

Marsh opened his mouth to argue, but no words came out.

"Get your stuff. Don't be here when I get back," Sydney snapped, and hurried to her car. She got behind the wheel, slammed the door, and took off quickly.

Marsh stood on the walkway watching Sydney's silver Beetle drive off. His relationship with her was the only good thing that had come out of the monstrous events of the summer. Now even that was slipping away. Strangely he wasn't sad. Or angry. Or even ashamed. At least not at that moment. His mind had traveled to a much more disturbing place . . . a place he didn't want to share, especially with those he cared about.

He was on his own again. And he had information. Something he hadn't explained to Cooper or Sydney.

Lignum vitae.

He knew what it meant.

If he was right, the game was about to change. But for that to happen he would have to perform an act that might damn him for all time. He didn't care. He was willing to do it. Sydney was wrong. It wasn't just about him. It was about his mother. And Cooper. And now Ennis. If he were to allow his thoughts to spin out of control, he would admit that it was also about every soul that now walked in the Light . . .

or existed in the Black. With that much at stake, most anything he did to stop Damon would be justified. He hoped. The real question was, could he do it?

Marsh wished Cooper had stuck around. They needed to make a plan. He hated that there was no way to contact him. It wasn't like he could pull the Ouija board out of the closet and use it like a Bat signal. Marsh could only wait and hope that Cooper got back to him . . . before Damon did.

Marsh needed to go home, so he jogged the familiar route through the neighborhood that he and Coop had taken thousands of times before. He made the trip quickly, then dragged himself and his stuff up the porch stairs and into his house for the first time in several days. It was only midafternoon but he was already exhausted. He had taken the day off from work at Santoro's Trophies and didn't want to do anything but sleep. There was no telling when he'd get the chance to rest again, and he needed to be fresh. He entered the empty house and went directly for the stairs to climb up to his room, and bed, when he heard a voice.

"Marsh? You out there?"

Marsh froze. His throat clutched. Someone was in the house.

"Marsh?"

His panic lasted no more than three seconds because he recognized the voice. His father was calling from the kitchen.

"Dad? You home already? That was fast."

Michael called back, "C'mon! Dinner's ready. GTH in here!"

Dinner? It was way too early for dinner. Marsh started walking toward the kitchen, when he heard someone running down the stairs from the second floor. He shot a surprised look up to see . . .

Himself. Marsh himself came running down the stairs.

But it was a young Marsh, who looked no more than ten years old.

"Coming!" Young Marsh called.

Marsh's mind locked. He was looking at a young version of himself wearing jeans, PRO-Keds, and a Boba Fett T-shirt . . . all clothes that he remembered well.

"Who are you?" Marsh managed to say with a gasp.

The kid didn't acknowledge him. Or even hear him. It was like Marsh wasn't even there, which made him wonder which Marsh was real . . . him, or the specter from the past.

Another voice called from the kitchen. A woman's voice. One that made Marsh's heart ache.

"C'mon! Dinner's getting cold!" she called. Not an unusual warning, except that the voice belonged to his mother.

"On my way!" Young Marsh called back as he hit the ground floor and sprinted toward the kitchen. He galloped through the dining room and disappeared through the swinging door, just as he had done thousands of times before.

Marsh fought to stay in control. He knew what was happening. It was Damon. It had to be. When he was haunted by Gravedigger, Marsh thought he was going out of his mind. Now he knew better. Damon was capable of creating visions to mess with his head. He had to hold on to the fact that they were nothing more than shadows. Illusions. The only way they could hurt him was if he let them, and he had grown too strong for that. After what he'd already seen, there was nothing that Damon could show him that would do any real damage.

With that in mind, Marsh got his feet moving and walked toward the kitchen.

As he drew closer to the swinging door, he heard the familiar sounds of a family sitting down to dinner. There was the clatter of serving bowls, the metallic chirp of silverware being placed, the scrape of chairs across a tiled floor. The voices were muffled, though Marsh could make out every word.

"Eat fast," his dad said. "Yanks and Sox on tonight."

"Excellent!" Young Marsh replied.

"Homework first," his mom cautioned.

"Aww, Mom!" Marsh complained.

"Yeah. 'Aww, Mom,'" Dad echoed.

"Don't 'Aww, Mom' me!" Terri said with a laugh. "Either of you."

All three laughed.

Marsh felt tears growing. Nothing about what he was hearing was horrifying, other than it was a painful reminder of a happier life that would never again be. It was one of Damon's more cruel illusions, but it didn't stop Marsh from wanting to see the scene and experience it once again, even though he knew it wasn't real.

"Wait," Terri called. "Do you hear that?"

"Hear what?" Young Marsh asked.

"Is somebody in the house?" Terri asked, concerned.

"I heard it too," Marsh's dad said. "It sounds like someone is in the dining room."

Marsh picked up the pace.

"It's okay. It's me!" he called out. "It's Marsh!"

He put his hand on the door and was about to push it open, when he heard a terrified scream come from his mother.

"Mom!" Marsh called out. "It's just me!"

Marsh pushed open the door and stepped into a gut-wrenching scene . . . that had nothing to do with dinner.

His dad and Young Marsh stood by the sink, staring up at his mother . . . who hung from the neck by a noose that was looped over the ceiling fan. The grisly sight made

Marsh take a step away in horror, hitting his back against the kitchen door. He could hear the gentle creak of the rope as her body swung, lifeless, over the kitchen table. He couldn't take his eyes off it, until the face of his mother twisted toward him, and he saw her bulging, lifeless eyes.

"It's up to you, Marsh," his father said.

At first he thought the illusion of his dad was talking to Young Marsh, but when he looked to the man, he saw that he was focused on him.

Young Marsh looked to him as well and added, "You can save her, just like Cooper told you."

"Wha—?" Marsh mumbled. "Cooper didn't say anything."

"He didn't?" Michael said with surprise. "What was that kid thinking? Holding that information from you? Typical."

"I wonder why he didn't tell you?" Young Marsh asked.

Marsh summoned his courage, trying desperately to stay connected with sanity.

"Get out!" he shouted, then looked around the room, hoping to see Damon. Or Gravedigger. Or anyone else that would prove he was seeing an illusion.

"Get them out of here!" Marsh screamed.

"But this is our house too," Young Marsh argued.

"No, it isn't! You aren't real," Marsh screamed, and stormed toward them.

His father shrugged, then he and Young Marsh disappeared.

Marsh turned quickly to see if the illusion of his hanging mother was gone. It wasn't. He took a step toward the grisly illusion, but rather than disappearing, the rope snapped and the body fell, hitting the kitchen table with a sickening thud while scattering bowls and plates that smashed to the floor.

The horrific sight revolted Marsh, making him back away. The body of his mother rolled off the table, hit a chair, and then thumped down onto the kitchen floor. When it landed, her head faced Marsh, though twisted backward on her body as if she were looking over her own shoulder.

"Save me, Marsh," his mother said.

Marsh screamed.

It was all his shattered mind could manage.

8

"Ralph! Whoa, what happened?"

Cooper stepped into the Light to find Marshall sitting on the floor of his kitchen, shaking. The illusion of his hanged mother was gone. There were no shattered plates or frayed ropes, though Marsh continued to stare at the spot where the illusion had been.

"Ralph!" Coop yelled, leaning down to his friend.

Marsh finally looked away, returning to the moment, and reality. He looked up at Cooper, at first not registering who it was.

"What do you see?" Coop asked, agitated.

"I, uh, nothing."

"You're on the floor shaking and staring like a zombie because of nothing?" Coop asked with skepticism.

Marsh shrugged. "It's been a rough day."

"Where's Sydney?" Coop asked.

"Not here." He stood up and went to the sink to get a glass of water to help calm himself.

"Wha—? You guys are supposed to stay together."

"We had a fight," Marsh explained with no emotion. "She thinks it was my fault that Ennis died."

"Well, that's just stupid," Coop said, scoffing. "How could you know Damon was going to get to him?"

Marsh took a sip of water and said, "She's right."

"Uh . . . what?"

"Ennis was on the edge. When we talked about the Black, his whole attitude changed. He saw it as a way out. And I saw it as a way to help my mother. I'm not gonna lie."

"But it's not like you pushed him out of that window," Coop offered.

"No, but I might as well have. We could have stayed with him. Now he's dead."

Coop watched his friend with concern, trying to read his thoughts. "You're sounding a little nutty, Ralph."

"I'm fine," Marsh said with no emotion.

"You don't sound fine. I mean, you just admitted to letting Ennis die so he could help us in the Black. That doesn't sound like you."

Marsh shrugged. "None of us are the same anymore. Except for you, Coop. Even in death you've stayed the same. You still get what you want, no matter what you have to do to get it."

"What are you talking about?"

"What did Damon say about my mother?"

Coop stiffened. "What do you mean?" he asked evasively.

"Don't make it worse," Marsh said coldly.

"Why do you ask? Was he here?"

"You could say that. Stop ducking. What were you supposed to tell me about my mother?"

"I don't know what you mean."

"No? You weren't supposed to tell me that I could save her?"

Coop shook his head, buying time, looking for the right words.

"Do *not* lie to me," Marsh said through clenched teeth.

"All right!" Coop blurted out. "He made a threat. He's always making threats. Who knows if he was serious?"

"*You* do, Coop. Or else you would have told me."

"Yeah, well, maybe that's why I came right back."

"Is it?" Marsh asked. "Do not lie to me."

Coop wasn't used to being backed into a corner, especially by Marsh. He started to argue, but thought better of it.

"No," he admitted. "I'm back because something felt off between you and Sydney."

"Maybe we're all keeping secrets," Marsh replied.

"C'mon!" Coop complained. "What would you have done if I'd told you? You don't know where the poleax is any more than I do."

"But I deserve to know the truth so I can make my own choices." He was shaking again but not from fear. Marsh was furious. "We're talking about my mother here."

"Okay, fine," Coop shot back. "Suppose you knew where the poleax was? What would you do then? Huh? Marsh, your mom means a lot to me too. In life *and* in death. I fought beside her to stop Damon. I know what's important to her, and I guarantee she wouldn't want you to give him the poleax."

"So then I should just let him destroy her?" Marsh asked.

"It's not like you have a choice," Coop replied.

Marsh winced.

"I'm sorry," Coop added sincerely. "That was cold. You're right, I should have told you."

Marsh glanced to the kitchen table. The same table

where he had seen the vision of his mother hanging from a rope.

"And this time she'll be gone forever," Marsh whispered.

"That's not a guarantee," Coop offered. "I'll find her. I got the others away from Damon, and I can do the same for her."

"No," Marsh said quickly.

"No?"

"It may already be too late," Marsh said. "But it's not too late for Sydney."

"What do you mean?"

"You were right. Something's going on with us. She was so angry with me for what happened to Ennis that she took off . . . without the crucible. Damon could be going after her right now. If I were you, I'd go find her."

Coop stiffened. "If you were me, you wouldn't have let her go in the first place."

Marsh took a threatening step toward Cooper. "You're the last person who should be passing judgment."

Coop stood his ground, and the two friends stood eye to eye, neither backing down.

"Where did she go?" Coop finally asked.

"She has a class at the junior high this afternoon."

"She's going to teach a class after a day like this?" Coop asked, incredulous.

Marsh shrugged. "She's probably still on the road somewhere."

"You shouldn't have let her go," Coop said.

"And you should have told me about my mother."

Coop was off balance. He didn't like the guy that Marsh had become. His naïveté was slowly being replaced by cold calculation. And something was off. He wasn't telling Coop everything, and Coop knew it. His friend wasn't a good liar. He hadn't had enough practice. Coop knew he would have to mend fences with his friend, but first he had to make sure that Sydney was safe.

"I'll be right back," Coop said.

"Good luck."

Marsh's words hung there, having been delivered with an obvious lack of sincerity.

Coop hesitated, unsure if he was making the right move, but he saw no other choice and stepped out of Marsh's kitchen to begin the search for his sister.

As soon as he disappeared, Marsh ran for the door. He knew he wouldn't have much time, so he had to act fast. He ran straight for the garage. The place hadn't been organized in years and was full of so much junk that there was no room for the car. Marsh wasn't entirely sure what he was looking for, only that he would know it when he found it. He grabbed a hammer off the cluttered tool bench, felt its weight, then tossed it back down. He found a garden spade with a long wooden handle. It hadn't been used to turn up soil in ages. Marsh didn't even bother to pick it up. He dug through the shelf beneath the tool bench, where he pushed past clippers, tangled snow chains, a rusted hand drill, and some cracked flower pots.

Finally he pushed aside a half-empty plastic bag of top-soil and found his prize. It was a black metal crowbar with a hook and claw on either end. He lifted the tool and tested its strength. It was solid. It was heavy.

It was exactly what he needed.

Coop took the most direct route to Stony Brook Junior High. Rather than simply disappearing from Marsh's house and reappearing at the school, he expected to find Sydney on the road, so he floated above the traffic, scanning the cars, watching out for her silver Beetle. Being a ghost had its perks. He wished he could have enjoyed using them a little more.

It was rush hour, so the traffic was heavy. He had to be careful not to miss the car. Every second counted. There was no telling what Damon might do to put her in danger again. It was an uneasy trip, not only because he was worried about his sister, but because of Marsh's behavior. Yes, his friend had been through a lot, but it was hard to believe that he would have let Sydney go unprotected even if they had had a fight. Sydney was tough to deal with, he knew, but Marsh cared about her. It didn't add up.

Her car was nowhere to be seen. Afraid that he might have missed it, he quickly took another route back toward their house but came up empty again. He took a third route back to the school and decided that she must have gotten there faster than he thought. He scanned the parking lot but didn't see her car. Something was definitely wrong. He floated into the school and went right to the classroom where she had been tutoring algebra.

It was empty. Most of the classrooms were empty. Only two classes were in session, and both of those were in the wood shop. Sydney was definitely not there. So then, where was she? Cooper chose to go to the most obvious place. Home. He didn't bother to track the car route. He wanted to get there as quickly as possible, so he imagined himself to be home, and two seconds later he was.

Sydney's car was in the driveway. His parents' car wasn't. That was bad news. It meant Sydney was alone. Coop didn't hesitate to swoop into the house, fearing that he would find Sydney battling one of Damon's visions.

What he found instead was his sister sitting on the couch, crying.

"Hey! You okay?" he shouted.

Sydney screamed and jumped up to run away from him.

"Whoa, whoa, it's me!" Coop assured her.

Sydney shot a frightened glance over her shoulder, recognized her brother, and relaxed.

"What is wrong with you?" she snarled.

"Hey, I'm a ghost. What do you expect? Are you all right?"

Sydney collected herself and sat back down. "Aside from the near heart attack, yes."

"Nothing spooky happened since you left Marsh?"

"Only you popping in."

Coop finally relaxed.

"So . . . you and Marsh had a fight?" Coop asked tentatively.

Sydney nodded. "I know what's at stake here," she said thoughtfully. "I'm just not willing to give up on my humanity to deal with it."

"He didn't kill Ennis," Coop said.

"He didn't try to save him either. And you know what? Neither did I. What does that say about me?"

"It makes us normal people trying to deal with really abnormal challenges."

Sydney looked up at her brother and gave him a small smile. "That was surprisingly eloquent."

"I have my moments. Why didn't you go to school?"

"I don't have classes today."

"But . . . you told Marsh you were going there."

"No, I didn't."

"He said you did."

"Why would he lie?"

Coop frowned, and paced. "Something's wrong."

"Gee, you think?"

"I mean he's keeping something from me. I think Damon paid him a visit. It twisted his head around and—"

"That's impossible," Sydney interrupted.

"Do you seriously think anything is impossible any-more?" Coop asked.

"In this case, yes. Damon couldn't have gotten to him."

"Why not?"

"Because the crucible would have kept Damon away."

Coop's eyes went wide as the realization hit him. "Jeez, you're right. Could that be why he was all shaky? Because the crucibles don't stop Damon anymore?"

"Maybe," Sydney said, thinking back. "Or maybe— Oh my god."

She leaped off the couch and ran across the room to get her shoulder bag. She grabbed it, jammed her hand inside . . . and pulled out the golden crucible.

"We were standing close together in the front yard," Sydney said, thinking back. "He must have slipped it in then."

The two stared at the round orb for a few moments, try-ing to understand the implications.

Finally Coop said, "I don't know if I should be relieved or horrified."

"Because Damon could go after him again?"

"No. Because I'm afraid he may not be as concerned about losing his humanity as you are."

9

Marsh had called for a cab. Ordinarily he would have taken his bike, but he knew he wouldn't have much time and he didn't want Cooper to track him down. Getting away from the house quickly was critical. Once gone, he felt certain that he was headed to the last place anybody would expect him to go. Even Cooper. Especially Cooper. Still, he had to be certain so he wanted to get there as quickly as possible.

"You visiting somebody special?" the cabdriver asked.

Marsh didn't answer.

The cabbie added, "I'm not sure when they close up. You might not have much time."

"I won't need much time," was Marsh's emotionless answer.

The cabbie stopped trying to make conversation. It was obvious to him that the kid in the back was upset. He figured it was better to let him deal with it on his own.

It was getting late in the afternoon but still hours before dark. That was one consolation for Marsh. He didn't like being alone in the dark . . . especially not where he was going.

The cab rolled to a stop, and the cabbie turned back to him. "I'll wait for you right here."

"Don't," Marsh said quickly as he dug for his wallet.

"You're in the middle of nowhere!"

Marsh threw a twenty-dollar bill at the cabbie. "Thanks. Good-bye."

"Whatever," the driver said with a shrug.

Marsh climbed out of the cab awkwardly. It was tough to move with a crowbar hidden along his leg inside his pants. He slammed the door shut and stood watching as the yellow car drove away along the country lane. The road was empty. There was never much traffic in this part of town. Once the cab disappeared and the whine of its engine died away, the only sound Marsh heard came from the early birds who had already begun to hunt for their evening meal. It was a peaceful, lazy late summer afternoon.

Marsh pulled the heavy crowbar out of his pants leg, then turned to see that the front gate was still open. He was relieved to know that he wouldn't have to break in. He walked up to the tall wrought-iron fence and stopped, flashing back to the last time he had been there. It wasn't a good memory, and he quickly shook it off. He knew that if he dwelled on the past, especially a past that was so disturbing, there would be no way he would be able to go through with what he had come to do. He had to clear his mind and keep moving. With a quick breath he stepped forward and walked through the open gate of Stony Brook Cemetery.

He knew exactly where to go, though it had been a few years since he had been to that particular area. He had seen the place many times . . . in his mind. It was burned into his memory, as disturbing images usually are. He walked slowly along the paved road that wound between the sea of head-stones and statues. It was an old cemetery, with graves dating back to the seventeenth century. The one small consolation was that he wasn't going to visit the older, Gothic section. The ancient mausoleums, tombstones, and statues in that area were the fodder for nightmares. Marsh had more than enough nightmare material to deal with already.

Because it was late in the day, there were no other people visiting graves. The only activity was a sole worker riding a backhoe, filling in a grave that was situated about fifty yards away from where Marsh was walking. Marsh didn't stop to watch. The idea of earth being dumped onto a coffin was a chilling one. It made him think of the term that Coop said his grandfather used for dying: "The dirt nap." It was a cavalier phrase that cheapened death. It didn't seem as clever or funny when you considered the literal meaning.

He wondered if it was Ennis's grave, since the funeral had been only a few hours before. The thought made him pick up the pace. He didn't want his imagination to play with that image. Besides, he didn't want the worker to know he was there.

He walked for another five minutes and caught the first glimpse of his destination peeking through a grove of cypress trees. It was a mausoleum, but not one of the crusty old ones that could be found in the ancient section of the cemetery. This was a modern structure made of marble and stone, with square lines and not a single forlorn statue in sight. Marsh had been inside exactly once and promised himself that he would never go back.

He was about to break that promise.

The building could have passed for a small modern church. Pots of colorful, well-tended flowers were to either side of the entrance, and the grass that surrounded it looked to have been trimmed that very day. The light gray marble walls were spotless. The glass doors were sparkling clear. It was a clean, inviting structure . . . for the dead.

Four marble steps led up to a short porch that had two tall, white columns guarding the entryway. Marsh fought the memories of his last visit as he climbed the steps and pulled on the gleaming brass handle. The door was locked.

It made him think of a joke from when he was a young kid.

"Why do cemeteries have fences?"

"Because people are dying to get in."

He never thought it was very funny, but all the same, in that moment, he was dying to get in. He dug into his jeans and pulled out a ring with two shiny brass keys. They had been gathering dust in the back of his father's desk drawer at home. He never forgot about them, but had never expected to use them either. He wasn't even 100 percent sure they would work. He picked one and slipped it into the lock. He held his breath and twisted.

The lock turned effortlessly. Marsh closed his eyes and pulled the door open. He was instantly hit by an overwhelming smell. A sweet smell. Flowers. People always commented on how wonderful flowers smelled. Marsh didn't agree. The fragrant aroma always brought back terrible memories for him, most of them having to do with funerals.

He entered quickly and closed the door. There were pull-down shades on each of the doors to block out direct light. He didn't want anyone to catch sight of him inside so he lowered both of the blinds. Not only was he hidden from curious eyes, but by lowering the blinds, the outside world ceased to exist. It was as if he had entered another world.

He listened. The mausoleum was quiet. He was alone. He had done it.

The easy part.

The ceiling was glass, which allowed in enough late-day light to see by. There was no need to turn on any lamps that might be noticed from outside. Directly inside the front entrance was the meditation chapel. There was a long marble bench on either side. On the wall behind each was a mosaic artwork that depicted a different tranquil countryside. Large vases filled with fresh flowers stood in each corner. It looked like a pleasant enough place to sit and think, if you wanted to sit and think about hanging out in a building full of dead people.

He walked to the far end of the chapel, where there were wide rooms off to either side. The walls of each were covered with rows of symmetrical marble-faced squares roughly two feet wide. These were the niches were people interred the cremated remains of their loved ones. Many had the names of the tenants etched into the marble and painted a rich golden color. Most of them had small bronze vases attached. Some held fresh flowers, others had the remains of petals that had wilted long ago. Most were empty. The majority of the niches at eye level had names. Many of the squares that were lower or much higher were blank. There was plenty of room for those who were dying to get in.

Though he had only stolen quick glimpses of the mausoleum the one time he was there, he remembered it all. He also remembered where he had to go. Halfway along the wall of the room to the right was another door. He turned and walked to it, passing the niches that held the urns of ashes that were once people. He arrived at the solid brass door and didn't bother checking to see if it was locked. He went right for the ring with the two keys and chose the second key. This lock turned as easily as the first, and with a loud click that echoed through the empty chamber, the door was unlocked.

The door was wider than normal in order to accommodate deliveries. He pulled it open to find that it was also heavy. Like a vault. Swinging it wide, he saw the set of stairs that led below. It was dark down there. He was scared. It was the fear that anybody would have if they were alone in a dark mausoleum, surrounded by the dead. He felt foolish for it. There was plenty for him to be afraid of, but not in the traditional sense. He was about to step into territory that would be unfathomable to the average person. Ghosts? They were the least of his worries. What waited below was far more horrible than any spirit. He steeled himself, stepped inside, and pulled the door shut behind him. He grasped the crowbar tighter and began his descent.

No sunlight penetrated the chamber. He needed to turn on a light. He stopped to let his eyes adjust, and after a few seconds he was able to make out faint, gray detail. To his relief, a row of light switches was on the wall to his right. He reached out and flipped the first in line. This triggered to life a row of lights that were recessed near the ceiling. It was a soft, unobtrusive light that created just enough illumination to navigate by. Slowly, he descended into the depths and stopped when he arrived at the bottom stair.

He had reached the final leg of his journey and turned to gaze into the subterranean crypt.

The room covered twice as much area as the structure above because most of the space had been created by burrowing underground. The ceiling was low, but the niches built into these walls were much larger than the ones on the ground floor. The receptacles up top were designed to hold a small urn of ashes. These crypts were built to hold full-size coffins. The facades that covered each of the crypts was made from the same material as above. White marble. But rather than being two-feet square, the symmetrical sections built into these walls were roughly seven feet long and two feet high . . . the standard size to hold a coffin that was slipped in sideways. As above, there were bronze vases that held flowers. Marsh was surprised to see that they all looked as fresh as if they had been delivered that day. It didn't take long to understand why. They were plastic. As above, many of the crypts were inscribed with names. Most had dates. Some even had prayers.

His destination was the far end of the room.

He took a step and started to shake. His stomach twisted, and he had all he could do to keep from getting sick. He thought he had gotten over that reaction to stress. It was just another hurdle he would have to overcome.

"Ralph," came a soft voice.

Marsh didn't react. He thought it was his mind playing tricks. It wouldn't have been the first time. He stopped walking, listened, then continued on.

"What are you doing?" came the voice again.

It was no inner dialogue. Marsh spun quickly to see Cooper standing on the stairs behind him. In just a few seconds his emotions ran from surprise, to fear, to anger.

"How did you find me?" Marsh asked.

Coop shrugged. "I can always find you . . . or did you forget that?"

He had.

"Besides, you left your cell phone at your house, and Sydney checked it. You called for a cab. The dispatcher said they brought you here. So Sydney knows too."

"Where is she?"

"I told her to stay put, which means she's probably on the way. I can move a lot quicker than she can."

There was an awkward silence.

"What's with the crowbar?" Coop asked.

"You can't stop me," Marsh said, his voice quivering.

"I don't even know what you're doing."

Marsh held up the tool to examine it. "I'm going to save my mother," he said.

With that he turned and strode for the far end of the burial chamber.

Coop ran ahead of him.

"Talk to me, Ralph," he said. "What's going on?"

"I'm a smart guy," Marsh said. "It took a while but I finally put it together."

"Okay, I'm not and I didn't. Enlighten me."

"My mother told you the story about what happened under that temple in Greece with her and Ennis. They found the poleax in Damon's tomb, along with the six crucibles."

"Yeah, it was all about protecting the Rift."

"Exactly. The Rift. That's how she died. She wasn't crushed in an earthquake. She fell into the Rift. And it wasn't really a tomb, was it?"

"No, I guess not. At least not Damon's tomb. He'd gone through the Rift too. Centuries before."

Marsh had reached the far wall of crypts. He stopped and looked to his friend. His eyes were wild and his heart was thumping frantically.

"I can't let her spirit die, Coop."

"I'm doing all I can."

"I know. But I haven't been. At least until now."

"And what is it you're doing?"

Marsh looked down at the marble slab that covered a crypt at waist level. Etched in the white marble were the words:

THERESA SEAVER. BELOVED WIFE AND MOTHER. BFF.

Coop gazed at the crypt, desperately trying to understand.

"Ennis was there," Marsh said. "In Greece. After Mom died, he handled all the details. All the paperwork. He dealt with the governments and the shipping companies and cut through all the red tape to bring her body home. Dad and I never questioned a thing. We were too messed up. But now I understand. I can't believe it took me so long."

"Understand what?" Coop asked, frustrated.

"You know what happened. She told you the whole thing. She didn't die in the rubble."

"But she did die! She's in the Black, Marsh!"

"I know. But it wasn't the earthquake that killed her. She went through the Rift."

"So?"

"So that means there was no body to bring home."

The realization hit Cooper like a freight train rumbling along the Morpheus Road.

"Jeez, you're right," he said with a gasp.

Marsh looked him dead in the eye and said, "Lignum vitae. Damon was right all along. I know where the poleax is."

10

"*Lignum* what?" Coop asked, reeling, trying to understand all the implications. "What does that mean?"

"Lignum vitae. The wood of life. That's what Ennis called it. He said it represented strength and asked if it was okay."

"You're losing me, man."

"I stood right there," Marsh said, pointing to a spot not far from the crypt. "I saw Ennis put a twisted sculpture of branches on top of the coffin before they slid it into the tomb. It was like a knot made out of wooden limbs. The perfect size to hide something."

Cooper looked to Ree's crypt, trying to calculate the facts that Marsh was throwing out.

"Ralph, you're dreaming," he finally said. "The poleax is a weapon. It's too big to hide in a twisted branch of wood."

"I'm sure it is," Marsh said calmly. "But it was the perfect size to hide a small golden ball."

Coop's eyes went wide. Everything that Marsh had been babbling about had suddenly snapped into perfect focus.

"Oh jeez," he said with a gasp.

Marsh nodded. "This is what it's been about from the start, Coop. Damon knew I would be the one to figure it out. It's why he came after you to come after me. The fifth crucible is protecting the poleax . . . in my mother's grave."

Marsh was breathing hard, his eyes glazed. His mind had gone to another place in order to process the horror of what he was about to do.

"So you want to break into the crypt and get it?" Coop asked, numb.

"I want to save my mother," Marsh answered. He clutched the crowbar and took a step back to line himself up.

"Ralph, no!" Coop yelled. "You can't. You just can't."

"I can. I have to," Marsh replied.

"Listen to me. Your mom is still okay. Damon needs her to try to control you, and it's working. You're doing exactly what he wants."

"He threatened to kill her spirit," Marsh said.

"And what would stop him from doing it anyway, even after he got the poleax? He is not an honorable guy."

"You could be right, but I'm not taking the chance."

"So what are you going to do?" Coop challenged. "Just hand him the poleax and hope he releases your mother? Trust me, that won't happen."

"I do trust you, Coop. That's why I'm giving the poleax to you."

"What!" Coop exclaimed, once again thrown by Marsh's thinking.

"This is your plan, remember? You wanted the Guardians to get the poleax and use it against Damon. From everything

I've seen, Damon is too powerful to be brought down like a normal spirit."

Coop backed off. "No . . . no . . . that's just . . . nuts."

"It isn't," Marsh said with authority. "Use the poleax, Coop. Use it on Damon."

Coop was reeling. "I . . . I don't know. That's like . . . like . . . playing with fire."

"Exactly. Your kind of fight."

Marsh focused on the crypt. Coop saw that he was getting ready to act, and jumped in front of him.

"No!" he shouted. "I can't believe I'm the voice of reason here but you're wrong. I was wrong. If the poleax is in there with the crucible, then Damon can't get it."

"But for how long?" Marsh cried. "Three crucibles are broken, and Damon's abilities have grown each time. He's not going to stop until he gets what he wants, so why should I?"

"I know, Ralph. I hear you. But this is way bigger than saving your mother. It's bigger than you and me and any of the spirits who've been fighting him. If Damon gets that thing, it'll be Armageddon."

"You may be right," Marsh said, still remarkably calm. "But sooner or later he's going to find this. Maybe it'll be a hundred years from now after he tortures some other poor sucker into getting it, but it will happen. The only difference will be that my mother will no longer exist."

"What if you're wrong?" Coop shouted, grasping at straws. "What if it isn't there? What if this is really your mother's tomb and her body's been in there for three years? Is that something you want to see? And live with?"

Marsh blinked, imagining the possibility. Coop had finally gotten through to him. He took a few steps back from the crypt and read the inscription. Tears grew in his eyes.

"I don't think I'm wrong," Marsh said softly. "But if I am, the worst thing that will happen is that I'll lose whatever is left of my mind. But if I'm right, we could hold the power to stop Damon."

Coop said, "Or bring on Judgment Day."

Marsh grasped the crowbar tighter.

"Are you going to move?"

Coop shook his head. "I can't stop you, but I'm not getting out of the way."

Marsh started breathing hard. The sound of his labored breaths filled the subterranean room. His eyes were focused on the stretch of marble that protected either the poleax . . . or his mother's remains.

"Don't do it, Ralph," Coop begged softly. "I promise I'll find her."

Marsh raised the crowbar, let out an anguished bellow, and charged for the crypt. True to his word, Cooper didn't budge. When Marsh swung the bar, it traveled right through his friend before smashing into the crypt's facade.

The very first blow sent a spiderweb of cracks through the name Theresa Seaver. Marsh screamed with agony and adrenaline as he continued, hammering away at the marble, desperate to get the job done quickly.

Each blow traveled through Coop's spirit. He closed his eyes, not wanting to witness the destruction of the tomb . . . and his best friend.

With a tortured howl Marsh gave one final swing. The crowbar made contact and shattered the marble facing. The arc of Marsh's swing continued into the uncovered crypt, where the hook of the crowbar snagged onto something. Marsh followed through like a batter swinging for the fences and pulled out a snarl of branches.

Lignum vitae.

He had caught the sculpture with the crowbar. As he yanked it out of the crypt, along with it came a golden orb that had been nestled in its branches. It was too late for

Marsh to stop the momentum. The glass ball flew across the room, landed on the marble floor . . ..

And shattered.

Red liquid exploded from the broken ball, spraying across the floor and the far wall of crypts.

Another crucible was history.

Cooper saw the eruption and deflated.

"And . . . here we go," he uttered with resignation.

The floor shook. Marsh knew the feeling. An earthquake was rocking the mausoleum, though both Marsh and Cooper knew that it wasn't a natural geological event.

Marsh staggered back a few steps, nearly tripping over a large, jagged chunk of marble. The stone veneer that had sealed Terri Seaver's final resting place was gone. Behind it, in a niche that was barely big enough to contain it, was a mahogany coffin.

Marsh stared at the casket, wide-eyed.

"Pull it out," Cooper commanded to Marsh.

Marsh didn't react.

The mausoleum continued to shake and rumble.

"Marsh!" Coop screamed. "If the poleax is there, you gotta get it! Now!"

Marsh shook himself into action. He jumped to the open crypt and reached for the brass handles of the coffin. He grasped them both, and froze.

"What's the matter?" Coop asked.

"I can't," Marsh said with a whimper.

Cooper jumped down next to his friend and got right into his face. "You started this. You can't bail now."

Marsh was in tears. "It—it's my mother," he stammered. "What if—"

"Too late!" Coop screamed above the rumbling of the quake. "The crucible's gone. He's coming. If the poleax is in there, we sure as hell better get it before he does. Pull it out!"

Marsh screamed in despair . . . and pulled. The coffin was heavier than he expected, but he was charged with adrenaline and the wooden casket slid out easily. Once out of the enclosure there was no place for it to go but down. There was one crypt below Ree's, so it was a three-foot drop to the floor. Marsh hesitated, looking for a way to gently ease the casket to the ground.

"Drop it!" Coop screamed.

Marsh obeyed and yanked the coffin off the ledge. The heavy casket fell and landed with a dull thud. The force cracked the seal, springing the lid open a small inch.

Marsh staggered back, overcome with grief. And fear. The rumbling continued, making it difficult for him to stand on legs that were already weak.

"Open it, Ralph," Coop commanded with calm force.

"What if I'm wrong?" Marsh cried, hysterical.

"I hope you are. Open it!"

Marsh wiped his eyes and staggered forward, his gaze focused on the narrow opening where the lid of the coffin had released from the bottom shell. Coop ran right up alongside him.

"I know, Ralph. It doesn't get any worse than this. But you know what? I think you're right. I think the only thing we're going to find in that box is a sword. Your mother is in the Black. She fell through the Rift. She's not in there. But the poleax might be, and if it is, you've got to get it before Damon does."

Coop's words gave Marsh strength. He approached the coffin, knelt down beside it, and grasped the lid. His hands were shaking. His tears flowed again.

He couldn't move.

"Open it, Marsh," Coop coaxed. "If I'm going to save her, I'll need the poleax."

Marsh steeled himself, took a deep breath, and lifted the lid to reveal . . .

. . . skeletal remains.

The last time Marsh had seen his mother was the day she had left for Greece and her rendezvous with destiny. Since that day the hurt had only grown worse as memories of her slowly faded. He often relied on pictures to remind him of the way she smiled or the shape of her eyes. He feared that someday he would have only memories of her pictures but not of the woman herself. He hated to think that might happen. He wanted to remember her. The person.

As he looked down into that coffin, he knew that no matter how fleeting his memories might be, he could be absolutely certain of one thing:

"It's not her," he said, the tension leaving his body.

"How can you tell?" Coop asked, squinting, trying not to look too closely.

"Because it's a man," was Marsh's simple reply.

Coop forced himself to look.

"Jeez, it is."

The remains had decomposed to the point where there was little skin left on the bones, but the hair and the clothing were fairly intact. Ree Seaver was of medium build and had long wavy brown hair. The poor man in the coffin had short, black hair and wore a gray suit.

Marsh couldn't take his eyes off the remains. "Who could it be?" he asked.

"Uh-oh," Coop said.

"What?"

"The rumbling stopped."

"You're right. Does that mean—"

Marsh felt a strong hand grab his arm and yank him forcefully away from the coffin. He half stumbled, half flew across the room, landed on his butt, and slid through the drying blood of Alexander the Great. Once he came to a stop, he twisted around to see . . .

Damon of Epirus was standing over the open coffin.

"Sometimes the most complicated question can be answered by the simplest of answers," he exclaimed, barely hiding his excitement. "This has taken far too long."

Cooper ran at Damon, desperate to tackle him and pull him away from the coffin. But instead of driving his shoulder into Damon's chest, Coop passed right through him . . . like a ghost. Coop stopped and spun around, stunned.

"How is that possible?" he shouted. "We're both spirits!"

Damon shrugged casually. "Yet I can manipulate physical matter like no other," he said. "Surely you know that by now."

"Marsh!" Coop yelled. "Stop him!"

Marsh didn't have to be told twice. He scrambled to his feet, ran at Damon, and dove at him with his arms out wide, ready to tackle him up and drive him into the wall of crypts. Instead he traveled through Damon as if he were . . . a spirit. Marsh slammed into the marble wall himself and grunted in pain as he smashed his shoulder into the unforgiving surface.

Damon chuckled. "It's quite futile, you know."

Marsh and Coop were helpless to do anything but watch in horror as Damon reached down into the coffin, grabbed the jacket of the skeleton, and pulled it up out of the casket. He appraised the remains briefly, the way one would examine a unique bug. It didn't hold his attention for long. With a dismissive shrug he tossed the remains to the floor behind the coffin, where it fell in a crumpled heap like a broken doll.

"Coop, do something!" Marsh yelled.

Coop didn't move.

"Like what?" he said. "We're done, Ralph."

Damon looked back down to the coffin, and his eyes lit up like a child's on Christmas morning.

When Marsh saw that reaction, he knew Cooper was right.

They were done.

Damon reached into the casket and removed a four-foot long black sword that was unlike any weapon Marsh and Coop had ever seen or imagined. Its tip came to a bayonet-like point, which could do plenty of damage on its own, but there was more. A foot down from the tip were two more equally dangerous devices. One was a curved pick a foot and a half long that came to a sharp point . . . perfect for impaling a skull. Opposite it was an eight-inch cleaverlike blade . . . the ideal tool for chopping the heads off defense-less enemy prisoners.

Damon held the weapon aloft with one hand, admiring his prize. "I never gave up hope," he said to the weapon, as if it cared.

"That's it?" Marsh exclaimed, incredulous. "All the horror, the deaths, the lives you've turned inside out? It was all for that sword?"

Damon gave Marsh a sly smile.

"Not just a sword," he said. "This blade is infused with the energy of every spirit that it tore from its living vessel. I cannot begin to estimate the numbers."

"The Butcher of Epirus speaks," Coop said with disdain. "You must be so proud."

"Foley," Damon said. "Perhaps you can help your friend understand. You've seen what the spirit swords are capable of. Those were once ordinary weapons that were brought through the Rift into the Black to become spirit-killers." He held up the poleax and continued, "This sword, this magni-ficent weapon, held that kind of power without having to leave the Light. Imagine what it will become once it jour-neys along the Morpheus Road. I believe that justifies all that I went through to retrieve it."

"All *you* went through?" Coop said sarcastically. "We didn't ask for any of this."

"Yet here we are," Damon said with no sympathy.

"What happens now?" Marsh asked tentatively.

"Now?" Damon asked, his voice booming through the mausoleum. He raised the poleax up high overhead, grasping it with both hands. "Now . . . we begin."

He spun around and with a single, violent swing brought the sword straight down and sliced the blade into the wall of crypts. The black blade tore through the marble like it was paper, sending a spray of blinding purple light through the tomb that forced Marsh and Coop to shield their eyes. The earthquake returned, knocking Marsh off his feet, but he kept watching as Damon ripped a vertical slice through the marble. The sound of the cutting was anything but natural. It was a chorus of howls and agony; pain and power all blending into a massive roar of sound that made Marsh want to cry out in despair.

The cutting was finished in seconds and the demonic howling ended, along with the firing lights. What was left was a gaping black hole in the wall through which could be heard the desolate sound of eternity.

A new Rift had been created.

His job complete, Damon turned to Marsh and Cooper and declared, "I trust I will not see either of you again."

"What about my mother?" Marsh cried.

Damon shrugged. "She is no longer my concern."

"You got what you wanted! Where is she?"

"Thank you both," Damon said, ignoring Marsh's plea. "This would not have been possible without your help."

He gave a formal bow, stepped backward, and leaped through the Rift.

"No, stop!" Marsh screamed at no one.

Cooper and Marsh stood staring at the tear in the seam of existence, stunned to the point of paralysis.

"He's going to rally his troops," Coop said, breathless.

"And now that he's got the poleax, he can open up as many Rifts as he wants."

"And I let it happen," Marsh finally said, dumbfounded.

"No," Coop corrected quickly. "You were right. He wasn't going to stop until he got that thing. This was bound to happen someday, with or without us."

"Except it happened today."

Coop stepped closer to the wall and stared into the abyss. The opening cut right through Terri Seaver's empty tomb along with the crypt below it. Coop feared that whoever the poor guy was who occupied the lower berth had been cut in two, but the edges of the opening had no thickness. It wasn't so much a physical gash in the marble as it was a tear in the thin fabric that separated two worlds . . . as it did on the floor of Ree's vision of Grand Central Terminal. It was as if the wall of crypts was a paper-thin curtain that had been sliced apart to reveal another existence beyond.

"Go home, Ralph," Coop said. "You're finished."

"What do you mean?"

Coop ran his hand back through his hair, quickly getting his wits back.

"Damon doesn't care about you anymore," he said. "Or Sydney or anybody else in the Light. He got what he wanted and now he's moving on."

"But . . . it can't be over."

"It's not, but your part in this is. Go find Sydney. Tell her what happened. And hang on to that crucible. I don't think you'll need it anymore, but I might."

"What are you going to do?" Marsh asked.

"I have no idea, except to keep my promise."

"What promise?"

"I'm going to find your mother, and not just for you. She has to bring the Guardians back together."

"But . . . I can't just sit around waiting. Pretending like nothing's going on."

"That's *exactly* what you're going to do," Coop ordered. "This battle has moved farther down the road."

"Yeah, until it comes back here."

Coop shot Marsh a pained look. "Let's hope it doesn't come to that."

"I'm sorry," Marsh said softly.

"Don't be. Find Sydney."

"She doesn't want anything to do with me."

"Then, convince her she's wrong. I can't believe I'm saying this, but you guys are good together."

Marsh nodded. "I don't like this. It's starting to feel like a farewell moment."

Coop scoffed and was ready with a quick comeback to tell his friend how wrong he was, but thought better of it and said, "It isn't. We'll see each other again."

Coop turned back to the Rift and squared off against the dark hole. "Let's hope no other spirit, living or dead, ever crosses through that thing . . . in either direction." He looked to Marsh, smiled, and gave him the double okay sign.

Marsh smiled in return, but it was forced.

Coop winked. The swirl of colorful fog appeared before him and he was gone.

Marsh was left alone in the mausoleum. He stood in the same spot, not moving, unsure of what to do. He stared into the dark hole that could very well have opened a pathway to a cataclysm. A doorway he helped create. He had been used and manipulated by someone smarter than he was. Marsh knew that he had fought back with everything he had, but in the end it wasn't enough. He was still a weak little boy who didn't have the smarts, or the courage, to do the right thing. Staring into that void, Marsh felt as though he was looking into his own empty future. He would always have to live with the knowledge that when challenged, he had failed on a colossal level.

It was something he couldn't imagine living with.

He glanced down to the broken body of the man who had rested in his mother's grave. Who was he? Where did Ennis find him? Did his spirit know of the role he had played in this tragic drama? Seeing him lying next to the open coffin, looking so vulnerable, pushed Marsh to imagine what might be in store for every living person if Damon succeeded in mounting an army to march into the Light. The man's broken body seemed so inconsequential compared to the spirit that once gave it life. How many others would meet the same fate when Damon returned, brandishing his villainous weapon? How many more spirits would be torn from their living vessels? The idea was unbearable to imagine, made more so by the knowledge that he had put the poleax back into Damon's hands.

Marsh knelt down close to the remains and said, "I'm sorry I disturbed you."

As he knelt there, at the lowest point of life possible . . . he felt a glimmer of hope.

If he had learned anything from his experience, it was about the amazing nature and power of the human spirit. It was a power that insured life would continue beyond the mortal time frame spent in the Light. Cooper's adventure proved that. Damon's existence proved that. Every stop along the Morpheus Road had meaning, every person's journey was a unique adventure. It was the natural course of existence. It was right. It was good.

Marsh knew he had to do whatever it took to make sure it wouldn't end.

He looked around the subterranean mausoleum and wondered how long it would take before somebody discovered the carnage. How often did people go down there?

With any luck it wouldn't be until Damon's quest had ended . . . one way or another.

He felt a surge of confidence. For the first time in a very long while he knew what he had to do. His only regret was that it would absolutely crush his dad. And Sydney. Maybe. He vowed to do all he could to make sure they both understood that everything was cool. Sydney would get it. Dad would take a little more work, but he trusted Sydney to help him through it. They would both have to understand that there were bigger issues at stake than any one person's life.

Or death.

Marsh looked to the Rift. He heard the hollow echo of the void, but saw nothing. Nothing but black.

He was more excited than scared.

Cooper was wrong. It wasn't over for him.

With that belief in mind, Marsh held his breath . . . and stepped into the Rift.

11

When Cooper stepped out of the Light and onto the beach of Zoe's vision in the Black, he was struck again by its simple perfection. The sun was setting, casting a golden glow over the ocean water as the palm trees rustled lazily in a warm breeze that carried the citrusy smell of oranges from a nearby grove. Making the scene appear even more ideal was the sight of his grandfather kneeling over the glowing coals of a fire, expertly cooking fish and vegetables on a spit.

"Hello, Cooper," came a welcoming voice.

Cooper turned quickly to see Maggie walking lazily toward him along the shore in ankle-deep water. She had her shoes in one hand while gripping the hem of her dress in the other to keep it dry.

Seeing Maggie approach him with the sweet smile that

she had finally found, Coop allowed himself to imagine what it might be like to forget he had ever heard of Damon the Butcher and stay on that idyllic beach to enjoy whatever time that was left of normal.

"I've been worried about you," Maggie said as she joined him.

"I'm fine. Sort of. What about you guys?"

Maggie gestured toward the village and said, "We've had a guardian angel."

Coop looked to where she was pointing and the illusion of paradise instantly vaporized.

Zoe sat on an overturned boat, grasping the black spirit sword, vigilantly watching over them. She was on alert and ready to roll. Her steely gaze told the real story: There was no way they could forget Damon.

Coop gave her a wave.

Zoe returned the gesture with a slight, businesslike nod.

"Did you find Ree?" Maggie asked.

Coop frowned and shook his head.

"Listen," he said, suddenly nervous. "I, uh, I've got some bad news, but before I tell everyone, I want you to promise me something."

"Sure. What?"

Coop ran his hands through his hair and stared at his Pumas.

"What's the matter?" Maggie asked innocently. "You're never at a loss for words."

"Yeah, well, I've never said something like this before."

Maggie reached out and gently lifted his chin so she could look into his eyes.

"Just say it."

Coop took a deep breath and said, "Things are going to get nasty. There's no way I can predict where we'll end up once the dust settles. If it settles."

Maggie didn't interrupt but kept her eyes locked on his.

"What I'm saying is, I don't want anything to happen to you."

She gave him a slight smile and said, "I don't want anything to happen to *any* of us."

"I know, me neither, but I feel as if I've just gotten to know you, and after all you've been through, it just doesn't seem right that you should have to risk your future when you're so close to getting out of the Black and—"

"How do you know I'm getting out?"

"I don't. Not really. But if anybody deserves to move on to a better place, it's you. You've paid your dues a couple times over and that's what gets you sprung, right?"

"I suppose," she said with a shrug.

"Well, that's what I think, so what I'm asking is that when things start to hit the fan, you do your best to stay out of it."

"And what if I want to be with you?" she asked.

Coop had an argument all ready, but in that moment, all he could think about was how much he cared for Maggie Salinger. He pulled her toward him and hugged her close.

"That's the last place you should be," he said.

The two stood together for a long moment. Coop pressed his cheek into her hair, sensing the vague sweet smell of freshly picked apples.

"Coop? Are you crying?"

Coop cleared his throat and pulled away from her.

"Jeez, no! Give me a break. I'm just . . . I'm just . . . Look, I'm not one for being all sentimental. I'm just not."

Maggie smiled coyly, "I think you're doing just fine."

"Yeah, well, all I'm saying is that after all you've been through, you've earned a free pass out of this mess and I want you to keep your head down. Okay?"

Maggie reached up, wrapped her hands around his neck, and whispered, "I love you, too."

She leaned up to him and the two kissed. For a moment they were back on the Ferris wheel at Playland, where nothing else mattered but the two of them.

And Cooper was indeed crying.

"Coop!" Gramps yelled from his spot farther down the beach. "Jeez, come up for air and get over here!"

Maggie and Cooper pulled back from each other, laughing.

"Awkward," Coop said, sniffing.

"I'm not promising anything, Coop," Maggie said. "But thank you for worrying about me."

Coop quickly wiped his eyes and said, "Let's go see what he's hollering about."

He held Maggie's hand and the two hurried along the shoreline toward his grandfather. Zoe left her station and they all joined together around the fire.

"The fishing here is pretty darn sweet," Gramps said with a sparkle in his eyes that Coop was glad to see had returned. "Alls I had to do was dip a net, and the critters practically jumped in, asking to be roasted."

Zoe and Maggie sat on opposite sides of Foley while Coop knelt in the sand, facing him.

"That is how I remember it, so that is how it is," Zoe said.

"And I've been picking some of the tastiest tomatoes and peppers I ever seen. Puts my garden to shame. Who's hungry?"

Nobody answered.

"Aww, c'mon," Foley cajoled. "We're all on borrowed time. Might as well enjoy ourselves."

"I'll eat," Maggie said diplomatically.

"That's my girl!" Foley exclaimed, and stripped off a flaky piece of white fish from the spit. He put it on a wide banana leaf along with a charred section of roasted red pepper and a juicy slice of tomato and handed it to her.

"Should be seasoned just right," he added. "I found all sorts of things up in Zoe's house."

Maggie sampled the food and smiled with appreciation.

Foley beamed. It struck Cooper that since the two had come to terms with their pasts, his grandfather was treating Maggie as if she too were a grandchild. It was one of the few positive results that came from their encounter with Damon the Butcher.

While they spoke of fish and vegetables, Zoe never took her eyes from Coop. She was searching for some hint as to what he may have learned since their escape from the Colosseum.

Coop didn't want to break the spell of the warm moment. It wasn't until he caught Zoe's questioning gaze that he finally gave in and allowed reality to return.

"I don't know how else to say this, so I'll just put it out there," he began. "Damon has the poleax."

All three erupted with stunned shouts of surprise and anger, none more so than Zoe. She sprang to her feet as if the news had sent a painful electric shock through her. She gripped the black sword in both hands, spun back to Coop, and through clenched teeth whispered one strained word.

"How?"

"Does it matter?" Coop answered.

"Too many souls have been lost trying to prevent this from happening," Zoe answered. "Including my father's. Yes, it matters."

Cooper didn't want to put it all onto Marsh's shoulders, but he didn't want to lie to Zoe either. She didn't deserve that.

"It wasn't any one thing," Coop said. "It was a series of events that started when Damon's tomb was discovered and the first crucible was broken. Once that happened, it was only a matter of time."

"But we defeated his army!" Zoe cried. "And the Rift was sealed!"

"Because the Watchers stepped in," Coop corrected. "Let's be honest here. The Guardians were noble and brave and all that, but they didn't beat Damon. The guy is too smart. And powerful. He was bound to find the poleax eventually."

"Where was it?" Maggie asked.

"Hidden in Ree Seaver's tomb," Coop answered with no emotion.

Foley whistled in awe. "So she was holding on to it the whole time . . . so to speak."

"No, Ree's body wasn't in her tomb. She went through the Rift, remember? And not that I want to pile it on, but you should know, once Damon got the poleax, the first thing he did was tear open another Rift."

Maggie and Foley looked to Zoe, waiting for her reaction.

This time she didn't respond with anger. It was as if the news had numbed her. She dropped down on her knees in the sand, unable to hold her own weight.

"It was all for nothing," she said, stunned. "He has won."

"Whoa, let's not go there," Coop cautioned. "This isn't over."

"What do you think he'll do now?" Maggie asked.

"He's going to assemble another army," Coop replied. "I think that's why he was in ancient Rome. He's pulling spirits from all over the Black, and from what I saw he won't have much trouble. That place is like a crossroads of the angry dead."

"And then what?" Foley asked.

"I don't know," Coop answered. "The guy is out to prove he can lead an army into battle and I think he's going to do just that . . . and march on the Light."

"Cripes," Foley said with dismay. "But he won't have the

same abilities in the Light that he does here. Will he?"

"No, but even if he gets his ass kicked, blasting open the Morpheus Road and allowing spirits to travel freely between dimensions would be . . . would be . . ."

"It would be the end of the world," Foley said soberly. He dropped his portion of fish into the fire.

"Then we *have* lost," Zoe said with finality.

"No, we haven't," Coop corrected. "I think if there's any chance of stopping Damon, we've got to let him have his battle."

"What?" Maggie said with surprise. "Why? I thought—"

"Not in the Light," Coop interrupted. "In the Black."

"I do not understand," Zoe said.

"If Damon can gather an army, so can we," Coop explained. "Many of the Guardians are out there. Most still have their weapons. Zoe, we've got to rally them. You said how many spirits have made sacrifices to protect the Rift and stop Damon? They're going to have to do it again. Start tripping through visions. Find them. Recruit more. Bring them here. We're going to have to fight again, and this time we've got to be a little smarter about it."

Foley said, "You're talking about destroying a whole lot of good spirits to do this."

"If Damon has his way, they're going to be destroyed anyway. At least this way we're fighting back."

Coop stood over Zoe and looked down at the young soldier who so recently saw her father's spirit destroyed battling the same forces that Cooper was asking them to face again.

"Will you do it?" Coop asked.

Zoe got to her feet and stood toe-to-toe with Coop. "Do you have to ask?"

Coop smiled.

"Where will we start?" Zoe asked.

"Not 'we,'" Coop said. "You. I'm going after Ree. The

Guardians have already lost one leader. They can't lose both."

"Agreed," Zoe said, and held out her black sword. "Take this."

Cooper backed off. "No, thanks. Not my style."

"But how will you get past Damon to free her without one?" Zoe asked.

"I don't think I'll have to. Now that he has the poleax, he's written us off. He doesn't think we're a threat anymore. That's the biggest mistake he could make."

"Then, we will be safe, but you will not. Not if you seek Ree Seaver. Take the weapon."

Coop hesitated, then reached out and grabbed the black sword.

"Thank you," he said. "You'll get it back."

"What about us?" Foley asked.

"I want you and Maggie to stay here and wait for Zoe to come back. She'll need help organizing the Guardians."

Maggie approached Cooper and held his hands. "Can I say something?"

"Sure," Coop replied.

"We're going to stop him," she said with confidence. "I've never felt more sure about anything."

"Well, good," Coop said awkwardly. "That makes one of us."

"No, it makes all of us. We have faith in you because you did something that nobody else has ever done. You convinced the Watchers to intervene."

"Yeah, well, I don't think they'll do it again," Coop cautioned.

"Don't be so sure. They did it once because we were in the right, and we still are. We will triumph because I believe we are all part of the same living being, and living beings heal. We are going to heal. I truly believe that and I believe the Watchers will eventually help."

"Can I quote you on that?" Coop said with a nervous laugh.

"You can," Maggie said. "I'm only going to ask one thing of you."

"What's that?"

"Wherever you end up, I want to be there with you."

Black.

It was all that Marsh could register. There was no up, down, sideways, or in between. There was no sound or sensation. Time had either stopped or was flying by. There was no way to tell. He wasn't even sure if he was conscious . . . until the first sensation returned. He could smell, and the smell wasn't good.

Zoo. That was his first thought.

He sensed that he was walking upright. On what? Air? His legs were moving but he couldn't feel the ground. Up ahead, he saw the first break in the black. It was a vague slash of gray that cut through the darkness.

As his eyes focused, so did his thoughts. He remembered. He had stepped into the Rift that Damon had slashed through his mother's tomb, and had never broken stride. He was still walking. But toward what? The gash ahead looked to be the same as the Rift Damon had created in the mausoleum. Had he made a U-turn and was headed back home? He had to know, so he stepped through the opening . . .

. . . and into a large, dark enclosure. The floor was dirt. The walls were stone. The animal smell was overpowering.

And he wasn't alone.

A low growl came from the shadows on the far side of the enclosure. He had stepped into a dark cell that was used to hold animals. Big animals. Marsh was ready to step back into the Rift when he sensed a presence to his right. He snapped a look to see a large male lion with a thick shaggy mane hunched down, cautiously headed his way.

Stalking him.

Marsh's reaction was to move in the opposite direction, away from the big cat. Unfortunately, it was also away from the Rift. Though his heart rate had gone through the roof, he was smart enough not to make any sudden moves. If he turned to run, the cat would be on him. He moved slowly, scanning for any other animals and, more important, a way out.

The cat's eyes were locked on him, ready to pounce.

"Help," Marsh called out weakly, barely above a whisper.

He didn't want to do anything that might push the cat over the edge. He glanced along the wall to his left to see that a wooden door was cut into the stone wall no more than ten feet away. It seemed like a mile. Marsh's sole focus was to get there.

The lion was twenty feet away and closing with caution and confidence as if it knew there was no way for its prey to escape. It kept moving steadily with its body tense, ready to spring. Marsh had seen the same behavior with his cat, Winston, when it was stalking. Cats were cats, whether their prey was a moth . . . or a man. He knew the lion would spring with no warning. All he could do was keep moving.

A few steps more and Marsh reached the door. He pressed his back against it, and while still facing the lion, he reached around to find a door handle. His hand moved across the rough wood but found nothing. He pushed against the door with his back in the futile hope that it would push open. It didn't.

"Help," he called again, but faintly, for fear it would trigger the attack. "I'm in the lion's cage."

The lion stopped, its eyes locked on Marsh.

Marsh saw its pupils widen and his butt waggle. It was about to pounce.

A vicious roar broke the silence, but it didn't come from

the lion that had been stalking him. Marsh spun quickly to see another lion approaching from the other side.

He was trapped between them. This second lion was a female. Females were the hunters and this one was on the prowl. His only avenue of escape was straight ahead, as futile as that might have been. He pushed himself off the door, ready to sprint across the room to . . . where? But as he pushed off the door, it swung open. The sudden movement threw him off balance and he fell backward, tumbling out of the room.

He felt strong hands grab the back of his shirt to pull him out of the animal pen. He fell hard on his back, outside of the cell. As he hit the dirt floor, he heard the sound of the door slamming shut and the angry roar of the lions who had just watched their meal abruptly snatched from under their noses. The two beasts threw themselves against the door, roaring angrily and scratching at the wood with thick claws.

Marsh focused and looked to see who it was that had saved him.

It was a woman. Her back was to Marsh as she looked through the door's window at the raging lions. She had long, wavy brown hair and wore a khaki work shirt and dark pants.

Zookeeper, Marsh thought.

"Thanks," he said. "A second later and I'd have been lunch."

The woman stiffened, as if Marsh's voice had the effect of a cold blast of air.

"Where exactly are we?" he asked.

The woman put her hand on the door, bracing herself.

"Hey, you okay?" Marsh asked.

"No, I'm not," the woman said. "Because where we are is the Black."

It was Marsh's turn to react. Not because he had learned that he was in the Black. That was the plan. That's where he wanted to be.

It was because he knew the voice.

"Why?" she asked. "Why are you here?"

She turned slowly to face him.

When Marsh saw her, his mouth fell open. He tried to speak but only managed to whisper two simple words.

"Hi, Mom."

12

Ree Seaver ran to her son, dropped to her knees, and threw her arms around him.

Both were in tears.

Marsh felt like a little boy again. Being hugged by his mother was like something out of a wonderfully cruel dream. It was a simple act he had come to accept would never happen again. At least not in life.

The two were locked together for several moments before Ree pulled away to look at her son, holding him at arm's length.

"You grew up," she said through her tears.

"You look the exact same," Marsh replied.

Ree hugged him close again.

"How could you possibly be here?" she asked through her tears. "What happened?"

"I wasn't killed, if that's what you're asking."

Ree tensed up. She pulled away from Marsh, her gaze turning sharp. "What do you mean?"

"I came looking for you. It was my choice."

Ree sat back, confused, trying to wrap her mind around what Marsh was telling her.

"Your choice?" she mumbled. "You committed suicide?"

"No!" Marsh cried quickly. "Jeez! I wouldn't do something like that."

"Then, what do you mean you came looking for me?" she asked, confused.

"I know all about the Black, Mom. And Damon. And the Guardians. Cooper told me everything."

His explanation only served to further confuse her. "Cooper told you? How is that possible?"

"The Watchers allowed him to be seen and heard by me in the Light. His sister can see him too."

"The Watchers allowed that?" she asked, incredulous.

Marsh nodded quickly.

"So you know about the Black," she said. "Which means you know there's only one way you can get here, and that's to die."

"Well, yeah, I guess but that's not exactly what happened."

"You aren't making sense, Marshall."

"I got here the same way you did."

Ree tried to let his words sink in, but still didn't understand.

"You couldn't have," Ree declared. "I got here by coming through a Rift that doesn't exist anymore."

Marsh stood and helped his mother to her feet.

"I'm sorry to have to tell you this. Damon created another one."

Ree backed away from him, shaking her head in disbelief.

"No. That's impossible. To do that he'd need the poleax and there's no way he could have . . ." She didn't finish her thought. She looked to Marsh, giving him the same stern look she always did when she wanted the complete truth and wouldn't stand for anything less.

"What happened?" she asked coldly.

Marsh had trouble looking directly at her. He was once again a little boy who had to answer to his mother for something he probably shouldn't have done.

"I took charge," he answered, going on offense. "Damon wasn't going to give up until he found the poleax. You know that. We all did. It was only a matter of time before he got it, and I wanted Coop to have it first so he could use it against Damon."

"So what did you do?" Ree persisted, fearing the answer.

"I found it," Marsh declared. "It was in your tomb. Ennis put it there along with a crucible to protect it. But I accidentally broke the crucible when I smashed open the crypt and—"

"You broke into my tomb?" Ree asked, aghast.

"I was pretty sure you weren't in it. I wanted Coop to have the poleax and put an end to this guy."

Ree took a deep breath, trying to control her anxiety.

"You weren't in it, by the way," Marsh said softly. "It was some guy."

"Some guy," Ree echoed, dumbfounded.

Marsh continued. "When the crucible broke, Damon showed up. Neither of us could stop him. He got the poleax."

"And he opened a new Rift," she declared, the truth finally coming clear.

Marsh nodded.

"And you came through."

"I came looking for you."

Ree leaned back against the stone wall of the wild animal enclosure.

"So you *did* commit suicide," she declared. "And Damon has the poleax. This isn't your finest hour, Marsh."

"Maybe not, but I'm going to make it right," Marsh stated boldly. "Damon doesn't care about us anymore. He's moved on. That's a mistake. Coop already found Zoe and Maggie and his grandfather and took them to Zoe's vision. They're going to bring the Guardians back together and—"

"Wait. What? Cooper found the others?"

"Yes. He took them to Zoe's vision." He glanced around the stone corridor and added, "Wait, is this where they were? Ancient Rome?"

"Somebody's vision of ancient Rome. We're in the bowels of the Colosseum. I haven't left because Damon threatened to destroy the others if I did."

"See?" Marsh declared. "They're long gone. Damon doesn't care about us anymore now that he's got the poleax."

Ree's mind raced. "This is . . . this is just wrong. Marsh, you are going back through the Rift. Maybe it's not too late to get your life back."

"No! I came here to help you."

"You killed yourself, Marsh! Do you understand that? You are dead!"

"I know how it works, Mom. I probably know more than *you* do. Did you know that Damon is hunting for some guy named Brennus?"

"No. Who is that?"

"I don't know, but I'm going to find out. I'm staying."

"And do what? Marsh, I love you for trying to help but you've made some serious mistakes."

"I know. It's my fault Damon has the poleax, but I truly believe he would have gotten it anyway. The guy is ruthless. He haunted Ennis until he couldn't take it anymore and . . ." His voice trailed off.

"What happened to Ennis?" Ree asked with trepidation.

"Damon was torturing him. It was horrible. He didn't have a crucible for protection because he wanted me to have it."

"Is he dead?" Ree asked, incredulous.

Marsh nodded gravely. "I think death was a relief."

Ree winced. "My god, this is never going to end."

"Yes, it is," Marsh declared. "Damon thinks we're done. He won't see us coming."

The sound of a trumpet fanfare blasted from the arena above.

"What's that?" Marsh asked, looking up.

Several soldiers ran past them along an adjoining corridor.

Ree said. "Something's going on up in the arena."

"Maybe we should see," Marsh said. "It could be Damon."

He started after the soldiers but Ree held him back.

"No," she commanded. "I want you to go back through the Rift."

Marsh didn't pull away. He stood his ground and looked his mother square in the eyes.

"Damon cut the Rift into this vision for a reason," he said with authority. "I'm going to find out what it is."

Ree searched her son's eyes, looking for the little boy she had left so long ago. All she caught was a faint, familiar glimpse that was quickly lost in the years she had missed and the horrors he'd seen.

"C'mon, Mom," Marsh cajoled. "I died for this."

Ree's eyes grew watery and she hugged her son once again.

"I'm so sorry," she whispered.

"It's okay. Be glad I'm here."

"Don't see that happening." She wiped her eyes, stood tall, and said, "C'mon."

She headed off and the two made their way through the

labyrinth of tunnels that made up the underworld of the Flavian Amphitheater.

Marsh didn't allow himself the luxury of stopping to marvel at the impossibility of it all. Though he was fascinated to see the Colosseum the way it actually existed in ancient Rome, he wanted to stay focused on the challenges ahead. He allowed himself one fleeting thought about the incredible dimension he had landed in: He promised himself that once he finished Damon, he'd come back and take full advantage of being in the Black. That is, if Damon didn't finish him first.

Ree led Marsh up a series of ramps until they found themselves standing under an arched tunnel that led to the arena.

"Oh man," Marsh gasped. As much as he had heard about how visions in the Black worked, he wasn't prepared for the sight in front of him.

It was night. The Colosseum was dark but the full moon cast enough light to illuminate details of the immense stadium.

"We're really here," he gasped. "It's the Colosseum."

"It's somebody's vision of the Colosseum," Ree corrected.

All four levels of seating that ringed the arena were dark. Marsh thought they were empty, until he saw a flame flicker to life. Followed by another and another. All around the stadium, flames ignited. Thousands of them. What at first looked like an empty stadium was soon revealed to be completely packed with people, each person holding their own burning candle. Marsh couldn't make out any of the faces, or details, but he assumed they were the same people from many eras that Cooper had described.

"It's like a vigil," Ree whispered.

Nobody spoke. The eerie silence sent a chill up Marsh's spine.

"Coop was right," he whispered. "I feel like I'm still alive."

Ree put an arm around his shoulders. She was surprised to see that he had grown taller than her.

Another trumpet fanfare sounded, heralding the entrance of a lone rider on horseback. He appeared through a tall archway, carrying his own flaming torch.

"Damon," she said, barely whispering.

Though Damon of Epirus was in full battle dress, his squat frame didn't give him the air of a formidable warrior. If not for the weapon that was strapped to his waist, he would have looked like a sad pretender wearing a costume. The weapon proved otherwise.

"He's got the poleax," Marsh said.

The black horse pranced into the arena as the trumpets continued their fanfare.

The crowd watched in silent reverence.

Damon rode to the dead center of the ring and spun his horse slowly so that he could see the entire assemblage . . . and they could see him. The light from the thousands of flames glistened on his horse's shiny black coat. Satisfied, he raised his free hand and the trumpets fell silent. Damon let the drama build for a few seconds more, then shouted for all to hear.

"You have been patient," he called, his voice echoing through the massive stadium. "We have all been patient and you will soon be rewarded. We have been thrown together by fate and given the opportunity to take charge of our own destiny. Our own futures. Our own eternity. We have been controlled by an unjust, uncaring power for too long."

He spun his horse in a tight circle, allowing each and every spirit to get a good look at him. To admire him.

Marsh whispered to his mother, "What is he talking about?"

Ree replied, "He's got these people convinced that they shouldn't accept being judged by the Watchers."

"I thought the Watchers were all about rewarding those who work on becoming better people."

Ree shrugged. "They are."

"And Damon doesn't like that?"

"Damon doesn't give a damn, but he's got his followers all worked up about it. He preys on those who have been in the Black the longest and fear they'll never get the chance to move on."

Damon rode back to the center of the arena.

"But freedom will not come easily," Damon continued. "For that, we must fight."

"Fight who?" Marsh asked Ree. "Who is their enemy?"

Damon bellowed, "I swear to you that when we are done, the oppression that has existed for centuries will no longer hold sway over us. Our future will be what we choose, whether we prefer to remain in our visions in the Black, or return to life in the Light."

Marsh and Ree looked to each other.

"He's going to do it," Marsh said soberly. "He's going to bring them all back into the Light. But they'll be wiped out by modern weapons."

"Of course," Ree answered. "But the damage will have been done. The Morpheus Road will have been blown wide open."

Damon reached to his waist, grasped the poleax, and raised it high over his head.

Finally the crowd erupted with the massive explosion of cheers that they had been holding back. A pent-up wave of emotion took over that shook the stadium to its stone foundation.

"There aren't enough Guardians to stop them," Ree declared.

Damon dropped his torch, silencing the crowd.

"If we are to succeed in breaking down the barriers that have held us prisoner, we must be willing to move in every direction and include all spirits. We are not alone. Before we fight, our numbers need to grow. They *must* grow. I will call upon those who stand the most to gain and invite them to join us. By standing together with our brothers and sisters who have been punished so unfairly, we will ensure our victory and our freedom."

"Who is he talking about?" Marsh asked.

Ree didn't say because she feared what the answer might be.

Damon kicked his dark horse into action. With the poleax raised, he galloped around the perimeter of the arena as the crowd cheered him on.

Ree and Marsh ducked back into the shadows so as not to be seen as he passed.

Damon reveled in the adulation. His chin was held high and the poleax even higher as his followers poured out their hearts to him.

Finally, on the far side of the arena from where Ree and Marsh stood, Damon pulled up and trotted toward the brick wall that ringed the floor.

The crowd continued their frenzied cheer.

"What is he doing?" Marsh asked.

"I'm afraid to even think."

Damon looked up at the poleax, raised it high, then drove it into the brick wall of the arena. Instantly a flash of purple light erupted from the spot where he had pierced the facade.

"My god," Marsh said with a gasp. "This is it. He's opening another Rift into the Light."

Still on horseback, Damon trotted forward, tearing open a seam in the wall.

"This is why he picked the Colosseum," Ree said. "It's a staging area for an attack on the Light."

"We have to do something!" Marsh declared.

Damon continued to trot forward, lengthening the cut. Bright purple light glowed from the edges, sending the crowd into a frenzy.

"Do not move!" came a command from behind Marsh and Ree.

They spun around to see two Roman soldiers with black swords charging toward them.

"Run," Marsh commanded to his mother.

"No, we'll step into another vision," Ree replied.

"What about Damon?"

Before Ree could answer, a dark figure jumped down in front of them from the stands, landing between them and the charging soldiers. The Romans were caught off guard and didn't react quickly enough to defend themselves. The dark figure slashed at them, turning them both into shadows, snuffing both of their spirits before they could take another step.

Ree and Marsh stood stunned, not sure of what had just happened.

The dark figure turned to them and said, "This sword is just flat awesome."

"Coop!" Marsh declared.

Coop focused on Marsh, and froze. "Ralph? No. No, no, you can't be here!"

Marsh ignored him and turned to watch Damon.

The warrior had completed his cut. The gash between worlds stood nearly twenty yards long and slowly melted vertically to open up a portal large enough for a small army to march through.

"He did it," Coop gasped. "He's going to attack the Light."

The crowd continued to roar its approval.

Coop grabbed Marsh by the front of his hoodie and went nose to nose with him. Both were surprised that his hands did not pass through.

"You see?" Coop snarled. "This is why I didn't want you to find the poleax."

"I—I know," Marsh stammered. "I didn't want this to happen."

"But it did," Coop spat back. "Look! He's about to attack the living and there's nothing we can do about it."

"But he isn't," Ree said.

"Of course he is," Coop spat. "Why else would he cut open a Rift into the Light?"

"I don't think that's what it is," Ree answered, numb.

Even through the cheers of the crowd, a sound could be heard spewing from the gaping hole. It was a horrifying howl that crossed between pain and anger. The wails of a billion tortured souls joined together in an outpouring of agony.

Coop and Ree had heard the sound before.

"No," Coop muttered. "This can't be happening."

He let Marsh go and took a few dazed steps farther into the arena. Marsh and Ree joined him and the three stood together, glaring at the newly created phenomenon.

"What?" Marsh asked, frantic. "What's happening?"

"He isn't ready to battle," Ree said hoarsely. "Not yet. That's what the speech was all about. He's still gathering his forces."

Damon trotted back to the center of the arena, and as the cheers rained down on him, he turned his mount to face the gaping hole between dimensions.

"This is exactly what the Watchers didn't want to happen," Coop said.

"What?" Marsh cried in frustration. "What's happening?"

"He's not going into the Light," Ree answered. "At least not yet."

"So what's he doing?" Marsh cried.

Damon kicked at his horse and took off with a fast gallop, headed directly for the Rift. The crowd cheered him on as he charged forward and through the opening between dimensions.

The answer came from Coop.

"He's going to hunt for more recruits . . . in the Blood."

13

The crowd continued to roar, though Damon was long gone.

"Uh-oh," Coop said, pointing.

Several Roman soldiers had surrounded them and were closing in fast . . . all with black swords.

Coop raised his own sword, ready to fight.

"C'mon," he taunted. "I'm ready."

Ree grabbed Coop by the back of his shirt. "No, you're not."

She pulled him backward, along with Marsh.

The soldiers charged.

The swirling cloud of color appeared behind the three and Ree pulled them in. A moment later they stepped backward onto the subway platform of Ree's vision . . . along with one of the soldiers. The stunned soldier looked around in surprise, which gave Coop the opening he needed. With one quick jab he drove his sword into the befuddled spirit, turning his image into the black cloud that quickly dissipated, which meant that he was no more.

Coop turned to Ree and declared, "Yes, I am."

Marsh was nearly as disoriented as the doomed soldier. He glanced around the empty subway platform with wide eyes, trying to grasp what had just happened.

"Where is this?" he asked, confused.

Coop threw the sword down, rushed at Marsh, grabbed him by the shirt, and pushed him until his back hit the side of Ree's subway car.

"I've been going nuts protecting you all this time and you just threw your life away? Are you serious?"

"I . . . I came here to save my mother," Marsh shot back, trying to gather his wits.

Coop pulled him away from the subway car by a few inches just so he could slam him back into it violently.

"I told you I'd find her and when I did, big surprise, you were there too!"

"I came to help," Marsh argued.

"Yeah, you're doing a great job," Coop said with disdain. "You gave Damon the poleax, you broke another crucible, there's another Rift into the Light along with a big honking Rift straight into hell, and all you've got to show for it is your own death. How is that helping?"

Ree put her hand on Coop's shoulder.

"Enough," she said firmly.

Coop was a raw nerve. He wanted to hit somebody and Marsh was the likely candidate.

"Cooper!" Ree barked.

"Damn," Coop blurted out as he pushed Marsh away and backed off.

"I did what I thought was right," Marsh cried.

"Seriously? I'd hate to know what you think is wrong. We're finished."

"Don't say that," Ree demanded.

"Give me a break," Coop shot back. "The Guardians got their asses kicked by Damon's soldiers once already. What do you think is going to happen when he recruits an even bigger army from the freakin' dark side? Whatever chance we had of stopping him is gone, thanks to Little Boy Boo-Hoo over there."

Marsh didn't defend himself.

Ree looked Coop square in the eye and firmly said, "Calm down."

Coop glared at Marsh, ready to start in on him again, but the tension left his body and he dropped his shoulders.

"You're right," he said, suddenly sounding tired. "It's over."

"Do not be so sure," came the calm voice of a woman that none of them recognized.

All three spun to see that another spirit had arrived. It was a beautiful, tall, dark-skinned woman who stood on the far end of the train platform with her arms at her sides. She wore a black robe that was tied at the waist, accentuating her athletic build.

She was a Watcher.

Once he got over the shock of seeing her, Coop took a few quick, aggressive steps toward the woman.

"Where have you all been?" he demanded. "Do you know what just happened?"

The woman stood firm with a slight smile on her lips. When she spoke, the words didn't come from her mouth. They simply existed.

"We had hoped it would not come to this," she said calmly.

"Well, it did," Coop shot back angrily. "Why didn't you stop him?"

"That is not what we do," the woman replied.

"And what happens when Damon marches out of that

Rift with an army from hell? You going to stand around watching and hope that doesn't go bad too?"

The Watcher didn't respond.

"Why are you here?" Ree asked. "Why now?"

"I came to inform you that there is someone who might help you," the woman replied. "Damon is not the first spirit who sought to create such chaos. He is not even the most powerful. Long ago another spirit entered the Blood in search of allies. Reluctantly we sent one of our own after him to prevent that."

"You sent a Watcher into the Blood?" Ree asked. "What happened?"

The Watcher raised both hands and gestured around her, saying, "The Morpheus Road was saved."

"What about the Watcher?" Marsh asked.

"He remained in the Blood. That was his sacrifice."

"So there's a Watcher in the Blood who stopped one bad apple and you're thinking he can stop Damon too?" Coop asked.

"He might be of assistance . . . if he knew of Damon."

"So tell him," Coop said quickly.

"Sending one of our own into the Blood was unprecedented. It will not happen again."

"But you already did it," Ree argued.

"A unique situation," the Watcher said with patience. "That spirit had the power to cause the destruction of all that is."

"Really?" Coop shot back sarcastically. "What exactly do you think Damon is up to?"

"Damon is not as powerful as that spirit once was," the Watcher said.

Marsh asked, "So this Watcher might be able to stop Damon, but only if somebody tells him about what's going on. Is that it?"

The Watcher nodded and said, "Perhaps."

"So tell him!" Coop shouted. "You've got to be able to do that. I mean, you're not even moving your lips and we hear what you're saying. Send him some kind of cosmic message."

"We cannot," the Watcher explained. "The Blood is a spiritual wasteland. We have no power there."

Coop shrugged, "So then what's the point? Why are you telling us this?"

"I think I know," Marsh announced. He turned to the Watcher and asked, "Are you suggesting what I think you are?"

The Watcher didn't respond.

Coop looked between the Watcher and Marsh, confused.

"You can't be serious," Ree said to the Watcher.

The Watcher remained silent.

Coop said, "Did I miss something here?"

"I'll go," Marsh said.

The light finally came on for Cooper. He spun to the Watcher and said, "Whoa, is that it? You want us to go into the Blood to find this guy?"

The Watcher didn't reply.

"No," Ree declared adamantly. "Nobody's going anywhere."

Marsh argued, "But if we don't, Damon's going to come out with an army that the Guardians have no chance of stopping."

"Jeez," Coop said, reeling. "The Blood? Seriously? Haven't we done enough?"

"Only you can answer that," the Watcher said. "The fate of the Morpheus Road will always be in the hands of those who walk it."

"Then, I'll go," Marsh said.

"No, you won't," Coop said quickly. "If anybody's going, it's me."

"Forget it," Marsh shot back.

"Trust me, Ralph. I'd love to see you go but you wouldn't stand a chance in hell . . . literally."

"And you think you can do better?"

"I won't even answer that," Coop replied with a laugh.

"Then, we'll both go," Marsh offered.

"No!" Ree shouted. "This is insane!"

Coop picked up the black sword he had tossed onto the subway platform and looked to the Watcher. "How do I find this guy?"

"Spirits in the Blood exist in an organic whole," the Watcher replied. "Much more so than in the Black or the Light. You will find your way."

"I have no idea what that means," Coop said.

"You will understand once you are there," the Watcher replied.

Ree stepped in between Cooper and the Watcher and squared off against the woman.

"You can't ask us to do this," she argued.

"I am not asking," the Watcher replied. "I am simply offering information."

"Right, information that could send innocent souls to hell for eternity," Ree said, scoffing.

"That would be so," the Watcher replied. "If not for the Rift. The opening is why this opportunity exists. It offers the means for a spirit to enter the Blood."

"And get back out?" Marsh asked.

"As long as it remains open."

"See?" Coop said with confidence. "I get in, find the good guy, point him at Damon, the Watcher takes out vampire-boy, and I come skipping out of Trouble Town. Armageddon averted."

"Not you," Ree declared. "If there's anybody who should go, it's me."

"No way!" Marsh shouted.

"He's right," Coop declared. "If I blow it, then the Guardians will end up being our last hope. You're their leader. You need to help Zoe bring them back together. Recruit a few more while you're at it."

Ree couldn't argue with the logic.

"You should be aware of one more thing," the Watcher cautioned.

"There's more?" Coop asked, incredulous.

"The evil spirit who entered the Blood in search of souls still exists. Damon may know that."

Coop said, "You mean the Watcher didn't destroy this nasty guy?"

The Watcher shook her head. "We do not destroy any spirit."

"So that means Damon could find an ally who is even worse than him," Ree said soberly.

"It is quite possible," the Watcher admitted.

"Does this bad boy have a name?" Coop asked.

The Watcher said, "He goes by the name of . . . Brennus."

14

Damon of Epirus found himself in unfamiliar territory.

For centuries he had wielded power over his minions through fear and intimidation. As far back as his life in the Light he had cleverly twisted those with weaker minds into obeying his every command. He had mercilessly executed thousands and cemented his dark reputation by occasionally eating the flesh of his victims for the sole purpose of creating a frightening aura that made the weak shudder . . . and obey.

Two thousand years later he found himself on the verge of fulfilling the glorious destiny that had eluded him in life. He was about to assemble a terrifying and powerful fighting force that he would lead into one glorious battle . . . something he never had the fortitude to do in life. For that he had torn a hole between dimensions. For that he had charged into hell. For that he found that for the first time since the beginning of his existence . . .

. . . he was frightened.

The exhilaration he felt from the cheering crowd that had so emboldened him in the Black instantly vanished the moment he galloped through the Rift. It was replaced by a powerful sense of dread that nearly paralyzed him.

The far side of the Rift was a mirror image of the vision he had left in the Black, though it was a decidedly different version of the Flavian Amphitheater than the one that belonged to the emperor Titus. The sky was a deep purple-black without a single star to provide light. It wasn't night, it was just . . . dark. He was hit with a putrid smell that made him gag and his eyes water. Was something burning? Or decaying? Then there was the sound. The Blood was engulfed with a constant white noise of agony, as if every last soul was in pain and couldn't help but wail in a massive chorus of despair.

The Colosseum was destroyed, much more so than the disrepair the actual stadium had suffered in the Light. Several sections had crumbled to the ground leaving only a small percentage of the circular building still intact. Several mounds of brick rubble lay scattered about, creating a snaking labyrinth that Damon had to carefully maneuver his horse through.

And he wasn't alone. Dark shadows weaved and darted through the rubble, flitting on the edges of his vision. Whenever he shifted his gaze to try and see one, it was gone.

"I am being hunted," Damon whispered to himself.

He wasn't used to being alone, especially not in a hostile environment without the protection of his minions. Looking back, he saw the wide gash of the Rift cut into the one remaining wall of the stadium. A soft gray light glowed from within, calling him back to the Black. Back to sanity. He was tempted to bring his mount around and gallop out of the nightmare, but forced himself to continue on. He had waited centuries for this opportunity. Retreat was not an option. He clutched the poleax and kicked his horse into a trot to get away from the claustrophobic ruins of the Colosseum.

His horse had barely begun to move when a shadow sprung from the top of one of the rubble piles and wrapped its arms around the animal's neck. The horse shied and whinnied in terror. Damon caught a quick glimpse of the attacker and saw a chillingly human face that was bone white with empty eye sockets. The four-foot-tall demon was covered with thick, matted fur that made it appear to be part animal, part human and all wrong. It snarled at him, showing sharp, cracked white teeth . . . that it sunk into the neck of the horse.

Damon was too surprised to do anything but freeze in the saddle.

His horse was more practical. The large animal shook its head and flung the creature away, sending it crashing into a pile of bricks where the impact caused it to squeal like an angry pig. The violent encounter snapped Damon back into the moment and gave him the presence of mind to kick the horse and get it moving. The horse didn't argue. It broke into a dead gallop, careening through the rubble, desperate to escape from its tormentors. Damon had all he could do to hold on so as not to be flung off. It wasn't horsemanship that kept him aboard, it was fear.

The horse weaved through the debris and broke out into the open beyond the shattered walls of the Colosseum. Damon gathered his wits and reined the horse down to a canter and ultimately to a stop. He glanced back at the Colosseum to observe the massive wreckage.

"Whose vision could this be?" he asked aloud.

He gazed forward to survey his surroundings. What he expected to see were the ruins of the Roman Forum and the giant statue of Nero that stood just beyond the stadium. What he saw instead was the carnage that was the Blood. He sat on his horse on the top of a small rise where he could see far into the distance. Though it was dark, he could make out some detail.

Before him lay the wreckage of multiple centuries of life. There were toppled modern skyscrapers next to mounds of broken marble statues. Cars were piled next to buggies and chariots. The sharp silhouette of a massive Saturn V rocket lay against a gargantuan, rusted cruise ship, which was surrounded by St. Louis's Gateway Arch.

Damon's fear was replaced by fascination. He gave a prodding kick to his horse and the animal walked forward slowly. As they moved, Damon found that they were constantly traveling between visions. Unlike in the Black, the transitions were seamless. Damon walked by the clock tower known as Big Ben that was lying flat on one side. The massive clock face loomed above him as he passed beneath the huge, bent minute and hour arms. A few short steps later he found himself in front of the Egyptian Sphinx with its decapitated head lying between its front paws. Still farther along he skirted the wheels of a 747 jet that was tilted back onto its tail with its nose pointing into the air like a hungry dog begging for treats.

He trotted through nondescript suburban neighborhoods, jungle villages, city streets, and crumbled cathedrals. It all looked to have been destroyed by age, neglect, and sorrow.

And there were the spirits of people. Lots of them. They walked, zombielike, through the visions, neither acknowledging Damon nor questioning his presence. They floated aimlessly, expressionless, moving about the visions in an endless, useless dance. They were the spirits of the Blood . . . the souls who were banished to this vile wasteland of sorrowful memories for eternity. Damon saw people from every era imaginable. They served no function and performed no tasks. They simply existed.

"Wretched" was the best word he could think of to describe them.

Seeing these pathetic spirits gave Damon new hope. These were just the sort of victims he could exploit to fulfill his quest. He would give them purpose. But to accomplish that he would need help. For that, he had to seek out the spirit who had once attempted the very same task. Between that spirit's knowledge of the Blood and his own ingenuity, Damon felt certain he would not fail. He needed to find that spirit. The one he had heard of for so long.

The spirit known as Brennus.

All he needed to do was keep from losing his mind, which was proving to be more difficult than he anticipated.

The only warning he received of the impending attack was a brief snarl, then a hiss. Damon barely had time to register the sound before his horse was set upon, this time by two of the hollow-eyed demons. One leaped onto the haunches of his horse, making it spin in surprise. The moment it turned its head, the other demon jumped for its neck. They had learned from their previous failure.

Damon caught a brief glimpse of the demon as it opened its mouth to reveal multiple rows of sharklike teeth. A moment later it sunk them into the horse's neck. The horse reared up as it whinnied in pain. The move was so sudden and violent that Damon was thrown from the saddle. He landed heavily on his back, rolled once, grasped the poleax, and sprang to his feet, ready to fight. He might have been too cowardly to enter a battle by choice, but when attacked, Damon was more than willing to defend himself.

The demons were more interested in his horse. The animal was on its side in the final throws of its existence. Like hyenas feasting on a downed zebra, the demons ripped into the horse's flesh, tearing it from the bone, devouring it. More demons arrived to join in the feast. It was a sickening display, even for Damon. Realizing that the horse was no longer of use to him, Damon staggered away, wanting to put as much distance between him and the ravenous ghouls as possible.

He stumbled through the dark with no destination in mind. He staggered through the wreckage of a modern-day airport with a caved-in ceiling and a shattered window, through which he saw the wreckage of hundreds of airplanes strewn across the rutted tarmac. The building was alive with the dead. Many wore the tattered uniforms of pilots and flight attendants. There were also passengers, trapped in the eternal waiting area for flights that would never arrive or depart.

Shadows skirted everywhere. Damon feared that the demons had finished their meal and were hunting down their next course. He left the building and found himself in waist-deep snow on a steep hill. He fought to keep his balance but tumbled forward, falling through the white powder until he landed in a small Tyrolean mountain town that looked as though it had been hit with an earthquake. Spirits skied along the snowy streets with no apparent means of propulsion.

Damon struggled to his feet and trudged through the snow, but had trouble making headway . . .

. . . which was exactly what his pursuers were waiting for. They attacked from the depths of the derelict buildings, circling Damon, ready to pounce.

"So be it," Damon announced, breathless.

He drew the poleax and held it at the ready.

"Which of you shall die first?" he asked with bravura.

Having his treasured weapon and knowing the power it possessed gave him the confidence to make a stand.

The hungry demons weren't impressed. With a screeching cry the first banshee jumped at him. Damon had the wherewithal to bring the poleax around in defense. A small part of him welcomed the attack. He wanted to see the damage the poleax could do against a spirit, knowing it was far more powerful than any of the black spirit-killing swords that had been brought into the Black.

The demon leaped forward and was instantly impaled on Damon's blade. Damon had a moment of satisfaction, but no more. The demon squirmed on the end of the blade, obviously in pain. What it *didn't* do was dissolve into a dark cloud, which could only mean one thing . . .

The poleax had no power in the Blood.

The demons closed the circle, prepared to feast.

Damon had the stomach-dropping realization that he was powerless, and about to be devoured. He wondered if being eaten would end his existence, and if it would be painful.

"Yaaaah!"

An aggressive, guttural cry pierced through the high-pitched screeches of the demons. Damon sensed the warm light from a flame that reflected off the bony faces of his attackers. The demons backed off, including the ghoul who had been impaled on the poleax. It pulled itself off the blade and fled into the darkness, followed by the rest of the marauders.

Damon was left standing alone, still clutching the useless poleax.

"Nasty little varmints," an unknown man declared with disdain.

Damon looked up to see a tall, thin man standing in the snow, holding a burning lamp.

"They hate the light, and the heat," he explained. "Just once I'd like to burn one of 'em just to see it shrivel."

Damon squinted to get a better look at his savior.

He wore a plaid flannel shirt and canvas pants. His hands were big and rough, like those of a working man. What Damon focused on was his face. His cheeks were sunken and the faraway look in his eye spoke of a long, difficult history. He vaguely reminded Damon of the American President Abraham Lincoln, though his eyes showed no kindness.

"Don't look so surprised," the man said. "You been looking for me."

"Brennus?" Damon asked with surprise.

"Brennus?" the man repeated, and laughed so hard it made him cough. "Nah, Sanger's the name. Not sure why. Fools around here picked up on it and it just stuck."

Damon cautiously approached the stranger. "If you are not Brennus, who are you and why would you think I am looking for you?"

"How about you first thank me for saving you from them critters?" Sanger said.

Damon glanced nervously in the direction of the fleeing demons. "You have my gratitude. What are they?"

"Figments," Sanger replied. "I think they come from our own thoughts, or some such thing. Just like this whole place. It's all just a version of what we had in life. A real nasty version."

"So they do not actually exist?" Damon asked.

"Oh they're real enough. They ate your horse, didn't they?"

"How did you know . . . I mean, yes they did."

"All part of the show, I guess," Sanger said knowingly. "All part of the torture. What you see around here is exactly what you don't want to see."

"So my horse is all right?"

"Your horse was never all right," Sanger snapped. "None of this is. It's all just a vision."

Damon took a deep breath. "I suppose that makes sense."

"About as much sense as all of us understanding each other's language," Sanger replied. "Far as I can tell, we don't all hail from the same place. Or time."

Damon said, "You still haven't told me why you believe I am looking for you."

Sanger stepped up to Damon and held up his lamp so that his eyes lit up. A chill crept up Damon's spine. It was an alien feeling for him.

"All spirits are drawn to their own destiny in the Blood," Sanger said. "I don't know you from a haystack, but I feel as though we should be together. Maybe you should tell *me* why."

Damon had regained his composure. He was now calculating the new rules of the Blood and how he could use them to his advantage.

"I seek a spirit named Brennus," Damon said with confidence. "Perhaps you could help me locate him."

Sanger looked Damon up and down as if he were no more impressed by him than the demons he had just scared away.

"Gets pretty dull around here," Sanger answered. "I've been looking for a little something to spark things up. Maybe putting you together with Brennus would be just the thing."

Damon's heart raced. "You can bring me to him?"

Sanger turned his head, spit, wiped his chin with his sleeve, and said, "Maybe. If there's something in it for me."

Damon tried not to smile.

Sanger was his.

Damon said, "What if I told you I could release you from the Blood?"

It was Sanger's turn to smile. His cracked lips parted into a wide grin, revealing yellow, chipped teeth.

"I'd say you just bought yourself a guide."

15

"I'm going with you," Marsh declared.

"Forget it," Cooper shot back. "I've been watching out for you all my life. And death. This time I'm watching my own back."

"I don't need you to take care of me," Marsh argued.

Coop laughed sarcastically.

They were aboard Ree's subway car in her vision. The Watcher was long gone. Ree sat on her couch, quietly listening to the boys.

"Look, Ralph," Coop continued. "You made a mistake. You were out of your head. I get it. But it's done. You don't have to try and make up for it. Move on."

"I'm just as much a part of this as you are," Marsh argued. "No, I'm *more* a part of it. The only reason Damon went after you was to get to me."

"Yeah, and when he did, you gave him exactly what he wanted."

"I thought we were moving on?"

"Stop! All right?" Coop exclaimed. "This isn't Xbox. We're talking about going to hell here. Literally. There's no reset button to hit and start over if things go bad."

"I know that," Marsh replied calmly. "I'm going."

"Not with me you're not. Look, I may be cheesed off at you but you are still my brother and I won't let you do this."

"I'm going," Marsh stated matter-of-factly.

"Why? What are you trying to prove?" Coop shouted with exasperation.

As Coop's frustration grew, Marsh actually became more calm.

"I'm not trying to prove anything," Marsh finally said, then added thoughtfully, "Except that maybe we're better than this."

"What's that supposed to mean?"

Marsh glanced to his mom, who was hanging on his every word.

"I've seen a lot of things I'm having trouble accepting, and I'm not talking about the Morpheus Road," he said. "What bothers me is seeing the depths people can sink to in order to get what they want . . . including me."

"Yeah, well, welcome to reality," Cooper said.

Marsh nodded sadly. "I guess. Maybe I'm naive but I'm beginning to realize that mistakes are part of life. It's impossible to always know the exact right thing to do. What's important is how we recover from bad choices."

Coop was ready to leap in with an argument, but didn't have one.

Marsh continued, "We've been challenged to stop Damon. We didn't ask for the job and made plenty of bad moves that only made things worse, but that doesn't change the fact that Damon must be stopped and the Watchers are looking to us to do it."

"I hear you," Coop said, his anger fading. "And you're right. But you gotta be realistic. This is going to get nasty and I don't think you're up to it. I'm sorry."

"My whole life you've been pushing me to take chances, and all I've done is push back. I'm not pushing back anymore, Coop. I'm going."

Coop ran his hands through his hair, searching for the right words that would convince his best friend to back off. In desperation he turned to Ree.

"Talk to him," Coop implored. "Tell him he can't do this."

Ree had been watching her son with pride throughout the argument. His words had rung painfully true to her.

"I don't think I'll ever get over the guilt of having helped unearth the poleax," she said. "We're facing the apocalypse and I bear much of the blame. I too hate to see the depths that we can sink to, and I am not as naive as either of you. But I also know that second chances exist. It's what the Black is all about. The worst thing we could do is not take them, because I think that's what the Watchers are waiting for us to do."

"But we *are* taking them," Coop said. "Round up the Guardians. Marsh can help you with that if he wants. Leave Damon to me."

Ree took a breath and said, "I will do exactly that, but I believe Marsh should go with you."

Coop whipped her a surprised look.

Marsh broke out in a broad grin.

"Seriously?" Coop shouted, stunned. "You're willing to send your son to hell?"

"I'm willing to let him grow up and follow his head, and his heart."

Marsh sat down next to his mother and held her hand. He didn't say a word. He didn't need to.

Coop paced furiously. "This is . . . this is just . . . wrong. You think you're feeling guilty now? What're you going to do if this turns out bad, which it probably will?"

Ree stood, pulling Marsh to his feet.

"I don't think it will," she said with confidence. She held out her hand to Coop. "Come with me, both of you. I want to show you something."

Coop hesitated, then reached out. Ree squeezed both their hands reassuringly as the colorful fog appeared before them. They stepped into the swirl of light on the subway car . . .

. . . and out onto a quiet street in a small Greek village.

Marsh and Coop looked around to get their bearings. It was Marsh who first understood.

"I know where we are," he announced, pointing to an ancient, crumbling temple that sat at the end of the winding street.

"Yeah, I know that building," Coop said. "I think."

"You do. We're still in my vision," Ree explained. "It's a remote corner that I've only been to once before, and once in the Light."

"The Temple of the Morning Light," Marsh said solemnly.

Coop did a double take at the structure. "Really?" he asked. "That's it?"

"It's how I remember the village of Ammoudia," Ree answered. "I have no idea what the temple looks like in the Light now, since the earthquake."

"Why are we here, Mom?" Marsh asked.

Ree's answer was to walk toward the crumbling building. Marsh and Coop exchanged glances and followed without a word. Ree led them along the same fateful route she had taken with Ennis Mobley on her last journey in the Light. They approached the tall, domed building and stepped through the soaring entryway.

"It's exactly like I pictured it," Coop said in awe.

They sidestepped the rubble of broken furniture to enter a corridor on the far side that led to the wooden framed opening that was the portal to an empty storage space . . . empty except for a hole in the floor that Ennis had created in his quest to uncover an ancient mystery.

A flashlight sat on the wooden frame, waiting for them. Ree grabbed it, flicked it on, and climbed through. The boys followed, staying close to her as she descended the stone stairs that brought them to the underground chamber and the snaking passageway that led toward the Necromanteio. The Oracle of the Dead.

They moved quickly through the twisting catacombs, passing the mummified remains of the long-forgotten. Neither had to ask what their ultimate destination was.

"That's it," Ree finally declared.

She stopped, shining her light on the stone sarcophagus that was supposedly the tomb of Damon of Epirus, but was in reality the seal over the Rift that Damon had created so many centuries before.

"This is how it appeared before we broke the seal and uncovered the crucibles," Ree explained.

"Is there a Rift in your vision too?" Marsh asked.

"No," Ree answered. "But there's something else."

She handed Cooper the flashlight and reached to the top of the crypt to grab a small stone container.

"The box that held the six crucibles," Marsh said in awe.

Ree slid off the heavy lid and tipped it so the others could see inside.

"I don't get it," Coop said. "I thought there were six."

"There were," Ree explained. "In the Light."

The box held only one of the golden orbs that contained the blood of Alexander the Great that were created as a curse by the ancients to keep Damon away from the Rift he had created. Ree took the orb from the stone box and placed the empty container back on top of the tomb.

"Sometimes the best way to hide something is to put it in plain sight," she explained.

The golden ball reflected the light from the flashlight like a shiny Christmas ornament. The boys stared at it, both mesmerized and confused.

The realization hit Marsh first.

"It's the real thing," he declared. "That's not part of your vision. It's the sixth crucible."

"What!" Coop exclaimed. "It's been here all along?"

Ree explained, "When I fell through the Rift into the Black, I had two crucibles. Once I learned of their power, I chose to hide one. I didn't tell a soul about it. Not even Adeipho or Zoe. I figured it was the best way to keep it safe in case things went bad . . . and things have gone very bad."

She took Marsh's hand and placed the golden ball in his open palm. "This will keep you safe from Damon. It's the only thing I can do to make sure you come back."

She turned to Coop and added, "That you'll both come back."

Marsh looked to Cooper, expecting a protest.

He didn't get one.

"I'm going to do exactly what you suggested," Ree continued. "I'm going to Zoe's vision and help her bring the Guardians back together. Go into the Blood. Both of you. Find the Watcher. Get him to help you stop Damon. If he doesn't help you, bring him back through the Rift."

"Why?" Coop asked.

"Because I'll use that black sword on him myself. You can tell him that."

"Yes, ma'am," was all Coop could say.

Ree faced Marsh and said, "Damon used you. He used all of us. Repay the favor."

Marsh glanced to Cooper.

Cooper raised an eyebrow and said, "Your mom's a badass."

Ree said, "I think it's come down to this. The Watchers look over all spirits, not just the good ones. Cooper was wrong. I think you *do* have something to prove, Marsh. We all do. We have to show the Watchers that mankind knows the right way."

"And then what?" Marsh asked.

"Then maybe they'll step in and end this. They've done it before."

"And what if they don't?" Coop asked.

Ree said, "Then at least we'll know we went down swinging."

Ree pulled Marsh close, hugging him, fighting the fear of losing her conviction. And her son.

"I love you," she said. She put her arm around Coop and added, "Both of you. I am so proud."

The three stood together in the dark vision, committing to memory those last few moments together.

Ree finally pulled back and said, "Now it's time to fight."

The Flavian Amphitheater was empty.

The cheering crowds had long since departed. Four Roman soldiers stood guard on the floor of the arena in front of the dimensional tear that continued to spew purple light.

"They've all got the killer swords," Coop pointed out.

Cooper and Marsh had crept through the darkened stadium unnoticed. They peered over the brick wall that surrounded the arena, directly opposite the Rift.

"And we've only got one," Marsh whispered.

"It won't be as tough as it looks," Coop replied. "We just have to pick our spot and get past one of them. No way they'll follow us through the Rift."

Coop clutched his own black sword. He knew he would have to use it to destroy yet another spirit. Or two.

"Don't worry," Marsh whispered. "I've got your back."

Coop gave Marsh a small smile. "You realize this is more important than either of us. If it comes down to taking out Damon or saving our own skins . . ."

He didn't complete the thought.

"I get it," Marsh said. "You realize this wasn't how I planned on spending the summer."

Coop chuckled. "You mean you'd rather be hanging out at the beach?"

"I'd pretty much rather be hanging out anywhere else. But I'm glad we're here."

Coop nodded, then took off running, crouching low, staying below the top of the wall. Marsh followed right behind him. The two circled halfway around the stadium until they were twenty yards from the Rift. Cautiously they both peered up and over at the guards below.

"This is cake," Coop whispered. "They're looking out at the arena, not back at the Rift. We'll get right above the opening, then drop down and—"

"Look out!" Marsh screamed.

The guards on the arena floor weren't alone.

A Roman soldier leaped at them from a tunnel that ran below the stands. He had a sword. A black sword. He slashed down at Cooper, who raised his own sword in defense. He deflected the blow then jabbed a punch to the soldier's gut. The beefy Roman spirit doubled over with a grunt.

"Go!" Coop yelled to Marsh.

Marsh didn't hesitate. He jumped up and ran along the

wall, headed for the top of the Rift. He'd only gotten a few steps when he glanced back to see that the soldier was back on his feet, and on the attack.

Coop swung at him but the soldier wouldn't be fooled twice. He dodged out of the way and Coop's fist caught nothing but air. The soldier countered with a swipe of his sword and Coop could only protect himself. He held his sword up and deflected another blow but he was no match for the more experienced soldier. The Roman parried Coop's defense and knocked his sword arm away, leaving Coop wide open. The soldier pulled his sword back to strike . . .

. . . and was hit from behind. Marsh had come back and launched himself at the guy, feetfirst. The soldier's head snapped back as he fell forward, out of control. Coop dodged around him and ran for the Rift.

Marsh got up and sprinted after him.

The soldiers down on the arena floor saw the fight unfolding in the stands above but stayed at their posts, standing ten yards in front of the Rift. They were no threat.

But the ten soldiers who were running along the stands from either side were.

"As soon as we land in the arena, the guys down there will attack," Marsh exclaimed, breathless.

Coop looked around, desperate for an idea.

"So let's not land," he exclaimed, and ran for the top of the Rift.

Lying across the seats that were directly above the Rift was the heavy rope netting that was used to protect the spectators from stray weapons that were thrown from the arena. It was attached to the top edge of the wall and spread out over several rows of seats, ready to be hoisted.

Coop stuck his black sword through his belt and grabbed at the netting several rows up.

Marsh saw what he was doing and followed his lead.

"Go no farther!" came an angry warning.

The soldiers were running fast, seconds from reaching Marsh and Cooper. The lead soldier in each group held a black sword.

Marsh grabbed the netting with both hands and nodded to Cooper. He was ready.

"Ralph?" Coop shouted.

"Yeah?"

"Go to hell."

Clutching the net, the two launched themselves over the edge of the wall.

The soldiers in the arena saw what was happening and closed on the Rift . . . too late.

Marsh and Cooper sailed down, the top edge of the net caught, the ropes pulled tight, and their fall turned into a swing that arced over the arena floor, past the guards, and flung them straight through the Rift.

Into the Blood.

16

Damon wasn't used to taking orders.

With each step his anger grew more intense as he stared at the back of the tall, wan spirit who called himself Sanger. He kept his rage under control, though. If Sanger could lead him to Brennus, it would be well worth swallowing his ample pride. There would be plenty of time to destroy Sanger once he was no longer of use to him.

Sanger held his lantern out as they walked, not to light their way but to keep the light-sensitive demons at bay.

They trudged through many visions . . . a battlefield crisscrossed with trenches, the dry dead garden of a crumbling castle, and a mall with no customers or merchandise. Sanger walked with authority. Damon wished he could say the same.

"How much farther?" he asked.

"We'll be there when we get there," Sanger replied, tweaking Damon's ego yet again.

"That sword you got," Sanger said. "Never seen nothing like it."

"And you won't see another," Damon replied with pride.

"It's useless here," Sanger said flatly.

"Do not be so sure about that," Damon replied with arrogance. "It may not have had any power over those vile demons but—"

Sanger spun around, grabbed the blade end of the poleax, and before Damon could stop him, he drove it into his own stomach.

"No!" Damon screamed. He hated the crude spirit but he wasn't done with him.

Sanger gritted his teeth against the pain, but managed a smile.

Damon was speechless. It was true. His mighty weapon held no power in the Blood.

Sanger stared straight into Damon's eyes. It took all of Damon's willpower not to look away from the man who showed more than a touch of insanity.

"You haven't been here long, have you?" Sanger asked.

"I—I have only just arrived," stammered Damon.

"You've got that look. No spirit here's got that look for long."

"What look is that?"

"You still got hope."

Sanger stepped back, pulling himself off the poleax. He spit, rubbed the wound, then turned and continued the journey.

Damon's confidence was shaken. For the first time in his life, or death, he felt as though he was not in complete control.

Soon after, Sanger held up his hand and the two stopped.

They had arrived at an old farmhouse with broken, glassless windows that allowed wind to whistle through and billow the tattered curtains. Across from the house was a large, nondescript gray barn.

"I do not understand," Damon declared. "This could not be the vision of the spirit Brennus."

"It ain't," Sanger replied. "This is my vision."

The house had no soul . . . a fitting home for Sanger, thought Damon.

"Why have you brought me here?" Damon demanded.

Sanger ignored the question and continued toward the barn. Damon had no choice but to follow. Sanger loped past the large closed barn doors and rounded the structure to where a long, wooden canoe sat upturned against the wall.

"Fetch it," Sanger ordered. "We'll go the rest of the way on the river."

"We will carry it together," Damon countered.

Sanger bent down and picked up two wooden paddles. "I got these," he said, and held up the lantern. "And this. Course I could always leave the lantern but I can't guarantee them demons won't come back."

Damon bit his lip to keep from raging at the man and lifted one end of the canoe.

"It is too heavy to carry," he announced. "I will drag it."

"Suit yourself," Sanger said with disdain and started off.

Damon quietly vowed to himself that he would destroy Sanger at the first opportunity. He dragged the canoe along the ground, following the light from the lantern as Sanger entered a narrow path that cut through thick woods. There was no telling what might be lurking to either side, waiting to pounce. Damon struggled to keep close to Sanger and, more important, the lantern.

The trail opened up to a stretch of rock and rubble. Ten yards beyond was a wide river with thick forest lining both banks. There was nothing treacherous about it, other than the fact that the water was glowing orange like molten lava.

Damon gasped and dropped the canoe. "We cannot navigate this waterway," he declared. "The wooden craft will surely burn."

Sanger ignored him, dropped the paddles and the lantern, and picked up the canoe, easily lifting it over his head. He walked to the edge and dropped the boat down into the glowing water.

It didn't burn.

"Paddles," Sanger commanded.

"I will go no farther," Damon announced petulantly.

Sanger pulled the canoe onto land to make sure it wouldn't be carried away in the current, then approached Damon. He stood facing the ancient warrior and without warning he lashed out and slapped him across the face.

Damon's head snapped to the side. He was more surprised than hurt. No one had ever dared to treat him like that. His hand immediately went to the poleax . . . and Sanger quickly slapped his other cheek.

"Who are you?" Sanger demanded. "You think you're strong enough to line yourself up with Brennus? All I've seen is a scared little fat man. Maybe that weapon makes people in the Black do what you say, but that holds no water here. Now either you pull yourself together and start showing some mettle or I'll leave you here and pick my teeth while watching those little banshees tear you apart."

Damon straightened his back and snarled, "Forgive me for causing you such inconvenience. There must be so many other things you'd prefer to be doing with your valuable time, you wretched little cretin."

Sanger's eyes flared.

"Now, that's more like it," he declared.

He turned his back on Damon and strode toward the canoe.

Damon wanted to leap at the spirit and snap his neck, but he fought the urge and did what he was told.

Sanger went straight for the bow of the canoe and sat there holding the lantern, waiting for Damon to launch them. Damon struggled, but managed to push the craft out onto the glowing water and get aboard without tipping.

"It's a ways," Sanger said. "Start paddling."

Damon knew nothing about paddling a canoe but managed to get the small craft moving with awkward strokes.

Sanger quickly realized that Damon was incompetent, so he propped the lantern up in the bow and grabbed the other paddle and worked to right their course.

They moved downriver with the slow current, passing burned-out towns, ruins of shattered glass skyscrapers, and the caved-in dome of the United States Capitol building. Damon chose not to question Sanger. He had committed to trusting the surly spirit. He was more concerned about retracing his steps back to the Rift. Getting lost in the Blood would prove to be an inglorious end to his quest.

The river emptied into a large lake that glowed as brightly as the river that fed it. The stark contrast between the dark purple sky and the orange glow would have been strangely beautiful, if not for the ever-present moans of the damned.

"There," Sanger announced, pointing to a dark structure on the shore.

Damon's spirits rose and he paddled faster, eager to finally meet Brennus and to destroy the spirit who'd led him there. As they drew closer to shore, the outline of a structure took shape. A high, stone wall rose up from the water like the battlement of a medieval fortress. Beyond the retaining wall was a low castlelike structure with triangular towers and misshapen arches.

Damon had witnessed the evolution of architecture from his time until the present and had never seen a building quite like this one. Massive statues of snarling, winged beasts lined the edge of the roof. It looked designed to intimidate and dissuade the curious. There was nothing welcoming about it in the least.

It was the exact sort of dwelling that Damon expected to be the vision of the spirit called Brennus.

Sanger expertly steered the canoe to the stone steps that led up from the water, then deftly grabbed the lantern and jumped out. With one mighty pull he yanked the craft up and onto the steep stairs, with Damon still aboard.

Damon dropped the paddle into the canoe, swearing never to touch such a crude instrument again, and stumbled out onto the stairs.

Sanger stood on top with his hands on his waist, snickering at Damon's awkward performance.

"Any day now," he called.

Damon climbed the stairs until he reached Sanger. He stood tall to try and regain some measure of dignity, and commanded, "Lead me to Brennus."

Sanger shook his head in disgust, turned his back on Damon, and walked toward the building.

Damon looked past him to see that a wide courtyard stood between the retaining wall and the sprawling stone mansion. He followed Sanger, past several fountains that were scattered about, spewing glowing water from the lake in decorative patterns. It wasn't until he got close to one of the fountains that he realized the statues within were stone versions of the demons that had attacked him.

"How do you know Brennus?" Damon called to Sanger.

Sanger stopped and surveyed the imposing, dark compound.

"Never crossed paths with him," he replied with a shrug.

Damon was rocked. "What? Then, how did you know to lead me here and—"

"Relax," Sanger commanded. "I said I never met him. That don't mean I don't know nothing about him. I've heard the stories. They say he'd be a rival to Satan himself, if there was such a thing as Satan."

"Then, how can you be sure this is his vision?" Damon asked.

"'Cause that's how it works here," Sanger replied. "I set my mind to finding him and here we are. We got as many different visions going on here as spirits that brung 'em. It's all one big stinkin' soup. You not only have to deal with your own misery, but every other fool's as well."

Damon took a look at the surroundings with new understanding . . . and dread.

Sanger said, "I've heard of spirits who went looking for Brennus, but never met one who found him. Yet here we are. Maybe there's something special about you that'll make us the first."

He broke into a crooked smile that offered no warmth.

Damon stared him down and Sanger dropped the smile. It was the first sign that Sanger wasn't completely comfortable with Damon.

"Tell me," Damon said. "What stories have you heard?"

Sanger shrugged. "Nothing specific. Just rumors and such."

"Are you aware that Brennus was a sin eater?"

"A what?"

"A sin eater. He would enter the home of the recently deceased where the body would be laid out next to a sumptuous feast. The food was his to enjoy. All he needed do was to reach over the dead body . . . and eat."

"That's a heck of a thing. Why?" Sanger asked, intrigued.

"With each bite of food, he would also be taking in the

sins of the deceased. The dead man's soul would be cleansed, avoiding any possibility of being sent directly to the Blood."

"And that worked?" Sanger asked.

"I do not know, but I understand it came with a great cost to Brennus. He was a poor laborer with only one brother. He was driven to eat sins so as not to starve. His body may have been nourished, but his soul took on the weight of the sins from multiple lives. He continued the practice after death brought him to the Black. That is when I first heard of him. He ate the sins of those in the Black who were desperate to avoid being banished to the Blood. Imagine a single soul that contained that much evil? It staggers the imagination."

"Maybe I wasn't so far off in thinking he's kin to Satan," Sanger said in awe.

"Ultimately he knew he was doomed for eternity and chose to take control of his destiny. His goal was to destroy the Morpheus Road. When he was finally banished to the Blood, he came willingly. His plan was to gather an army of the damned and break down the barrier between dimensions. That is the last I heard of him, which tells me that he failed in his quest. But knowing he was here, and knowing what he intended to do, I have decided to allow him to join me in my own quest."

"And what is it you're after?"

"The very same thing."

"I may have misjudged you, friend," Sanger said nervously.

"Indeed," Damon replied. "My army stands ready in the Black to take control of our own destiny. Do you wish to wander aimlessly for all time through this dark hell? Or return to the Light and the life of your choosing?"

"That's possible?" Sanger asked, genuinely surprised.

"It is, but to ensure that victory I need more than the spirits from the Black. I need those who stand the most to win. I need the damned, and to get them I need Brennus. That is why I entered the Blood."

"Wait, you came here of your own choosin'?" Sanger asked.

"Does that demonstrate my, what did you call it? Mettle?"

"It demonstrates that you're a crazy fool," Sanger said with awe, then smiled. "I like that."

An unholy chorus of howls broke out as the statues inside the fountains sprang to life. The hollow-eyed demons transformed from stone into the fur-clad shadow banshees. Before Damon could react, a dozen monsters descended on them, knocking out their legs and pinning them to the ground.

Damon didn't bother reaching for the poleax. He knew it would do no good.

While four banshees held his arms, a fifth sat on his chest leering down at him, staring with empty eyes.

"What is your purpose?" the demon shrieked in a horrific squeal that sounded like shattering glass while strings of thick drool dripped from its mouth into Damon's eyes.

Damon blinked it away as he forced himself to stay focused . . . and sane.

"I seek the spirit named Brennus," he answered.

The demon looked to the others, and they all began chattering like angry monkeys.

"Bring me to him," Damon demanded.

The demons fell silent.

"There is no reaching Brennus," the figment on Damon's chest hissed.

"Why? How can that be?"

"He has been imprisoned."

Damon deflated. It was a wrinkle he hadn't expected. How could a spirit be imprisoned if he were already in the Blood?

"You will not see him, unless you are able," the banshee asked.

"Able to do what?" Damon shouted, grasping.

"To free him."

17

Marsh and Cooper landed together in a tangle of arms, legs, and netting.

No sooner had they stopped tumbling than they quickly fought to free themselves and jump to their feet, ready to take on any of the Roman soldiers who were brave or foolish enough to follow them into the Blood.

None appeared. Their allegiance to Damon had its limits.

Realizing they were alone, Marsh and Cooper gave each other a quick nod to acknowledge that all was well and turned to get their first look at the Blood. They were faced with the same image Damon had seen . . . the wreckage of the Roman Colosseum. As impossible as that vision appeared, it wasn't as impactful as the oppressive feeling of dread that overwhelmed them both, compounded by the constant chorus of agonized moans.

Coop tugged on Marsh's arm. He wanted to get moving.

Marsh nodded in agreement and the two walked quickly away, weaving their way around the piles of shattered limestone that had fallen from the Colosseum walls. Shadows darted everywhere, just beyond the edge of sight. Marsh sensed a presence on top of one of the rubble piles and spun quickly, but saw nothing. Without a word he picked up the pace. Neither said it, but they both wanted to be out of the confines of the Colosseum as fast as possible.

When they finally passed the outer wall, they stopped and stood together, scanning the horizon, getting their first view of the limitless decay of so many lives that was the Blood.

"It's just . . . tragic," Marsh said in a small voice.

"Are these visions?" Coop asked. "Is this what the poor bastards remember from their lives?"

"It makes me feel, I don't know, empty," Marsh said.

"Seriously. No wonder they're all moaning. Where is everybody, anyway?"

"I think they're everywhere," Marsh replied.

Once their eyes adjusted to the dark, they clearly saw spirits wandering about. There were untold numbers, all lost, aimless . . . and hopeless.

"That's who Damon came for," Coop said. "If he got those spirits in the Black all fired up about taking control of their lives, convincing these losers should be a no-brainer."

Marsh pulled the crucible out of the pocket of his hoodie and held it for security. "And what if he finds this Brennus character?"

"Go back, Ralph," Coop said firmly. "No harm, no foul."

Marsh stiffened. "I didn't say that because I was scared."

"You should be," Coop replied. "I sure as hell am. And this place is about as sure as hell as it gets."

"Let's find the Watcher," Marsh declared.

"I don't even know where to start."

Marsh surveyed the horizon. "The Watcher said that we'll find our way."

"That's a little cosmic for me. I'd rather have a map. Or a GPS."

Marsh stayed focused on the dark distance, looking for a clue that might help guide them.

"Nothing," Coop said dismissively. "No arrows. No beacons. No signs saying 'This Way to the Watcher.' How are we supposed to know where to go?"

"Follow me," Marsh ordered, and began walking.

"To where? We can't just start wandering around."

"This feels right," Marsh replied, and walked on with confidence.

Coop followed, but wasn't as certain and kept glancing back toward the remains of the Colosseum. "I wish we could, like, leave a trail of bread crumbs or something."

The two passed through timeless remains of shattered lives. They walked across a footbridge that spanned a foul-smelling canal in what looked to be the remains of Venice, Italy. On the far side they passed through a doorway and stepped into a classroom that was packed with adults, all sitting in children's chairs, staring vacantly ahead . . . at nothing.

Coop shuddered. "I thought this place was supposed to be all fire and pitchforks. It's more like we're walking through the nightmares of these poor bastards."

Leaving the classroom, they stepped into a wide-open desert where the bone-white sand glowed bright in contrast to the deep purple sky. Huge piles of rusted, damaged musical instruments were buried in the soft sand. Pianos were upended, a harp with broken strings lay grotesquely twisted, countless rusted horns poked up from below, never to be played.

The two stood on the edge of the expanse, staring in wonder.

"There's no end to it," Marsh said, awestruck. "These souls have to live with the horrible memories of what their lives had become."

"I think I'd rather deal with fire and pitchforks," Coop said.

They soon found themselves walking down the street of a small town, passing broken and burned storefronts, inside of which were the dark souls who'd frequented them in life.

"My god," Marsh said with a gasp. "It's Stony Brook."

Coop looked around with renewed interest, trying to find some sign that Marsh could be wrong.

"Why are we seeing home?" Marsh asked.

"Why not?" Coop shot back. "I'm sure plenty of people from Stony Brook end up here. I can think of a few who deserve to."

"I'd go out of my mind," Marsh added.

"You wouldn't be alone. These spirits just seem . . . lost."

Marsh and Cooper stared for a moment at the men and women who wandered the streets of Stony Brook, helplessly trapped in a memory that could only taunt them with images of a life that would never again be theirs.

"Keep moving," Coop said. "This is way too depressing."

They left the corrupted image of their hometown to pass through many others that weren't recognizable, all while constantly crossing paths with hundreds of aimless souls. Every so often a spirit would look to them and open his mouth to let out a chilling moan that added to the white noise of sorrow and lament.

"Tell me you know where you're going," Coop said. "If I have to take much more of this, I'm gonna start wailing too."

"I don't know how much farther," Marsh answered. "But we're headed the right way. Don't you feel it?"

Coop shrugged. "I don't like anything I'm feeling right now."

They soon found themselves in a wooded park. A broken and burned gazebo had fallen on its side, never to host another performance. Black fountains spewed glowing neon orange water. Twisted bicycles lay haphazardly on the dark grass, their bent wheels spinning slowly with haunting squeaks.

"We're getting close," Marsh announced.

"Seriously? The Watcher hangs out in a haunted park?"

Marsh turned onto a worn footpath that meandered through drooping trees. After a few turns the path emptied into a large clearing where a broad pond was waiting. The water glowed orange, the same as the water that sprang from the fountains. An island loomed in the dead center, upon which was built a clock tower that stood three stories high. Near the top were four white clock faces, one on each side of the tower. Each showed a different time. Beneath it, the tower walls were made of glass to reveal the clockwork within. A giant pendulum swung incessantly, moving the gears and creating a mechanical whirring sound that mercifully helped to drown out some of the moans.

"That's the first thing we've seen that isn't a wreck," Coop observed. "Do you think the Watcher is in there?"

"One way to find out."

A narrow, rickety wooden walkway was built from the shore and spanned the few yards of pond water to end on the island. Coop took the lead and strode for it. He was about to set foot on the first plank, when Marsh grabbed him from behind.

"Wait," he ordered. "We're not alone."

They had been so focused on the mysterious clock tower that they hadn't realized they were slowly and quietly being surrounded. A half-circle of spirits had appeared between them and the surrounding forest. There was a mix of people of every age and race who stood shoulder to shoulder, their dead eyes focused on Marsh and Coop as they moved slowly toward them.

"Zombies," Coop gasped.

"No, spirits of the damned," Marsh corrected.

The spirits had cut them off from going anywhere but out toward the island. Coop turned onto the footbridge and started across, with Marsh right behind. Halfway to the island he looked ahead and stopped suddenly.

"Uh-oh," Coop exclaimed.

Another spirit, a heavyset biker dude with a long beard and a tattoo of a snake on his cheek, stood on the bridge ahead of them.

"Trouble Town," Coop declared.

Marsh called out to the biker, "We're looking for the Watcher."

The guy didn't react. None of the spirits did. They simply continued to inch their way closer, tightening the noose.

Coop pulled his black sword from his belt and held it low, ready to fight.

"Don't go there," Marsh cautioned him.

"Me? They're the ones moving on us."

Marsh called again, "Can you help us? We're here to find the Watcher."

This time he got an answer. Every last spirit opened their mouth and let out a single, sustained moan.

Marsh and Coop drew closer to each other for support.

"What are they doing?" Marsh asked nervously.

"I think maybe Damon has already done some recruiting."

"So what do we do?"

"We get outta here," Coop answered.

He spun toward the biker and went on the attack with an adrenaline-fueled scream.

"No, don't!" Marsh warned.

Too late.

The spirit didn't react or try to defend himself against the crazed guy with a sword who was headed his way.

Cooper didn't hesitate. He thrust the blade forward and skewered the spirit square in the chest. The spirit flinched, its moan suddenly cut off.

But he didn't disappear.

"Oh this isn't good," Coop said with dismay.

The spirit stared right at Coop with dead doll eyes, then opened its mouth and continued to moan. Coop snapped. He pulled the sword out of the spirit and threw a punch to the snake tattoo on its ashen face. The biker staggered, fell over the wooden railing, and landed in the orange water of the pond.

"Coop!" Marsh screamed.

Coop turned to see Marsh on the walkway behind him, fighting off several spirits that were trying to pull him back toward land. Coop dropped the sword on the walkway and tried to free Marsh, but the spirits outnumbered them. With continual mind-numbing moans they grappled Marsh back to land while others descended on Cooper. Cooper swung and kicked but only managed to land a few satisfying shots. It was as if the spirits were numbed into feeling no pain. They swarmed Cooper and held him tight.

The crowd of spirits moved as one, pulling Marsh and Cooper away from the bridge and along the shore of the pond. Marsh and Coop fought to free themselves, but it was useless.

The spirits dragged them along the shore and into the orange water.

"Whoa! Wait!" Coop bellowed.

"Why are you doing this?" Marsh screamed.

The water was hot. Coop turned toward the island and saw the biker spirit surfacing from below, his dead eyes once again fixed on his prey, his mouth still open and moaning as orange water drooled over his lips.

The spirits pulled them deeper into the water.

"They're gonna drown us!" Marsh screamed.

Coop's mind couldn't comprehend what was happening. Could they be drowned? Could their spirits be destroyed that way in the Blood?

"Help!" Marsh screamed toward the clock tower. "Are you in there? We were sent by another Watcher!"

The spirits forced Marsh's and Cooper's heads under the glowing water. Marsh fought to get back to the surface and kept on yelling.

"Where are you?" he screamed, desperately hoping that the Watcher was within earshot.

The biker dude reached out for Coop, clutching his neck with strong, cold hands.

Coop was helpless against the big spirit's strength. He desperately tried to pull the guy's hands away, but it was no use. The spirit was driving him under the water.

Suddenly the moaning ended. A moment later the spirits released their hold.

Marsh and Coop scrambled away from the spirits while tripping and splashing their way to shore.

"You okay?" Coop sputtered.

Marsh coughed, and nodded.

"What happened?" Coop asked.

"I think he did," Marsh said, pointing to the island.

A man stood on the wooden walkway. The light from the clock face was directly behind his head, throwing him into silhouette. He stood with his legs apart, staring down at the boys. His hair was shaggy, falling well below his ears. He wore a long, black coat over dark clothing.

"Who sent you?" the man asked in a deep, confidant voice.

"A Watcher," Marsh answered. "A woman. She sent us here to find the Watcher who stopped Brennus from destroying the Morpheus Road."

"Why?" the man asked.

Unlike the other spirits, this spirit showed presence and intelligence.

Coop answered. "Because there's another spirit running around trying to finish what Brennus started."

"Many spirits have come here seeking vengeance for what happened to Brennus," the man said.

The attacking spirits stood still and quiet, like robots that had been shut down.

"Look, chief," Coop called out. "We're not here to bother you, whoever you are. We're looking for some badass Watcher who took Brennus down. So either point us in the right direction or get out of the way."

The man stood still for a long moment, then walked slowly along the walkway toward shore. The leather soles of his black cowboy boots fell heavily on the wooden planks.

The rest of the spirits didn't move or moan. They stood motionless in the water, staring at nothing.

As the man strode across the bridge, he reached down and retrieved Coop's black sword. After examining it like a curious prize, he shrugged and said, "This has no power here."

"Yeah, we found that out," replied Coop.

"Where did you get it?" the man asked as he stepped off the bridge and walked along the shore toward Marsh and Coop.

"There's been a standoff going on in the Black for centuries," Coop explained. "Both sides have those swords. We thought the good guys had won, but Damon had bigger plans."

"Damon?" the man repeated.

"That's the spirit who's looking for Brennus," Marsh said. "He's got a weapon that he used to rip open a Rift into the Blood, and another Rift between the Black and the Light."

The man shot a surprised look to Marsh. "You're saying that spirits can travel freely along the Morpheus Road?"

Coop answered, "Yeah, but that's nothing compared to what Damon wants to use them for. Stop with the questions. Who are you?"

The man felt the weight of the sword, then raised it high and drove it into the ground.

"I'm the one you've been looking for," he said. "Now who the heck are you?"

18

"He ate people's sins?" Coop asked, incredulous. "Like . . . munching on a turkey leg?"

"The power of the human spirit has few limits," the Watcher answered. "I don't know if the whole feasting ceremony was necessary other than to help Brennus believe he was actually taking on the negative history of the dead. But he thought it worked, so it did."

Cooper and Marsh were sitting in the dwelling of the Watcher. They had crossed the rickety footbridge to the island, where a small door at the base of the clock tower opened to reveal a narrow set of circular stairs leading down. The Watcher led them to a subterranean room that was decorated with bits and pieces taken from many ages and visions. Most of the furniture was wooden and heavy as if it belonged in a mountain cabin. The artwork looked as if it had come from a museum, with works by past masters that the boys recognized from field trips to New York. Classical Greek busts stood next to a bronze pirouetting ballerina that danced beneath an alien-looking mobile. It was an eclectic oasis that showed no signs of the sad decay that characterized every other aspect of the Blood. It wasn't at all what Marsh and Cooper expected.

Neither was the Watcher. He sat in a chair with his boots up on a desk, flipping a basketball back and forth, looking every bit like somebody's youthful dad.

Or uncle.

Marsh asked, "And he kept on eating sins in the Black after he died?"

The Watcher nodded. "It destroyed whatever shred of humanity he had left. When he was finally sent to the Blood, he was in his element. He rallied thousands of desperate souls with the promise of escape."

Unlike the Watcher who had sent them there, this man spoke normally with his words coming from his mouth.

"But you stopped him," Marsh said.

"Many spirits didn't go along with him. A good number fought back because of the trouble he was causing."

"Trouble?" Coop exclaimed with a laugh. "How can this place get any worse?"

"You have no idea," the Watcher said. "With no true order, the visions overlap."

"We've seen that," Marsh said. "You don't know when you're moving from one to the next."

"Exactly. Spirits try to maintain some sanity by keeping to their own personal vision, which is bad enough, but when you pile on the horror of other visions, it makes being here unbearable. Brennus agitated the spirits and moved them around, which created chaos by jumbling multiple visions together and making it impossible for any spirit to stay within their own space. So yes, he made the Blood worse than it already was."

"He made it hell to be in hell," Coop said.

"I guess you could put it that way," the Watcher said. "A group of spirits banded together to try to return some sense of balance. They captured Brennus and put him in a place where he can't use his influence. He's in a prison within a prison."

"Why didn't you just destroy him and be done with it?" Coop asked.

"I would never end a spirit's life," the Watcher said with total conviction.

"So what exactly *do* the Watchers do?" Marsh asked.

"We help spirits evolve. That's what the Black is all about. Every spirit's journey is different. There's no set time to spend in the Black. One spirit could exist there for a very short time, others may be there for centuries. We observe and ultimately decide when they are ready to move on."

"So where do you come from?" Marsh asked.

"We're not an alien race, if that's what you mean," the guy answered. "We're the evolved spirit of mankind. We're you. Unfortunately, not all spirits evolve, no matter how much time they spend in the Black. That's why the Blood exists."

The Watcher flipped the basketball into the air and spun it on one finger.

Coop gave Marsh a "Not bad" look of approval.

Marsh said, "But you seem so . . . normal."

"I'll take that as a compliment," the Watcher said with a laugh. "Coming here put me on the same level as every other spirit. I have no unique powers or abilities in the Blood."

Coop said, "You had plenty of power over those spirits who were trying to drown us."

"Those are some of the spirits who fought back against

Brennus. I think they're afraid of me. I'm not sure why but I'm sure as heck not going to tell them otherwise."

"Why you?" Coop asked. "How did you get this mission?"

The Watcher shrugged. "It wasn't the first time I was called upon. It's rare that we step in to try and offer direct guidance to mankind, but it has happened in a few dire situations. The last time was when one of our own felt he was better suited to determine the path of human events than mankind itself. He caused quite a stir in the Light for a while by working to influence the natural course of entire societies, and not for the better."

"What happened?" Marsh asked.

"Mankind triumphed, as it always does." He gave a sly smile and added, "I just helped nudge it in the right direction."

"If it's so rare, why did you come here to help the spirits of the damned?" Marsh asked.

"Brennus posed a threat like no other," the Watcher explained. "If he had succeeded the entire Morpheus Road would have been at risk, which meant all of humanity was in danger."

Marsh said, "But even if he rallied every last soul in the Blood, it wasn't like he could leave. Could he?"

"Not likely," the Watcher said. "But there's no telling what he might have accomplished with the combined strength of that many spirits. Mankind is always evolving, as is the Morpheus Road. The risk was too great. But I still wouldn't have intervened if not for the fact that so many spirits had already chosen to stop him. That's what tipped the scale. That's why I came to help them."

"And haven't left," Coop said.

The Watcher shrugged. "Like I said, Brennus still exists."

"And the Morpheus Road is in danger again," Marsh said gravely. "Except this time there's a way out of the Blood."

The Watcher's expression turned dark. "You were sent here to tell me everything. So tell me."

Coop and Marsh laid out the whole story: Damon's atrocities in life, his using the poleax to tear open a Rift into the Black, and the cursed crucibles that had kept him away from the poleax. They told him how Ree and Ennis's discovery of the poleax in the Light put it back on Damon's radar and how Damon pulled Marsh and Cooper into his web of horror to try and find it. They told of the battle between Damon's forces and the Guardians of the Rift and how the Watchers intervened to send Damon's minions into the Blood. And ultimately, they told of how Damon finally retrieved the poleax and ripped open two new Rifts.

Coop ended the story by saying, "So Damon is here, looking to team up with Brennus and whatever spirits he convinced to follow him."

The Watcher listened to the saga without interrupting. The only sign that he was disturbed by what he was hearing was when he occasionally fired the basketball from hand to hand.

"So that's it," Coop said. "The whole twisted story. What happens now?"

The Watcher shrugged. "I don't know. You tell me."

"But . . . the other Watcher said you'd help us," Marsh said.

"Okay. What would you like me to do?"

"What do you think?" Coop exclaimed. "Stop Damon."

"I think maybe that's *your* job," the Watcher replied.

"What!" Coop shouted. "No! You've got to do it."

"I'm sorry. We don't interfere."

"Yes, you do," argued Marsh. "That's why you came here in the first place."

"I came here to help the spirits of the Blood find their own way," the Watcher corrected. "If you expect me to wave my hand and send the bad guys to oblivion, you're mistaken."

"But . . . why?" Coop demanded.

"Because we only reflect the wishes of mankind."

"Okay, fine!" Coop shouted. "Here's my wish: Destroy Damon. How's that?"

The Watcher chuckled and said, "I'm afraid your wishes don't carry more weight than any other spirit's."

"But don't most spirits want to defeat the bad guys and reward the good guys?" Marsh asked, confused.

The Watcher tossed the basketball to him and said, "Good and bad are subjective concepts. Ultimately spirits like Brennus and Damon decide their own fate . . . no matter how wrong other spirits may think they are."

"So then, why are we here?" Marsh asked. "Why are *you* here?"

"I can guide you into making choices that will help get you what you want," he answered. "That's all we ever do. As to why you're here, well, that's up to you to decide."

"This is just stupid!" Coop shouted, angrily jumping to his feet. "We're facing the apocalypse and all you can say is, 'Well, it's your choice. Sorry.' Give me a break."

The Watcher said, "When I came here, it was to help the spirits deal with Brennus. I didn't do it myself. If Damon is going to be stopped, it will be up to the spirits here to do it . . . and to you."

Coop and Marshall both stared at the floor, stunned.

"So we're done," Marsh said.

The Watcher stood and put on his long coat. "I didn't say that. I'm just telling you that the playing field is level. So what's the deal? Do you want to try and stop this Damon character?"

"Of course!" Marsh replied.

"Okay. Then we should find him before he gets to Brennus."

Coop looked to Marsh, stunned. "This guy is making me nuts."

"So you'll help?" Marsh asked, brightening.

"I never said I wouldn't help," the Watcher chided. "I just said it's ultimately going to be up to you. You need to understand that."

Coop nodded. "Okay. I can live with that. I think."

"Good," the Watcher added. "Who's up for a little hunting?"

Coop grinned. "Dude, now we're talking."

The Watcher looked to Marsh.

Marsh stood up quickly. "I am. I owe that guy."

"Then, let's go find him," the Watcher said, and strode for the spiral stairs that led up and out of his sanctuary.

"Wait," Marsh said. "What do we call you?"

"Whatever you'd like," the Watcher replied.

"C'mon," Coop cajoled. "You're an evolved spirit. Can't you at least come up with a name?"

The Watcher thought for a moment and said, "Perhaps you should use the name I took when I was last called upon to help. In the Light."

"What is it?" Marsh asked.

The Watcher smiled, as if lost for a moment in a pleasant memory.

"Call me . . . Press."

19

A slow-moving flotilla of boats drifted along the glowing river of orange.

Damon was in the lead, this time in the bow of the canoe that was being powered by Sanger in the stern, who paddled with authority. Damon held the lantern forward, trying to make out details onshore.

Floating behind the canoe were four small flat-bottomed barges. Each held a dozen of the small, furry demons with sunken eyes. There was one paddler to the rear of each barge. The rest of the figments sat quietly, staring ahead, their eyes locked on Damon.

Damon scanned both shores, not knowing exactly what he was looking for, though confident that he would know it when he saw it. The banshees were barely capable of communication, but Damon had learned enough to know that Brennus no longer existed in the vision of the Gothic mansion but had been imprisoned in another area of his own vision. Damon didn't care how it had happened or why. All he wanted was to find Brennus and unleash him.

They passed a small city, and then a navy battleship that lay listing on its side with guns pointing harmlessly to the purple sky. After passing the remains of a huge suspension bridge that led to nowhere, Damon spotted something on the left bank that made his heart leap.

"There," he called back to Sanger. "That way. Quickly."

The silhouette of a massive stone cathedral loomed up above gnarled trees. Its single tall tower stood as an impressive, ominous sentinel.

"You sure?" Sanger asked.

"He's there," Damon declared. "As you so quaintly put it, I set my mind to finding him, and here we are."

"Suit yourself," Sanger replied, and navigated the canoe toward shore.

The other boats followed obediently.

Cooper, Marsh, and Press walked quickly down the midway of an amusement park, surrounded by the wreckage of rides and attractions that provided no joy for the wandering, moaning souls that shuffled past.

Press carried a long, well-worn wooden stave that was covered with ancient-looking carvings.

"Good-luck charm?" Coop asked.

"A present from another spirit who means a lot to me," Press replied.

"The Watchers have friends?" Marsh asked.

Press laughed. "What good is an existence that can't be shared with others?"

"How does that work?" Coop asked. "Where do you go after the Black if—"

Press cut him off, saying, "One challenge at a time, all right?"

"It's no big deal," Coop argued. "I'd just like to know what we're fighting for."

"You're fighting for your life," Press answered soberly. "And for the lives of everyone who came before you and will come after."

Coop and Marsh exchanged looks.

Coop shrugged and sarcastically said, "Oh is that all?"

They arrived at the edge of a lake that was glowing orange. Press led the way as they stepped across a series of floating docks where several small, burned-out boats were tied up.

Marsh shuddered. "Reminds me of the marina on Thistledown Lake. Last time I was there, Damon sent a guy to kill me."

Tied to the farthest float was a small, wooden fishing boat with an outboard engine.

Coop said, "The last time I was in one of these, I died."

Press hopped aboard the craft, fired up the engine with ease, and looked at the other two.

"Coming?"

Coop and Marsh jumped aboard and they pushed off. As Press motored quickly across the glassy orange lake, both were grateful that the steady sound of the engine drowned out the distant wailing moans.

"What did you have to do?" Marsh asked Press. "I mean, to capture Brennus?"

"He wasn't about to go down without a fight. Like I told you, physical existence here isn't much different than in the Light. It came down to an old-fashioned battle between Brennus and the spirits who stood against him."

"Been there," Coop said knowingly.

"I doubt that," Press shot back. "Brennus was protecting himself with these figments. I'm not sure how to describe them other than to say they are physical manifestations of fear."

Marsh asked, "You mean like living nightmares?"

"You could say that. I think they're more of a nuisance than a danger but Brennus was able to corral them and influence them into helping him."

The lake narrowed down to a river that snaked through a dark forest and eventually merged with another, wider river that glowed as orange as the lake.

"Did you actually get in the fight?" Coop asked. "With that stick?"

"I helped," Press said evasively. "They ambushed Brennus and sealed him in a vault that's part of his own vision. In the Light the guy lived near a cathedral full of ancient tombs."

"Well that's . . . creepy," Coop said.

Press said, "They forced Brennus into one of the cement tombs and sealed him inside."

"They buried him alive?" Marsh asked.

"So to speak," Press agreed.

"I don't know which is worse," Coop added, "being destroyed or living in a box for eternity."

Press didn't comment.

Sanger guided the canoe expertly to the riverbank and beached the craft. Damon jumped ashore quickly and stood in awe of the sight before him.

It was an immense cathedral made of gray stone. There was a massive single tower that dominated the structure, beneath which was an arched roof that was mostly collapsed. Whatever wooden elements had been part of the structure were long gone, leaving only the imposing stone shell. The building stood nearly a hundred yards back from the shore. The space between held the forlorn remains of a lush garden with winding paths, toppled walls, and curved arbors.

"He's here," Damon said eagerly. "I know it."

"What's the plan?" Sanger asked, his voice barely above a whisper.

Damon gave him a dismissive glance. "The plan is for you to follow me and do exactly as I say."

He looked back to shore to see that the barges had all landed and the dozens of small demons were standing silently, shoulder to shoulder, ready. He allowed himself a small smile. He had only been in the Blood for a short while and he already had a following. His confidence soared.

He grabbed the poleax and held it up, if only for show.

"I will now free the spirit known as Brennus," he bellowed. "And take command of his legions."

Damon expected the figments to let out a cheer of encouragement. Instead they remained chillingly silent, staring back at him with empty eyes.

Damon looked to Sanger, who shrugged and offered a weak, "Hooray."

Damon wanted to slash him with the poleax. Instead he kept his anger in check, turned, and strode toward the cathedral. Sanger glanced at the figments nervously and followed.

"Gotta tell ya," Sanger said. "I don't trust them little beasts."

"They are loyal to Brennus," Damon replied. "That is all that matters. Once Brennus joins me, their loyalty will be with me."

Suddenly the entire group of demons let out a collective, earsplitting shriek.

Damon spun in time to see the figments rushing toward

him. He held out the poleax, ready to fight, but the demons wanted nothing to do with either of them. They ran past Damon and Sanger and continued on toward the cathedral.

Sanger said, "Now, what do you s'pose got into them?"

"Look!" Damon ordered, pointing to the cathedral.

The dark, empty building showed no signs of life . . . until spirits began pouring from the crumbled doorways and gaping windows.

"What is this?" Damon asked, stunned.

Sanger said, "I do believe we're in for a fight."

"What's that?" Marsh asked, listening.

"More wailing spirits," Coop said dismissively. "I'm getting used to it."

"No," Press said, his attention focused. "I think Damon may have beaten us here."

"Why do you say that?" Marsh asked nervously.

"The spirits who imprisoned Brennus have stood guard over the tomb. It sounds as though they have visitors."

Coop and Marsh looked downriver to see a cathedral tower looming in the distance.

"Is that it?" Coop asked.

"That's it," Press said as he gunned the engine.

He turned the small craft quickly and sped toward the building.

Marsh's heart started to pound.

Coop pulled out his black sword.

"What's the plan?" Marsh asked nervously.

"Stay in the boat," Coop ordered. "I'll go after Damon."

Marsh didn't argue but had no intention of being left out. As frightened as he was to enter the battle, he had something that gave him confidence. He reached into the front pocket of his hoodie and grasped the crucible.

The sounds of battle grew louder as the boat neared shore.

"Avoid the spirits," Press said to Coop. "If they haven't stopped Damon, then you've got to get by them and stop him from unsealing the tomb, and you don't want to have to fight your way through them."

"Where is the tomb?" Coop asked.

"Inside the cathedral in the floor along the right aisle."

"Okay. What are you going to do?" Coop asked.

Press held the wooden stave out and said, "I'm your backup."

Marsh kept quiet.

Moments later they hit the riverbank. Press drove the boat up onto shore, grabbed his wooden stave, and leaped from the craft before it stopped moving. He was already running toward the cathedral before Marsh could reach back to kill the engine.

"That's how he backs me up?" Coop said, incredulous.

"I like that guy," Marsh said.

"Okay, Ralph, this is it. Wish me luck."

Before Marsh could respond, Coop jumped from the boat with his black sword out and ready.

Marsh clutched the golden crucible, waited until Coop was out of sight, then climbed out of the boat and ran toward the cathedral. His only plan was to get to Brennus's prison before Damon and hope that the crucible would prevent Damon from breaking in and releasing the spirit. He ran along the darkened, winding path, skirting skeletal bushes and dead trees, drawn to the sounds of clashing metal against shields and the screams of wounded spirits. When he shot through an opening in a mostly collapsed stone wall, he came upon the mayhem.

Dozens of human spirits battled the small animal-like figments. There was nothing elegant about the fight. The furry creatures clawed and bit at the spirits. The spirits were armed with short, crude clubs that they swung to keep the demons off them. The sound of the weapons hitting the figments was sickening. Spirits felt pain in the Blood, which was obvious from the agonized screeches coming from both sides.

The Watcher named Press had jumped into the thick of it. He spun his wooden stave expertly, knocking the figments aside, working his way through the battle to get to the cathedral.

Marsh saw that Cooper was in the midst of it as well, but he wasn't fighting the demons. Coop was in a fistfight with one of the human spirits. Marsh feared that he might have been fighting someone who was trying to protect the tomb, which is why Press told him to avoid the spirits. The tall, thin spirit was an old guy who threw punches with authority. Unlike most of the other spirits, it looked as though he had been in a few fights before, which wasn't good for Coop, because he had dropped his black sword. It lay several yards away from where they were fighting. Marsh thought of running to grab it for Coop, but realized he had a more important mission.

Damon was nowhere to be seen. There was only one possible explanation for where he could be, and it wasn't a good one. Marsh knew he had to get to the cathedral quickly and plotted a route that would skirt around the battleground to avoid getting caught up and slowed down by the conflict. He was about to take off running, when he felt a sharp point in his back.

"You are the absolute last person I expected to see here," came an all-too-familiar voice.

Marsh had been wrong . . . Damon wasn't in the cathedral.

Marsh took a quick step forward and spun to face his tormentor. His stomach turned when he realized that the weapon that was now held to his chest . . . was the poleax.

"I do not understand," Damon said. "I was done with you, yet here you are. What did you hope to accomplish by sacrificing your life after you fought so hard to protect it?"

"I . . . I'm going to stop you," Marsh said, trying to keep his voice from cracking.

Damon chuckled dismissively. "I admire your tenacity, but you have no hope of deterring me from my quest."

"Quest?" Marsh shot back. "Quest for what? To prove you weren't a coward in life? You can't change history."

Damon stiffened.

"And what is it *you* hope to prove by coming here?" he said coldly. "That you are something other than a coddled mother's boy who shies at the realities of a cruel world? Let me offer you one last dose of reality. Your misguided act has doomed you to forever remain the pathetic, frightened little boy you so wished to leave behind."

Marsh grabbed the crucible, yanked it out of his pocket, and held it out toward Damon threateningly.

Damon was taken aback at the sight of the crucible, but didn't drop his sword.

Marsh held the orb out farther, expecting something to happen. *Hoping* for something to happen. The two stood facing each other, with Damon holding the point of the poleax at Marsh's chest.

Nothing happened.

Finally Damon offered a condescending smile.

"You do know that this is a dead existence," he said, smug. "There is no spiritual power in the Blood."

Marsh's stomach fell. The crucible was useless.

Damon swung the poleax without warning and knocked the orb out of Marsh's hand.

Marsh tried to catch it . . . too late. The golden ball hit the ground and shattered, splashing the blood of Alexander across the stone walkway. There was no earthquake or any other sign of the power that the crucible possessed in other dimensions. In the Blood it was no more powerful than an ordinary piece of shattered glass.

Marsh stared at the thick blood that trickled down and disappeared between the stones of the walkway, not wanting to believe that another crucible was gone.

Damon smiled in triumph. "I believe there is one last crucible still in the possession of the lovely Sydney."

Marsh looked up to the warrior, steeled himself, and said, "Which means you'll never get close to her."

"Not at first," Damon replied. "But these wretched crucibles hold no power over other spirits. Once my army marches into the Light, rest assured there will be no shortage of volunteers to hunt her down and destroy the infernal trinket that has kept me at bay for so long. Once it is gone, there will be nothing left to protect your lovely friend . . . from me."

Marsh screamed and jumped at Damon.

Damon quickly and calmly swung the poleax back toward Marsh . . . and drove the blade directly into his heart.

20

Marsh had never known such pain.

His entire body was racked with an excruciating agony that radiated out from the center of his chest. He couldn't even catch enough breath to scream out. The feeling of an alien object inside his body, cutting his flesh, nearly made his mind snap.

Damon pulled his lips back in an unconscious gesture, revealing the points of his two sharpened front teeth.

Marsh feared that Damon was going to rip out his heart and eat it, as he had done with so many of his enemies in the Light.

Damon shook his head, as if forcing that very desire from his mind. He pulled the poleax out of Marsh and examined the blade. It was clean. Spirits didn't bleed. Marsh fell to his knees, clutching his chest, holding his hand to the wound in a vain attempt to stop the searing agony.

"You are fortunate," Damon declared. "Pray I will not have this same opportunity in the Black."

With Marsh dismissed, Damon sidestepped him and strode toward the cathedral.

Marsh fell onto his side, gasping for air, willing the pain to go away. The sounds of the battle meant nothing to him. The battle itself was inconsequential. What mattered was that he had stood up to Damon and lost. The hurt that came from his pathetic failure rivaled the pain that tore through his chest. The only difference was that the pain from the injury slowly diminished. He blinked back the tears and dared to take his hand away from his wound. He examined it, expecting to see blood but not surprised when he didn't. Injuries were only a temporary setback. A *painful* setback, but minor nonetheless.

Marsh didn't want to have to go through anything like that again. He wanted to run off, find the Rift that led back into the Black, find his own vision, and crawl under his bed to hide.

He might have done just that, if his head hadn't cleared enough to once again register the sounds of the battle that was still raging. A quick look toward the cathedral showed that it was a standoff. The figments hadn't gotten any closer to the cathedral, but they hadn't been turned back either. Press was still spinning his stave like an attack helicopter, and Coop was still sparring with the old spirit. Nothing had changed . . .

. . . except that Damon had made his way through the battlefield and was entering the front doors of the cathedral.

Marsh jumped to his feet, the pain forgotten. His first thought was to run to Coop and Press to let them know that Damon was inside, but he dismissed it. He couldn't afford to waste the time.

He had to stop Damon.

Rather than plunge straight ahead, he took the widest route possible around the battle. It took time but not nearly as much as if he had had to fight. He moved stealthily between the crumbled remnants of the garden, past broken statues and crumbled walls, dry fountains and empty trellises. He felt like a coward, but stayed focused. He had no idea how he would stop Damon from releasing Brennus, but he knew he had to try.

Finally he reached the bottom of the stone stairs that led up to the front door of the cathedral. He waited for a moment, making sure that the banshees were too busy to notice, then sprinted up the stairs and jumped through the dark doorway.

"I knew plenty of boys like you," Sanger spat at Cooper. "Good for nothing but trouble."

"I'll bet you were a real prince," Coop shot back. "That's why you landed here."

Sanger lashed out at Cooper, swinging hard. Coop ducked the punch easily, but Sanger came back with an uppercut that drove straight into his gut. Coop was surprised by the skill of the old man. In life he must have been a real battler. Coop was also surprised by how much the punch hurt. He staggered back but Sanger was on him quickly. He leaped at Cooper and tackled him, driving his knees into his chest. Coop landed on his back, and Sanger grabbed his arm and flipped him over, wrenching the arm up and behind his shoulders.

Sanger leaned down to him and spat in his ear with vicious intensity, "You're a smart-ass, kid. I'm gonna enjoy seeing the likes of you eating dirt when the rising comes. I'll be lookin' for you in particular . . . and for the ones who killed me. You're all gonna suffer, I'll make sure of that."

Coop's other arm was free. He held his breath, forced himself not to think of the pain, and drove his hand up and backward, jamming his palm into Sanger's nose. Sanger squealed and let go. Coop spun and was on him fast, first throwing a side kick to his head that sent him sprawling, then leaping on him and jamming his knee into the old spirit's throat.

"I don't know who you were in life, you old dog, but this is where you belong and this is where you're staying."

Sanger's eyes were wild as he let out a laugh that chilled Cooper. In that one second, Coop realized that if these were the kind of spirits that Damon was gathering to stage his war, Ree's Guardians wouldn't stand a chance.

The vast cathedral was dark and quiet. The sounds of the battle grew faint as if it were miles away. Marsh stood just inside the front door, taking in the ancient, crumbled structure. The ceiling that would have been several stories above was long gone, allowing him to see the stone tower that stretched into the purple sky. A balcony ringed the space a story above.

From where he stood, the altar looked to be fifty yards away. Marsh had been in similar colossal structures when his family had toured England, but never had he seen one that was so foreboding. So ominous. So dead. Rows of wooden pews stretched all the way to the front, defining the aisles: one directly down the center, one to either side of that, and two more along the left and right walls.

Where did Press say the tomb was? The left aisle? The right aisle? Marsh swore at himself for not remembering. He stood quietly, hoping to hear Damon moving about but the old church was as quiet as a tomb.

Or many tombs.

As terrified as he was, his hope grew. Damon couldn't have found Brennus's prison, or Marsh surely would have heard the sounds of him breaking into it. All he could think to do was find the tomb and stand guard as best as he could and hope that Coop and Press would soon be there. Before moving, he picked up a broken chunk of wood that was once the leg of a chair. It was the only weapon he could find.

He started to walk down the center aisle, feeling vulnerable. Damon could be hiding anywhere, watching him from the shadows. He chose instead to move to the far side and keep a wall at his back. He walked cautiously to his right, trying not to create too loud a footfall, but every time his toe touched the floor, it felt as though he were creating a booming echo that reverberated off the stone walls.

He reached the far side and, with his shoulder to the wall, slowly moved forward. As with the cathedrals in Europe, he passed by several stone crypts that were built into the walls. He didn't understand the practice of creating such garish displays for the dead. A statue to a revered person would have been plenty. Why did they have to have their bodies stuck right into the walls? It seemed barbaric. Most of the crypts had ancient writing that he couldn't read. It seemed to be some form of Old English. Or Celtic. Or whatever. All he knew was that he couldn't decipher any of it. He held out hope that he would come upon one that simply said BRENNUS, but that didn't seem likely.

Complicating matters was that there were hundreds of crypts covering the walls and the floors. If he had any hope of finding Brennus's prison, he would have to trust in what the Watcher told them. He would have to just "know."

He remembered that Press said the tomb was in the floor. That reduced the number of possibilities by at least two thirds. He passed over several rectangular sections that were flush with the floor but were actually inlaid tomb coverings.

None of the inscriptions were any easier to decipher than the ones on the walls. Marsh had the brief hope that Damon would have just as much trouble figuring out where Brennus was. Maybe neither of them would find the tomb before the cavalry arrived. That would have been okay.

He didn't put much faith in that, though.

Farther up the aisle he came upon a heaping of pews that were piled on top of one another as if they were the discarded LEGO toys of a giant. An angry giant. Some were splintered as if split in two by a massive force. Jagged pieces of wood created a sharp labyrinth for him to make his way through. It was as though the pile had been placed there deliberately as a deterrent to keep the curious away.

Marsh felt sure that he was getting closer.

He wove his way through the jutting points of splintered wood until he came to an area where only a few broken pieces were scattered on the floor. Marsh stepped forward and scanned the space, realizing that it was a clearing of sorts and he was surrounded by a wall made of splintered seats. The pews formed a ring, perhaps to act as a final, defensible barricade. Marsh stepped to the dead center to see that the barrier had been arranged around a tomb in the floor that looked to be about seven feet long and four feet wide and was covered by scattered pieces of broken pews.

Marsh knelt down on one knee and put his palm on the corner of the marble slab. It was warm. He reached forward, grabbed the edge of a long wooden plank, and pulled it aside to reveal the inscription. In simple three-inch-high letters was inscribed:

JAMES BRENNUS 1642–

It confirmed what he already sensed: The sin eater was imprisoned below.

His mind raced to the next step. Damon would surely find the tomb. Marsh would have to protect it until Cooper and Press got there. He clutched the splintered chair leg and looked around for something else to use as a weapon. He knew that anything he might find would be pathetic compared to the poleax, but he had to try. He grabbed another length of sharp wood off the floor, and froze. Something had dropped onto the back of his hand. Something wet. Had it started to rain? Did it rain in the Blood?

Marsh slowly looked up to see where it had come from . . .

. . . and saw that he wasn't alone. Leaning over the balcony railing, staring down at him from above, were a dozen of the hollow-eyed demons. Drool fell from their open mouths. They had been watching him the whole time.

Marsh clutched the chair leg, ready to fight, as the monsters vaulted over the railing.

Outside the cathedral the figments were tiring.

The spirits who were defending the cathedral had been spurred on by the arrival of Press, their spiritual mentor, and were finally able to push the demons back toward the river. Every inch of ground was hard fought, but the demons were losing.

Press was attacked from behind by two of the small monsters. He spun quickly, flinging one off before rapping it on the side of the head with his stave. The second grabbed him around the throat. Press went with it. He fell into a backward somersault, crushing the little monster with his body weight and then continuing the roll to his feet, bringing the stave around again and knocking the demon senseless.

Coop saw the whole thing and ran to join Press.

"Nice," he declared. "I didn't think Watchers went there."

Press shrugged. "I guess that's your answer."

"Answer to what?"

"To why I'm the one who gets these jobs."

Coop was impressed.

"Where's Damon?" Press asked.

Their conversation ended when the banshees made a last-ditch assault, charging en masse. Coop and Press were ready, Press with his stave and Coop with the powerless black sword. Together with the spirit guards, they stood their ground and drove the small demons back to the water. Several fell in and floundered while others boarded their flat-bottom boats and paddled away quickly.

Press and Coop stood together on the shore, breathing hard, then looked to each other.

"Damon," Press declared.

Coop glanced to the lake and boat the they had arrived in. The empty boat.

"Yeah," he added. "And Marsh."

Marsh swung the wooden chair legs wildly and managed to knock a few of the figments back, but it was a futile effort. There were too many of them. One grabbed his arm and wrenched the weapon from his hand while another threw him to the ground and held him on his back. Others quickly pinned Marsh's arms. The figment on top of him leaned in close and smiled, revealing sharpened teeth.

Marsh struggled but the best he could hope for was to keep his mind from snapping.

The demon opened its jaws wide and leaned in, ready to take a bite out of Marsh's cheek.

"Enough!" Damon commanded.

The figment snapped its mouth shut, angered that it had missed out on its snack. It jumped off Marsh's chest, revealing to him that Damon was standing on the far side of the tomb.

"It seems your family is quite skilled at finding hidden tombs," Damon said, bemused.

Marsh struggled to lift his head but the demons kept his arms pinned to the floor.

"Of course I would have found it eventually," Damon said. "But it is so much more poetic that you have saved me the trouble."

The warrior strode around the edges of the tomb, gazing down at the marble covering. He let the point of the poleax scrape across its surface. The sharp hiss of blade on stone filled the empty cathedral.

"Interesting," Damon said thoughtfully. "I expected the poleax to slice through this effortlessly."

"Don't do it," Marsh begged. "You're not going to prove anything by destroying the Morpheus Road."

"I disagree," Damon replied. "I am the champion of those spirits in the Black who no longer accept the unfair judgment of supposed superior spirits. I am their redeemer. And to the spirits in the Blood, I will be their avenger."

"But you're just using them," Marsh argued.

"We all have something to gain," Damon said. "As does Brennus."

"And what if he doesn't go along with your plan?" Marsh asked.

Damon smiled and said, "Let us find out."

He gripped the poleax with both hands, raised it high overhead, and brought the chopping blade down hard.

The sharp metal edge hit the marble tomb, cracking the surface.

Cooper and Press sprinted through the garden, headed for the cathedral. Alone. The spirit guards had remained by the shore to prevent the figments from circling back.

They hit the bottom of the stairs that led up to the front door and climbed quickly. When they were nearly to the top, they were met by Sanger, who leaned casually against the frame of the open door.

"Hello, boys," Sanger said calmly. "I'm afraid you're a wee bit late."

Cooper ran right up to the old man and grabbed him by the collar.

Sanger didn't fight him.

"I'm coming back for you," Coop growled.

Sanger gave him a smile full of yellowed teeth. "I'll be waitin'."

Cooper threw him aside as he and Press continued on into the cathedral.

Marsh struggled to free himself from the grip of the figments but it was futile. All he could do was watch in horror as Damon chopped away at the tomb.

The poleax may not have had spiritual power in the Blood, but it was strong enough to break through the marble seal. Damon whaled away as if possessed. Bits of marble flew everywhere as the surface cracked and crumbled. Each strike was painful for Marsh. It was further proof that once again he had failed.

"Stop!" Coop shouted as he and Press dodged through the piles of benches.

The demons holding Marsh were confused. Should they stay with Marsh? Or go for the intruders?

Coop and Press jumped into the clearing. Coop went right to help Marsh, swinging his sword, scattering the figments like cockroaches.

Marsh rolled away, and Coop helped him to his feet.

"You okay?" Coop asked.

Marsh nodded.

Press raised his stave threateningly toward Damon, who had stopped chopping and stood on the far side of the tomb, his chest heaving.

"And who is this?" Damon said through gasps. "Another misguided soul who has taken pity on those annoying boys?"

"You have no idea what you're doing," Press warned.

"Oh I think I do," Damon said with a smile. "The question is, do *you* know what I'm doing?"

With that he lifted the poleax high and brought it down hard, crashing through the last of the marble seal and sending the shattered pieces falling into the depths of the tomb below.

The prison door was open.

Nobody moved. Nobody spoke. All eyes were on the dark hole in the floor. Even the figments crowded together to stare in wonder.

Damon stood over the hole, staring down, his eyes alive with anticipation.

The only one not looking into the depths was Press. He didn't need to. He knew what was inside.

"You'll regret this," Press said to Damon.

Damon didn't take his eyes off the open tomb.

"Brennus!" he called down to the depths. "Come! Take your place by my side as we—"

A shadow leaped up and out of the hole, landing directly in front of Damon.

Marsh took a stunned step backward.

Coop gasped, "Oh jeez. This isn't good."

The sin eater was free.

21

Marsh couldn't be sure if he was looking at the spirit of a human or an animal.

The spirit called Brennus stood hunched over, his back twisted into an unnatural hump. Though he stood on two feet he could easily reach down to walk on all fours. Tangled gray hair fell over his shoulders, joining a straggle of long gray beard. His skin was shriveled and brown, looking more like a dried leather shoe than human flesh. He wore the clothes of a peasant farmer, with dark ragged pants and a cloth coat that hung in shreds to below his knees. His feet were bare and filthy, his toenails clawlike. His hands were twisted like tree roots with fingers that overlapped arthritically. As grotesque as he looked, he appeared frail, as if a slight breeze would knock him over.

His eyes told a different story. They were sharp and alert. And angry.

Damon was momentarily taken aback at the sight but quickly regained his composure and announced, "Welcome back to the Blood."

Brennus didn't acknowledge Damon. His gaze bore directly at Press.

Coop looked between the two.

"Dude," he whispered to Press. "That guy's got some serious hate on for you."

Press returned Brennus's gaze, unwavering. "You've been given a second chance, Brennus," he said. "Make no mistake, you can end up back in there just as easily."

Damon took a threatening step toward Press.

"Who are you to interfere?" Damon asked with arrogance.

"He's a Watcher," Coop said.

Damon froze. He hadn't expected that answer.

"Surprise," Coop added.

Damon was left momentarily speechless, but regained his composure quickly and strode back to Brennus.

"Ignore him," Damon said to the sin eater. "He has no power here."

Press and Brennus remained with their gazes locked like two gunslingers.

Press said, "If the spirits of the Blood wish it, you can remain free, but only if you agree to exist in peace."

Brennus's response was heavy, wheezy breathing.

Damon moved quickly and stood between the two.

"You have no control here!" he shouted to Press. "I have freed Brennus to join me in my quest."

His words finally caught Brennus's attention. The crippled spirit shuffled slowly toward Damon, the bones in his back cracking and crunching with every movement.

Marsh winced, imagining the pain.

"*Yer* quest?" Brennus asked in a soft, pained whisper.

"I know of your failed mission," Damon said. "You have

gathered many followers. I need them. Once joined with my own army, I will lead them straight up the Morpheus Road."

"How?" Brennus asked, his voice like gravel on sandpaper.

Damon raised the poleax and exclaimed, "I have the power to tear down the walls between worlds."

Press leaned toward Marsh and whispered, "Go to the front of the cathedral. Tell me what you see outside."

"What? Why?" Marsh replied.

"Just go," Press commanded.

Marsh turned and ran.

Coop asked Press, "What's that about?"

Press's answer was to take a firm hold on his wooden stave.

Coop noticed and grasped the handle of his own sword.

Brennus's breathing grew rapid. He let out short, quick gasps that turned into a painful laugh. He looked back to Press and said, "This be true?"

Press didn't reply.

"Of course it is!" Damon announced. "My army waits in the Black for my return along with—"

Brennus threw up a gnarled hand, silencing Damon.

Damon was so stunned that someone would dare show him such disrespect that he actually fell silent.

Brennus glared at Press. "You knew it be coming to this."

Press shrugged. "It's why I'm still here."

"You will address me!" Damon bellowed. "Both of you!"

They ignored him.

"Enough," Damon said, his frustration growing. He motioned to the figments and commanded, "Seize the weapons of the Watcher and the boy!"

The demons didn't move.

Damon lifted the poleax threateningly and shouted, "Now!"

The figments moved, but not toward Press and Cooper. They quickly gathered together and moved behind Brennus.

"Uh-oh," Coop muttered.

Marsh ran up, wide-eyed and out of breath.

"They're coming!" he announced frantically.

"Who is?" Coop asked.

"Spirits. Thousands of them. They're appearing out in the garden and headed this way."

"Wonderful!" Damon exclaimed. "Exactly what I expected."

Brennus again looked to Press and said, "Did ya really think there be any other way?"

"No," Press replied, resigned. "I didn't. This will end badly."

Brennus smiled, revealing blackened, cracked teeth. "I be counting on it."

"Time to go," Press said to the boys.

"Where?" Marsh asked.

"Anywhere but here," Press replied, and leaped forward, jumping over the empty tomb, headed toward the rear of the cathedral.

Marsh and Cooper were right behind him.

"Stop them!" Damon commanded the figments.

Two demons made a move for Press and regretted it. Press expertly jabbed the end of his stave into the first, then flicked the pole to the right and knocked the second off its hairy feet.

"Damn," was all Coop could utter, totally impressed.

The front doors of the cathedral crashed open as spirits began pouring in. They were the restless damned of a dozen centuries, moving forward together as if being drawn by an unseen, irresistible force.

"Perfect," Damon whispered at the grisly sight.

Press, Cooper, and Marsh ran past the circle of pews and deeper into the cathedral.

"Who are they?" Coop asked as they dodged chunks of fallen ceiling that lay in piles on the stone floor.

"Brennus's followers," Press replied. "They sensed his release."

"How many are there?" Marsh asked.

"You don't want to know," was Press's sobering answer.

Coop added, "And now they've got a ticket out of the Blood."

His words stung Marsh. Up until that moment the threat of Damon marching an army back along the Morpheus Road was just a frightening concept. Seeing Brennus's army of the damned had made it all too real. The war that could bring about doomsday was beginning to take shape and all because he had given Damon the poleax.

They ran through winding corridors until they came upon a door that led out of the cathedral. Stepping outside, they entered a ghost town straight out of the Old West.

Coop glanced back and announced, "They're not coming after us."

The three slowed but kept moving along the dusty, deserted street while casting quick glances back to make sure they weren't being followed.

"How did the spirits stop Brennus before?" Marsh asked Press.

"When I first came to the Blood, he was preparing for a major battle. He wasn't expecting a small group of spirits to challenge him. It wasn't hard for the few spirits who opposed him to get close enough to wrestle him into that tomb."

"Okay, cool. Let's do that again," Coop exclaimed.

"This time he'll be ready," Press said. "We'd never get close to him."

"But we have to do something," Coop exclaimed. "Did you see that guy? I don't know what evil looks like, but if there was a picture in the dictionary—"

"We fight," Marsh announced with such adamancy that it made the others stop moving.

"Fight?" Coop exclaimed. "He's got an army. We don't. Do we?"

Press answered, "There are spirits in the Blood who oppose Brennus, but rallying enough of them to oppose a force like that . . . I don't see it."

"I'm not talking about finding an army in the Blood," Marsh said. "We already have one . . . in the Black."

Coop laughed sarcastically. "You can't be serious. There's no way we'd convince the Guardians to come into the Blood. I still can't believe *we* did it."

"They wouldn't have to," Marsh said.

Coop stared at Marsh, uncomprehending.

"What are you thinking, Marsh?" Press asked.

"The Guardians protected a Rift for centuries. They can do it again. Zoe could bring them to the mouth of the Rift between the Black and the Blood and stop Brennus's army from coming through. The spirit swords don't work in the Blood. But in the Black . . ."

"We could wipe them out the moment they stepped through," Coop said, finishing the thought. "It's a small battlefield. The width of the Rift. Totally controllable."

Marsh added, "And it's not like Damon can create another Rift. The poleax is useless here."

"What about Damon's soldiers in the Black?" Coop asked.

"Damon isn't there to lead them," was Marsh's answer.

"Jeez," Coop said. "Could this work?"

They both looked to Press, who stared at the ground, thinking.

"C'mon, man," Coop cajoled. "Unless you've got some higher-spirit kind of idea, I'm thinking this is our best chance."

Press took a deep breath and said, "It would mean the destruction of so many souls."

"Not as many as if Damon marched an entire army back into the Black," Marsh said.

Press nodded thoughtfully and said, "I never thought I'd see the day."

"What day is that?" Marsh asked.

"The day I'd leave the Blood."

"Bonus!" Coop exclaimed. "You get sprung from Trouble Town. Maybe you can get some of your Watcher friends to give us a hand, like the one who gave you that stick."

"That won't happen," Press said adamantly.

"Then, all the more reason to get out of here," Marsh said. "It really is up to us."

Press looked to the two boys, and smiled. "I'm not entirely sure why you two guys got involved in this, but I'm glad you did."

"That makes one of us," Coop said. "Can we leave now?"

Press led the group quickly back through the Blood. Though there was no map and no obvious route through the haunted world, all three knew they were headed in the right direction. They passed through empty towns and crumbled cities, past toppled Mayan pyramids and barren forests, with no obvious borders between visions.

"This is strange," Marsh observed.

"You're just figuring that out?" Coop replied.

"Why hasn't Brennus tried to stop us?" Marsh asked. "If he's got followers everywhere, why haven't we run into any?"

Coop scanned the surroundings. Up until that moment the spirits of the Blood had been everywhere, wandering through the visions like the lost souls they were. Now not a single spirit could be seen.

"Jeez," Coop declared, looking around. "Where did everybody go?"

"They're moving toward Brennus," Press said.

"All of them?" Coop declared. "How's that possible? The Blood looks deserted!"

The implication was sobering.

"How many Guardians do you think Zoe and my mom can gather?" Marsh asked Coop.

"I don't know. Enough. I hope."

None of them said what they were thinking: *How many was enough?*

It wasn't long before they saw the silhouette of the Flavian Amphitheater and entered the wreckage of the once mighty stadium.

"There," Marsh said, pointing to the gash in the wall that was the Rift.

"That's it?" Press asked. "Simple as that?"

"Be careful when you go through," Coop said. "There might be some of Damon's Roman pals waiting for us." He held up the black sword and added, "And on the other side, these things have juice."

The three hurried right up to the tear through dimensions. Press stopped and looked back, taking one last look at the ghastly world.

"Don't tell me you're getting nostalgic," Coop said.

"In a strange way I am," Press answered. "I accepted my fate and made the best of it. It's possible to find beauty everywhere, even in the most horrific place that exists."

"I'll take your word for it," Coop said. "You can visit anytime you'd like."

"I'll pass on that," Press said. "Let's go."

Press held his stave up and ready, Coop raised his sword, and the three stepped into the Rift.

They kept moving forward, though it didn't seem like they were walking. In no time they approached the jagged gray shape that was the other side of the Rift. It grew larger as they drew near, rising up higher than their heads. Without a word, they all moved through . . .

. . . and stepped into the arena to face three Roman soldiers.

"Let's go!" Coop declared.

He immediately went for the soldier closest to him, attacking violently.

The soldier could only lift his shield to protect himself. He knew what the black sword could do.

Press went to work on the other two soldiers. They were more aggressive with him, for they didn't fear his wooden stave. Press swung left, clipping one, then ducked down and swung the stave low, knocking out the other soldier at the knees.

"Why are we fighting?" Coop called. "Go to your vision!"

"How?" Marsh exclaimed.

Coop ran to him and grabbed his arm as the colorful swirl appeared in front of them.

"You'll learn," Coop declared, and all three stepped into the fog.

22

Sydney had to force herself to drive safely.

Getting into a wreck while careening around a corner doing eighty wouldn't have done anybody any good. Least of all her. Still, she pressed her silver Volkswagen Beetle to the limits of her driving ability and prayed that she wouldn't be pulled over. It helped that she was headed to the remote northern end of Stony Brook, where traffic cops rarely patrolled.

She was angry at her brother, which wasn't unusual. In this case it was because he had the ability to get to Marsh long before she could. He was a spirit and she had to rely on common old ground transportation. She knew it was silly to be angry at him for that but she needed to be angry at someone and Coop was always a solid choice. She originally wanted him to ride in the car with her but agreed that speed was what mattered, so he vanished and went on his ghostly way while she was left to negotiate the winding roads of town in the hope that she wasn't too late to stop Marsh from doing whatever he planned on doing.

The taxi dispatcher said that a cab had taken him to Stony Brook cemetery. She didn't relish the idea of going back there alone, but if that's where Marsh was headed, that's where she needed to be.

It was late in the afternoon when she rolled through the front gates, relieved to see that they hadn't yet been closed for the day. She parked the car near a work shed, hoping nobody would notice that there was a late visitor. She wasn't in the mood to offer explanations, or to walk through the lonely cemetery, for that matter, but the fear of what might be happening to Marsh trumped any other concerns.

"Cooper?" she whispered to nobody, hoping that her brother's spirit might be watching over her.

There was no answer, ghostly or otherwise, so she steeled herself and walked quickly for her brother's grave. It was the only place she could think of to go.

She arrived without incident. It was an odd experience to be standing over Cooper's grave. He had been buried only a few weeks before, which was enough time for young grass to begin poking up through the turned soil. Though her brother's broken body lay several feet beneath the earth, it was hard to feel sadness. She was too busy dealing with his spirit, which was every bit as arrogant and obnoxious as his living self. It gave her a strange feeling of comfort to know that life didn't end with the death of one's living body.

Though, given recent events, she wasn't entirely sure how much longer anybody would be able to rest in peace. Anywhere.

"You here?" Sydney called out. "Hey? Anybody?"
No answer.

It wasn't a huge surprise. She couldn't think of a single reason why Marsh would have come to Cooper's grave. She was only there because she didn't know where else to go. Sydney was smart. Brilliant. The answers to so many questions that had been plaguing her since the adventure began felt tantalizingly close. It was frustrating for her not to be able to grasp them. As she stood over her brother's grave, she rolled the events of the summer over in her head. Why would Marsh come to the cemetery? He didn't have to hang out there to speak with Cooper. Even in death, Coop was never far away. No, he wasn't there because of Cooper, but he might have been there because of Ennis Mobley.

Ennis had been buried in the same cemetery that very day. Was that why Marsh had come? Sydney had no idea where Ennis's grave was and knew she wouldn't find it on her own. She decided to find somebody who worked there and hope they had a directory of the dead.

She had started back toward the parking lot, her mind still churning, when her eye caught sight of something that was oddly familiar. It was a mausoleum. She had almost forgotten about the one other time she had been to this cemetery. It was for Marsh's mother's funeral. She hadn't wanted to go but the Seavers were close friends and her parents insisted she be there, so she sucked it up and went, and hated every second of it. As much as she hadn't wanted to be at the sad service, her heart went out to Marsh who stood next to his mother's coffin in the lower level of the mausoleum. It pained her then, and it pained her now to think about the chain of events that his mother's death had set in motion. So much sadness. So many deaths. Cooper, George O., Mr. Reilly, and now Ennis Mobley.

Sydney stopped short. Her mind went back to Terri Seaver's funeral. She remembered standing in the back of the small group that had gone into the mausoleum for the interment. She had to stand up on tiptoes to see what was happening near the crypt. The priest had mumbled some prayers, then Ennis Mobley stepped forward and put something that looked like a tangle of branches on top of the coffin, announcing to the gathered that it was "the wood of life."

Lignum vitae.

Ennis's last words to Marsh.

Sydney turned quickly and sprinted for the mausoleum. She blasted through the trees and ran up the marble steps to the front door. Did they lock these things? She pulled on the handle, and the door swung open easily. She remembered the place all too well, and why not? It was the only mausoleum she had ever been in. She hurried through the meditation area and went right to the door that led down the stairs to the crypt where Marsh's mother was interred. The door leading to the stairs wasn't locked either. That meant one of two things: Either they didn't bother locking the place, or somebody had opened them recently.

"Marsh?" she cried, hurrying down the stairs.

She hit the floor . . . and froze. Her heart went into her throat. Sydney didn't know what she expected to find down there, but it wasn't what she saw in front of her.

A coffin lay on the floor, having been pulled from a destroyed tomb. The lid was open. Lying in a heap on the floor next to it was the owner. Sydney swallowed hard. Was she looking at the remains of Terri Seaver?

She forced herself to step forward to take a closer look. Fighting back fear and a twisted stomach, she stared down at the remains . . . and realized the truth. Whoever the skeleton was, it wasn't Marsh's mom. It was definitely a man.

"What the hell?" she whispered.

Lying next to the remains was the tangle of branches that Ennis had placed on the coffin.

Lignum vitae.

The coffin belonged to Ree Seaver, though the skeleton did not.

As grisly a sight as that was, it didn't affect her as much as the sight of the glowing tear in the wall of crypts. She may not have seen one before, but she knew exactly what it was. She was too late. Damon had the poleax and had torn open another Rift into the Black.

Sydney backed away in a daze from the grisly scene. The pieces of the puzzle were falling quickly into place. Ennis's last words to Marsh had led him to the truth. The poleax had been hidden in his mother's grave. It made total sense. Ennis had brought the poleax back from Greece in the coffin. He wanted to keep it away from Damon and gave Marsh the crucibles for protection. But Damon was too smart. He killed Cooper, haunted Marsh, and tortured Ennis until he got what he wanted.

Sydney stood looking into the glowing portal in awe of the fact that it was a conduit into the afterlife. What had happened? Where was Marsh? And Cooper? And for that matter . . . Damon? There was no way of knowing.

Or was there?

She took a step closer and gazed into eternity. The playing field was no longer in the Light. It had moved into the Black. She figured Cooper was there, doing his best to hunt down Damon. But where was Marsh?

She took another step closer to the portal. The answers were just beyond its glowing border. The Black. The stories she heard from Cooper sounded as if it was an incredible place, a place out of your own imagination and experience. You could meet and interact with spirits from every time. When the time came for her to enter the Black, she would see her grandparents again. And her aunt Theresa. Or even President Kennedy! She wondered if you would be reunited with your pets. She wouldn't have minded cuddling up with her cat Abigail one more time. Even if it was an illusion. The Black seemed like a place full of nothing but possibilities. You could correct your mistakes and become the best possible person you were capable of being. No more pressure. No more expectations to live up to. It could be whatever you wanted it to be. It didn't make sense to her that Damon was trying so hard to come back into the uncertainty of the Light when the Black had so much more going for it.

Sydney stepped even closer, mesmerized by the glow from within. It would be so simple to step inside and begin her own adventure. Everyone had to do it sooner or later. Everyone walked the Morpheus Road. She stood inches from the opening and put her hand on the marble wall of the crypt. It felt solid. And real. What lay beyond was just as real. Maybe more so. Answers to so many questions lay just beyond the opening. She tried to focus deeper inside to see if she could make out shapes. She looked up, to the sides, and then down.

What she saw on the floor just beyond the edge of the Rift made her catch her breath and jump back.

It was a hand. A lifeless hand. She got down onto her knees and peered into the bright light to see if she could see who it belonged to.

"Marsh!" she exclaimed.

Marsh's lifeless body lay just beyond the opening of the Rift. Sydney fought panic and acted out of instinct rather than logic. She reached inside, grabbed Marsh's wrist, and dragged him out into the mausoleum.

She put her head to his chest, hoping to hear a heartbeat . . . and didn't. His skin was still warm to the touch, but his spirit had left his body. For the first time in her life, Sydney lost control and broke down sobbing. She had gotten the answer to one of her questions and wished she hadn't. The room seemed to spin beneath her.

"Are you here?" she cried, looking around the tomb.

"Are you with me? Talk to me. Cooper? Where is he?"

There were no answers. Sydney was alone. She sat with Marsh's head in her lap for a good long time, weeping. In the span of a few short weeks she had lost two people who couldn't have been any closer to her. It made her feel painfully alone. She looked up to the Rift, staring into the inviting light.

Gently resting Marsh's head down onto the marble floor, she stood up on shaky legs and walked toward the opening. She wanted to see Marsh again, not just his body. She wanted to hold him. She even wanted to hold Cooper. The two meant everything to her and she couldn't imagine being without them. Not anymore. Never before had she felt so utterly powerless and alone.

She took a step closer to the gash, ready to step through . . . when she stopped.

There was a weight in her jacket pocket. A familiar weight. It made her remember that there was more going on than simple life and death. There was so much more at stake. She remembered that as lonely as she felt at that moment, she wasn't. If she had learned anything over the past few weeks, it was that she would never be alone.

She knew the right thing to do.

Sydney knelt down and slipped her arms under Marsh's body. It was an awkward struggle, but she managed to lift him enough so that she could slide him back through the Rift. Once she was certain that every part of him was beyond the threshold, she reached out and grabbed the lignum vitae sculpture that was resting against the coffin. She stood up, faced the Rift, and wiped her eyes.

"I don't know how you died," she called into the Rift, her voice shaking. "It might have been Damon or it might have been your own choice. But I know that one way or another, I'll see you again. We're fighting to save the Morpheus Road and I'm the only one left in the Light who knows that. I'm here. I'm ready to do whatever it takes."

She reached into her pocket . . .

"I think you guys need this more than I do."

. . . and took out the sixth crucible.

The last crucible.

"I love you guys," she said.

She grasped the crucible, kissed it . . . and rolled it into the Rift.

23

Damon stood high on the altar of the cathedral, hands on hips, proudly observing the impressive influx of spirits. They flowed into the ruins by the hundreds, filling the grand space. Thousands more followed, unable to enter the already overcrowded structure. The number of damned spirits that had been drawn to the cathedral dwarfed any army Damon had commanded in life, or in death. By comparison the loyal minions who fought for him in the Black seemed pitifully inadequate. Though they had triumphed over the Guardians, those spirits had been sent to the Blood by the uncharacteristic interference of the Watchers.

He had lost a battle but was confident he would soon win a war.

The spirits would bow at his feet, he knew that. He would then galvanize the horrific force and march them to the Rift, where they would join the spirits in the Black that he had lured to the vision of the emperor Titus. Most important, unlike every other battle he had been involved with, he planned to be at the forefront of this combined army. Brandishing his poleax, he would fulfill his true destiny. He would lead his troops into a glorious battle, charging through the visions of those who once questioned his bravery. They would all be mercilessly destroyed but not before kissing his feet and declaring his superiority. When they begged for pity, he would drive the poleax into their bodies, relishing their momentary flash of pain while making sure they understood that their existence had ended . . . by his hand.

Once victory was assured in the Black, he would turn his army on the true prize.

The Light.

The scenario he had played over in his mind for centuries was no longer a dream. Revenge was at hand. Glory was at hand. His patience had been rewarded.

Brennus stood beneath Damon, also observing the arrival of the throng. It seemed impossible that he could even stand, given the unnatural angle of his misshapen spine. He leaned on a gnarled crutch, his knuckles white from gripping its handle.

Damon wondered how best to use this twisted spirit. There was no doubt that the arriving spirits had come in response to his release from captivity. Brennus had done his job well. He had created a movement . . . a yearning for vengeance and freedom. But ultimately he had failed. He could not provide the leadership of a warrior. It made Damon's confidence swell even further. Whatever slights he had received in life had only prepared him for this moment. He was meant to be there and to offer these cursed souls what Brennus could not.

He was going to lead them back to life.

The cathedral was packed, though strangely silent. Damon scanned the thousands of faces and saw their resolution. They were ripe. They wanted direction. He chuckled to himself, remembering the reaction he elicited from the spirits in the Colosseum when he had told them exactly what they wanted to hear. He had fired their passions to the point where they wanted nothing more than to follow him into battle. It was time to do the same to the spirits of the Blood.

He raised his arms as if to embrace the assemblage.

"Welcome!" he bellowed. "One and all. Your torment is about to end. I have come to lead you from an existence you have been so unjustly forced to accept and bring you to a better place. The Blood will be no more. We will never again return to this hell. The opportunity is upon us. Follow me and fight for your life. Fight for your future. Fight for the Light!"

He stretched his arms out, waiting for the crowd to erupt with wildly enthusiastic cheers. Instead he was answered with silence. Each and every spirit stared up at him silently, as if not understanding what he was saying.

Brennus shuffled to the stairs leading up to the altar where Damon stood. He dragged one foot behind him and had to lean on his crutch for support. Damon did not make a move to help him as the old spirit made his way slowly and painfully up the steps toward him.

Damon addressed the crowd again, saying, "My first goal has been achieved. I have freed Brennus. What he promised you, I am now prepared to deliver. He has brought you here and I will lead you on. Thank you, Brennus. Your dream of freedom is about to be realized."

The crowd remained silent.

Damon looked about, confused. They had come because

of Brennus, but invoking his name brought no reaction. Were these spirits capable of understanding? Could they even hear?

Brennus shuffled up to Damon and stood uncomfortably close to him. His breathing was raspy. Climbing the few stairs had taken an immense amount of effort.

"I give you Brennus!" Damon shouted. "He has been your heart; now I will be your soul."

Brennus looked up to Damon through his tangle of gray hair. The old spirit was frail, but the intensity of his gaze froze Damon.

"There be a way into the Black?" Brennus asked, barely above a whisper.

"Yes!" Damon answered, but to the crowd. "I have created the means for us all to leave this nightmare and return to the—"

Brennus flashed his crutch toward Damon, hooking him behind the neck and pulling him down so their eyes met. Damon was so shocked by the audacity and the strength of the move that he didn't resist.

"Where?" Brennus asked.

Damon finally pulled away from the old spirit, his anger rising.

"You dare!" Damon bellowed. "I have freed you. I offer to lead you to glory in the great battle and you lash out?"

Brennus moved quickly, no longer shuffling like a twisted old man. He was on Damon before Damon could defend himself. He grabbed the warrior by the hair and yanked his head down so once again they were on the same level.

The multitude of spirits didn't react.

Damon reached for the poleax but Brennus grabbed his wrist with such strength that Damon feared he would snap bones.

"Hear me words," Brennus hissed. "This not be a battle for glory. There be no noble victory to be won. No wrong to be righted. There be only one thing."

"What is that?" Damon asked, through clenched teeth.

"Escape."

Damon couldn't move. He looked hopefully to the figments who had helped him get there, but the little devils stood impassively. The realization finally dawned on him: He was alone. He had no army and no allies. The glorious battle he had anticipated for centuries was slipping away.

"We have the same goal," Damon argued. "I too wish to escape this horror and lead these spirits to freedom."

Brennus jerked Damon's hair, making him scream.

"Where be the way?" Brennus demanded.

"No," Damon snarled through the pain. "The Rift was of my making. If these spirits are to pass through, I will lead them."

Brennus let go and Damon fell to his knees. Brennus then motioned to the figments, who swarmed in quickly, grabbed Damon, and dragged him away. He struggled to free himself but there were too many hands on him.

"Do not be a fool!" Damon shouted. "Only I can lead you to the Rift to join my army in the Black."

The figments dragged Damon down off the altar. Damon dug in his heels but he was no match for the little demons.

Brennus watched impassively.

"I freed you!" he shouted to Brennus, his desperation growing.

Brennus looked down on him from above and said, "What is it you want, then? Gratitude? Reward? Justice? You be in hell now. Those words be having no meaning."

"Then you will rot here, for I will not reveal the location of the Rift!" Damon shouted back defiantly.

Damon looked around desperately for anyone who

might help him and caught sight of Sanger, who stood on the edge of the crowd with his arms folded.

"Where have you been?" Damon demanded. "Do you see what's been happening to me?"

"I do," Sanger said with a sly smile. "Ain't nothing compared to what's *about* to happen to ya."

Sanger motioned down to the floor.

Damon followed his gaze and saw that the demons were dragging him toward the open tomb that had been Brennus's prison. Several more banshees appeared with a perfectly milled slab of stone . . . just the right size to seal the opening of the tomb.

"No!" Damon screamed to Brennus. "You dare not imprison me!"

The figments held Damon on the edge of the tomb. He struggled desperately but it was no use.

Sanger stepped up to him and pulled the poleax from its sheath.

Damon's eyes blazed with anger as he was relieved of his precious weapon, but he was helpless to stop it.

Sanger held the point of the weapon to Damon's neck.

"Don't be a fool," Sanger whispered. "You may have been the nastiest fella to walk the face of the earth, but you're just one man." Sanger motioned to Brennus and added, "With him, you're dealing with the sins of thousands. Don't fight it. Just go along. Like I did. Like they all did. Ain't no shame in following somebody stronger than you."

"No!" Damon screamed. "Damon of Epirus will not bow."

Sanger shrugged and said, "Just as well. You ain't gonna have much room for any bowing in there anyhow."

He nodded to the figments and they roughly tossed Damon into the tomb. Damon fell the few feet down and landed hard. He took one quick look around at the solid walls that would soon be his universe and felt the panic rise. He quickly jumped to his feet and reached up, wrapping his fingers on the edge to try and pull himself out.

"Bad idea," Sanger said as he slashed at Damon's fingers with the poleax.

Damon quickly pulled back and fell to the bottom of the tomb.

"Don't want to go losing fingers," Sanger teased. "It'll be tough enough spending eternity in the dark. Can't imagine not being able to scratch an itch when you get one."

He chuckled at his own cruel joke.

"Do not do this!" Damon shouted to the spirits who stood surrounding the tomb. "I am your only hope. Brennus could not lead you out of the Blood, but I can. Seal me away, and you'll never find your way out."

"Don't be so sure about that," Sanger said. "Might take a while, but we'll find it. That is, if it really exists."

"It does! My followers are on the far side, waiting to form an army for the ages."

The figments laid the stone slab down and began sliding it over the opening, slowly cutting Damon off.

"Sounds promising," Sanger said. "Too bad you won't be around to see it."

The figments slid the stone over the marble floor, scraping it into position.

"It isn't just about the Black!" Damon shouted in desperation. "I can bring you back to the Light. To life! Brennus cannot say that."

"Good night," Sanger said.

"Wait!" Damon shouted in tears.

Sanger held up his hand. He looked down at Damon without pity and said, "If you got something to say that means something, better say it now."

Damon was breathing hard, his eyes wild. He looked up

to Sanger but the old spirit showed no hint of compassion.

"All right," Damon said through tortured gasps. "All right. I will bring you there."

Brennus made his way down off the altar and dragged himself to the edge of the tomb, where he glared down at Damon.

"Now," Brennus wheezed.

24

"You gotta do something," Cooper railed. "Talk to the guy in charge. Make the case. The Watchers shut down one Rift already. If they did it again, this would be over."

"It doesn't work that way," Press replied. "There's nobody in charge. No governing council. No king. No president. I know that's hard to understand but it's the way it is."

"You're talking all normal, like a regular spirit," Foley said to Press. "You sure you're a Watcher?"

"Yeah, pretty sure," Press replied.

"Who *are* the Watchers?" Maggie asked.

"I told you before, we're you. We exist because mankind exists."

"Well, that's all nice and cosmic," Coop snarled. "But if you don't step in, then mankind might not exist much longer, so you're in just as much trouble as the rest of us."

"I understand that," Press said softly. "And I'm here to help, but do not expect any more than that."

They had gathered in Zoe's vision in the small house in Greece where she had lived as a girl. Also there were Ree Seaver, Maggie Salinger, Eugene Foley, and of course Zoe.

"So where did you come from?" Foley asked. "Where do any of you Watchers come from?"

"The place you're all trying to reach," Press replied. "The end of the Morpheus Road."

"I've been there," Coop spat. "It ain't pretty."

"The other end," Press said with a chuckle.

"Is it heaven?" Maggie asked.

"It's been called that, but it's not really a reward. It's a place that's just . . . right. I don't know how else to describe it. I don't doubt that you'll all see it eventually."

"If we're lucky," Marsh said.

"If we stop Damon," Coop added.

The ominous reality caused everyone to fall silent.

"All right," Coop said, jumping to his feet. "We're on our own. I get it. The only thing we can do is keep Damon from coming back through the Rift. If he doesn't get through, the poleax doesn't get through and he can't tear open any more highways, but there are a whole lot of bogeymen ganging up back there, so it's anybody's guess as to how long we can keep him back."

Marsh said, "The Rift is being guarded on this side by Damon's spirits from the Black. We might not even get to it before Damon starts sending them through."

All eyes went to Ree.

"So?" Coop asked. "That brings us to our last hope. The Guardians. Did you find any of them?"

Ree glanced to Zoe. Zoe gave her a nod and Ree stood up.

"I'd like you all to come with me," she said.

The colorful fog appeared behind her. Ree stepped into it and disappeared. The others followed without question.

Seconds later they found themselves standing in the garage in lower Manhattan where Cooper and Maggie had first encountered the Guardians. The place was empty.

Ree waited until they had all arrived before speaking.

"We lost many of the Guardians during the battle for the Rift," she declared. "It was devastating. Once Damon's soldiers were sent to the Blood, the surviving Guardians scattered and went back to their own visions."

"Their mission was complete," Zoe added. "My father's mission was complete. Though we lost many good spirits, the Rift was no more."

"But things changed," Cooper said.

"Yes," Zoe agreed. "Things changed. I have been through many visions, searching for the remaining Guardians, trying to bring them back together. It was not an easy task."

Coop glanced around the empty garage. "Looks like it was impossible."

"Not impossible," Ree said.

The large garage door leading to the street began to rise, revealing several people standing outside. They stepped into the garage and stood together as a group. Maggie and Cooper recognized a few . . . veterans from the battle for the Rift. There were men and women from many different eras and walks of life, and though they represented widely diverse races and times, they all shared one trait . . . a grim look of determination.

Cooper gave Marsh a dark look. Marsh shrugged.

"That's great," Coop said. "Seriously. I'm glad they're back. But, uh, there's like forty of them. That won't be enough to get past the soldiers at the Rift, let alone fight back an army of thousands. If this is the best we can do, we might as well hang it up right now."

"These are the seeds," Ree said. "They're here to fight, but also to gather those who are willing to do whatever is necessary to save humanity."

Marsh said, "They better get started. Who knows when Damon will start moving through the Rift."

Ree gave her son a smile, touched his cheek, and walked through the group of Guardians toward the open door. Marsh followed and the others fell in behind. Ree led them all outside, where they were greeted by a stunning sight.

The street to both sides of the building was teeming with people.

The crowd stretched in both directions for as far as could be seen. There were soldiers whose uniforms dated back to the American Revolution and others who looked as though they had sacrificed their lives in Iraq and Afghanistan. There were gladiators and policemen, tribal warriors, and many, many civilians. Most were armed with conventional weapons, from swords to rifles to cudgels.

Many also held the black spirit-killing swords. These spirits were the veterans of the last battle with Damon and were fully prepared for the next.

Ree said, "We have all seen the worst that mankind has produced, those who are willing to destroy in order to achieve their goals." She gestured to the huge, silent crowd. "These spirits are the best that mankind has become. They are ready, and they will fight."

It was an awe-inspiring sight . . . the polar opposite of the army that had gathered in the Blood.

Marsh stepped up to Press and said, "Is this what you meant by us having to save ourselves?"

Press looked over the group with a proud smile.

"I've seen it before," he said. "There will always be those who take the dark path. It's part of what we are. But we survive because there are also those who will never bow. Never settle. Never choose to rise at the expense of others. Yes, this is how mankind will save itself."

Coop said, "Then, we better get started."

The first group of Guardians knew what to do. They dispersed through the crowd, breaking the masses down and organizing them into smaller, more manageable teams.

"So many people," Marsh said to nobody in particular. "How is this going to work?"

The answer came from Ree. "Zoe has assumed command."

"Zoe?" Coop said, surprised. "She's, like, a girl."

"I am the daughter of Adeipho," Zoe said sharply, making Coop jump. "I am more than capable of leading the Guardians."

"Okay, okay," Coop said, holding up his hands in defense. "Just askin'."

"What can I expect to find at the amphitheater?" she asked.

"Depends," answered Marsh. "There are only a few guards protecting the Rift but Damon had the place full of spirits ready to follow him. If those spirits rally, we're in for a big fight."

Zoe said, "I do not see a problem. With Damon trapped in the Blood, they have no one to direct them. We will take the Rift. I am more concerned about keeping Damon and his minions from marching through."

"This is all about him," Marsh said. "The only way to end this battle, for good, is to end Damon."

"Agreed," Zoe replied. "But first we must secure the Rift."

As Zoe left to help organize the Guardians into smaller, tactical forces, Cooper pulled Marsh aside.

"What do you think?" Marsh asked.

"I think you were right, Ralph. This is our best chance. Nice going."

"Thanks."

"But it ends here."

"Let's hope so."

"No, I mean for you. I don't want you in this fight."

Marsh bristled. "What? Why?"

"Take Maggie and my grandfather and bring them some-where safe. Maybe back to your own vision. You haven't been there yet. It's a kick. Grab some Garden Poultry fries."

"They can go on their own," Marsh argued. "I'm not missing this."

"You have to."

"Why?"

Cooper hesitated before answering, as if not wanting to say what he felt needed saying.

"Because this isn't you."

"Oh. But it's you?"

"I've been in plenty of fights. Hell, I've already gone toe-to-toe with Damon. I'm looking forward to getting another shot at him."

"If there's anybody who deserves that shot, it's me."

"I know, but don't be stupid. You already dodged one bullet in the Blood. Don't push it. Take Maggie and my grandfather outta here and pray this ends quickly."

Marsh clenched his fists, trying to control his anger. "I told you, I don't need you to take care of me."

"I hear you but this is different. We're talking about an all-out battle. Heck, it's your plan! Be proud . . . but get outta the way."

"He killed my mother, he killed my best friend, he tor-tured me and twisted my life inside out. I can't let that go."

"Nobody's letting it go," Coop argued. "But you already gave up your life in the Light to get this guy. Don't risk los-ing your spirit too."

"That's my choice," Marsh said, and pushed past Cooper, headed back toward the Guardians.

Cooper grabbed him and spun him around.

"C'mon, Ralph—"

Marsh responded by throwing a punch. Coop ducked the punch easily, grabbed Marsh's arm, and twisted it behind his back.

"Don't be an idiot," Coop said.

"I am not leaving," Marsh bellowed with anger and frustration.

"You have to. Take the others and find someplace safe. You've done too much already."

Cooper pushed Marsh away so roughly that Marsh had to scramble to keep from falling down. He got his feet under him, then planted and squared off against Cooper.

"You mean because I gave Damon the poleax," he said, seething.

"That's not what I meant."

"Yeah, it is," Marsh said angrily. "You're afraid I'll do something stupid."

"That's ridiculous—"

"You've done plenty of stupid things too. More than most. But you don't see that. No, not you. You always get out of Trouble Town and end up looking good. Except when you died. That didn't turn out so hot for you, did it?"

"Just shut up, Ralph."

"You shouldn't be part of this either," Marsh added. "He just used you to get to me. This is way bigger than you too, Coop. You don't stand any more of a chance to get to Damon than I do. So maybe we should both just take off and watch this from the sidelines."

"That's not what I do," Coop said soberly.

"It's not what I do either. Not anymore."

Coop strode up to Marsh and held a threatening finger to his face. "Go. Anywhere. Now. I don't care where. Just stay away from this."

Cooper turned on his heel and hurried away.

Marsh was ready to explode. He was so angry at Cooper for so many reasons that he wanted to scream. He paced furiously, drawing the attention of some of the Guardians. He didn't want them to see him like that so he took the few steps down a side street until he was out of sight.

He needed to calm down. He needed a plan. There was no way he would be left out of the endgame. Not after having come so far. He needed to talk to someone who understood . . . who would see his side and help him find the right thing to do.

There was only one person he knew who could help him do that.

25

Damon of Epirus rode high in the saddle at the front of a powerful army that was marching toward a glorious battle. It was everything he had imagined it would be . . .

. . . except that he rode atop a miserable, weak donkey and he had no authority to command the massive spirit army that Brennus had gathered to conquer the Morpheus Road. Glancing back, he saw more soldiers than he had ever commanded in life. Though not an organized military machine, the sheer numbers made him believe it was an unstoppable force that would easily march straight into the Black and destroy the boundaries between life and death . . . without him.

Brennus had given him little choice. Either Damon would direct the army to the Rift or he would be imprisoned and forgotten in the underground tomb. Damon chose to swallow his pride and live to fight another day.

With each step closer to the Rift his anger grew. Digging at his gut was the knowledge that he had only himself to blame. He prided himself on his ability to outmaneuver his adversaries. It was difficult to accept that he had so grossly underestimated Brennus. He wouldn't let that happen again. His chance would come, of that he was certain.

He rode slowly though the Blood, past the ruins of so many lives, deliberately taking his time in the hopes that he might find an opportunity to seize the command he so desperately wanted.

The sin eater traveled several yards behind him, riding in a horse cart that was being pulled by several small figments. He wasn't capable of walking on his own or even riding a horse, because of his grotesquely twisted body. He was flanked on either side by beefy spirits on horseback. No other spirit could get close to Brennus, least of all Damon. Not that it mattered. Damon had no intention of attacking Brennus.

At least not yet.

He needed to get back to the Black. He needed to recharge the poleax. Sanger had returned the weapon to him, knowing it was of little use. Damon vowed that the surly spirit would pay for that mistake.

The shadow of the Flavian Amphitheater appeared in the distance. Time was running out. He made a snap decision. He kicked at the donkey and galloped forward, ready to charge into the Colosseum and through the Rift.

He didn't get far. The pitiful donkey was no runner. The two warriors who were escorting Brennus gave chase and caught up with him quickly. They grabbed his reins and slowed him to a trot, then to a stop. With one escort on either side of him, Damon was pinned in place. He considered pulling the poleax and attacking the two, but realized it was futile and backed down.

The squeaking wheels of the wooden cart signaled Brennus's arrival.

"The Rift be in there?" he asked, glaring at the humiliated general.

Damon didn't respond, which was all the answer that Brennus needed.

"What was it you were trying to do?" Brennus asked. "Get away from me?"

Again, Damon answered by not answering.

Brennus wheezed a disdainful laugh.

Damon gritted his teeth and took the humiliation. He had to wait for his chance.

"You say you was a general?" Brennus asked. "What general flees like a pitiful schoolgirl?"

Damon stared him in the eye, but didn't say a word.

"I have changed me mind," Brennus wheezed. "Ya don' deserve to enter the Black with us."

"What?" Damon screamed, stunned. "We had an agreement."

"And now we don'," Brennus said, and gave a dismissive wave with his gnarled hand.

Instantly the spirit warriors to either side of Damon lifted him off the donkey, dangling him between them.

"Do not be a fool," Damon warned. "You have no idea what waits for you in the Black."

Brennus shook his head in pity. "If they be creatures as wretched as you, I don' expect to be having much trouble at all."

"You will regret this," Damon said, seething with anger as his feet dangled in the air.

"No, I do not believe I will," Brennus said, and waved Damon off.

The two warriors rode together, with Damon between them struggling to get free. They galloped off into the dark, away from the Colosseum and the massive spirit army.

Damon gave up struggling and closed his eyes. Did he hear the spirits laughing? It was the first sign of intelligent life that they had shown, and the ultimate indignity. The worst that humanity had ever produced was mocking him.

Finally, mercifully, the soldiers pulled up and tossed Damon to the ground with no more concern than they would have given to a bag of trash.

Damon fell hard in the dry sand and covered his head so as not to be stomped by the horses' hooves. The spirit soldiers turned quickly and rode back the way they had come without so much as giving a final look back to him.

Damon slowly looked up to see that he had been dumped . . . in a dump. He was surrounded by mounds of putrid garbage that had been accumulating through all time. In the distance, he saw the dark outline of the Colosseum and the mass of spirits that would soon march to the Rift.

Without him.

Marsh learned fast.

He had listened to everything Cooper told him about moving through dimensions. He didn't have time for skepticism, or wonder, or fear. He had to take action so he imagined being at Sydney's house in the Light and stepped through the curtain of colorful fog . . .

. . . to arrive in her bedroom. He didn't stop to marvel at the incredible nature of it all. There would be time for that later—he hoped. He needed support and advice and wanted it from Sydney.

She was sitting at her desk, reading. He allowed himself a moment to watch her. He always thought she was the most beautiful girl he had ever seen. Seeing her with her long black hair falling onto the pages of her book, and her reading light glowing warmly against her pale skin, reminded him that he was the luckiest guy alive.

Except that he wasn't alive.

He suddenly felt like an intruder. He had been in her room plenty of times over the last few weeks but had always been invited. Now he had suddenly popped in as a spirit. Did Sydney even know he was dead? How could she? Suddenly, coming to her room seemed like a bad idea. He made a snap decision and took a step back to get out of there . . .

. . . when Sydney spun around. Marsh froze, feeling like a little boy who had just been caught doing something very wrong.

"Uh, hi," was all he managed to get out.

Sydney stood up and walked quickly toward him.

"I didn't mean to sneak up on you like this but—"

Sydney walked right past him, grabbed a notebook off the table near the door, and went back to her desk. She seemed angry. The last time they had seen each other, they had argued. She had accused him of being no better than Damon, someone who used others to get what he wanted.

Her words stung all the more because he knew they weren't far from the truth.

"A lot has happened," Marsh said. "I need your help."

She ignored him. Marsh expected her to freeze him out for a while longer, make him sweat, then finally give in and talk. He was willing to let her anger play out, but not for too long. Time was wasting. Damon could attack at any time.

"So much of what you said was right," Marsh said. "I've done things I could never imagine myself doing normally. But what's happening isn't. Normal, I mean."

Sydney sighed. Was she softening? Marsh slowly approached her.

"I've got to tell you something," Marsh said. "You're not going to like it. At least I *hope* you're not going to like it."

He stood right behind her.

"I don't know how to soften this, so I'll just say it: I'm dead, Sydney."

He put his hand on her shoulder . . . and it passed right through. He jumped back in surprise.

"Whoa!" he exclaimed.

Sydney didn't react.

"Can you hear me?" Marsh asked.

Sydney stayed focused on her book.

Whatever powers the Watchers had given to Cooper, they hadn't done the same for Marsh. He was a spirit in the Light, unable to be seen by the living. Up until that moment the concept that he was actually dead hadn't truly sunk in. As far as he was concerned he had simply stepped through a portal and arrived in another place where the rules of reality didn't apply. It had seemed like a magical dream.

Being back in the Light made the dream a reality. He was really dead. Not just gone. Dead. He was suddenly hit with a wave of sadness that he wasn't prepared for. It was an overwhelming feeling of emptiness that brought tears to his eyes.

He couldn't help but feel as if he had made another stupendous mistake. He wasn't needed in the Black. Cooper pretty much laid that one out. There was nothing he could do in the Light. Spirits only had the power to visit and observe. He had given up his life, and for what? Punishment for letting Damon get the better of him? Nobody cared about that. The chance to be a hero and make things right? He was powerless to do that. All he had succeeded in doing was to create more pain for those he loved.

Marsh feared that Cooper was right. He wasn't up to this. He could only make things worse.

He had no idea where to go or what to do next. He had hoped that Sydney would help him sort it all out but Sydney was unreachable. He turned to leave the room to go somewhere, anywhere, when his eye caught something incongruous.

Sitting on the end of Sydney's bed was a dark tangle of branches that looked oddly familiar. Sydney wasn't much on decorating with plants, which made its presence strange enough, but the gnarly roots looked anything but decorative. He stepped over to the bed to get a closer look.

Lignum vitae.

It was the sculpture that Ennis had put on his mother's casket. The sculpture that contained the sixth crucible.

Marsh shot a quick look to Sydney and ran to her desk.

"Where did you get that?" he asked.

It didn't matter that she didn't answer. He knew the truth. Sydney had been to the mausoleum. He had forgotten that she was headed there when Coop confronted him at his mother's grave. That meant Sydney had seen the open tomb, and the skeleton . . . and the Rift.

He glanced down to see what she was reading. It was an encyclopedia. She was reading about Alexander the Great. Marsh smiled. Sydney was doing research. She was still in the game. He glanced around the room quickly, looking for her purse. He saw it lying on the floor next to the door. He ran to it and fell to his knees to look inside. He desperately wanted to reach inside, or pull it open, but he wasn't capable. All he could do was peer in as best he could, looking for the crucible that he had slipped inside to protect her.

It wasn't there.

"What did you do with it, Syd?" he asked her futilely.

Marsh raced through the possibilities. Why would Sydney not have the crucible, especially if she knew he was dead and had no use for it? If she'd been at the Rift, she'd know that.

The Rift. The possibility struck Marsh hard. Could it be? There was only one way to find out. He closed his eyes, imagined where he wanted to be . . .

. . . and stepped into the mausoleum that held his mother's tomb.

Nothing had changed since he had been there, other than the fact that he was now dead . . . and the lignum vitae sculpture was gone. Sydney had definitely been there. He looked into the opening between lives and was stunned to see his own body lying just beyond the portal. He was momentarily transfixed by the sight of his own dead body and had to force himself to look away. He needed to focus on what it all meant.

Sydney had been there, that much was certain. She knew that Damon had the poleax, had opened up another Rift, and that Marsh had gone through . . . to die. His body was proof of that. He tried to think like Sydney. What would she do with that information? She obviously hadn't sounded any alarms, or the place would have been full of people, wondering why a grave had been desecrated and there was a mysterious portal between universes. No, Sydney wouldn't have rung that particular bell.

But she wouldn't pretend like it hadn't happened either. She would do something proactive. She would try to help. But how? There wasn't a whole lot a living person could do to help a spirit in the Black who wanted to destroy another spirit.

Or was there?

Marsh smiled. The possibility seemed more like a probability. He walked toward the Rift and without hesitation stepped over his own lifeless body and through the portal. A few steps later he emerged on the far side, in the Black, in the lion pen beneath the Roman Colosseum.

The two lions were on the far side of the enclosure, sleeping. Marsh wasn't afraid. When he had arrived the last time, he'd only been a spirit for a few seconds. He didn't know the drill. This time he was prepared. If the lions attacked, he'd simply step away to another vision. His only concern was that they'd give him enough time to find what he was looking for.

It didn't take long. Lying on the floor against the far wall, covered by some dirty straw, was the crucible.

The last crucible.

The globe was resting directly between the two sleeping lions. Without taking time to overthink the situation, Marsh strode directly for the crucible and picked it up. He clutched the golden orb and kissed it.

"I love you, Sydney," he whispered to himself, and stepped into the colorful fog that took him away from the animal pen before the lions even realized they had had a visitor.

26

Zoe had learned from her father's mistakes.

The Guardians had lost the battle for the Rift because Adeipho had underestimated the resolve and ruthlessness of Damon's soldiers. He chose to hold back the Guardians with the black spirit-killing swords as a last line of defense, expecting the others to repel the invaders with conventional weapons before they could get close to the Rift.

It was a tactic that failed miserably.

Damon's soldiers attacked with furious abandon, leading with their own spirit-killing swords, mowing the Guardians down by the dozens. By the time Adeipho and the Guardians brought their own black swords into play, it was too late. The Rift was taken and Adeipho was destroyed. If not for the uncharacteristic intervention of the Watchers, Damon would have controlled the Rift.

Zoe was not about to make the same mistake.

"Our attack will come from several directions," she explained to her captains. "We will surround the Colosseum with groups of thirty. Each Guardian with a spirit sword will be escorted by two others with conventional weapons. When an enemy is encountered, the two escorts will engage him, allowing the bearer of the spirit sword to find the right moment to strike. We may lose many escorts this way, but it will ensure that the Guardians with the spirit swords will reach the Rift, for that is where the true battle will take place."

The captains of each Guardian unit understood and agreed. They had all been through the previous battle. They didn't want to repeat that disaster any more than Zoe did.

Cooper and Press listened intently to Zoe's plan. They would both be in the same group. Cooper with his spirit sword and Press acting as one of his escorts.

The army of Guardians was still on the street in Ree's vision, but it was now divided into small attack groups. Cooper had drawn a rough map of the Colosseum, showing where the Rift was and where the soldiers were stationed. The map was redrawn several times and given to the captains. Zoe assigned each group to a location and point of entry into the Colosseum.

"Our attack must be swift and merciless," Zoe declared. "Our only hope of stopping Damon in the Blood is to control the Rift. Are we all in agreement?"

The captains shouted "Aye!" as one.

"Join your teams," Zoe ordered. "And good luck."

The leaders hurried off to present the battle plan to the brave volunteers who were willing to fight for the future of mankind.

"I'm sorry," Cooper said to Zoe.

"For what?"

"For thinking you weren't capable of leading them."

"I understand," Zoe replied. "And I will turn it back. How capable are you?"

The question surprised Cooper. Nobody had ever questioned his ability to fight. But then again, he had never been in a fight quite like this one.

"Don't worry about me," he said with a cocky smile. "See you at the Rift."

Zoe left to join her own attack group, leaving Cooper with Press.

"Pretty sure of yourself, aren't you?" Press asked teasingly.

"No, but that's never stopped me before," Coop answered.

Cooper hurried away from his group, headed for the garage. He ducked inside to find Ree, Maggie, and his grandfather sitting together.

"We're about to head out," Coop announced. "Ree, are you coming?"

"Of course."

Coop knelt down next to her and said, "I, uh, I let Marsh have it pretty good. I didn't want him anywhere near this battle."

"Why not?" Ree asked, surprised.

"Because he's not a fighter. You know that. I let you talk me into bringing him into the Blood. This time I'm not backing down."

"But it's not your decision," Ree complained. "That's what the Black is all about."

Coop glanced around the garage. "Yeah. The Black. Kind of feels like everything's on hold for a while."

"That's just it," Ree said. "It isn't. I told you before, I believe the Watchers know exactly what's going on. We've reached a crossroads in the evolution of mankind. I'm afraid if we aren't strong enough to turn back this threat, they may end up supporting the wrong side."

"Are you serious?" Coop asked, stunned.

"They're a reflection of us," Ree answered. "If the majority wants Armageddon, they may have no choice but to deliver."

"Jeez," Coop said.

"We can't let that happen," Ree continued. "We've got to show our strength and resolve. Marsh isn't a warrior, but he's been battling Damon from the start. Keeping him out of this fight could be a very big mistake."

Coop shot her a surprised look.

Maggie and Foley sat staring, stunned.

Coop shook it off and said, "Yeah, well, I guess we'll find out."

"Good luck, son," Foley said. "I'm proud of you."

Coop gave his gramps a quick hug.

"Wish I was coming with you," Foley said.

"We'll be back on your front porch soon enough," Coop replied.

As Cooper left the group to head back outside, Maggie jumped up quickly and walked with him.

"Do you think Ree's right?" she asked. "Could the Watchers come in on the other side?"

"I don't know," Coop answered. "I don't know anything except that half the lowlifes that ever existed are about to bust out of the Blood to try and bring down these nice little visions we've built for ourselves. How could the Watchers let that happen?"

"Maybe they're doing exactly what they're supposed to be doing," Maggie offered.

"How? By letting Press fight with us? I like the guy but there's only one of him."

"Or maybe they're waiting to see what we do. Like Ree said, isn't that what the Black is about? I mean, everything that's happened so far is our fault."

"How is it *our* fault?" Coop questioned quickly.

"Not yours or mine, but all of mankind's. Damon was human once. So were those who follow him. They're no different than you or I."

"Don't lump me in with that freak," Coop cautioned.

"But you *are* like him. We all are. What's happening goes beyond any one person. Any one spirit. Mankind let this happen, so mankind has to stop it."

"And what if we can't?" Coop said. "Do you think the Watchers would be willing to let mankind destroy itself?"

"I don't know. Maybe. If that's what we want, and a lot of spirits seem to want that. All we can do is fight for what we believe is right."

Maggie hesitated a moment, and then added, "Maybe it would be better if Marsh were here."

Coop was ready to argue the point, but held back. "I hope you're wrong about that. If the future of mankind depends on Marshall Seaver becoming a warrior . . ."

He didn't finish the thought.

Maggie said, "Maybe it just depends on him being him."

Coop reached out and wrapped his arms around her.

"Stop thinking so hard," he said. "Go somewhere safe. I don't want to lose you."

"I don't want to lose you either, but nowhere is safe."

He lifted her chin and the two kissed.

Both feared it was for the last time.

Marsh moved quickly but cautiously.

One step at a time. That was his mantra. He didn't want to think too far ahead because he had no idea what he would do once he got there. He had to focus on each new step and worry about the rest later.

His goal was to get to the Rift and into the Blood . . . to find Damon. He believed that stopping him was the only way to end the insanity. He only wished he knew how. His lone weapon was a single crucible. The last one. Though he knew full well it had no power over Damon in the Blood, he clutched it as insurance in case his enemy made it back through to the Black. He hoped it wouldn't come to that. When he got to Damon—*if* he got to Damon—he would have to find some way to end him. It was the only way.

He made his way from the depths of the Colosseum, taking the same route as when he had made the journey with his mother. With each step his anxiety grew. What would he find up there? Were Damon's forces gathering in anticipation of his triumphant return from the Blood? Had Brennus's legion of the damned already come through? And what of the Guardians? When would they attack to try and seize control of the Rift?

He climbed up from the dark stairwell to ground level, turned into the tunnel that led to the arena, and peered out from the shadows.

It was daytime. The arena was quiet. The stands were empty. Guards were still stationed in front of the Rift but they didn't seem to be on alert.

He wasn't too late. The attack hadn't come, but time was moving. Several more Roman soldiers were scattered across the arena floor and more were arriving from the outside. When the Guardians attacked, they would have a battle on their hands.

The Roman soldiers moved without urgency. They had no idea that a storm was brewing . . . on both sides of the Rift. From what Marsh could see, it was the perfect time for the Guardians to attack.

Keeping close to the walls, he climbed the few stairs up to the first level of seating and once again made his way around the circle of spectator seats, headed for the Rift. He reached into the front pocket of his hoodie for the hundredth time to make sure that he still had the crucible.

He was halfway around to the Rift . . . when the sound of blaring trumpets tore through the silence.

Marsh froze.

This was no fanfare to signal the start of a game. These trumpet calls were harsh and frantic. One word came to his mind: *alarm.*

He peered over the brick retaining wall and down into the arena to see that the Roman soldiers had tensed up. Several more sprinted into the arena with their weapons drawn, but once they arrived, they did nothing more than glance around in confusion. Still more soldiers ran in. This group was armed with the black spirit swords. The trumpets had definitely touched off a panic, but seemingly for no reason. There was no attack. The soldiers with the black swords gravitated toward the Rift, joining the other handful of soldiers who were guarding it. The rest of the soldiers stood in a loose group in the center of the arena, unsure what to do.

Their confusion didn't last long.

Marsh saw it before any of the soldiers did. To his far right on the edge of the arena, the air rippled and a colorful fog appeared. Directly opposite it on the other side of the arena another fog appeared. Halfway around a third materialized, followed by a fourth.

The Guardian's siege was about to begin.

From out of the swirling mist came Zoe's attack groups. Their weapons were raised high, with many carrying their own black swords. The stunned soldiers were surrounded in the center of the arena. Those soldiers with the black swords quickly moved to the front, knowing what was coming. Others sprinted directly for the Rift. They knew what was coming too, and why they were being attacked.

The second battle for a Rift had begun.

The attack teams burst from the fog in a dead run, screaming from the rush of adrenaline.

The soldiers to the center could do nothing but wait.

The four groups descended on them, attacking with the kind of fury that was missing when they had defended the Rift in Ree's vision.

"Coop!" Marsh said aloud without thinking when he saw that his friend was leading one of the attack teams.

Alongside him was Press, who was armed with his wooden stave. Compared to the experienced soldiers, Cooper wasn't proficient with the black sword. He hacked away with power, but with amateur skills. If not for Press, he might have been wiped out in the first minute. Press was his guardian angel. His wooden stave twirled and spun as he knocked away any soldier who attempted to rush Cooper.

Cooper may not have been proficient with the sword, but he wasn't afraid to use deadly force. No sooner did Press knock a soldier off balance than Coop would be right on him with the black sword, thrusting it forward and turning the spirit to shadow.

The cries of battle and agony were louder and more dense than any other spectacle that had ever played out in the arena, either in the Black or the Light. The clash of swords was constant, followed by a cry of despair in the instant before a spirit was no more.

Zoe fought with a vengeance . . . for her father and for all the Guardians who had lost their spirits to Damon's soldiers. Her sword was quick and merciless. She alone ended the spirits of a dozen soldiers.

Her battle plan was brilliant. The soldiers were taken completely by surprise and trapped in the center of the arena, where the Guardians could pick them off, one by one.

The Guardians suffered their own casualties as well. Many had survived the battle for the Rift in Ree's vision only to fall this second time around.

Marsh watched the carnage with horror . . . and awe.

The idea that so many spirits were dying before his eyes was hard to comprehend. But he couldn't allow himself to be a spectator. He had his own mission.

The Guardians hadn't yet made a move toward the Rift and the soldiers who waited for them with their own black swords. With the soldiers to the center being quickly wiped out, Marsh knew that the Guardians would soon turn to their objective.

The soldiers in front of the Rift knew it too and tensed up, ready for the attack.

Marsh scrambled along the ring of seats to get closer to the Rift. His hope was that the Guardians would draw the soldiers away from the opening and he could use that moment to slip through and into the Blood. It would be about as risky a maneuver as he could imagine, but he felt it was his only chance.

The fighting to the center of the arena was winding down. Only a few of Damon's soldiers remained. The Guardians were already gathering together, preparing to turn their attention to the Rift and charge the last line of the soldier's defense.

Marsh's heart raced. Could he do it? Would he have the guts to jump down into the fight and dodge his way through the slashing swords and into the Rift?

"What do you plan to do, Marshmallow?" came a familiar voice.

Marsh spun quickly to see that another spirit had arrived.

"Ennis!" Marsh called. "Get down!"

Ennis calmly sat down on the bench in front of him.

"I wish I could say I was happy to see you," Ennis said.

"I'm sorry, Ennis," Marsh said. "I should never have left you alone."

"There is no need to be sorry," Ennis said. "What happened to me was inevitable. I welcomed it. But seeing you here makes my heart ache."

"It was my choice," Marsh said breathlessly. "Damon cut another Rift into the Black and I went through. I wanted to. Now Damon's in the Blood and I'm going after him."

"No, you cannot," Ennis said sternly. "This is not your battle."

"Yes, it is," Marsh argued. "I didn't ask for it, but it's mine now."

"You stand no chance against that devil," Ennis argued.

Marsh reached into his hoodie and pulled out the crucible. He held it out to Ennis and said, "Maybe a little."

Ennis's eyes grew wide. "How is that possible? Why is it here?"

"Sydney tossed it through the Rift from the Light."

Ennis glanced down at the battle that was nearly complete . . . and about to begin anew.

"Help me, Ennis," Marsh begged. "Help me get through the Rift."

Damon was not about to accept defeat.

He picked himself up from the dirt, stood tall, and marched his way back toward the Colosseum with growing resolve. He would not allow the peasant sin eater to triumph at his expense. As he drew nearer to the Colosseum, he saw that the spirit army had already entered the ruins. Was he too late? Had the battle begun? Damon picked up the pace and ran the rest of the way, snaking through the piles of debris until he entered the remains of the colossal ring and saw the Rift within.

Brennus sat in his cart at its mouth, staring into the opening between lives. Listening.

The sounds of a raging battle could be heard coming

through from the Black, yet the spirit army was not moving. Damon's hope soared. There was still a chance. With one hand on the hilt of the poleax he stood tall and strode toward Brennus.

"You hear the sounds of battle?" Damon bellowed. "That is what awaits you. They are armed and they answer to me."

The two burly escorts stepped forward, blocking Damon's way. Damon raised the poleax, ready to fight them.

"Leave him be!" Brennus growled.

The two guards reluctantly stepped aside. Damon sheathed the poleax and cautiously approached Brennus.

"This army of yours," Brennus said thoughtfully. "Who they be fighting?"

Damon laughed. "Did you think there would be no resistance? Listen. What you hear is the sound of two armies clashing. Two trained armies. How could you not realize there would be those who would fight to protect the Morpheus Road?"

"No matter," Brennus said dismissively. "They could be destroying a thousand of me spirits and a thousand more after that and me still will be having the means to overrun the Black."

"That is your master plan?" Damon asked, incredulous. "Simply throw these spirits at them like so much dirt?"

"It be more than they could hope for here," Brennus replied. "A single moment of freedom be far better than eternal suffering. And for those who make it through . . . the prize."

"There is no prize without me!" Damon bellowed. "I have created this way into the Black. You could send countless spirits through and destroy every last obstacle that stands in your way but that is where your journey will end, for I alone hold the power to open the way into the Light."

Brennus turned away from the Rift to look directly at

Damon, his brittle bones crackling with every movement.

"That may be," he said with a sly smile. "If the Light be the prize."

Damon frowned and shook his head.

"Why else would you be waging this war?" he replied. "A second chance at life is all these spirits care about. It is all about the Light."

Brennus chuckled, the effort making him cough. He spit a wad of black phlegm onto the ground and wiped his mouth with a tattered sleeve.

"The Light be a place of corruptible flesh," he declared. "Primitive it is. Ugly. It be holding no interest for me."

"I . . . I don't understand," Damon said, genuinely confused. "Your only goal is to escape from the Blood? For what? To exist in the false illusions of the Black?"

"The prize be far greater, fool," Brennus wheezed. "But what would a cowardly soldier know of such glorious things?"

Damon's mind raced. Nothing the old spirit was saying made sense.

"Explain it to me!" he bellowed. "What prize is more coveted than life?"

"Imbecile!" Brennus bellowed. "I will not be looking back. The way is forward to conquer those who caused our pain. Who banished us to suffer in the Blood."

"The Watchers?" Damon said with a gasp. "You are going to attack the Watchers? But . . . how?"

"There be many stops on the Morpheus Road," Brennus declared slyly. "The Blood be one end. There be another."

Damon was so stunned he could barely speak.

"Another? Does this place have a name?"

"It do," Brennus said. "It be called . . . Solara."

27

The final push to the Rift was fast and brutal.

Fired by their own success and still driven by the bitter memory of their previous loss, the Guardians turned their attention to the soldiers who guarded the portal into the Blood. Though the Guardians vastly outnumbered the guards, the outcome was very much in doubt, for the twenty soldiers who protected the Rift each carried a black spirit-killing sword.

The toll of this endgame was sure to be heavy for both sides.

Zoe let out a guttural scream that spurred the Guardians on. They charged, en masse, from the center of the arena to the line of soldiers who stood waiting.

Cooper was out in front of the charge, ready to do some damage, but as he began to run, he felt a strong hand on his shoulder.

"No," Press said, holding him back.

Coop was wide eyed and breathing hard, flush with the anticipation of battle.

"C'mon!" he shouted to Press. "This is it!"

"No, it isn't," Press said calmly. "This is only the beginning."

Coop shot a look toward the Rift to see that the Guardians had reached the soldiers and had begun the fight. It was chaos, with swords both conventional and deadly flashing every which way. Anguished cries of pain and triumph filled the arena.

"It would be senseless for your spirit to end now," Press added. "The ultimate battle is still to come."

Coop fought the urge to charge into the mix while Press kept a firm grip on his shoulder. His head cleared slowly as the Watcher's words sunk home.

This battle was only a prelude.

He'd get the chance to fight again.

Marsh and Ennis worked their way through the tiers of seats, growing ever closer to the Rift. They didn't bother to try and stay out of sight, because the warriors on the arena floor were too busy to be concerned with a few spectators in the stands above them. They moved quickly, making it to within a few feet of the right edge of the Rift. It was close enough to feel the body heat coming from the warriors below.

"Impossible," Ennis declared. "We cannot make it through that."

The brutal battle centered directly in front of the twenty-yard-wide Rift.

Ennis added, "We could be destroyed, by either side."

Marsh couldn't argue. There didn't seem to be any way to get through the melee.

In the stands above, a crowd was gathering. The battle

over the future of mankind had become yet another spectacle taking place in the Flavian Amphitheater. The emperor Titus arrived to take his place in the royal box, where he could observe the violence.

Marsh saw the growing crowd. He wondered if any of the spectators truly appreciated what was unfolding in the arena, or if they had just come to be entertained.

There was at least one spectator who understood. Marsh's mother stood alone, directly above the Rift, gazing down at the carnage. Her look of anguish said it all.

"We should leave here," Ennis said, and made a move to go.

Marsh grabbed his arm to stop him.

"No," he said. "There might be a way."

The Roman soldiers guarding the Rift fought out of desperation.

What began for them as a mission to defend the portal quickly became a struggle for survival. They no longer battled to keep the Guardians back, but instead fought to escape and save themselves. Their allegiance to Damon and his quest didn't extend to suicide.

The Guardians showed no mercy. One by one the soldiers were destroyed, leaving behind their spirit-killing swords. Others dropped their swords and fled as their weapons were quickly scooped up to become part of the Guardians' arsenal.

Finally, after the last soldier was sent to oblivion, the Guardians stood looking to one another, their chests heaving with fatigue, their swords ready to strike again. It took a few moments for them to realize that the fight was over.

The Rift was theirs.

There were no joyous cries. No shouts of victory or any other display of bravura. There was only a brief moment of relief, which they shared with knowing glances. There wasn't time to savor the victory.

"Form a line!" Zoe shouted. "Spirit swords to the fore."

She ran across the mouth of the Rift, holding her own sword high for all to see. Her command was obeyed instantly. Each of the Guardians who held a black sword came forward and joined in a line that reached across the length of the Rift. There were enough swords to form two lines, one behind the other.

The rest of the Guardians filled in behind them. Many more continued to arrive from Ree's vision until the arena floor was nearly filled.

The defense of the Black was set.

Marsh and Ennis watched as the stands continued to fill with spectators.

"They have come to witness an unprecedented spectacle," Ennis marveled.

"Or maybe they've come to be part of it," Marsh said.

"What do you mean?"

"Damon has a lot more followers than those soldiers who were guarding the Rift. I saw this stadium full of them, all fired up and ready to fight."

Ennis scanned the growing crowd with apprehension.

"That means the Guardians are being surrounded," he said with a gasp.

"And an army of the damned is about to march out of the Rift."

Ennis nervously wiped sweat from his forehead. "They will be slaughtered."

"Not yet they won't," Marsh said with confidence. "I don't think these spirits will do a thing unless Damon tells them to."

"So we must get to him and make sure he does not come back," Ennis said. "But I do not see how."

"I think we'll get the chance," Marsh said thoughtfully. "We just have to be ready for it."

Cooper and Press joined Ree in the level directly above the Rift.

"They did it," Coop declared.

"They are a valiant group," Ree said with a touch of sadness. "But simply fighting for what you believe is right doesn't guarantee victory." She gestured to the rapidly growing crowd of spirits that were filling the Colosseum, and added, "Not when there are so many who have their own agenda, no matter how wrong-minded it may be."

"Don't underestimate the power of noble beliefs," Press replied. "Many conflicts have been won without much more than the inspiration that comes from the knowledge that what you're fighting for . . . is right."

"Lofty words," Ree replied. "I'd trade them for a few more of those black swords."

"Does this count?" Coop asked Press.

"What do you mean?"

"I mean, what more proof do the Watchers need that the Guardians are dedicated to saving the Morpheus Road?"

"Are you asking me if they will intervene now?" Press asked.

"That's exactly what I'm asking," Coop said impatiently.

Press took a tired breath and said, "As I told you before, the ultimate battle is still to come."

Zoe joined them, her eyes still blazing from the thrill of combat.

"We are ready," she declared. "If Damon so much as pushes a toe through that opening, it will be the last action he takes."

"It won't be enough," Cooper declared.

All eyes shot to him.

"It will," Zoe said defensively. "They'll be walking straight into a trap."

"I know we can hold them off," Coop said. "But for how long? I was there, remember? I saw. There were thousands of spirits. Many thousands. Every last loser from the beginning of time could be lining up to blast out of there. And why not? The place sucks. They're fighting an eternal sentence and it's not like any of them were good guys to begin with. They don't care about fighting for what's right. They want *out*. I'm sure the Guardians will knock off plenty of them, but there'll be thousands behind them, and thousands more. Face it, we can't protect the Rift forever."

"What else can we do?" Ree asked.

"Marsh was right," Coop said with absolute conviction. "The only way to stop this is to stop Damon."

"Don't forget Brennus," Press warned. "He's the one who truly controls the spirits of the Blood."

"Right," Coop said. "That guy's no picnic either. If we sit here and let them come at us, it won't be a question of whether or not we can save the Black. It'll be about how long it'll take to fall."

"Damon will be the first to be destroyed when he comes through," Zoe said.

"Don't you think he knows that?" Coop shot back. "He's got an ego, but he's not an idiot."

"What do you suggest, Cooper?" Ree asked.

Coop smiled and said, "I say we go on offense."

Damon pulled the poleax from its sheath and stood in front of Brennus.

"I have waged many a successful campaign," he announced.

"I can lead you to victory. Release your spirits to me and I will achieve all that you wish with far fewer casualties than if you simply drove them blindly through the Rift. There is an art to waging war, and I am an artist. I humbly ask that you allow me to be your general, as I was to Alexander so long ago."

Brennus didn't move. His eyes stayed focused on Damon, their gazes locked.

Damon didn't flinch. He didn't want to show weakness of any kind. He knew this was his last chance.

"I believe ya," Brennus finally croaked. "Ya must have been a brilliant general. A leader of men."

"I was," Damon said, trying not to show his relief that he was finally getting through to Brennus.

"And yer soldiers? Were they loyal to ya? To the death?"

"Indeed they were," Damon replied, swelling with pride. "To the death and beyond."

Brennus leaned forward, though the movement caused him to wince with pain.

"Then you, being such a fine general, must know that in battle there can be only one leader."

"I could not agree more," Damon said quickly. "Loyalties cannot be divided."

"Good," Brennus said with finality. "Then you'll understand why I won't be needing your services."

The smile instantly dropped from Damon's face.

"What?"

Brennus declared, "There be only one leader of this rising, and that be me."

Brennus gestured to his escorts, who immediately descended on Damon.

Damon was too stunned by the sudden turnaround to defend himself.

"No! You'll lose thousands of spirits!"

The burly guards lifted Damon up into the air and carried him toward the sea of the damned. Damon struggled, trying to get to the poleax, but too many hands kept him contained.

"Thousands?" Brennus cackled. "That be all?"

The guards handed Damon over to the masses. The spirits accepted him, holding him above their heads, handing him farther and farther back. Damon squirmed and fought to break free, but it was useless. He was under their control. The indignity was made complete by their total disrespect, and their laughter.

Damon gave in. He let the hands take him away. Fighting was useless. The spirits handled him like a toy, laughing and tossing him farther back, away from the Rift and out of the Colosseum. Damon closed his eyes and tensed his body, refusing to fight back and give them the satisfaction of knowing how truly helpless he was. After what felt like an eternity, they tossed him to the side of the road, where he hit hard and came to rest by the remains of a crumbled statue.

Damon lay there without moving. He didn't look up. He didn't want to see the spirits who were moving on without him. He didn't want to admit that his glorious quest had come to a decidedly inglorious end in the dry dust of hell.

The Colosseum was eerily quiet.

There were over a thousand Guardians on the arena floor and tens of thousands of spectators in the stands, but the only discernible sound was a hollow wind that blew through the wide empty corridors of the stadium.

All eyes were trained on the Rift.

No group was more focused than the few dozen Guardians who stood before the opening, armed with the spirit-killing swords. They knew the importance of their task.

Each and every one had vowed not to let a single spirit pass from the Blood into the Black.

Emperor Titus sat forward in his throne in anticipation. He had every reason to believe that this spectacle would be the most glorious ever to have been staged in the Flavian Amphitheater . . . no matter what the result.

Marsh and Ennis peered over the retaining wall, not twenty yards from the Rift. Ennis was nervous, his gaze shifting from the Rift to Marsh.

Marsh kept his eyes on the Rift. He was confident they'd get the chance to move and didn't want to miss it when it came.

Cooper, Press, and Ree stood above the Rift, their attention focused on the Guardians and in particular on the first two rows, for they held the black spirit swords. They were the first and last line of defense. In their hands was the future of the Morpheus Road.

Ree was torn between feelings of pride and guilt. She was tortured with the knowledge that none of this would have happened if she and Ennis hadn't gone into the Temple of the Morning Light. But they did go and it did happen. The best she could hope for now was damage control. Seeing the selfless intensity of the Guardians gave her the slight hope that maybe, just maybe, it would be enough.

Zoe was with the Guardians, front and center, ready to defend the Black as she knew her father would have. As he would have wanted her to.

They all waited. And waited.

It was Zoe who saw it first.

A vague shape appeared deep within the purple glow of the Rift.

"They come!" she bellowed.

Every last person in the Colosseum tensed up.

Another shape appeared, and then another. They seemed like misshapen silhouettes, but the Guardians knew the truth. The amorphous forms would take shape, and when they did, multiple spirits would be coming through the Rift.

Zoe raised her sword.

The others followed suit. They were more than ready to cut the interlopers down the moment they stepped out of the Rift.

"At the ready!" Zoe commanded.

The first spirit was about to appear directly in front of her, which Zoe was grateful for. She wanted to set the tone and be the first to destroy one of the spirits of the damned. She wanted to draw first blood. She hoped it would be Damon.

The spirit stepped out of the Rift, showing itself to be a grizzled, bearded man with piercing blue eyes. Zoe raised her sword, ready to strike.

The spirit smiled at her.

Zoe was momentarily taken off guard.

The spirit took a step forward.

Zoe sliced down with her sword . . .

. . . too late. The spirit disappeared in a swirl of colorful fog.

Zoe froze. The front line of Guardians stared in shock. What had happened?

Another spirit stepped out of the Rift on the far right end. A Guardian made the move with his sword but the spirit vanished, leaving the Guardian flailing at air.

"They're not going to fight!" Cooper called from above. "They know the deal. They're already moving between visions."

Two more spirits stepped out of the Rift and disappeared before the Guardians could attack. More appeared and then disappeared as soon as they arrived. The Guardians were left flailing at air.

"We must go through!" a Guardian yelled, and made a move for the Rift.

Zoe grabbed him and stopped him before he could enter.

"No!" she shouted. "They will tear you apart in there. The spirit swords have no power."

Spirits started arriving quickly and disappearing just as fast as they could come through. The Guardians started slashing wildly, hoping to strike a spirit before it could vanish, but there was no way to anticipate where they would appear. With all the flailing swords they were more in danger of destroying one another than any spirit coming through the Rift.

"It's chaos," Ree said in a dazed whisper.

"No, it's not," Coop said darkly. "Those spirits know exactly what they're doing. Question is, where are they going?"

The Guardians began to have some success. The spirits from the Blood became victims of their own numbers as many were pushed from behind into the Black and cut down before they had the chance to move on. The Guardians became more selective with their attacks. They stood at the ready and lunged the moment they saw the whisper of a shape coming through. It was an effective maneuver. They began destroying spirits by the hundreds.

It wasn't enough. The Guardians had hoped to stop them all from leaching into the Black, but even with their successes, just as many spirits were making it through as were being destroyed. And they kept coming. And coming. The Guardians had no hope of stemming the flow.

The crowd of spectators didn't know what to make of the scene. They had expected a battle. Instead they were presented with the scene of the Guardians having as much success with the fight as if they were trying to swat at vanishing hummingbirds.

"Now." Marsh stood up, ready to leap over the wall and down to the arena floor.

"Now?" Ennis exclaimed. "It is insanity down there!"

"Exactly. But the spirits don't have swords and the Guardians are focused on stopping them from coming out of the Rift, so . . . we're going in."

Marsh vaulted over the low wall and landed on the sandy floor. He made a quick check to ensure the crucible was safe, then began dodging spirits on his way to the Rift. His plan was to approach the far right side of the Rift, wait for an opening, and dash through. He tried not to focus on the horror of the battles that were taking place, and the loss of life. He had to treat them only as obstacles he needed to skirt in order to move forward and get to the Rift.

He got to within five yards of the far right corner and knelt down on one knee. It was close enough that he could spring forward the moment there was an opening. Two spirits from the Blood stepped out on that same side. Their visit was short-lived, for a Guardian leaped forward and slashed through them both with his black sword, turning them to shadows that instantly vanished. But as the Guardian followed through with his swing, another spirit leaped out from behind the first two. His timing was perfect. The Guardian couldn't swing back fast enough to strike.

Though at first the spirits had been recklessly leaping through the Rift and hoping for the best, they had soon changed tactics. A spirit would make it safely into the Black by using another spirit as a shield. The first spirit would be cut down, allowing the second to leap out of the Rift and instantly move to another vision.

Marsh saw this success and expected the spirit who had made it through safely to disappear like the others, but the spirit caught sight of Marsh first.

"You," the spirit snarled.

"Sanger," Marsh said with a gasp.

"You ain't gettin' away from me again," the wretched

old man growled, and made a move toward Marsh with his fists up.

Marsh stood to defend himself but Sanger never got to throw a punch. Before he could get a step closer, the old spirit was hit with a flying tackle and knocked off his feet.

"Coop!" Marsh yelled.

Cooper scrambled to his feet, picked Sanger up by the shirt, and nailed him with a vicious punch to the chin. Sanger stumbled backward and slammed into the wall next to the Rift.

"What are you doing here?" Coop screamed at Marsh.

"I'm going after Damon."

"You can't go with me, Ralph!" Coop argued.

"With *you*?"

"I'm going back to the Blood."

"Marsh!" Ennis screamed.

Marsh and Coop both looked up in time to see Sanger lunging toward them . . . with a black spirit-killing sword up and ready to strike. It was Coop's sword. He had dropped it when he had tackled Sanger. There was a frozen moment. Neither Marsh nor Coop could think fast enough to move.

But Ennis did. He threw himself in front of the boys, and Sanger skewered him with the deadly weapon.

"Ennis!" Marsh screamed.

In his last seconds of existence, Ennis Mobley turned his head toward Marsh with his mouth open to scream, but no sound came out. He made eye contact with Marsh for the briefest of moments and then his body turned to shadow.

Ennis Mobley's spirit was no more.

Sanger stood there, still clutching the deadly sword, momentarily stunned by what he had done. He then lifted the sword in triumph, his eyes blazing.

"Now we're talkin'!" he howled with delight.

Marsh lost control. He lunged at Sanger, ready to take the guy apart.

Sanger raised the sword to claim his second victim . . . but Coop got to him first. Before he could swing, Coop hit him hard and wrestled him to the ground as the old spirit dropped the sword.

Marsh didn't move. He wanted nothing more than to tear into the guy who had just killed Ennis . . . but something else had caught his attention.

The edge of the Rift was clear. No spirits were coming through, which momentarily focused the Guardians' attention elsewhere. There was no telling how long that would last. Certainly no more than a few seconds. Marsh had his chance . . .

. . . and took it. He pushed aside the anguish over Ennis's sacrifice and sprinted for the Rift.

Coop was on the ground, struggling with Sanger.

"Marsh, no!" he screamed out.

Too late. Marsh jumped into the Rift.

Coop's attention was on Marsh, and Sanger took advantage. He rolled away from Coop, headed for the spirit sword.

Coop saw him and jumped ahead, reaching the sword the instant before Sanger did. He brought it up, ready to skewer the surly spirit.

Sanger didn't give him the chance. He backed away and disappeared in a swirl of color.

Coop didn't care. He turned back to the Rift, ready to go after Marsh.

It was at that moment that a flood of spirits came through, directly in front of Cooper. The Guardians fought them off, ending some but losing others. The struggle made it impossible for Coop to get through. It was a dangerous spot to be in. He had no choice but to back off and accept what had happened.

Marsh was back in the Blood . . . alone.

28

Marsh was confronted by a sea of desperate fleeing spirits.

As he pushed into the Blood, he felt like a fish swimming upstream . . . against a sea of fish swimming downstream. None of the spirits bothered to give him a second look. They moved, zombielike, as if hypnotized by the draw of the light coming from the Rift, and its promise of escape from their infernal prison.

Marsh couldn't fight the flow, so he pushed his way to the side, clawing to get out of the stream of souls. It wasn't until he gave up trying to dodge the spirits and instead lowered his shoulder to knock a few of them down that he was able to force his way out of the crowd. He barged forward, jumped from the stream, and ran for protection next to a pile of rubble, where he was finally able to catch his breath and take a look back to where he'd come from.

"Unbelievable," he said to himself, breathless.

It was a daunting sight. The line of spirits was twenty wide and snaked back from the Rift and out of the ruins of the Blood version of the Colosseum. There were spirits from every walk of life, every era and society on earth. There were old bent men, strapping boys, and women of all types and ages.

Marsh wondered if they knew the odds of their survival on the far side, and decided it probably didn't matter to them. If there was a chance to escape from this hell, even if it were a small one, they would take it.

He looked up to the spectator box that in the Black was the private viewing area of the emperor Titus. Hunched in the rotting throne was Brennus, proudly observing the snaking flow. What Marsh didn't see . . . was Damon. Marsh stood up on a marble pedestal and scanned the area, searching for his adversary, but Damon was nowhere to be seen. Marsh closed his eyes and put his faith in what the Watchers had told him. It had worked in the past and he had to trust it would work again. If he needed to find Damon, he would. He cleared his mind, trying to sense Damon's presence, or get a clue, or receive any kind of inspiration that would tell him where Damon might be. It didn't take him long to come to at least one conclusion.

He's not here.

It made no sense to him. Damon had waited centuries for this moment of glory. Why wasn't he out in front, leading the way?

Marsh's mission hadn't changed. He had to find Damon, no matter where he was. He took one last look at the stream of damned spirits as they marched into the Rift, and shuddered. Dozens were moving through every second, with no sign of slowing. He knew he had to move fast, so he jumped off the pedestal and ran out of the Colosseum. When he cleared the outer wall of the structure, he stopped short and stood staring in awe at the sight in front of him.

A line of spirits extended across the otherwise empty expanse and wound like a meandering river back through the hills of Rome before disappearing far in the distance. There was no way to estimate the number of spirits who were lined up, eager to risk their existence for the chance to escape from the Blood.

He tore himself away from the impossible sight and jogged deeper into the dark terrain. He didn't know exactly where he was going, but felt confident that his journey would eventually bring him to Damon.

He moved through decimated city streets, overgrown jungle villages, and the wastes of suburbia. At one point he found himself walking down the quaint main street of a small town. It stopped Marsh cold. The street was familiar. But it wasn't Stony Brook. Where was he?

He took another look around and his jaw dropped.

There was a castle at the end of Main Street that had been caved in by the toppled Matterhorn mountain. Several yellow submarines were piled at the base of the mountain next to a handful of giant colorful teacups.

"Disneyland," Marsh said, horrified.

In many ways it was the most disturbing image he had seen in the Blood, but he couldn't let it affect him. He had done his best to ignore the reality of the ghastly visions. He couldn't let anything stop him from his mission, least of all his own fear and revulsion. Without another thought he turned off Main Street, ran past a pile of discarded Dumbos, and hurried on.

Another disturbing realization soon followed. He had passed through many different visions and had yet to see another spirit. The implication was mind-numbing:

Hell was being emptied out.

He moved past a shattered car factory filled with the twisted remains of a hundred half-finished vehicles, to find himself on the edge of an ancient village of stucco homes.

Marsh stopped. It wasn't the sight of the village that froze him, it was a sound. It was faint but unmistakable and it brought back disturbing memories.

Drip . . . drip . . . drip.

It was the sound of dripping water.

This time the incessant sound didn't frighten him, for he knew it could mean only one thing: His search was over. He stepped forward, turned the corner of a small house, and immediately knew where he was.

The vision was just as Coop had described. He was on a dusty street in ancient Greece that was lined on either side with small stucco buildings. At the far end of the street was a domed church. Halfway to the church was a fountain that held the massive statue of Alexander the Great. As in the Black, the slight stream of water coming from the fountain created the dripping sound that had haunted Marsh since this nightmare had begun. The street was a ruined version of what Coop had seen in the Black. The buildings were empty, the church's dome caved in. Oddly, the statue of Alexander was unscathed.

It was the vision of Damon of Epirus.

Marsh walked forward slowly. He knew Damon was there. Somewhere. He felt his presence. This was the moment he had hoped for, and as he feared, he had no idea what he would do once he confronted his tormentor. He felt the weight of the crucible in his hoodie pocket. It was useless to him in the Blood. He was feeling very much alone, and vulnerable. But he kept walking.

Halfway to the fountain, Marsh saw something that at first made him catch his breath in surprise, but then gave him the slightest bit of hope. Stuck in the street, like a dark version of

Excalibur, was the poleax. The monstrous weapon was the root from which all his troubles grew, and it was there for the taking. It may not have spiritual power in the Blood, but it was a weapon and Marsh wanted it. He picked up his pace, eager to get his hands on the sword that he would use against its owner. He was no more than five yards away, ready to reach out, when Damon appeared from the far side of the fountain, now wearing his armor, prepared for battle.

Marsh stopped in surprise and cursed himself for doing so. He should have kept going. The poleax would have been his. Now it was a standoff. Both had an equal chance of reaching it first. They stood facing each other like two gunslingers, waiting for the other to make the first move.

"Why have you come?" Damon asked.

"I . . . I'm not going to lie," Marsh said. "I came to end you."

"For what purpose? Revenge?"

"I don't care about revenge. This is about the Morpheus Road."

Damon laughed. "Then, yours is a misguided mission. Destroying me will not salvage the Morpheus Road. The campaign now belongs to Brennus. I am no more than a spectator. But if you still care to do battle, I would be more than willing to oblige."

Damon made a quick move for the poleax.

Marsh was caught by surprise and reacted too late. Damon would easily reach it before him.

Damon reached forward . . .

. . . and was knocked off his feet by a flying shadow.

Marsh didn't hesitate a second time. He jumped for the weapon and pulled it out of the ground before he understood what had happened. Taking a few steps back to give himself time to defend himself, he saw two spirits wrestling on the ground. One was Damon.

The other took control, pulled Damon to his feet, and hissed, "I've been *so* looking forward to this."

Cooper nailed Damon on the chin with a vicious punch that sent the warrior stumbling backward until he crossed his feet and fell against the fountain.

Coop stalked forward quickly and stood over him, poised for a fight.

"Get up!" he screamed.

Marsh ran up next to Cooper, holding the poleax threateningly toward the downed general.

Damon wiped his chin and laughed. "This must be so satisfying for you, Foley. Finally, the chance to take sweet revenge the way you know best, with your fists. And you, Seaver, holding my own weapon on me. So poetic, and so futile."

"Futile?" Coop screamed, his rage growing. "How's this for futile?"

He picked Damon up by the edges of the body armor he now wore, lifted his squat frame until he was standing, and then nailed him with another punch that spun the general around and dropped him to his knees.

"I got a whole sack of futile to unload on you," Coop taunted.

He made a move to pull Damon to his feet again, but Marsh held him back.

"Wait," Marsh said. "This is wrong."

"Wrong?" Coop exclaimed. "It's why we came back. Thanks for waiting for me, by the way," he added sarcastically. "I thought my head would explode when I saw Disneyland."

"What do you mean the campaign belongs to Brennus?" Marsh asked Damon.

Damon sat down and leaned his back against the fountain.

"My quest has come to an end," Damon said with resignation.

"Liar," Coop spat. "The spirits are moving into the Black right now."

"They are," Damon said, sounding tired. "Without me."

He made a move to stand up, but Marsh kept the sword pointed at his chest.

Damon sat back and gave him a dismissive wave. "You understand that has no power here."

Marsh held it on him just the same.

"The battle for the Morpheus Road is indeed imminent," Damon said. "But leading the charge will be Brennus, not I."

"I don't get it," Marsh said. "Why?"

"The spirits of the Blood are as loyal to him as those in the Black are to me," Damon said with resignation. "Centuries of planning have resulted in nothing more than my exchanging eternity in the Black for eternity in the Blood. So you see, whatever pitiful revenge you exact with your fists is but a trifle to me."

"So that's it?" Coop asked. "Brennus takes over and you're just . . . done?"

Damon glanced up at the statue of Alexander, as if it stood in silent judgment.

"As in life . . . yes."

"Oh no," Coop snarled as he lunged at Damon and picked him up by his breastplate. "You can't just walk away."

"You may prefer that I be destroyed, but as you have seen, the poleax has no power here. I am afraid my sentence will be to remain in the Blood. That is, until Brennus destroys the Morpheus Road, and in spite of his amateurish military skills, I have no doubt that he will succeed."

Coop screamed in rage and threw Damon back to the ground.

Damon hit hard, facefirst. He spit dirt, coughed, and

said, "Is this how you plan to spend what little time you have left?"

"If Brennus is such an amateur, why do you think he'll succeed?" Marsh asked.

"Because he has the brute strength that comes with numbers. He will lose millions of souls knowing he has millions more to draw from . . . an inelegant strategy, to say the least."

"And what strategy would you have used?" Marsh asked.

"Who cares?" Coop bellowed.

"I am a general," Damon said with pride. "A tactician. You may see me as brutal but I treat each battle like a game of chess that requires strategy and cunning."

"While people die around you," Coop said, scoffing.

"People die in battle, yes, but death is not the ultimate goal. Wars are waged over territory or power or riches—"

"Or glory," Marsh said.

Damon wiped the dirt from his face and said, "Yes, you are correct, Seaver. I sought glory. But no matter what you may believe, mankind would have survived my adventuring. Changed perhaps, but I would not have brought about the end of days."

"And Brennus will?" Marsh asked.

"His goals are very different than mine. Where I sought glory, he seeks chaos."

"What's the difference?" Coop scoffed. "He can't win a battle in the Light any more than you can. I don't care how many spirits he's got behind him."

"Agreed. He would not triumph in the Light . . . if the Light were his objective."

"It's not?" Coop asked quickly.

"What other objective is there?" Marsh asked with trepidation.

"Brennus has accumulated the evil of untold souls,"

Damon cautioned. "Even I shudder at his dark thoughts. His aim is to conquer the place that holds the collected wisdom and knowledge of mankind. It is the final destination of every completed soul."

Coop and Marsh exchanged looks.

"I don't like the sound of that," Coop said.

"You mean like . . . heaven?" Marsh asked.

"The other end of the Morpheus Road," Coop said, numb. "Where Press said the Watchers are from."

"It has a name," Damon said. "Solara. Brennus intends to destroy the spirit of mankind that has existed there since the beginning of time. When he succeeds, it will truly be the end of days."

"But . . . how can he do that?" Coop asked. "I mean, he can't open up a Rift into heaven. Can he?"

"He needs only to find the Threshold," Damon replied. "It is the portal that the Watchers employ to pass along the road and into Solara."

"Is that a real place?" Coop asked.

"It is. Even I would not have dared to attempt a crossing. There was no reason. I have no true quarrel with the Watchers."

Coop paced nervously. "So you're saying he's going to take those millions of spirits from the Blood and . . . conquer heaven?"

Damon shrugged and said, "Simply put, yes."

There was a long moment of silence as the grim reality set in.

Coop finally broke the tension and grabbed Marsh's arm. "We gotta get back."

"Wait," Marsh said, pulling away from Cooper. "I . . . I have to think."

"He's done, Marsh," Coop argued. "I can't stand looking at him anymore."

Marsh nodded, his mind spinning out of control at the implications.

"Yeah," Marsh mumbled, dazed. "We have to warn Press."

The two backed off and turned away from the broken general. They took only a few steps, when Marsh suddenly spun around and stalked right back and stood over Damon.

"Ralph!" Coop exclaimed.

Marsh ignored him. He got right into Damon's face and said, "You assembled an army in the Black and came searching for more recruits to do what? Battle the Guardians? A force you already defeated once?"

"That was but a minor skirmish," Damon said, scoffing.

"So why battle them again? There's no glory in that. You saw yourself sitting high on a horse in front of an army of spirits that you could lead straight into the Light, didn't you?"

"A splendid dream," Damon said wistfully.

"It was a dream all right," Coop said. "You'd have been cut down in a heartbeat by modern weapons."

"It was never about victory, you obnoxious thug," Damon spat at him. "It was about the glory of the battle."

"A battle you had no chance of winning," Marsh argued. "Not a whole lot of glory there."

Damon was ready to disagree, but remained silent.

"Let's go, Marsh," Coop said.

"Tell me," Marsh said to Damon, "which is more effective? The brute strength that comes with numbers? Or the skills of a master tactician?"

Damon smiled. "You know how I will answer that."

Marsh pressed on. "Then, why not wage a campaign that is truly worthy of your skills?"

"Easy, Ralph," Coop cautioned. "Where are you going with this?"

Marsh stayed focused and said, "Defeating the Guardians

again wouldn't change history's perception of you. And the glory of marching into the Light in front of an impressive army wouldn't last long. Is that all you wanted? A brief moment? Or would you rather battle the greatest force ever assembled . . . with a chance of actually winning?"

"You can't be serious," Coop said with dismay.

Marsh had Damon's full attention.

Keeping his eyes on Marsh, Damon slowly got to his feet.

Coop ran forward to stop him but Marsh put his hand out, keeping Coop back.

"Am I hearing correctly?" Damon said. "Are you suggesting I wage war against Brennus?"

"I am."

"Marsh!" Coop screamed. "He's probably lying through his pointed teeth about Brennus and Solara and all that."

Marsh finally focused on Cooper and said, "Does it matter? You saw those spirits flooding into the Black, and the millions more waiting their turn. The Guardians can't stop them."

Coop was flustered. "But . . . after all he's done to us. Do you realize who you're talking to?"

Marsh glanced to Damon and said, "Yeah. Maybe the only guy who can stop them."

"No!" Coop screamed. "How can we trust him after all he's done?"

"The Watchers won't stop Brennus, and the Guardians are outnumbered a thousand to one," Marsh barked. "Even if he's lying about Solara, do you seriously think the Guardians can stop Brennus, no matter what he's up to?"

Coop started to answer quickly, but held back and softly said, "No."

Marsh pointed to Damon. "But *he* might."

"I don't believe this," Coop muttered under his breath.

Marsh stood directly in front of Damon and said, "So?

Are you willing to gather your spirits and fight the war that you've been waiting centuries for?"

Damon stared at Marsh for several moments, then stepped away, lost in thought. He strolled around the fountain, surveying the Blood version of his ancestral village and contemplating the statue of Alexander.

"You are clever, Marshall Seaver," Damon said. "You have used my weaknesses in an attempt to influence me, as I have played on your fears to do the same to you. Bravo. But as I see it, you need me more than I need you. You are still fighting for your eternal souls, while I have nothing more to lose."

"But a whole lot to gain," Marsh said quickly.

"Do I?" Damon asked. "These are my terms—"

"Terms?" Coop screamed. "He's giving us terms? I'll kick his ass to—"

Coop went for Damon but Marsh held him back.

"What terms?" Marsh asked.

Damon said, "If I were to wage this battle, I would need your assurance that you will do everything in your power to ensure that I will not end up back here."

"How are we supposed to do that?" Coop shouted. "We're not Watchers."

"But you have their ear," Damon argued. "It is the least you can do."

"No, we can do more," Marsh said.

"We can?" Coop asked, surprised.

"If you battle Brennus, I'll plead your case to the Watchers but I can't guarantee what they'll do," Marsh said. "But there's something I *can* guarantee."

Marsh reached into his hoodie and pulled out the crucible.

Damon stood stiff at the sight of it. "The final crucible," he said with reverence.

"Win or lose, when the battle is complete, I promise that I'll destroy this. You'll no longer be cursed by the blood of Alexander."

Damon let the hint of a small smile cross his lips. He glanced up to the statue of his former general, then back to Marsh.

"Very well," he said. "I accept your terms."

"Oh my god," Coop lamented. "I don't believe this."

He pulled away from Marsh and stalked toward Damon. "Are you serious about this? Or is it just another one of your lies?"

Damon stood straight, brushed the dirt from his armor, and spoke with a crisp, confident voice.

"I will not insult you by pretending to be anything other than what I am. I do not justify my actions nor deflect responsibility. But I am proud to say that I am a motivator of men and a superlative tactician. I would welcome nothing more than the opportunity to prove my worth and to show that if anyone is up to the task, it is I."

"And then what?" Coop said, scoffing. "March your army into the Light anyway?"

Damon held Cooper's gaze. Neither blinked.

"No," Damon said with finality. "Defeating Brennus would be adequate . . . so long as the crucible is destroyed and I am free of its hold."

"It will be," Marsh assured him.

"This is just nuts," Coop said, kicking at the ground angrily.

"There is one more thing," Damon said.

"More?" Coop said, incredulous.

Damon looked to Marsh. "If I am to have any hope of succeeding, I will need the poleax."

"No way!" Coop screamed. "Jeez, you got brass."

Marsh looked to the dark sword that he had been holding at his side.

"Why?" he asked.

"You know the power it holds in the Black," Damon said. "It has opened up Rifts between lives . . . and it can close them."

Coop shot Damon a surprised look. "Seriously? You can close the Rift?"

"No matter how brave and accomplished a general may be, a battle against an infinite army cannot be won. To defeat Brennus I must first stop the flow of souls from the Blood."

Marsh looked to Cooper. "What do you think?" he asked.

Cooper shrugged. "I have no idea. It's your call, Ralph."

Marsh raised the poleax and looked it over.

"Are you sure you know what you're doing?" Coop asked.

"Yeah," Marsh replied. "I'm taking the only chance we have."

He held the poleax in both hands and offered it to Damon.

"I have to trust you," he said.

With that, he handed the powerful weapon over to Damon a second time.

29

Marsh and Cooper huddled together inside the Flavian Amphitheater in the Blood, hidden behind a pitted column, watching as the endless stream of spirits continued to move into the Rift.

"Brennus is gone," Coop said, pointing to the empty throne in the royal box.

"He went through," Marsh said. "He's not in the Blood anymore. Don't you feel it?"

Coop nodded. "Yeah. I do. Let's hope he was one of the lucky contestants who got whacked fast on the other side."

Marsh ran from behind the column, moving quickly forward and closer to the Rift, where he ducked down behind a pile of shattered arms and legs that once belonged to statues. Coop was right behind him.

"You realize we made a deal with the devil," Coop said.

"I do."

"We're risking it all for the guy who killed me and your mother and a few thousand other innocent people. And ate some of them, by the way."

"Yup."

"And you think he's going to keep his word?"

"I think he's going to fight because that's what he wants to do. He's never lied about that."

"And what if he wins, Ralph?"

"I don't know. Let's hope we get the chance to find out."

Marsh moved around the pile of marble body parts and sprinted to a spot along the brick retaining wall not five yards from the left edge of the Rift. None of the spirits paid them any attention.

"I'll go first," Coop said. "The Guardians know me. Wait a few seconds and then follow. If I'm not there when you get through, wave your arms and scream your head off."

"What should I scream?"

"I don't know. Your mother's name. Or Zoe's name. Or anything that'll make them realize you aren't like the other drones coming through."

"And then we both start screaming," Marsh said.

"Yeah. Man, I hope you know what you're doing, Ralph."

"Me too. And would you do one thing for me?"

"What?"

"Stop calling me Ralph."

Coop stared at his friend for a long moment, then gave him a big smile and the double okay sign.

"See you on the other side."

"Good luck," Marsh called, but Coop was already up and running for the edge of the Rift.

Coop pushed his way into the line, not caring that he had cut in front of about eight million others waiting to go through, and disappeared into the Rift.

Marsh took one last look back into the Blood, hoping he would never have to see the wretched place again. For any reason. He counted to five, then jumped up and followed Coop. He first had to shove his way into the flow of spirits before riding the wave into the Rift. He was sandwiched between two spirits who were moving quickly. Too quickly. Marsh didn't have time to prepare himself. He held his breath, ready to scream out at the Guardians to avoid getting mowed down by a black sword. Seconds later he was pushed through the gray opening and back out to the arena floor.

In the Black.

After having spent so much time in the dark of the Blood, Marsh was momentarily blinded by daylight. He felt an electric charge jump through his body and realized that the spirit who had come through in front of him had taken a sword hit directly to his chest and been vaporized.

"Hey! It's me! Marshall Seaver!" he yelled, waving his arms.

He saw the silhouette of an attacker move toward him. All he could think to do was fall on his knees and hope that the black sword would miss him.

"I'm Ree Seaver's son!" Marsh yelled, holding his arms up to block the sun and whatever else might be coming his way.

He expected to feel the same tingling sensation as when the spirit had been destroyed, only a thousand times more powerful. He braced himself, ready for his existence to end.

Instead of the stinging shock, his arm was grabbed by strong hands and he was pulled to his feet.

He had made it.

"Where's Cooper?" Marsh asked the Guardian as he was being pulled along.

"Right here, idiot," Coop replied. It was Coop who had grabbed Marsh and was pulling him away from the Rift.

Marsh's eyes finally adjusted to the light and he recognized his best friend. As they moved away from the fighting, he glanced back to see that the defense of the Rift was ongoing. Spirits were still pouring through. Some were quickly destroyed; others escaped in a cloud of color.

"We don't have much time," Marsh cautioned.

"We can't do anything without Zoe's help," Coop replied.

He let go of Marsh, and the two sprinted to the far side of the arena, where Ree and Press stood observing the battle.

Ree threw her arms around Marsh. "Oh thank god," she cried.

"What happened?" Press asked.

Cooper started to answer but Marsh cut him off.

"We've got to clear the Guardians away from the Rift," he said breathlessly. "Now. Right now."

"Why?" Ree asked, confused.

"Because our best hope of beating Brennus is about to come through the Rift, and if the Guardians get to him first, we're done."

"Brennus came through a while ago," Press declared. "He was surrounded by a dozen figments. The Guardians cut down most of them but Brennus escaped."

"All the more reason to clear the Rift," Coop said.

"What's going on, Marsh?" Ree asked.

"If I tell you, you're going to ask more questions and then it will be too late. Please, just trust me."

Zoe ran up to the group, still brandishing her black sword and out of breath from the battle.

"Did you destroy Damon?" she asked.

"Not exactly," was Coop's calm answer.

"Pull back the Guardians," Ree commanded Zoe.

"Pull back?" Zoe shouted with surprise. "Why?"

"Somebody is coming out who can help us," Marsh answered.

"Who?" Zoe asked.

"Just do it!" Marsh yelled with frustration.

"But that will allow hundreds of spirits to come through," Zoe protested.

"A few hundred more won't matter when there are millions lined up to get out of there," Marsh said.

"Millions?" Ree repeated, aghast.

"Give or take," Coop said with a casual shrug. "Pull them back, Zoe. It'll only be for a short while."

Zoe was torn. She glanced between Marsh and Cooper, trying to understand.

"You have to trust us," Marsh said.

Zoe committed. She turned and sprinted back for the Rift.

"She's not going to like this," Coop cautioned.

"Nobody will."

"Who's coming through, Marsh?" Ree asked.

"You wouldn't believe me, so you're just going to have to see for yourself . . . and have a little faith."

"Or a lot of faith," Coop added.

Zoe rounded the Guardians until she came to the edge of the Rift, and the battle zone. She raised her sword and screamed, "Hold back! Hold back! Let them through!"

The Guardians responded with confusion. How was it possible that their leader would be ordering them to back off? They ignored the command and continued to mow down as many spirits as they could.

Zoe lifted her sword and strode across the mouth of the Rift, forcing the Guardians to back off.

"Give way!" she commanded. "Do not attack!"

Some obeyed begrudgingly while others continued to slash and stab. Zoe had to swing her sword threateningly at her own people, forcing them to understand that she was dead serious.

"I said stand down!" she screamed.

Eventually every last Guardian obeyed and backed off, grumbling. They knew better than to challenge Zoe.

Making the situation more confusing was the fact that as soon as they stopped their defense, spirits came flooding through the Rift unhindered. They appeared by the dozens, taking one step into the Black and then disappearing in a cloud of color.

Zoe kept her back to the Rift. She knew what was happening from the horrified looks on the faces of the Guardians but didn't want to see it for herself. She had put her faith in Marsh and Cooper and had to believe she was doing the right thing.

The Guardians continued to retreat until there was a ten-yard buffer between the line of those holding spirit swords and the mouth of the Rift.

"We will stand down!" Zoe shouted so all could hear. "But stay ready. On my command, the defense will continue. Until then, do not attack any spirit that arrives."

Fearing that the temptation to continue the defense would prove to be too much for some of the Guardians, Zoe positioned herself in the dead center of her front line. She faced many inquisitive looks but didn't have the explanation they desperately needed, so she steeled herself and turned to face the swarm of spirits that poured from the Rift.

Seeing the arrival of so many spirits of the damned made her want to raise her sword and cut them down herself, but she held back. It was a difficult test of willpower . . .

. . . that was about to become much more difficult.

Seeing the Guardians retreat and the sudden flood of spirits, the crowd in the stands had grown quiet. They sensed that something dramatic was about to happen.

Marsh held his mother's hand and said, "Believe me, this may be our only hope."

Ree didn't question Marsh. She knew the answers would come soon enough.

All eyes were on the Rift. Even the Guardians settled

down, realizing that they were about to witness something important.

Spirits continued to appear and dissolve. With each passing second, dozens of spirits arrived and escaped. It was as though they knew the defenses were down so they decided to pour in even faster. Hundreds arrived. Multiple hundreds. Then, without warning, they stopped. The Rift remained clear. The flow had ceased. Completely.

Nobody looked away. Nobody questioned. The Colosseum was eerily quiet until . . . the faint yet unmistakable sound of a walking horse was heard coming from the Rift.

Marsh squeezed his mother's hand.

Coop scratched his head nervously.

"Jeez, I hope this doesn't suck," he said to nobody.

A large shadow appeared inside the Rift. It was a rider on a black stallion walking slowly toward the light of the arena.

The front line of Guardians tensed up.

"Let him through," Zoe called to her defenders.

The shadow grew more defined. It was a warrior in full battle armor who boldly strode through the Rift with his chin held high . . . and the poleax on his hip.

Zoe turned and looked back toward Marsh with dismay.

Marsh held both hands up to her as if to say, "Relax. It's okay."

There was a moment of stunned silence, and then the spirits in the stands erupted with shouts of joy.

Their leader had returned.

The outpouring of emotion set the Guardians in motion. They surged forward to attack Damon. Zoe had to draw her own sword and fight to keep them back.

"No!" she screamed. "Let him be!"

She didn't understand why their nemesis was being allowed a free pass back into the Black, but she had put her faith in Marsh and knew she had to follow through.

Ree barely reacted. She kept her eyes on Damon and uttered one simple word. "Really?"

Marsh didn't know how to answer.

Damon looked up at the crowd and basked in the glory for a long moment. He reached for his hip and pulled out the poleax, holding it high in the air in a show of victory. The crowd loved it and cheered wildly.

"Maybe this wasn't such a hot idea," Coop whispered to Marsh.

Damon waved the sword to his adoring minions, then kicked his horse and galloped to the far right side of the Rift as the flow of spirits escaping from the Blood began again. They spewed from the Rift with even more urgency, as if they knew the end was near. Damon did a tight one-eighty until his horse faced the length of the opening that was disgorging spirits. With the roar of the cheering crowd as background, Damon leaned down with the poleax, tearing into the wall of the Colosseum just to the side of the existing opening.

"I guess the thing's loaded again," Coop said.

"What is he doing?" Ree asked.

Marsh hoped he knew, but didn't dare offer an answer.

Damon slapped the reins and trotted forward, dragging the tip of the sword through the opening of the Rift. It was the same move he had made when he had created the Rift, but this time the brilliant light that trailed the poleax closed the opening down. Like two pieces of cloth being sewn together, the Rift was being sealed off as the last few desperate escapees pushed their way through the rapidly shrinking portal.

The Guardians drew back even farther, shocked at the development.

The dramatic gesture quieted the crowd. The only sounds that came from the masses were gasps of surprise . . . and awe.

"Is this really happening?" Ree asked.

Damon made his way to the far side and pulled his sword out of the wall. The Rift was no more. There would be no more spirits escaping from the Blood. Damon trotted back to the center, looked up at the stands, and thrust the poleax into the air.

The spirits went wild, cheering for their hero.

Coop said, "I'm really not liking this."

Damon turned and looked directly at Marsh.

Marsh waited for an acknowledgment, or a salute, or anything to let him know that Damon was going to make good on the rest of his promise.

Instead Damon slashed the poleax down violently, kicked his horse, and took off at a gallop, headed for the archway that led out of the Colosseum.

The Guardians could only watch with wonder.

Damon didn't make it all the way to the archway. The air rippled and the colorful swirl of fog appeared in the opening, swallowing him as he charged through.

"Look!" Coop declared.

The same mist of colors rose up from the cheering crowd, enveloping them. One moment the stands were packed with fifty thousand spirits, the next the seats were empty, the cheers fading to a distant echo.

The hundreds of Guardians on the arena floor remained motionless, all looking up in stunned silence at the now empty seats of the stadium.

"Well . . . that was interesting," Coop said. "Now what?"

"There's going to be a war," Marsh answered.

"I know that," Coop replied. "But are we fighting one army . . . or two?"

30

"Why?" was the question on everyone's mind, though Zoe was the first to ask it.

She came running back to Marsh and Cooper, followed closely behind by many of the other Guardians, who crowded behind her. They had recovered from the shock of seeing Damon march proudly out of the Rift, seal it, and then escape . . . along with a stadium full of his minions.

"He's going to take on Brennus," Marsh said quickly, trying to keep his voice steady.

Zoe's eyes were wild as she struggled to make sense of what had happened.

"But we could have ended him right there!" she shouted. "This could all be over."

"It wouldn't be!" Marsh argued. "Damon doesn't control those spirits that escaped from the Blood. Brennus does, and they're going to cause more problems than Damon ever could."

"But he is the one who created the Rift to allow them to escape," Zoe argued.

"And he closed it," Marsh bellowed. "You saw. You all saw."

The crowd of Guardians was not in an understanding mood. Most couldn't hear what Marsh had to say and saw him as the reason that Damon had slipped through their grasp. The crowd of angry Guardians moved in behind Zoe, their eyes focused on Marsh, their swords ready to begin a new battle right then and there.

Marsh threw up his hands to stop them.

"Please! Trust me! It's the only way."

Instead of accepting Marsh's explanation, his words fired them up even more. They wanted somebody's head for what had happened, and Marsh's was the likely candidate.

"We better skip outta here, Ralph—uh, Marsh," Coop said.

"Come with me," Ree said, and took Marsh's hand. "You come too, Zoe."

Before the Guardians could take another step closer, Ree disappeared in a cloud along with Marsh, leaving Coop to face the angry mob of Guardians.

"It's true," he announced feebly to the emotional group. "Freeing Damon is our best chance and . . . Jeez, I can't believe I just said that."

The crowd didn't care. They moved in on Coop, ready to take him apart. Cooper didn't bother trying to convince them anymore. He stepped out of the vision . . .

. . . and arrived on the train platform next to the subway car in Ree's vision. Press, Ree, Marsh, and Zoe were already inside of Ree's subway car and he quickly joined them.

"I believe you," Press said to Marsh. "Why else would Damon close the Rift?"

"I'm telling you, all he wants is a battle," Marsh said. "It doesn't matter who the enemy is."

"So he says," Coop announced as he entered the train car. "But I still don't trust him."

"Did we have another choice?" Marsh asked.

Coop thought for a second, then replied, "No. It was the only thing we could have done."

"Thank you."

Zoe was so worked up she couldn't stand still. "We could have ended him right there!"

"But the Guardians can't protect the Threshold without help," Marsh shot back.

Press stood up straight, surprised at Marsh's statement.

"Threshold? What threshold?" Zoe asked.

Coop answered, "According to Damon, Brennus is really looking to conquer a place called Solara."

Marsh looked to Press and asked, "Is there such a thing as a Threshold? And Solara?"

Press hesitated as if unsure whether to answer.

"You're here to help us," Marsh demanded. "You can at least give us a little information."

Press opened his mouth but no words came out. He was shaken. Finally, after what seemed like an eternity, he said one simple word: "Yes."

"Thank you," Marsh shot back, all business. "If Brennus takes control of the Threshold, would it be as bad as it seems?"

Press stared at the floor to allow himself time to process the information.

"What is the Threshold, Press?" Ree asked calmly.

Press spoke slowly and deliberately. "It's the conduit through which we pass between Solara and the Black. Call it a Rift, if you like. A permanent one. It has existed since the beginning of mankind."

"That's what the next life is called?" Ree asked. "Solara?"

Press nodded. "It's the spiritual center of the universe. All life eventually becomes part of Solara."

"Unless they get dumped into the Blood," Coop offered.

"Life did not begin in Solara. It's where all spirits are drawn once they are complete."

"So the Watchers exist in there?" Ree asked.

"Yes."

Marsh asked, "Why can't you just move back and forth the way we go between visions?"

"The Threshold is a way to protect Solara," Press explained. "It wouldn't do for spirits to come and go whenever they please."

"Right," Coop said. "You gotta pass the test first."

Marsh asked, "So what would happen if Brennus got to the Threshold?"

Press had trouble finding the words. "What you're talking about is the worst that mankind is capable of creating, overwhelming the best. That's why I went after Brennus in the Blood, and stayed to make sure he wouldn't escape. There was the fear that if he was successful, he would set his sights on Solara."

"Is it even possible?" Ree asked. "Could he get to the Threshold?"

"Spirits stumble on the Threshold all the time, but they are gently turned away. I can't say that a determined army of thousands from the Blood would be so easily dissuaded."

"But the Watchers must have the power to turn them away," Coop said. "I saw them suck an entire army into the Blood!"

"The power to do it and the *right* to do it are two different things," Press said. "We aren't a separate race. We are mankind. If the collective will of so many spirits is determined to enter Solara, they will."

"And what would happen then?" Ree asked.

Press sat down on Ree's couch and stared ahead, imagining the scene.

"This will be hard for you to understand. It's hard for any spirit to understand until they've experienced it for themselves. Solara is a place of infinite possibility. Spirits are no longer bound by the rules of the lives they have lived. What you've seen here in the Black is only a taste of what's possible. Solara was created by the spirit of man and represents the ultimate perfection. It's not just about Earth, either. All the worlds that exist in the universe are equally part of the spiritual fabric of existence. Energy flows from everywhere. From the Light and even the Black. Each and every spirit holds the very essence of mankind in their hands."

Coop, Marsh, and Ree exchanged glances.

"Oh," Coop said casually. "Multiple worlds, spiritual fabric, infinite power. That's pretty much what I figured."

"I know it's hard to grasp," Press said. "But you will. You *all* will. But to disrupt that balance and give that kind of power to spirits who want to bring it all down, well, you might not get that chance because Solara would cease to be the positive influence it has always been. In other words, it would no longer exist as it has . . . and mankind wouldn't be far behind."

There was a long silence as everyone tried to work through what they'd heard.

"Help me understand," Zoe said to Marsh. "Why do you believe Damon will help us?"

"Because it's not about us," Marsh answered. "It's about him. It's always been about him. He's been fighting his own personal demons for centuries. He wants to lead his army into the ultimate battle, something he never did in life. He gathered his army to fight the Guardians and then march triumphantly into the Light. That was the plan, but freeing Brennus changed things. Brennus stole his thunder, just like your father did in life. And Alexander. To him, fighting Brennus would be the ultimate victory and would mean his own salvation. His life would finally be complete."

"And you truly believe this?" Ree asked.

"There's a bigger question," Coop interrupted. "How many spirits came through from the Blood? I thought Marsh was nuts for trusting Damon and giving him the poleax, but I'm changing my tune. The question is not whether we can trust Damon, it's if anybody can stop that army from hell."

All eyes went to Zoe.

The normally confident girl looked pale.

"There is no way to know how many of those spirits came through from the Blood," she said.

"Thousands," Ree interjected. "Many thousands."

Zoe swallowed hard.

"We will fight," she said, her voice shaking. "The spirit swords can destroy untold numbers. But no matter how valiantly we fight, with so many coming at us, eventually we will be overwhelmed."

"So like it or not," Coop said, "we need Damon."

Ree added, "And what if he chooses his own course? Like you said, it's not about us, it's about him. Who's to say that the chance to overrun Solara won't tempt him the same way it did Brennus?"

"It might," was Marsh's sober answer.

"Well, whatever happens," Coop said, "the one thing we know for sure is that somebody's going to attack this Threshold place, so we'd better move the Guardians there before it happens."

"It's like . . . paradise," Marsh said in awe.

He, Cooper, Ree, and Press had left Ree's vision and stepped onto the soft grass of a breathtaking green valley.

High cliffs rose up on either side, blanketed with moss and tropical greenery that cascaded over the rocks like water-falls. The valley floor was narrow and dotted with tall palm trees and flowering bushes.

"It's been called that," Press explained as he led them through the lush surroundings. "This is the last vision that spirits see in the Black before moving through into Solara."

"Nice," Coop commented. "Kind of like taking a victory lap."

The sweet smell of fruit trees filled the air as colorful butterflies danced on the light, warm breeze. The only sound was the far-off roar that came from the many waterfalls that dotted the steep cliffs.

Ree said, "It gives me a feeling of, I don't know . . . calm."

"That's the idea," Press said.

"Don't get used to it," Coop warned.

His words broke the brief spell of euphoria that the group had been enjoying.

"Where's the Threshold?" Marsh asked.

"On the far end," Press replied. "It won't take long."

The four walked for several minutes, marveling at the spectacular, soaring cliffs that rose to either side. The ground was covered with a vast green carpet of soft grass that stretched to the base of the steep cliffs. With each step the valley narrowed as if they were walking into the point of a massive V. After traveling for nearly a half mile, they came upon a dense stand of palm trees that seemed to stand guard across the end of the gorge.

"We're here," Press declared.

He led them along a path that twisted through a stretch of soft brush that was thick with foliage. As they rounded the final bend, all three caught the first glimpse of their destination, and stood frozen.

"Uh . . . wow," was all Coop could say.

A series of shallow stairs, cut from natural stone, rose before them. The wide flight of steps continued up for another thirty yards to top off at a summit that was nearly three stories high. It was a massive plateau, hugged from behind by the two steep valley cliffs that had come together as one. A massive archway stood on the summit that was built from stones so large they seemed to defy gravity. The base of the arch was roughly ten yards wide, half the size of the Rift that Damon had cut into the Blood. Soft light shone from within, revealing no detail and giving the arch a warm, welcoming glow.

"So," Coop said. "Are we talking Pearly Gates here?"

Press chuckled. "Call it what you want. It's the Threshold to Solara."

"Only way in?" Coop asked.

"This is it."

"Don't suppose we could sneak a little peak inside?"

Press grinned at Cooper. "Yeah . . . no."

"Big surprise," Coop said sarcastically.

Ree said, "This is where the Watchers enter the Black?"

Press nodded. "From here we can travel through the Light and the Black the same as you. But there's only one way in and out of Solara."

They heard a rustle of bushes from behind them, and all three spun quickly to see . . .

Zoe had arrived and stood, wide-eyed, staring up at the Threshold.

"Ta-da!" Coop exclaimed.

"Can I walk up?" she asked Press.

Press motioned for her to climb the stairs. Zoe went first and the others followed.

"Don't try sneaking in," Coop said to her. "That's a big no-no."

Zoe ignored the comment and said, "It's good that the

valley is narrow. And closed. There's only one direction an attack can come from."

Marsh asked, "Do the Guardians still want my head?"

"Yes," was Zoe's honest answer. "But we have other things to worry about."

"So they're willing to defend the Threshold?" Ree asked.

They had reached the top of the platform.

"There is your answer," Zoe said, pointing back toward the valley.

From the lofty vantage point they could see over the top of the stand of palm trees and out to the majestic gorge they had just traveled through.

"Oh yeah," Coop said with surprise and relief.

The valley floor was crowded with hundreds of Zoe's Guardians.

"They understand that one way or another, this will be the last stand," Zoe said. "They are ready."

"What's your plan?" Press asked.

"It isn't complicated. We must do the opposite of what we did at the Rift and keep the invaders from going through."

She pointed into the light of the Threshold, and stood staring. Mesmerized.

"Is that really the way into heaven?" she asked.

"No," Press answered quickly. "That's the entrance. The way in is much more difficult."

"Ooh, deep," Coop said.

"Every spirit that exists should eventually step through this portal," Press said. "If they don't, it's by their own choosing."

"And you guys are the judges," Coop said.

"Hey, we don't make the rules," Press said quickly. "We just reflect the desires of mankind. What's happening here is unprecedented. It's nothing less than a battle between philosophies."

"Between good and evil," Marsh said.

"Not exactly," Press replied. "Mankind has always defined itself. We are who we want to be. Spirits are sent to the Blood because they don't accept the wishes of mankind. But if they succeed in overrunning Solara, the definition of what is good and what is evil will change because they will change it."

"And life turns upside down," Coop said. "Trying to be good might land you in the Blood."

"We will not let that happen," Zoe said with total confidence. "Our defenses will begin beyond the line of trees. I will also commit several Guardians with spirit swords to stay back and form a second defense at the base of the stairs, should some of the attackers make it through. I would prefer if you all remain here."

"Whoa, no. I'm going to fight," Coop protested.

"And you will get the chance," Zoe said darkly. "But here."

Coop didn't argue. He knew the odds that the Guardians were facing.

Zoe stood facing the others, looking to each in turn. "I am proud to have known you all," she said. "I will fight in your honor. And my father's."

She made a point of not looking to Marsh.

"Good luck, Zoe," Ree said.

Zoe gave them a quick nod, then turned and hurried down the stairs to rejoin the Guardians.

"She doesn't trust me," Marsh said.

"What did you expect?" Coop asked. "You helped the bad guy."

"But—"

"Hey, you don't have to convince me," Coop said quickly. "I get it."

Ree said, "So now what do we do?"

Press answered. "We wait."

The valley was calm and quiet, in spite of the hundreds of Guardians who had fanned out in front of the line of trees at the base of the Threshold.

Marsh wandered about the platform. He glanced behind the arch to see nothing but the end of the valley. The Threshold had no depth. Gazing through from behind, he could see the valley spread out before him. Looking through from the front, there was only the warm light of Solara. Marsh walked to the front of the arch, in the dead center, and stared inside.

"Maybe we should make a run for it," Coop said as he walked up to stand beside him.

"It's tempting," Marsh said.

"Ah, we'd probably get spit back out like a couple of underweight fish."

The two stood silently.

"Heck of a summer this turned out to be," Coop finally said.

Marsh smiled and shrugged.

"That last day of school seems like such a long time ago," Coop added.

"Yeah," Marsh agreed. "A couple of lifetimes. Ours."

They both let the impact of those words hang for a moment, then . . .

"I'm sorry, Marsh," Coop said.

"For what?" Marsh asked, bristling. "For not protecting me like you always do?"

"No. For coming down on you for living in the past. If there's anybody guilty of that, it's me."

"How do you figure that?"

"Think about it. One of us didn't want to grow up."

"Yeah, and?" Marsh said skeptically.

"And the other one wanted to build model rockets."

Marsh shot Coop a quick, surprised look.

Coop added, "What you've been through these past few years? I couldn't have handled it. Or I would have dealt by causing trouble. But you? You took it and learned . . . and kept moving. You know what I think? You could probably step through this Threshold right now and they'd welcome you with open arms. Why don't you give it a shot?"

Marsh shook his head. "Nah, I'll wait till I get the invite."

"See? That's like . . . wise. I'm ready to just run through and take my chances."

The two chuckled.

"You're my brother, Marsh. You always will be no matter how much we go at each other."

Marsh smiled and nodded sincerely.

"You know something else?" Coop added. "I think all that's happened, to us I mean, I think there's a reason for it."

"Yeah," Marsh said, scoffing. "Seriously bad luck."

"No. This wasn't some random accident. Damon's sword was hidden for two thousand years. He could have chosen anybody to find it. But he didn't. He chose you. And me. And your mother and Ennis and everybody else who got sucked into this nightmare. I don't think that was an accident. I think the Watchers are doing a little more than Press admits."

"Why would they do that?" Marsh asked.

"Because I think they believe we can save them."

Marsh snapped a surprised look to Coop.

Coop followed with, "And one more thing. Maybe the most important thing."

"What's that?"

"I don't care what you say. To me, you'll always be Ralph."

Marsh couldn't help but smile.

The moment was broken by the sound of a horn. A signal. Press and Ree ran up to join Marsh and Coop at the mouth of the Threshold. They stood together to look out over the valley.

"What was that?" Coop asked.

"The call to battle," Ree answered. "Something's about to happen."

"So who's attacking?" Marsh asked. "Damon or Brennus?"

The answer came seconds later. At the opposite end of the valley, several hundred yards beyond where the Guardians were ready to make their stand, the air in the center of the gorge began to ripple and move.

"Whoever it is," Marsh said. "They're coming."

31

Moving like a massive tidal wave, dozens of spirits erupted from the swirl of color that stretched across the valley. Their arrival point was more than a hundred yards from the first line of Guardians who stood nervously waiting for them. It was a gap that closed quickly. The flood of spirits moved ahead to make room for the thousands of others who arrived behind them.

"Brennus," Marsh said.

"How can you tell?" Coop asked.

"It's random. They aren't organized. Damon wouldn't be so reckless. Those are definitely the spirits from the Blood."

Most of the spirits were armed with simple weapons . . . swords, clubs, axes, and cudgels. They raised them high, screaming wildly, ready to tear into the defenders.

"So many," Ree said, barely above a whisper.

They kept coming, pouring out of the fog in mind-numbing volume.

"They're fighting for their lives," Press said. "For their futures. They've escaped from the Blood and want to make sure they'll never get sent back. That's strong motivation."

"We cannot stop them all," Ree said, putting into words what everyone was thinking.

The first wave of spirits hit the Guardians, and the mayhem began. There was nothing creative about their tactics. They fought like animals, using their weapons to try and beat a path through the Guardians and make it to the Threshold of Solara.

The Guardians kept the spirit swords up front. The brave defenders slashed back at their attackers, destroying them by the dozens. But the spirits kept coming. And coming. Those that broke through the first line of defense were met by many other Guardians with conventional weapons. The battles that followed were vicious. Though no injury could end a spirit's existence, the pain was every bit as intense as if it were a battle being fought in the Light. It took incredible courage for the Guardians to stand their ground and fight back. Whenever possible they would drag one of the spirits back toward the front, where a Guardian with a spirit sword would end them. More often a battle ended with one fighter or the other falling in a daze, then fighting back the pain in order to heal and continue on.

It was a low-tech, violent, mutual massacre.

"This can't go on," came a familiar voice.

Maggie Salinger had arrived on the platform. She ran to Coop and threw her arms around him.

"You can't be here," he scolded. "Go back to your vision."

"Not with this going on," she argued.

Coop glanced back into the Threshold, then to Press.

"Help me out here," he called. "If there's anybody who deserves to enter Solara, it's her."

"I know her story," Press said.

"She suffered for years because my grandfather . . . Wait, how could you know her story?"

Press shrugged.

"Then, let her go through," Coop begged.

"No!" Maggie argued. "I'm not going anywhere."

"It's heaven, Maggie," Coop said. "They call it Solara. You belong there."

Maggie gave a quick look into the Threshold, but turned to Coop and said, "But where I *want* to be is here with you."

The Guardians who had stayed back as the last defense tightened up. They formed a line at the bottom of the stone stairs in anticipation of the spirits who were sure to break through. Most held black spirit swords.

Blood spirits continued to pour from the swirling mist.

"Is this how it's going to be?" Ree asked Press. "Because they have the greater numbers, they can change the course of human existence . . . no matter how wrong-minded they may be?"

"Mankind chooses its own course," Press said. "There's nothing I can do, or the spirits of Solara can do, to change that."

"I'm going down there," Coop announced, pulling the spirit sword from his belt.

"Don't!" Maggie begged.

"Why not? The least I can do is take some of those guys down. What are they going to do? Kill me?"

He'd started to move down the steps, when Marsh called out.

"Wait! Look!"

He pointed out to the valley.

"Yeah, we see it. The Guardians can't hold out much longer."

The leading edge of the spirits from the Blood was about to break through the first line of defense. Hundreds were being destroyed, but there were many hundreds more to take their place.

"No!" Marsh yelled. "Look beyond. To the valley."

"I see it," Ree declared. "On both sides."

Two more gateways between visions were materializing. One to either side of the colorful fog that was disgorging the Blood spirits.

"Seriously?" Coop complained. "How many more can they send?"

To the far right of the valley, behind the battling spirits from the Blood, a helicopter appeared from out of the newly created fog. It was a military helicopter that blasted out of the mist, moving fast and low.

"It's a nightmare," Ree said with a gasp.

A gunner was poised inside the fuselage door, ready to open fire.

"This is about to get very ugly," Coop declared, and ran down the stairs.

The helicopter swooped past the battle, then gained altitude and flew out over the far rim of the canyon before circling back to begin its attack run. If the spirits fighting on the valley floor were aware of the incoming marauder, they didn't react or change their tactics.

Ree put her arm around her son's shoulders.

"I'm sorry, Mom," he said.

"Don't be," she said. "We are very small players in this drama."

She hugged him tight and stared at the battle below, ready for the final attack to begin.

The helicopter gunner opened fire . . .

. . . not at the Guardians but at the spirits from the Blood.

"Whoa, wait!" Marsh exclaimed.

The spirits scattered. Some fell, others used their temporarily fallen comrades as shields. The clatter of the machine gun echoed across the valley as the attack continued and bodies fell. The Guardians used the opportunity to regroup and tighten their defenses.

A loud explosion rocked the ground, followed by an eruption of fire and dirt that spewed from the dead center of the Blood spirit army. Bodies flew. Spirits scattered.

Coop came charging back up the stairs. "It's the tank!" he declared. "From the first Rift!"

Rolling from the mist on the left side of the valley was the vintage military attack tank that the Guardians had encountered when they were guarding the Rift in Ree's vision. Only this time, the Guardians weren't the target.

"What is going on?" Ree asked.

Her answer came in the form of a battle cry, and the sight of hundreds of mounted soldiers erupting from the swirling fog to either side of the valley. Armed with swords, lances, and maces, they charged to attack the Blood spirits from either side.

"This is it," Marsh said calmly. "The battle he's waited centuries for."

Leading the charge from the right, on horseback, was Damon. Holding the poleax up high, his dark armor gleaming in the sun, the squat warrior led his soldiers to war.

The two-pronged attack divided the spirits from the Blood. Rather than charge straight ahead at the Guardians with full force, they now had to battle on three sides. And against enemies from above. The helicopter continued to circle back and strafe the thousands of the Blood spirits as they appeared out of the fog.

Without having to repel the full force of the Blood spirits, the Guardians were able to regroup and make a more effective stand. A handful of spirits made it all the way through the gauntlet and past the trees, but they were quickly snuffed out by the Guardians who waited at the base of the steps to the Threshold.

"Divide and conquer," Coop said. "They don't know which way to turn. Damon knows what he's doing."

Damon fought from atop his black horse, slashing down with the poleax, wiping out multiple spirits with every swing. He fought with anger . . . and confidence. He spun his horse every which way, never standing still long enough for a spirit to do any damage. Between the crashing hooves and the swinging blade, no spirit survived an encounter with the poleax of Damon of Epirus.

The influx of Blood spirits spewing into the valley didn't slow down.

The tank turned its gun toward the mist from which they were appearing . . . and fired. The shell hit directly at their point of arrival, exploding on contact, throwing them into such disarray that it significantly slowed the steady stream of reinforcements. The confusion and mayhem it caused was enough to keep each of the battlefronts under the control of Damon's soldiers and the Guardians.

The entire valley floor was turned into a killing field. Bodies were everywhere. Though most returned to fight again, others weren't so lucky and fell to the black swords before they could recover.

Damon directed his troops from horseback, pointing out groups of spirits that were vulnerable. His soldiers responded quickly and efficiently.

"It's everything he wanted it to be," Marsh said in awe.

"And what happens if he wins his battle?" Ree asked. "If he no longer wants to attack the Light, what could he have promised his army to get them to fight?"

"Hopefully he told them the truth," Marsh answered.

"They're fighting for their lives as much as the Guardians are."

"Or maybe he'll still go for the Light," Coop threw in.

Nobody responded to the ominous possibility.

Though Damon's soldiers, and the Guardians, were fighting valiantly and effectively, the battle had been going on for too long.

"They're getting tired," Press pointed out. "Some can barely lift the swords."

While the Guardians and soldiers had the upper hand on the spirits, the spirits still had the superior numbers. With each spirit that was destroyed, its place was taken by a new, fresh fighter.

Even Damon was slowing down. Where at first he had been spinning his horse and slashing like a crazed tornado, he now circled the battle, occasionally sweeping down with the poleax to destroy an unprotected spirit, but no longer engaging in combat.

And more spirits kept flooding in through the fog.

"He had his moment," Press said. "But he's losing it."

They watched soberly as the three-pronged defense weakened, allowing the spirits from the Blood to focus back on the Guardians . . . and the Threshold.

"All it did was prolong the inevitable," Ree said soberly.

At the foot of the steps the second line of Guardians had to battle an increasing number of Blood spirits who made it through.

One spirit came crashing through the brush on horseback headed directly for three Guardians, who were ready and waiting for him.

"Stop!" Marsh shouted down to the Guardians. "Let him go!"

The invader was Damon, looking dazed and barely able to stay on his horse.

Reluctantly the Guardians backed off and allowed Damon to ride up the steps.

"Should we be letting this happen?" Coop asked nervously. "I mean . . . the Threshold."

"Let him come up," Press said with confidence. "A single spirit cannot take down Solara, even if he was foolish enough to try."

Damon's horse looked worse than he did. It was covered with sweat and breathing hard. Its skin was crisscrossed with the slashes from many swords. The dark horse hobbled to the top of the platform and, with a tired exhale, stood in place obediently.

Several Guardians had trailed him and stood behind the horse with spirit swords at the ready in case Damon did anything foolish.

Press, Ree, Cooper, Maggie, and Marsh faced him.

Damon stared into the light of the Threshold, taking an extended, longing look.

"That is one journey I will never be making," he finally said with sad acceptance.

"You kept your word and fought Brennus," Marsh said.

"But to what end?" Damon shot back.

Cooper grabbed his sword, ready to protect Marsh if Damon lashed out with the poleax.

"This is a war that cannot be won," Damon added, then chuckled ironically. "I suppose in hindsight it was not wise to make this my one and only battle."

"You led your army bravely," Marsh said. "You don't have anything more to prove."

Damon looked down to the fighting in the distance.

"A noble effort that ultimately was for naught," Damon said wistfully.

"It's not over," Ree said.

"But soon," he warned. "Look down there. The spirits

from the Blood cannot be held back. They will break through and begin their final assault of the Threshold."

"I don't believe that," Marsh snapped at him. "There must be something more we can do. You're the genius general. Come up with something!"

Damon gave Marsh a small smile. "It is ironic that the person who hates me the most has the most faith in me."

"So do something!" Coop shouted. "I'm not a big fan of yours either, by the way."

Damon looked down to the battle and spoke as if he was thinking out loud.

"Without a dramatic change this battle will soon be over," he began. "As I see it, there is only one last move that can be made."

"So make it!" Coop shouted.

Damon shook his head. "No. I would most certainly fail."

"What is it?" Marsh asked impatiently.

"The spirits of the damned are driven," Damon said. "Brennus has turned them into a single entity with a common goal . . . survival and revenge. Look at them fight. No one spirit matters. They are sacrificing themselves willingly in the hope of making it through to the heart of the enemy. To Solara. No fighting force could possibly have come to this on their own. It was Brennus. He has gathered them and brought them to this moment. He is the force that guides their hand as if they were a single living being."

"So where is this Brennus?" Ree asked, surveying the field. "I don't see him leading the way."

"I am sure the sin eater will make his triumphant arrival once the battle has been won and the Threshold has been secured. It is something I have done many times. Until then, I believe he is directing this battle from his own vision . . . the small village where he performed his unholy art."

"And your point is . . . ?" Coop said.

"To kill this beast you must cut off its head," Damon snapped. "Without Brennus, they will be lost."

The group exchanged encouraging looks.

"Yeah," Coop said. "Makes sense. So go after him!"

"I cannot," Damon replied. "He knows me too well, as do his minions. I would not get within a whisper of him. It would take an innocent to end Brennus. Someone unexpected."

Damon reached to his belt, grabbed the poleax, and pulled it free. He held up his beloved, infernal weapon and admired it once again. He then grabbed the blade with his other hand and swung the sword down slowly until the handle was pointed directly at Marsh.

"I am returning this to you with my gratitude for your trust," Damon said. "I honor you for the faith you had in me, for your courage, and I say to you in all sincerity that after all you have seen, all that you have encountered at my hand, it is only fitting that you be the one to end this."

All eyes went to Marsh.

Marsh stood with his mouth open, stunned, looking up at his nemesis.

"You have been tested more than most," Damon said. "Both physically and spiritually. You are ready. Take the sword and cut the head from the beast."

Marsh focused on the poleax . . . the source of all his troubles. It led to the death of his mother and his best friend. It caused him to be haunted by the demons that lurked in his own imagination and in worlds beyond.

Marsh looked to his mother, desperate for her wisdom.

"What do I do?" he asked.

"You've led this battle from the beginning," Ree answered calmly. "Now you can end it. What better way to demonstrate to the Watchers that we represent the true spirit of mankind?"

Marsh stared at the offered sword.

"Is that true, Press?" Marsh asked. "Will this convince the Watchers to—"

He looked to Press, but the Watcher was gone.

"Nice," Coop said sarcastically. "When the going gets tough . . ."

"Take it," Damon said to Marsh. "What I began, you can end."

Marsh swallowed hard. With a steady hand, he reached up and grasped the handle of the monstrous sword.

It was an unholy weapon that had changed his life forever.

And now it was his.

32

It was dark. And cold.

Marsh had stepped out of the swirling fog into a dense pine forest. He stood still and listened, hoping for a clue as to where he was and where he should go.

"Been here, done this," Coop said.

Marsh spun quickly to see Coop step out of the fog.

"Go back," Marsh ordered. "I've got to do this alone."

"Why?" Coop asked. "Because Damon thinks it's your destiny or something? Bull. You need me, Ralph."

"You still think I'm not capable?"

"Don't get all huffy," Coop replied. "You're plenty capable. Or as capable as anybody who never threw a punch in his life and has to fight the nastiest guy in existence."

"I don't plan on fighting him," Marsh said as he held up the poleax. "All I need is an opening."

"And I'll make sure you get it. I've been here before. I know where he lives. I even know his brother. Are we going to do this together or are you still trying to prove something?"

Marsh kicked at the ground anxiously.

"C'mon, Marsh," Coop argued. "It's us. You and me."

Marsh looked straight at Coop and said, "I think you're right. There may be a reason why we're in the middle of this. But if that's true, then I've got to be the one to end it."

"Agreed. And I'm going to make sure you do."

Marsh gave him a slight smile.

"Excellent," Coop said. "Follow me."

He led Marsh through the woods along the same route he had taken when he had been there before, hunting for Damon.

"Over there!" Marsh declared.

"No," Coop said. "The village is this way."

"But something's going on over there."

Coop listened and heard it too. There was the sound of activity coming from a spot deeper in the woods. The two changed direction and wound their way through the trees until they broke out onto a huge meadow that was full of anxious spirits jockeying to enter a wall of swirling color. There were multiple thousands, all crowded together, all pushing toward the fog . . . and the battle that waited for them on the other side.

"This is where they landed when they came through," Coop whispered. "Jeez, there's still a ton of them."

"Makes sense they'd come to Brennus's vision," Marsh said. He looked around and added, "So where's Brennus?"

Coop glanced around, but the twisted spirit was nowhere in sight.

"I doubt that he needs to be pointing the way for these guys," Coop said. "He's got them totally programmed."

"So then, where is he?"

They sunk back into the woods and continued through

the moonlit labyrinth. Along the way they passed several spirits from the Blood who wandered aimlessly as if having lost track of the others, and their minds. They would focus on Marsh and Cooper for a second, then move on, uninterested.

"Damon was right," Marsh said. "They would have recognized him and stopped him."

"Yeah, we're nobodies," Coop added. "But not for long."

They continued until they came upon the low stone wall that surrounded the village.

"This is where Brennus lived in the Light," Coop explained. "And did his sin-eating thing."

They cautiously hopped the wall and, with their swords drawn, crept past the stone huts until they reached the village center, where a ring of huts surrounded a single well. The village was dark and quiet. There was no sign of life anywhere, except for one hut. Light glowed from within. Smoke rose from the center chimney.

Two heavyset characters stood guard out front.

"That's where his brother lives," Coop whispered. "He's an old man named Riagan. He's no threat, but those two bozos out front are trouble."

"Get them out of the way," Marsh said flatly.

Coop gave Marsh a playful shove. "I told you you needed me."

Marsh wasn't in the mood for kidding around. "Just get them outta there," he commanded.

"Done."

Coop left Marsh, quickly skirting around the back side of the huts to circle closer to the sentries.

Marsh followed, but not too closely. He wanted to be in position for when Cooper got the burly guards away from the door. His heart pounded. He forced himself not to think about what he was there to do. He had never hurt anyone in his life. He feared that when the moment came, he would hesitate. Or worse, fail. He had to keep telling himself that Brennus wasn't human. He was the sum of so much evil that he could coerce legions into destroying the spirit of mankind. Marsh kept the vision of the battle at the Threshold in mind. So many spirits were willing to fight for what was right. How could he not do the same?

Cooper crept around the back side of the hut next to Riagan's. He was behind the sentries, but ten yards away. It was a long distance of open ground to cover. He held his black sword with one hand, the blade pointing skyward. He knew he didn't have to win a battle, he only had to get a piece of them. The sword would do the rest. He looked back to see Marsh crouched on the far side of the hut, behind him. He gave him a wink, then sprinted for the guards.

Coop covered the ten yards quickly and destroyed the first guard before the sentry even realized he was being attacked. With a powerful swipe of the sword he lashed it across the doomed spirit's chest, barely feeling the impact as the unsuspecting guard was turned to a shadow that quickly vanished.

The second spirit, Maedoc, reacted quickly. Rather than attack, he jumped back in order to buy time to defend himself.

Cooper didn't attack either, but kept the spirit sword high.

"Remember me?" Coop taunted while waving the sword.

Slowly he backed away from the hut toward the well.

Maedoc's eyes blazed. He glanced to the door as if unsure if he should leave his post.

"Looking for help?" Coop taunted. "Don't think you can take me yourself?"

The baiting worked. Maedoc growled angrily and stalked toward Cooper . . .

. . . leaving the door unguarded.

Coop didn't dare to glance in Marsh's direction for fear that he would alert Maedoc.

"C'mon, Bluto," Coop teased. "You're dying to take me

apart, aren't you? Nobody's gonna stop you this time. It's just you and me."

Maedoc crouched low, looking for an opening.

Coop knew it would be no contest. Maedoc was unarmed. His only goal was to keep the brute's attention on him and not on the hut.

Maedoc faked a move, as if he was going to charge.

"Ooh," Coop taunted. "Slick move. Didn't see that coming."

Maedoc let out a low growl. His anger had reached the boiling point.

Coop held the blade close, ready to nail the big guy the moment he sprang.

Maedoc jumped forward . . .

. . . and Marsh made his move toward the door.

Coop glanced to his friend, and immediately wished he hadn't.

Maedoc saw Coop's look, pulled up, and glanced over his shoulder.

"Damn," Coop swore.

Maedoc forgot about Coop and took off after Marsh. He was fast for a big guy and would have caught Marsh before he got to the door . . .

. . . if Coop hadn't gotten to him first. He lunged at Maedoc, blade first. The tip of the spirit sword caught the huge man in the back. Maedoc froze and tried to turn back to see what it was that had skewered him, but he never saw his attacker. A second later the burly spirit floated away as shadowy vapor.

Marsh didn't notice or care. He pushed open the door and leaped inside.

Coop started to follow but didn't get far. He sensed more than saw a quick shadow flash by his face. A second later he felt searing pain stretch across his arms. He had been holding out the spirit sword with both hands as the shadow flashed down, hitting his wrists, knocking the weapon from his grasp. His instinct made him recoil from the attack, which was the worst thing he could have done. By the time he caught his balance and recovered enough sense to retrieve the sword, his attacker had swept in and scooped the blade from the ground.

"What have we here?" the man said as he quickly directed the blade toward Cooper.

Cooper froze, now facing the point of his own weapon.

"Didn't expect to see you again," the man said with a smile that showed stained teeth.

"Sanger," Coop said with disdain.

"Aye," replied the old man. "Don't know when to quit, do ya?"

Marsh stepped inside the large hut with every sense on alert. He kept his back to the door and the poleax ready. The first thing he registered was music. The soft sound of a single recorder filled the room with a haunting tune.

A fire burned in the dead center, surrounded by a ring of stones. Its light was so bright it threw the walls of the round hut into deep shadow. Brennus could have been lurking anywhere.

Marsh moved cautiously around the perimeter, keeping his back to the wall so that everything was in front of him. Once he moved a few feet, he could see past the fire to the far wall of the hut, and froze.

Lying on a wooden table was Brennus. The grotesque, twisted spirit was on his back, staring up at the ceiling. The only movement came from his short, quick labored breaths. Marsh's confidence soared. Brennus was in no shape to put up a fight. Whatever was wrong with him, he didn't seem capable of joining his spirit army, let alone leading them into Solara. But the battle was still raging and whether he was physically there or not, he still had influence over the Blood spirits. That wouldn't end until Brennus was ended.

Marsh gripped the poleax tighter and continued to move around the wall to get closer to his target.

Beyond Brennus was another table that was pushed right up against the wall. On this table were the partially eaten remains of a huge feast. There were empty bowls, loaves of bread with large chunks torn off, a half-eaten chicken, and loads of fruit, all with single bites taken out. Was this Brennus's downfall? Had he gorged on a huge meal and it had somehow made him sick?

The recorder music stopped.

Marsh had been so focused on Brennus that he had nearly forgotten about it. It wasn't until it ended that he realized it wasn't Brennus who was playing the music.

"Me brother be near the end of his existence," came a man's voice from the shadows directly across the hut from Marsh. It was a deep, intense voice that barely spoke above a whisper.

Marsh stopped moving.

"Are you . . . Riagan?" he asked tentatively.

"Aye," the deep voice whispered.

"What's wrong with Brennus?" Marsh asked.

"He carried the weight of sin for too long," Riagan replied. "No spirit be able to survive with such a dark burden forever. Returning to the Black be his undoing."

Marsh's heart hammered. Could it be? Was Brennus going to die on his own?

"The weapon you carry," Riagan said. "I heard tell of its power. Brennus sought such a weapon, but alas, it be of no use to him now. Perhaps . . . you should be giving it to me."

Coop dodged away from Sanger, who teased him with the spirit sword, waving it in front of his eyes. Coop kept backing up, making sure to keep the lethal weapon a safe distance away . . . and Sanger away from the hut.

"What are you doin' here?" Sanger said. "The fight for the Threshold's as good as over. You looking for mercy?"

"Yeah," Coop said. "That's it. If you can't beat 'em, join 'em, right?"

"Liar," Sanger spat.

He swung the sword, forcing Coop to dodge out of the way.

"Why would I lie?" Coop asked. "Brennus is in charge now. Nothing I can do about that."

"Is that what you think?" Sanger said teasingly. "Shows what you know."

Sanger lunged at Cooper. Coop dodged to the side and made a move to grab Sanger, but Sanger pulled the sword back quickly, regaining the advantage.

"You're a fighter," Sanger said. "That's good. I enjoy a good dustup now and again."

Marsh inched closer to Brennus, his mind racing. Brennus looked helpless. It would have been easy to simply thrust the poleax into him as he lay there, but Marsh couldn't be certain if Brennus was as weak as he looked.

"Brennus treated me like a servant, he did," Riagan said with disdain. "A common slave. In the Light and then here. I would bring the dead here for him to do his work and collect his fees. It was the devil's work, but he gave me no choice. Me own brother. Now look at him. Crushed under the weight of his own making."

Marsh squinted, trying to find Riagan in the shadows.

"You have a choice now," Marsh said. "He can't make you do anything. Not anymore. Help me stop the attack."

"Stop it?" Riagan said with surprise. "Why would I be

doing that? I dreamed of this day. I planned for it. Unlike me brother, I have stayed strong. His fate will not be mine, for I be prepared."

"Prepared for what?" Marsh asked nervously.

Marsh finally saw movement in the shadows. A hulking figure rose up from the floor and stepped forward into the firelight. Marsh's knees went weak. Coop had said that Riagan was an old guy and not a threat. That couldn't have been further from the truth, for the man towered over Marsh with a grotesquely wide face and eyes that blazed with insanity. He wiped his greasy-slick face with hands that were twice the normal size.

"To take command of his army," Riagan hissed. "He had not the strength to continue, so I relieved him of his burden."

"You . . . what?" Marsh asked, aghast.

"All that Brennus was, all that he took on, be resting with me now."

"I . . . I don't understand."

"He be as good as dead, so I ate the sins of a sin eater," Riagan snarled, gesturing to the half-eaten feast. "And with that weapon I will enter Solara. So if you please . . ."

Riagan sprung at Marsh, grabbing for the poleax.

Marsh dodged away, tripped over a bench, and knocked over a small table.

Coop continued to maneuver Sanger farther away from the hut.

Sanger was happy to oblige, enjoying the fact that Cooper feared him . . .

. . . until they heard the sound of crashing furniture. Sanger spun toward the hut with surprise, and Coop attacked. He grabbed the wiry man in a bear hug, pinning his arms to keep him from swinging the sword.

"I shoulda known," Sanger said.

He was far stronger than Coop expected. He took a deep breath and forced his arms forward, breaking Coop's hold. Then he drove an elbow back, nailing Cooper square in the jaw.

Coop saw stars and reeled backward. He fought to stay upright and clear his head but the force of the blow knocked him off balance and he fell flat on his back.

Sanger pounced quickly, jamming his foot down onto Cooper's chest while holding the sword to his throat.

"I shoulda finished you in the Blood," Sanger said, taunting. He drew the sword back and was about to drive it into Cooper to end his existence when . . .

"Stop!" came a girl's voice.

Sanger looked up to see that Maggie had arrived. He blinked, as if not entirely sure of what he was seeing.

"Wha—?" he muttered, confused.

Maggie was just as shaken as Sanger. She opened her mouth to speak, but no words came out.

Coop took the opportunity and knocked Sanger's foot off his chest. He quickly rolled away and sprang to his feet, expecting to feel the bite of the spirit sword. The attack didn't come and Coop spun back toward Sanger, ready to defend himself.

Sanger stood with the sword up, ready to swing. His eyes were wild and confused as he looked between the two of them.

"Put it down," Maggie commanded.

Sanger nodded knowingly as he struggled to get his wits back.

"I get it now," he said. "S'pose I shouldn't be surprised. That's how it works. We all just keep coming back around to each other."

Coop moved away from Maggie, not wanting her to be near him when Sanger attacked.

"What are you babbling about?" he said to Sanger.

Sanger chuckled and coughed. "This is just perfect. What goes around, comes around. Are you sweet on her, boy? You must be or I wouldn't have run into you in the Blood. Guess this is just my lucky day."

Coop looked to Maggie, confused.

Tears streamed down her cheeks.

"What are you talking about?" Cooper demanded.

Sanger smiled and cackled a laugh. "This just couldn't be better. I get sprung from the Blood, I'm about to ride into Solara . . . and best of all, I get payback for what she done to me."

Coop's blood ran cold. He looked to Maggie for confirmation.

Maggie nodded and through her sobs said, "He's my father."

Riagan ran through the fire to get to Marsh, knocking aside an iron pot and kicking out flaming logs. Taking on Brennus's cursed soul had changed him, both physically and mentally. He was like an enraged animal as he grabbed at furniture and utensils and anything else he could grab to fling at Marsh.

Marsh backed off, desperately swinging the poleax to defend himself.

"Drop it now!" Riagan bellowed. "Or I promise you will suffer."

Marsh lashed at him with long swings, not the tight controlled jabs of an experienced warrior.

Riagan easily avoided the pathetic attacks.

Marsh took a few steps back . . . and a hand grabbed him

from behind. He spun to see that he had hit the table where Brennus was lying, and the weakened spirit had grabbed hold of his hoodie.

"Sanger?" Coop said, stunned. "Or Salinger?"

"I answer to both," Sanger said. "And now you'll both answer to me."

"Stop!" Coop shouted, his mind spinning, desperately trying to stay focused and process what he was seeing. "It wasn't her fault that you died."

"No?" Sanger snarled. "She locked me in the barn and lit the place on fire. That girl's the devil, I tell ya!"

Coop slowly stalked toward Sanger, his anger rising as it finally sank in that he was facing the monster who had made Maggie's life miserable for so long.

"She unlocked the door," Coop said. "It was the neighbor kids who relocked it and then accidentally knocked over a lamp."

"And she cheated me! She was going to run off with my money!"

Maggie fell to her knees, sobbing. The sight of her father had overwhelmed her.

"She was your daughter!" Coop yelled. "And you beat her. She was trying to escape from you."

"Escape? If only that were true. The witch killed me . . . and her mother."

"It was an accident! It wouldn't have happened if you hadn't been beating her. That's why those kids were there. They heard you yelling. They were there because of you. It was *your* fault it happened."

Sanger looked to Maggie with no sympathy.

"She's your daughter, man," Coop said.

The look in Sanger's eyes turned hard.

"She stole from me," he said with a snarl. "And then she killed me."

The old man raised his sword as if to swing at Cooper, but abruptly turned and went for Maggie.

Maggie screamed and cowered.

Cooper lunged at Sanger, leaving his feet as he tackled the old man.

Sanger fell hard, dropping the sword. Cooper was so enraged he didn't notice and wouldn't have cared. He flipped the old man over and began swinging.

Marsh didn't know if Brennus was trying to pull him down or was using him to get up. Either way, he didn't want anything to do with him so he twisted away. But Brennus's grip was strong. He held on and Marsh ended up pulling him off the table. The skeletal spirit fell to the dirt floor, finally releasing his grip so that Marsh was able to stumble away from the table.

Riagan stayed after Marsh, carelessly kicking his frail brother out of the way with one sweep of his boot.

Marsh did all he could to protect himself. He pulled over tables and chairs to slow Riagan down, or trip him up so that he could come back at Riagan with the poleax.

But Riagan was too fast and powerful. He continued to attack, ducking Marsh's feeble attempts to defend himself, looking for the opening he would need to grab the poleax and turn it back on Marsh.

Sanger responded like a trapped animal. He howled and threw Cooper off him. But rather than attack, he looked around quickly, saw the black sword in the dirt, and jumped for it.

Cooper had no chance to get it first . . .

. . . but Maggie did. She scooped up the sword and backed away quickly, holding the weapon out to protect herself from the vengeful spirit of her father.

"Go away!" she screamed, her tears clouding her vision. "Go back to whatever hell you came from!"

Cooper ran for Sanger, but Sanger sensed that he was coming. He spun quickly and threw a vicious roundhouse punch that knocked Cooper to the ground, senseless. He then turned back to Maggie, his emotions in check. Slowly he moved toward her.

"You want to finish what you started, don't you?" he taunted. "You want to kill me again."

Maggie shook her head violently. "I didn't kill you," she sobbed. "It wasn't my fault."

"But you did. You killed me and your mother. If I belong in hell, then you should be right there with me."

"No!" Maggie screamed.

"Then, do it!" Sanger snarled. "Cut me down. This is your chance."

He moved closer.

Maggie kept backing off, sobbing uncontrollably.

"This is the end, girl," Sanger said. "I'm about to live the glory of Solara while you get what you deserve . . . an eternity of suffering."

Maggie couldn't move.

Sanger stood with his hands on his hips and laughed.

"It's a lot tougher killing somebody when you have to look 'em in the eye," he said.

Maggie tried to raise the sword against her father, but instead she shook her head and let her hands fall. The tip of the sword hit the dirt.

"Can't do it, can ya?" Sanger said with disdain as he started forward to finish her.

He lunged at his daughter . . .

. . . as Cooper swept in, grabbed Maggie's hands, and lifted the sword.

"But I can," Coop said.

Sanger tried to stop . . . too late. He had already committed. With Coop and Maggie both holding the sword, Sanger impaled himself on the end.

The look of shock lasted only a second, and then he was gone.

Coop didn't stop to see if Maggie was okay. He wrenched the sword from her hands and ran for the hut.

Marsh's luck had run out. He was exhausted.

Riagan wasn't. He was fueled by the newly acquired dark energy he had stolen from Brennus. He grabbed one of the wooden legs from the table that Damon had destroyed and used it as a weapon to ward off the increasingly feeble attacks that Marsh was offering.

With one final desperate maneuver, Marsh swept the poleax at him, hoping to catch him with the chopping blade.

Riagan didn't even bother to try and dodge the blow. He blocked it with the table leg, then quickly swept the wooden club backward, cuffing Marsh on the side of the head. The powerful blow sent Marsh reeling. He fell backward onto the table that held the feast of the sin eater, knocking it over and sending the food flying. The poleax was wrenched out of Marsh's hands and clattered to the floor.

"Why did ya even try?" Riagan snarled. "That weapon be useless in the hands of the likes of you."

Marsh struggled to clear his head.

Riagan went for the poleax.

Marsh had no chance of getting to it first.

"Riagan!" Coop called.

Riagan spun in surprise to see Coop standing inside the door with the black spirit sword up and ready.

"You," Riagan growled. "You who sought Damon of Epirus."

"And now I'm coming after you," Coop threatened.

"You don't stand any better a chance than your weak friend," Riagan said with arrogance.

He turned back to retrieve the poleax . . .

. . . opening himself up to Marsh, who stood holding Damon's sword with the point aimed square at Riagan's chest.

Riagan froze in surprise.

"As last words go," Marsh said with confidence, "not so great."

Riagan made a move to escape . . .

. . . and Marsh drove the poleax into his chest.

Riagan opened his mouth to scream but didn't get the chance. Before the sound could cross his lips, Riagan's existence ended in a shadowy cloud.

Coop was too stunned to move.

Marsh held the poleax tight and turned around. He wasn't finished. On the floor before him was the broken body of the monster named Brennus.

Brennus looked up at him, square in the eye. His body may have been weak, but Marsh could see the evil that still lurked behind his gaze.

"This doesn't end until you do," Marsh said.

"You do not have the courage," Brennus whispered.

"Well . . . yeah, I do," Marsh replied, and drove the poleax into the sin eater.

Brennus's eyes flared with anger as his body disintegrated into a dark cloud . . . and disappeared.

"Now it's over," Marsh said with finality, and dropped the poleax to the floor.

Cooper ran to him and stared down at the empty space where Brennus had just been.

"Jeez," Coop said in dismay. "You did it. I knew you could."

"No, you didn't."

"You're right, I didn't."

"Now what?" Marsh asked.

"Now we see what it all means," Coop replied, and ran for the door.

Marsh picked up the poleax and followed him outside to where Maggie was waiting.

She stood tall. Her tears were gone.

"Thank you," she said in a strong, confident voice.

"Believe me, it was my pleasure," Coop said.

He took her by the hand as the swirling fog of color appeared before them. All three stepped into the mist . . .

. . . and stepped out onto the platform of the Threshold.

In the valley below, the battle continued. The Blood spirits were dangerously close to breaking down the Guardians' first line of defense. They would soon hit the trees and then the stairs that led to the Threshold.

Damon remained on his horse, alone, on the far side of the platform.

Ree stood on the opposite end, also surveying the carnage. When she saw the three appear, she let out a sigh of relief and ran to Marsh.

"It's done," Marsh said in a soft voice.

Coop and Maggie joined them.

"Doesn't look so done to me," Coop said, pointing down to the battle that raged below.

Zoe came up the stairs, half running, half staggering. She was exhausted. Her armor was in tatters, her face covered with welts.

"I am going to order the Guardians to pull back and

regroup at the base of the stairs," she declared. "That is where we will make our final stand."

"Wait," Marsh declared. "Look."

He pointed out to the valley. The battle was continuing as before, with one significant difference.

"It's gone," Ree said with surprise.

"What is?" Coop asked, confused.

"The gateway between visions," Ree exclaimed. "It's closed."

All eyes went to the far end of the valley and to the colorful fog that had been disgorging thousands of spirits from Brennus's vision. It was no longer there.

"Ending Brennus must have ended his vision," Coop said with growing hope. "The Blood spirits can't get through anymore."

Cooper looked to Marsh and gave him the double okay sign. "Jeez, you really *did* do it, Ralph."

"Now it's up to the Guardians," Marsh said. "And Damon's army."

"And the Watchers," Maggie said.

"Forget that," Coop replied with bitterness. "We can't count on them."

"I'm not so sure," Maggie said as she pointed back to the Threshold.

Everyone turned to see that the warm light from the Threshold was growing brighter, as if the archway was slowly coming to life. A stiff wind blasted from within, followed by a chorus of sharp whistles. From the depths of the Threshold, thousands of small black streaks flew out, each making a shrill sound as they flashed past those standing on the platform.

"What is this?" Marsh asked in awe.

They all watched in wonder as the black streaks shot high over the valley like a flock of birds headed toward the far end, traveling high above the battlefield.

On the valley floor, the fighting ended abruptly as the spirits stood frozen, staring up at the spectacle in the sky.

"I've seen this show before," Coop said as he put his arm around Maggie. "You're gonna love it."

The dark shadows reached the far end of the valley, then made a wide turn until they were headed back in the direction they had come from. Once all the shadows had made the turn, they quickly swooped downward like a fleet of attack planes. When they reached the spot where the colorful fog had been, there was a ground-rattling explosion as if the spirits had hit an invisible barrier. The eruption resulted in a massive black cloud that drifted down toward the ground, creating an enormous, dark wall.

The flying shadows continued on, flying low to the ground headed directly for the multitude of soldiers that stood frozen, watching in wonder. The shadows passed harmlessly through the Guardians and Damon's soldiers. The Blood spirits weren't as fortunate. When the black shadows hit the spirits of the damned, they acted like a demonic force that pulled each of them toward the giant black wall . . . that was no longer a wall.

The black fog had opened like a curtain to reveal another reality beyond. It was a gaping portal into the desolate, dark world that existed on the wrong end of the Morpheus Road.

The Blood spirits fought. They screamed. They begged the Guardians to help them.

They were done.

Each spirit was lifted off the ground and instantly transformed into a dark shadow. But rather than dissipating and blowing away, the small clouds were pulled into the opening and back into the Blood.

"Listen," Marsh said.

The familiar sound of forlorn moaning had returned. It drifted from the open curtain and filled the valley with its plaintive wail. The Blood was once again occupied.

"I don't know who's worse off," Coop said. "The ones being pulled back or the ones who were destroyed."

"What about the spirits still in Brennus's vision?" Marsh asked.

Coop said, "I'll bet you a nickel they're getting the same treatment."

It took only a few moments for every last spirit who had escaped from the Blood and survived the battle to be returned. When the last shadow was swallowed up, the curtain of smoke drew together and swallowed itself, disappearing as if it had never been there.

The swarm of black shadows continued back toward the Threshold, joined together, and flew inside like a swarm of bats returning to their cave. Within seconds the bright light dissipated and the Threshold had returned to normal.

The valley was quiet for a long moment . . . until a single soldier began to cheer.

He was followed by another, and another. Soon, all of the remaining Guardians and soldiers erupted into a joyous celebration, hugging and congratulating one another. It didn't matter which leader they had followed into battle. They had faced a common enemy and survived.

And the Threshold was safe.

"The battle is over," Zoe announced. "But will the war continue?"

All eyes went to Damon, who sat tall on his black horse, quietly observing the celebration below.

33

Damon dismounted, stood tall, and strode boldly toward the others.

Zoe went for her sword, but Marsh grabbed her arm and held her back.

Marsh stepped forward to face Damon. The others stood behind him, all on alert for anything Damon might try.

Coop kept his hand close to his spirit sword.

Marsh held the poleax by the handle with the point down.

Damon walked directly up to him, stopped a few feet away, and said, "I assume that Brennus's spirit is no more."

"That's right," Marsh answered.

Damon gave him a slight, respectful nod. "Then, I salute you."

"How did it feel?" Marsh asked Damon.

"How did *what* feel?" Coop said, confused.

Damon gazed out onto the valley. Onto the battlefield.

The celebration had died down and the thousands of spirits stood together, looking up toward the Threshold, toward them, waiting for a sign as to what they should do next.

Damon surveyed the scene with satisfaction.

"As I hoped it would," he said. "And now, would you be so kind as to return my weapon?"

He reached out, ready to accept the poleax.

Coop and Zoe stiffened.

Marsh didn't move. "Not a chance," he said flatly.

Damon smiled and dropped his hand. "I did not think so."

"But we made a bargain," Marsh added.

He reached into the pocket of his hoodie and retrieved the last golden crucible. He held it out to Damon, who took a defensive step backward as if it were diseased.

"Last one," Marsh said, and casually tossed the crucible over his shoulder.

The golden orb arced into the air and came down on the stone platform. It shattered on contact, spewing forth the final remains of Alexander the Great.

Coop winced, as did Ree, but neither said a word.

Damon stared fearfully as if the cursed blood might rise up and drown him, but the thick liquid did nothing more than trickle through the cracks between stones . . . and disappear.

"Thank you for that," Damon said. "And our other arrangement?"

Marsh shrugged. "You're still here, aren't you?"

Damon looked around, as if realizing for the first time that he had not been swept back into the Blood with all of the other spirits.

"Indeed," he said with a satisfied smile. "To whatever extent you were responsible, I thank you."

"I think you have yourself to thank," Marsh said.

"Indeed," Damon said, satisfied. "Then, I will take my leave."

"There's one thing," Marsh added. "Stay the hell away from me. From all of us. Wherever you travel, whatever you do, I don't ever want to see you or hear of you again."

"Understood," Damon said with a slight deferential bow.

He turned and headed back for his horse. The others watched tensely as he mounted, adjusted his armor, and was about to trot off when . . .

"Damon," Marsh called out.

Damon looked back to him.

"I have to know. This could have happened to anyone for two thousand years, but it happened to us. Was it all just random or was there some purpose?"

"I have asked that same question myself," Damon answered. "I do not pretend to understand all there is to know of the forces that influence us, but after having observed them for so long, I believe I know more than most."

"So what's the answer?" Marsh pressed.

"I do not know," Damon said with a shrug. "Perhaps there is no explanation. It may be as you say. Random. But if one needs more understanding, perhaps you need look no further than where we find ourselves. I set out to disrupt the Morpheus Road, and what was the result? I was defeated, yet received exactly what I was seeking. And all has returned to the way it was."

"Except for a couple of dead people along the way," Coop said with disdain.

"Death is a part life," Damon said. "Perhaps it took those sacrifices, and yours, to ensure the future of mankind. It was no small accomplishment and makes me think of the possibility."

"Possibility of what?" Ree asked.

"That what happened here was not random at all.

We may all have been guided more than we realize. The choices we make are our own, but so much of what we do is influenced by what we see, and feel. I tried to challenge that, and failed. Why? Because I was not up to the task? Because I was wrong? Or was it because I chose the wrong people to try and influence? I understand your question, Marshall Seaver, and I will be wondering the same thing for as long as I exist. Why was it you? I do not know, but I feel there may have been more forces at work than we will ever know."

Damon kicked his horse and broke into a gallop, running across the front of the platform. As he was about to hit the stairs on the far end, the colorful fog appeared in front of him and he disappeared.

"Look!" Zoe called.

In the valley below, each of Damon's soldiers disappeared into their own personal mist, leaving only a confused army of Guardians.

"Simple as that," Coop said. "Now he goes off somewhere and starts stewing again, and maybe a few generations from now he starts feeling a little less philosophical and starts looking for the poleax again. Then what?"

"Then nothing," Marsh said. "This time it's going where he'll never find it."

"Is there such a place?" Maggie asked.

Marsh raised the poleax, the sword that was the tool of untold death and destruction, reared back, and flung it into the Threshold.

There was a quick flash of light where the poleax entered, and it was gone.

Coop laughed. "Nice."

"What's that?" Zoe asked.

From deep within the light of the Threshold, a shadow appeared.

"Uh-oh," Coop said. "Are they throwing it back?"

The one shadow became two and quickly took human form.

"Somebody's coming out," Ree declared.

The two shadows walked quickly from the depths of the Threshold and stepped out into the light of the valley.

"Press," Marsh declared.

Press walked with a beautiful dark-skinned woman who was as tall as he and moved with the grace of an athlete. It was the same woman who appeared to Ree, Marsh, and Cooper in Ree's vision to tell them about Press being in the Blood. Both wore the plain black clothes of the Watchers. They stepped from the Threshold and moved off to the side, where they stood silently.

"Uh-oh," Coop said. "I think they're back in Watcher mode."

"Why?" Marsh called to them. "What made the Watchers finally intervene?"

When Press "spoke," they heard his words though his lips didn't move. He had returned to a higher level of existence.

"Because the positive spirit of mankind prevailed," Press answered.

"You mean because Marsh ended Brennus and cut off the flow of spirits," Coop said.

"That is true in part," the dark woman said. "There were two very powerful forces vying for control. But what finally turned the tide wasn't a weapon, or a battle, or any act of violence."

"Then, what was it?" Marsh asked.

"One of the simplest positive qualities that defines mankind," Press answered. "Trust."

"Trust?" Coop repeated, disbelieving. "What's that got to do with—?"

"It was Damon," Ree said, realizing. "Marsh put his trust in Damon and he delivered."

"Seriously?" Coop exclaimed, incredulous. "You finally took our side because of freakin' Damon?"

Press said, "The evil that Brennus and Damon had been building for centuries no longer exists for one simple reason. Marsh trusted Damon to make the right choice and Damon's humanity prevailed. That is what made the difference."

Coop shook his head with wonder and said, "Unbelievable."

Marsh said, "So what happens if Damon goes back to being Damon?"

Press gave them a knowing smile and said, "Maybe you should just enjoy this moment."

Another shadow appeared from inside the Threshold. As it moved closer, it took the shape of a person who was much taller than Press and had long dark hair.

When the features of the person became clear, Zoe took a quick surprised breath.

"Adeipho!" she said with a gasp.

"It can't be," Coop exclaimed. "I saw his spirit destroyed."

"Not my father," Zoe exclaimed. "My brother."

The young Adeipho stepped from the light of the Threshold, looking very much like his father. Rather than the leather battle armor, he wore simple cotton pants and a shirt . . . the clothes of a fisherman."

"You fought well, Sister," Adeipho said.

Zoe made a move to run for him, but stopped herself as if not sure what was proper.

"Can I . . . ?" she asked Press.

Press nodded.

Adeipho held out his arms and Zoe ran to him. She was no longer the angry soldier who commanded an army. She was once again a happy young girl.

"Have you come to stay?" she asked, her head buried in his chest.

Adeipho laughed. "Of course not. You are coming with me. Mother is waiting."

Zoe shot a quick, questioning look to Press.

Press nodded and gestured toward the Threshold.

Zoe hugged her brother even closer and whispered, "Father is gone."

"I know," he said softly.

Adeipho looked to the others and said, "You have all fought well. We could not be more proud."

Coop called, "So, uh, what's it like in there?"

Adeipho smiled and said, "Thanks to what you have all done, you will be able to find out for yourselves one day."

Coop looked to Marsh and said, "I knew he wouldn't tell us."

Zoe pulled away from her brother and called to the others. "I know we will meet again."

Adeipho put his arm around Zoe and the two turned and walked through the Threshold.

"I guess she earned that," Coop said to Press.

Press responded with a small smile, and a wink.

"Hey, look," Marsh called out.

Everyone turned to look back at the valley to see that the Guardians were no longer there. All signs of the battle that had torn apart the idyllic gorge had disappeared as well. It was once again . . . paradise.

"Somebody else is coming out," Ree announced.

Another shadow appeared within the Threshold. This one was much smaller than Adeipho and was clearly a woman. She had long, dark hair and wore a dress that came down to just below her knees.

It was Maggie's turn to gasp.

Coop saw her reaction, and his throat clutched.

"Maggie?" her mother called as she stepped tentatively into the light.

She looked like an older version of Maggie, with gray-streaked dark hair that she wore tied back into a braid. She wore a simple blue-checked dress with a red coat-sweater over it. Her brown eyes had just as much life as Maggie's, with no hint of the sad, tortured life she had lived at the hands of her brutal husband.

Maggie stood behind Coop as if for protection.

"Maggie, sweetheart, let me see you!" her mother called.

Maggie didn't budge. She trembled with fear as she had done when she first met Cooper in the Black.

"It's okay," Coop said soothingly. "Go to her."

"I . . . I can't," Maggie whimpered.

"I know the truth," Maggie's mom said. "It wasn't your fault. I was so upset to see how you were treated after the accident."

"I'm sorry, Mrs. Salinger," Coop said. "For what my grandfather did."

"Thank you, Cooper, but there's no need for apologies," she said. "My daughter has made her peace with him."

Coop gently held Maggie and coaxed her to go to her mother. Maggie hugged her own waist and stepped forward reluctantly.

"I want to tell you it's over," her mom said. "But the truth is, it's just beginning, and that's a good thing. Come with me, Maggie. This is where you belong."

Maggie's mom stepped forward with her arms out. Maggie stood stiffly for a moment longer, then finally broke down and ran to her. The two hugged as the tears flowed. Her mother rubbed her back soothingly, whispering to her little girl the way she had done so many times in life.

Maggie's mom looked to Cooper and said, "Thank you for

helping to take away her burden, and your grandfather's."

Coop opened his mouth to speak, but no words came out.

"Wow, that's a first," Marsh said, laughing. "Cooper speechless. Mark the day."

Maggie pulled away from her mom and went to Cooper. She held his hands and said, "Come with us."

Coop looked to Press.

Press responded with a slight shake of his head.

"Soon enough," Coop said to Maggie. "You didn't think I'd skate through the Black this quick, did you? In spite of all my amazing heroics. I guess I've still got some work to do."

He threw another look to Press to see if he'd get a reaction. He didn't.

"I'll do my time, and then we'll see what happens," Coop added.

Maggie threw her arms around Cooper and hugged him close. "I love you, Cooper Foley. Thank you for saving my life."

Coop had to blink back tears himself. His reply was to squeeze her back.

"Okay," he said, holding her at arm's length. "The sooner you get out of here the sooner I can start working on doing the same thing."

Maggie nodded, then looked to Marsh and Ree. "I know I'll see you all soon."

"I hope so," Marsh replied.

"Good-bye, Maggie," Ree said.

Maggie gave a quick kiss to Cooper. "Say good-bye to your grandfather."

"I will."

"Don't forget me."

"I think I should be saying that to you. You're the one who's about to become some higher form of life."

Maggie giggled, then turned and took her mother's

hand. Together the two walked into the Threshold. Maggie gave one last look back to Cooper, blew him a kiss, and the two disappeared.

Cooper took a step closer to the Threshold and stared expectantly into the light.

No more spirits appeared.

"I guess that's it," he declared. "Looks like we get the consolation prize . . . time in the Black."

"Could be worse things," Marsh said.

Coop spun back to them and said, "Who wants to come with me to visit Gramps? He'll want to know about Maggie."

"Among other things," Ree said with a chuckle.

"I'll go," Marsh said.

"We'll all go," Ree added.

"No."

They all turned quickly to see that the two Watchers had moved to the mouth of the Threshold.

Press said, "There's one more thing to be done."

34

The lions were gone. The pen was empty. The Roman Colosseum was deserted. There was nothing to prevent access to the last remaining Rift.

Marsh, Cooper, and Ree stood facing the portal between the Black and the Light.

"Tempting, isn't it?" Coop said.

"You know we can't go through," Ree cautioned. "It would go against everything we fought for."

"Yeah, but . . . we just saved humanity," Coop argued. "Shouldn't that earn us a couple of get-out-of-jail-free cards?"

"I guess I don't see this as jail," Ree argued. "Our lives haven't ended."

"Yeah, I get it," Coop said with resignation. "I don't love it, but I get it."

"The Rift has to be closed," Marsh said. "How do we do that?"

"You don't," Press replied without actually speaking.

Press stood behind the others on the far side of the lion pen, along with the woman Watcher.

"It will close once we have finished," he added.

"You mean you had the power to close the Rifts all along?" Coop asked.

"The negative spirit that created the Rift no longer exists," the woman answered. "Therefore the Rift will no longer exist."

Coop said, "And I'll never understand how any of this works."

"What else has to be finished?" Marsh asked.

"First, I must commend you all," Press said. "I have no doubt that you all will soon be moving through the Threshold yourselves."

"Yeah, get on that, would ya?" Coop said. "Put in a good word to somebody."

"I still want to know," Marsh said, "was this all random? I mean, could this have happened to anybody and we were just the unlucky ones?"

"Damon was right," the dark-skinned woman said. "We all make choices based on the influence of others. Anyone could have found the poleax. But they didn't. It was you, Ree. And that brought you all to this point. At any time you could have made different decisions and Damon might have triumphed, or Brennus, but you didn't. None of you did. Sometimes things simply happen because that is the way they were meant to be. The positive spirit of mankind is strong. Was it random? Yes. But circumstances brought the exact right people together, and that was no accident."

"Uh . . . did that answer the question?" Coop asked.

"Close enough," Marsh answered.

"So close the Rift," Coop said.

"Not just yet," Press replied. "Cooper, you arrived in the Black the way all spirits do. You died in the Light."

"Yeah, thanks for the reminder," Coop said.

"Ree and Marsh, yours was a different route. You came through unnatural Rifts that Damon created. You did not die to get here."

"So what?" Coop asked. "They're just as dead as I am."

Neither Press nor the woman responded.

"Aren't they?" Coop asked.

"Their journey was not the same," the woman answered.

"Whoa, what are you saying?" Marsh asked. "We're not dead?"

"Your spirits came through, but your physical bodies remained in the Light."

"They did?" Coop exclaimed.

"So what does that mean?" Ree asked, her excitement growing.

"Oh man," Coop said, stunned. "Can they go back?"

Press stepped closer to Ree and Marsh and replied, "Ree, you fell through the Rift quite some time ago. I'm afraid that too much time has passed. Your physical body still exists in the Light, but it has deteriorated to the point that it cannot be salvaged."

Ree nodded in understanding, but was then hit with a realization.

"So you're saying . . . ?"

Press turned to Marsh and said, "Your coming here has turned the course of this conflict. Without your guidance and trust in the better nature of mankind, I dread to think what Damon would have accomplished. Or Brennus. "

"Just tell me he can go back through the Rift," Coop exclaimed.

Press focused on Marsh and said, "Your physical body

is still sound. Yes, you can go back to the Light."

Everyone stood in stunned silence. Ree and Coop looked to Marsh, waiting for his reaction.

"I . . . I . . . I'm not sure I *want* to go back," Marsh said. "I mean, we all end up here eventually, right? You said it, Mom. This isn't jail. It's not a punishment. It's just part of life."

"It is," Ree said. "But your first life isn't over yet."

She took Marsh's face in her hands and through tears said, "Go home, sweetheart. Your father is going to need you. There are so many things you can do before coming back here."

"But I *will* be back here!" Marsh said. "So what's the point?"

"Life begins in the Light," Press said. "It isn't just the first step. In so many ways it's the most important step. This is a journey for everyone, and everyone's journey is different. Where you are is as important as where you're going. Embrace the life you were given, and the rest of your journey will be that much richer for it."

"But . . . I don't want to leave you," Marsh said to Ree. "And Coop."

"You have to," Coop said sincerely. "Think of how much cooler things will be now that you know what you have to look forward to. Talk about stress-free."

"And we'll be with you," Ree said, holding back her tears.

"Not all the time," Coop interjected. "That could get uncomfortable."

"Will Coop still be able to talk with me?" Marsh asked Press.

"No," the woman said. "We took a great chance in giving him that ability. It won't happen again."

"That's cool," Coop said brightly. "Every once in a while I'll move stuff around and freak you out. We'll be great at parties. Everybody will think you're magic."

Coop was trying to be casual, but his tears proved that he was anything but.

Ree hugged her son and said, "You have to go back. You know that."

Marsh nodded. He knew.

Press said, "You know more about life and death than anyone else alive. It's a great gift to have that knowledge. Be careful how you share it."

"Yeah," Coop added. "Don't go making some reality show about the great beyond or anything. People will think you're nuts."

Marsh pulled his mother close.

"I don't want to lose you again," he said, his voice cracking.

"You're not, sweetheart. You're going to live your life, and then come back."

Marsh took a deep breath to calm himself, then kissed his mother on the cheek.

"Yeah," he said. "Soon enough."

"No!" Ree said quickly. "Not soon. Live a long life. I'm counting on that."

She wiped Marsh's eyes and said, "Now go."

Marsh turned to Cooper.

"How twisted is this?" Coop said. "Instead of being sad because somebody's gonna die, we're all weepy because somebody's about to live."

Marsh laughed. "Yeah, well, we never did things the normal way."

"Seriously," Coop said, then added, "Would you do me one favor?"

"Sure. Anything."

"Live for the both of us."

Marsh fought back tears and said, "I will."

The two best friends hugged. For the last time.

"So long, Ralph," Coop said. "I'll be watching."

Marsh nodded and backed away.

"How does this work?" he asked Press.

"Just walk through," Press replied.

Marsh walked up to the tear in the wall that was the seam between lives. He took one last look back at the Black, at his mother and at his best friend.

Cooper gave him the double okay sign.

Marsh smiled, turned, and stepped into the Rift.

When Marsh opened his eyes, he was completely disoriented. He saw nothing but black and wondered if there had been some mistake. Perhaps Press was wrong and it was too late for him to go back after all. He found himself lying on his back staring up at nothing.

To his right he saw a jagged, gray hole. Instinctively he knew what it was. He pulled himself to his feet and stood up to face the gray opening. Behind him was nothing . . . and everything. In front of him was life. He stepped out of the Rift . . .

. . . and into the mausoleum that held his mother's grave, that wasn't his mother's grave. On the floor was the open coffin and the remains of the mystery man who had been transported from Greece. As Marsh stepped out of the Rift he immediately felt heat at his back. He jumped forward and spun around to see the Rift healing itself. The seam between lives was closing up as if an unseen hand were sewing it back together. In seconds, the wall of tombs had returned to the state that Marsh had first found it in. The marble facade of his mother's crypt was again intact, the coffin and the remains were gone. All was as it had been.

"Whoever you are," Marsh said. "Rest in peace."

Marsh ran to the stairs leading up and out of the basement crypt. He climbed quickly, ran through the mausoleum, and out the front door. He stood on the roadway in front of the mausoleum, breathing hard, hoping that nobody had seen him. It was daytime, but what day was it? How long had he been in the Black? One day? Two? A century?

He walked quickly through the cemetery, headed for the front gate. With any luck, he'd be out of there before anybody saw him.

"Hey!" somebody shouted.

Luck wasn't with him.

Marsh froze.

A maintenance worker in coveralls strolled toward him.

"Here kinda early, ain't ya?" he asked. "I just opened the gates."

Marsh took a quick look around and realized that the shadows were long and the grass was covered with dew. It was early morning.

"Just wanted to pay a quick visit," Marsh said, trying to control his voice. "I'm leaving now."

The maintenance worker gave him a curious look and continued on, "Okay. Have a good one."

Marsh started for the entrance but then stopped and turned back.

"Hey, could you call me a cab? I thought I'd be staying longer but realized I can't."

The ride from the northern border of Stony Brook to the center of town was familiar to Marsh, though this trip seemed anything but. He stared out of the cab window at the trees, the birds, the people . . . marveling at the fact that they were all alive. This was no vision. It was all very real. He rolled down the window and sucked in the orangey smell of jasmine. It smelled like heaven. It smelled right.

Sydney Foley was asleep. It was nearly nine thirty but she didn't have to be to class for another few hours. She wanted to sleep. It was the only way she could keep her mind from spinning out of control, wondering what was happening to Marsh. And Cooper. And life as she thought she knew it.

She felt a slight breeze on her face that gently nudged her awake. She was lying on her back and through half-open eyes saw that someone was standing over her bed. She wasn't shocked or scared. She smiled.

"Good dream," she said lazily, and rolled over for another few minutes of sleep.

"Good morning," Marsh said.

Sydney's eyes snapped open as she went from half asleep to about as awake as you can be in less than a second. She sat bolt upright to see Marsh standing over her.

"Sleeping in?" Marsh asked.

Sydney threw herself at Marsh and hugged him tight. She then pushed him away just as quickly.

"You're real!" she exclaimed. "You're not . . . not—"

"A ghost? No. It's me. In the flesh."

"But . . . I saw you dead."

"And I came back. Special privilege."

Sydney threw herself back at him and squeezed him until he squirmed.

"Easy," Marsh said, chuckling. "Or you'll put me back there."

"If you could come back, what about . . . ?"

Marsh shook his head. "Just me, Syd. I'm sorry."

The news only made Sydney hold him closer.

"Thanks for sending the crucible," Marsh said. "It helped."

"It kept Damon away?"

"No, I broke it for him. As a reward."

Sydney pushed Marsh away, stunned.

"You . . . reward for what?" she asked.

"For saving the Morpheus Road."

"Uh . . . what?"

Marsh held her close and laughed. "There's so much to tell you but the bottom line is, it's over. For good this time."

"So what happens now?"

"That's easy," Marsh replied. "We live our lives."

Marsh had a new mission that he pursued with dogged determination.

The man who was in Ree Seaver's coffin was identified as a homeless man with no family. He had died of natural causes and his body had been waiting for burial in a mortuary in Greece when it had mysteriously disappeared. Further investigation turned up a series of local officials as well as customs workers who confessed to accepting bribes and allowing his body to be released under the name of Theresa Seaver to an American named Ennis Mobley.

Ennis had needed a body to be Ree Seaver in order to move the poleax to a place where he thought it would never be found.

The news caused a scandal that helped Marsh and his father accomplish their true goal. If not for the embarrassment it brought to various government agencies, they may not have had the same level of cooperation that they received.

The Necromanteio was not only a sacred, historic site, it was a popular tourist destination. A search through the rubble left by an earthquake on such a site needed to be approved by many different government agencies and carried out under tight scrutiny. Marsh and his dad had the benefit of the international press on their side but it was still a long, frustrating process. Finally, one year to the day after Marsh had come back from the Black, search teams located the body of the lone victim that had been buried in the rubble of the Ammoudia earthquake: Theresa Seaver.

Her second funeral in Stony Brook was much different

than the first. Only a few people attended the very private service. Marsh was a rock, helping his father get through the difficult experience. He thought of telling him the truth, but decided not to throw something else at him that would seem so impossible. He knew the time would come, but it wasn't then.

Sydney had held on to the lignum vitae branches and made sure to place them on top of Ree's coffin before it was slipped into the crypt.

Marsh was the last to leave the mausoleum that day. He wanted to be alone for one final moment with his mom. It wasn't a sad parting. Marsh actually felt relieved. He leaned into the crypt, kissed his hand, and touched his mother's coffin saying, "*Now* we're done."

As they were leaving the cemetery, Sydney held Marsh by the arm and said, "Promise me something?"

"Sure, what?"

"Let's never come back to this freakin' cemetery ever again."

All Marsh could do was laugh.

Marsh went on to do exactly what Coop had asked him. He lived a life for both of them. A very long life. He had learned a great deal from his premature exposure to the afterlife, not the least of which was the realization that life was precious. Every life. It was up to each person to live it the best way they could. For Marsh, it meant doing the things that he loved best, no matter what anyone thought of it.

Or of him.

One of the things he loved was his art. Rather than brush it off as the folly of a juvenile sensibility, he embraced it. Marsh went on to art school and became a successful fantasy writer and artist. He was responsible for creating many characters that lived in the pages of graphic novels, movies, and television. His work created a legion of fans who waited eagerly for his newest creation and followed the adventures of his popular characters with fan-boy glee.

His most famous and successful creation by far was his first. After having drawn Gravedigger in so many incarnations with no connective narrative, he finally found the story by creating a nemesis for the demon. A hero. It was a spirit who battled Gravedigger's dark, Gothic magic by drawing upon the positive power of the spirit world. Their adventures and battles spanned dimensions, worlds, and times. Marsh wrote and drew thousands of stories, many of which became successful movies, introducing Gravedigger to legions of fans who loved to be surprised . . . and scared.

As a joke that only he and Sydney could appreciate, the ironic name he chose for Gravedigger's spirit nemesis was Damon. Whenever he drew the handsome and noble general, he always chuckled to himself and thought: *I'll bet Cooper's turning over in his grave.*

Marsh wrote many stories and created hundreds of characters throughout his life, but he always came back to drawing Gravedigger and Damon for the simple reason that it made him happy. Not only because it kept him connected to his roots, but it also acted as a comforting reminder of the larger reality of life. That knowledge was indeed a gift.

Of course, there was only one name he could have given to the series.

He called it: *Morpheus Road*.

THE END

PENDRAGON

Bobby Pendragon is a seemingly normal fourteen-year-old boy. He has a family, a home, and a possible new girlfriend. But something happens to Bobby that changes his life forever.

HE IS CHOSEN TO DETERMINE
THE COURSE OF HUMAN EXISTENCE.

Pulled away from the comfort of his family and suburban home, Bobby is launched into the middle of an immense, interdimensional conflict. It's a journey of danger and discovery for Bobby, and his success or failure will do nothing less than determine the fate of the world. . . .

From Aladdin • Published by Simon & Schuster